T H E   W A K E F I E L D

GILBERT MORRIS

The
RAMPARTS
Of
HEAVEN

TYNDALE HOUSE PUBLISHERS, INC.
Wheaton, Illinois

Library of Congress Cataloging-in-Publication Data

Morris, Gilbert
    The ramparts of heaven / Gilbert Morris.
        p.   cm. — (The Wakefield dynasty : 5)
    ISBN 0-8423-6233-9 (pbk.)
    1. Great Britain—History—George II, 1727–1760—Fiction.
2. Methodist Church (England)—History—18th Century—Fiction.
I. Title.   II. Series: Morris, Gilbert. Wakefield dynasty : 5.
PS3563.08742R35   1997
813′.54—dc20   96-32142

Printed in the United States of America

00   99   98   97
5   4   3   2   1

CONTENTS

To David and Audrey Coleman.

God has blessed Johnnie and me with many fine friends.

You two have been a blessing to us both!

[THE MORGANS]

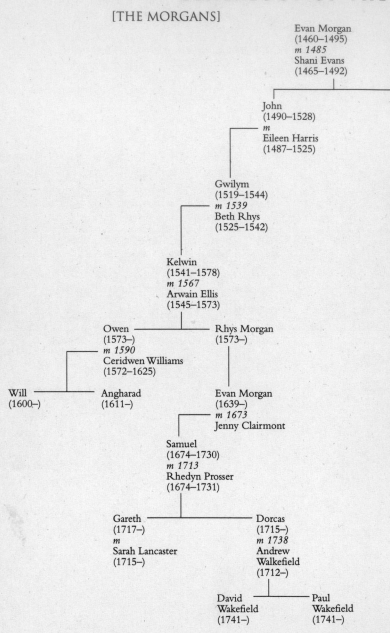

Evan Morgan
(1460–1495)
m 1485
Shani Evans
(1465–1492)

John
(1490–1528)
m
Eileen Harris
(1487–1525)

Gwilym
(1519–1544)
m 1539
Beth Rhys
(1525–1542)

Kelwin
(1541–1578)
m 1567
Arwain Ellis
(1545–1573)

Owen
(1573–)
m 1590
Ceridwen Williams
(1572–1625)

Rhys Morgan
(1573–)

Will
(1600–)

Angharad
(1611–)

Evan Morgan
(1639–)
m 1673
Jenny Clairmont

Samuel
(1674–1730)
m 1713
Rhedyn Prosser
(1674–1731)

Gareth
(1717–)
m
Sarah Lancaster
(1715–)

Dorcas
(1715–)
m 1738
Andrew
Wakefield
(1712–)

David
Wakefield
(1741–)

Paul
Wakefield
(1741–)

WAKEFIELD DYNASTY

[THE WAKEFIELDS]

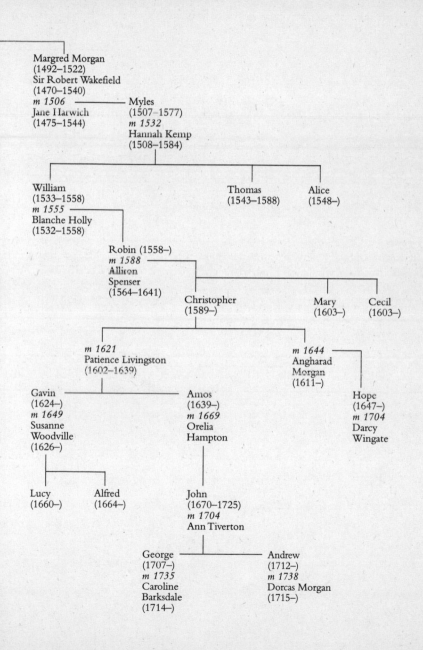

Margred Morgan
(1492–1522)
Sir Robert Wakefield
(1470–1540)
m 1506 ——— Myles
Jane Harwich   (1507–1577)
(1475–1544)   m 1532
                    Hannah Kemp
                    (1508–1584)

William   Thomas   Alice
(1533–1558)   (1543–1588)   (1548–)
m 1555
Blanche Holly
(1532–1558)

Robin (1558–)
m 1588
Allison
Spenser
(1564–1641)
            Christopher   Mary   Cecil
            (1589–)   (1603–)   (1603–)

m 1621   m 1644
Patience Livingston   Angharad
(1602–1639)   Morgan
                                (1611–)

Gavin ———————————— Amos   Hope
(1624–)   (1639–)   (1647–)
m 1649   m 1669   m 1704
Susanne   Orelia   Darcy
Woodville   Hampton   Wingate
(1626–)

Lucy   Alfred   John
(1660–)   (1664–)   (1670–1725)
                          m 1704
                          Ann Tiverton

          George ——————————— Andrew
          (1707–)   (1712–)
          m 1735   m 1738
          Caroline   Dorcas Morgan
          Barksdale   (1715–)
          (1714–)

The Holy
Club

Part ONE

1 7 3 1 — 1 7 3 4

MISTAKEN IDENTITY

In the year of our Lord 1731, England faced enormous problems—cultural, international, and moral. But on a fine late spring afternoon, sitting before her dressing table, Caroline Barksdale was more concerned about the dress she had donned to wear to a ball than she was about international intrigue.

Miss Barksdale, a petite but well-proportioned young woman, seventeen years of age, leaned forward, studying her reddish blonde hair and practicing a smile. As she blinked her large brown eyes overshadowed by heavy lashes, there was a pertness in her expression attractive to the young gentlemen who had begun to discover her.

Caroline turned sideways, looked over her shoulder, then back again. Her French gown was so expensive that she'd gasped when her mother had named the price. A flowing cherry-colored *sacque* with loose-fitting elbow-length sleeves, it was caught up and pinned back, exposing a quilted and embroidered petticoat. A small linen cap with lace over her powdered wig completed her dress.

"It *is* rather daring—" she whispered, staring at the low-cut bodice. Just then a sound behind her brought her head up, and her mother swept in. "Why, you're not dressed, Caroline! Your father's ready with the carriage."

"Oh, Mother, I'm not sure about this dress!" Caroline tugged at the neckline but the dress remained firmly anchored. It hadn't seemed particularly low-cut when she'd bought it but now that she was ready to face the public in it, there seemed to be an inordinate amount of white skin exposed. "This dress isn't too low-cut, do you think, Mother?"

"Low-cut? Nonsense!" Lettie Barksdale, a short, plump woman with rosy cheeks and small blue eyes, slapped Caroline's hand away from the dress. Several of Lettie's pudgy fingers were adorned with large-jeweled rings, including an enormous red ruby. They were hands that had seen hard work, for no amount of lotions or manicures could quite conceal this part of Lettie Barksdale's past. Now she snorted, saying impatiently, "The owner of the shop assured us this is the very latest in Paris fashions, so stop fussing with it!"

Caroline smiled slightly, the corners of her full lips turning up. "Very well, but if I wore this dress out in the sun, I would be sunburned in a most embarrassing fashion." She turned, picked up her cape, and draped it around her shoulders. "I'm ready, Mother."

"How do you like my dress?" her mother asked.

Caroline eyed her mother's gown, a plum-colored affair decorated with so much ribbon and lace that every movement made Lettie look like a rippling flower garden. It was an expensive dress but not at all suited to her mother's florid complexion or her figure. Caroline almost said, "You look like a barrel wearing an expensive gown." But she was much too tactful. Instead she smiled and responded, "It's a beautiful dress, Mother. I'm sure everyone will admire it."

"They should! It certainly cost enough." Leaving the room, Lettie led her daughter down the stairs and as they reached the bottom, announced rather loudly, "We're ready to go, Lofton, as soon as I get my coat."

"You've had time enough to prepare for a royal coronation." The speaker, Lofton Barksdale, a tall man of forty-five with brown hair beginning to thin in front, had shrewd brown eyes set close together and a sensuous mouth that now turned up into a smile. "I feel like a fool in this outfit," he complained. "Like some jackanapes Frenchman." He was wearing the latest fashion, including white knee breeches and stockings, a double-breasted coat, and a plaid waistcoat. Being a large man, he looked as though he'd been stuffed into his garments but he dared not disregard his tailor.

"It's going to drive us bankrupt, Lettie, if we have to dress for any more of these confounded balls!"

"Oh, don't be silly, Lofton!" Lettie took his arm possessively and pulled him toward the door. "We've got to keep up with the standards in London. We're not in some little village now. You're an important man. Come along, Caroline. Don't dawdle."

A large servant opened the door, then bowed slightly as the trio stepped outside. The waiting carriage cost more than Lofton Barksdale had made during the first five years of his business life—and more than some small houses in the village where Lofton Barksdale had lived for years. Still, Lettie had insisted they had to arrive in style—"I can't go around London in a donkey cart!" she had put it. As the driver assisted the ladies inside, Barksdale snapped, "Don't waste time, Jenkins. We don't want to be late."

"Yes, sir!" The driver closed the door and scrambled like an agile monkey up on the box. Then, snatching his whip, he cracked it with a flourish and called out to the horses, "Step lively!" The matched set of bays leaped forward and the carriage moved down the street at a rapid clip.

Lettie peered out the window, her inquisitive eyes taking in the features of London. After moving from a small town in Sussex, she was fascinated by the enormity of this city of six hundred thousand inhabitants. The carriage wound its way through a medley of dwellings and businesses on serpentine narrow streets and past alleys that looked dark and rather dangerous. Here in London, the Barksdales had discovered, the rich and the poor sometimes rubbed shoulders. A noble lord might live in the same neighborhood as a butcher and a tallow chandler. As they passed many gin houses, Barksdale gloomily looked out the window and remarked, "I heard a chap say yesterday that five million gallons of gin were consumed last year in England." He shook his head with displeasure. "They're fools for drinking that poison!"

"Certainly they are, but what can you expect of the lower classes?" Lettie said, sniffing condescendingly. She had conveniently chosen to forget that she'd been one of the "lower classes" during her childhood and youth. Even after she had married Lofton Barksdale, an up-and-coming young merchant, she'd only reached the lower realm of the middle class. But as Lofton's business prospered, she'd begun to pressure him for a house in London. Her constant chipping away at her husband's resistance had achieved its aim a month earlier, when they'd finally moved to the city.

Now Lettie reached over and brushed her hand against Caroline's face. "You need to use a little more rice powder, Caroline. You have a good complexion but it doesn't hurt to help nature."

"Right!" Barksdale grunted. He nodded and made a heavy-handed attempt at humor. "If you're going to snare a husband, you've got to make yourself look as good as possible."

"You make it sound like someone trying to sell a house!" Caroline said, smiling. A quick-witted young woman, she added, "So getting married is like trying to sell a house, is it, Papa? You put some paint on it and patch it up so prospective buyers are taken in by it?"

"It's not like that at all!" Lettie snapped with little humor. Then she shook her head, uttering a further admonition. "You must marry, of course. What else is there for a woman to do?"

"Right. Just see to it that you marry well," Barksdale added.

"And how much must this young man be worth to qualify?" Caroline asked with a straight face. "I don't think you've mentioned what income would be acceptable."

Neither of her parents found this the slightest bit humorous. Lettie pursed her lips, did some rapid arithmetic, then said firmly, "At least ten thousand pounds a year and not one penny less."

"I'll keep that in mind," Caroline said and turned to look out the window, covering her smile with her hand. At a time when most women were instructed only in the areas of embroidery and painting miniatures, Caroline was quite well educated—much more so than most young women of her class. Her father had seen to it that she had tutors in literature and even the sciences.

As Lofton Barksdale stared at his daughter, suddenly he wished she'd been born a boy. It was too late for that, of course. Since he had no son, there would be no one to carry on his name. But if he worked his plan right, his blood could still be carried on. Though he had not mentioned it to either his wife or to Caroline, Barksdale had moved to London for one purpose: to place Caroline where suitable husbands might be more available than in a tiny village.

Leaning back in his seat, he contemplated with satisfaction the future that lay before him and his family. He had been brought up poor, but by his own efforts had lifted himself out of manual labor. Now he felt God was rewarding his efforts with wealth—and hopefully with a wealthy son-in-law!

Lord and Lady Fairfax felt it fitting to invite a few up-and-coming businessmen to the balls they held. Although they were not upper nobility themselves, they were respectably set in their world. Lord Fairfax had served in the army without great distinction but as the son of a previous Lord Fairfax, he had been given a title. None of the Fairfaxes had distinguished themselves at anything except, perhaps, dancing. All the Fairfax men seemed to be born with a dancing leg—sometimes even two. The house Fairfax had built in London had been constructed around an enormous ballroom that took up more floor space than the rest of the house altogether. As the afternoon waned and darkness came on, the crystal chandeliers overhead gleamed, throwing their pale beams over the dancers, who moved across the polished floor to the music of a lively six-piece orchestra.

This was another of the Fairfaxes' demands—that the music be the *very* best, which usually meant hiring Italians, some of whom spoke practically no English. Nevertheless, a pleased Lord Fairfax leaned across to his hawk-faced wife, adorned in an orchid dress that was clearly unsuitable for her sallow complexion, and commented, "I say, that new fiddler does quite well."

After attending hundreds of balls, including those she and her husband gave, Lady Fairfax had become almost jaded. Now she looked languidly toward the musicians ensconced in a balcony at the far end of the room. She listened for a moment and then murmured almost grudgingly, "They do very well, I'm sure." Then, after a pause, she looked around the room and said, "There's no one here tonight."

This was a remarkable statement, for the floor was almost packed. The colors of the women's dresses made a kaleidoscope of flashing reds, greens, and blues so that the men, condemned to wear the darker colors according to fashion, were outshone completely. But when Lady Fairfax said there was "no one" there, she meant there were no crowned princes, no foreign ministers from the court at France, no conquering hero or a general or an admiral. No, it was just your usual run of pleasure-seekers who swam in the waters of London's social life almost like schools of fish in an aquarium.

"Who's that coming in?" Lord Fairfax demanded abruptly. "Oh, yes. It's that new fellow. What's his name?"

"Barksdale, I believe." Lady Fairfax nodded. She had a hawkish face with a hook nose and a mouth like a knife. "Common looking, aren't they, Henry?"

"The girl looks very good."

"You *would* notice her! What is he—a butcher or something?"

"Oh, no. He's in bonds, stocks—that sort of thing—very clever. That's why I asked him here. We may want his help in case we need to invest."

"I suppose such people are necessary," Lady Fairfax commented.

Caroline Barksdale was impressed by the ballroom. She and her mother were deserted almost at once by Lofton Barksdale, who was approached by a business associate and taken away to the billiard room.

"I suppose that's the last we'll see of him this evening," Lettie complained sharply. "Well, come along. Let's take a seat over there." She towed Caroline to a section of chairs placed along the wall and the two were seated. "I wish we'd see someone I know," Lettie said disconsolately. "It's so difficult to break into conversations or associations that began before one arrived."

Her wish was granted almost at once, for a tall, angular woman with a heavily painted face came to say, "Mrs. Barksdale, how good to see you here."

"Why it's Mrs. Smith. How good to see you, Dora. I don't believe you've met my daughter, Caroline." Lettie introduced Caroline and added, "This is a lovely place."

"Oh, it does very well, I suppose." Mrs. Smith eyed Caroline and smiled. "I suppose you're enjoying yourself in London, Miss Barksdale. Have you met many people yet?"

"No, not so many."

"Well, there's one right over there," Mrs. Smith said, with a careless nod of her head. "Through the dancers there—over by the refreshment table."

"Who's that?" Lettie demanded at once.

"Sir George Wakefield, a *very* eligible young man." Mrs. Smith turned to Lettie Barksdale and smiled, making her look remarkably like a crocodile. "Quite a catch for some enterprising young lady."

Caroline tried to peer through the dancers but saw only a glimpse of the man Mrs. Smith had indicated. He seemed to be of average appearance and height but his face was interesting. "He looks intelligent," she remarked, keeping her voice bland.

"No man who's worth thirty thousand pounds a year has to be intelligent," Mrs. Smith said, utterly believing her own words. Because she was on the lowest rung of the social ladder, Mrs. Smith spent her days moving from one tea or ball to another, doing what she could to gain status and standing.

As Mrs. Smith pointed out various celebrities to Lettie Barksdale, Caroline felt increasingly more awkward. She was approached only twice, and then by older men who came to greet her mother and spoke to her in passing. This was a new and painful experience; back in her own village she'd been the belle of every ball.

"I wonder if I might introduce myself?"

The sound of a male voice startled Caroline, who'd been looking down the long room to her right. She turned swiftly and blinked in surprise. Sir George Wakefield, the man Mrs. Smith had pointed out, was standing in front of her, looking down at her with a smile.

"Why, I think that's permissible," Caroline responded quickly. Her mother had walked off with Mrs. Smith, so Caroline took the occasion to study Wakefield and make a quick evaluation. He

10

was lean and athletic. His plain gray coat, black knee breeches, white stockings, and black shoes with silver buckles were finely made and fit him well. He had dark blond hair and a pair of direct, blue, wide-spaced eyes. Although he wasn't exactly handsome, he had strongly masculine features—a broad forehead, small ears, a short English nose, a firm mouth with a full lower lip, and a pronounced chin. When he smiled, she noticed that he had unusually good teeth.

"My name is Wakefield," he said easily. "I believe we've never met, so I'd like to take this opportunity to introduce myself."

"My name is Caroline Barksdale. My father and mother are here somewhere," she said.

"You're new to London?" he queried, his eyes alight with interest.

"Oh, yes. We've only been here a month."

Wakefield smiled and asked, "May I have the honor of this dance, Miss Barksdale?"

"Certainly, sir."

Caroline rose with alacrity, and for the next fifteen minutes the two enjoyed one of the slower dances of the evening. Caroline was a good dancer and somehow it pleased her that she was much better than her partner. He was certainly not her idea of a lord, for there was a simplicity about him, almost a humility, that she hadn't expected. She almost asked him what it felt like to be a lord but wisely controlled her impulse. It didn't take long to discover that he was quite a good conversationalist.

At the end of the dance, Wakefield said, "I trust I'm not being too forward—but may I get you some refreshments and then perhaps have the next dance?"

Caroline was most agreeable. While the man was gone, her mother came to sit beside her, asking rather sharply, "Who was that?"

"Sir George Wakefield," Caroline said, smiling. Then she added,

"He's worth thirty thousand pounds a year—or so Mrs. Smith says. Do you think he'll qualify as a suitor for my hand?"

"Don't be foolish, Caroline! What did he say? Tell me *everything . . . !*"

But before Caroline could satisfy her mother's curiosity, Wakefield was back, bearing two glasses of punch. When Caroline introduced her mother, he bowed from the waist and smiled. "I'm happy to meet you, Mrs. Barksdale, and I'll look forward to meeting your husband."

Aware that her mother was bursting with curiosity, Caroline finished her punch quickly, then said, "I think the music's starting again."

"Yes. Excuse us, Mrs. Barksdale."

Caroline was pleased with her "conquest," as it were. So much so, that later, when she had been escorted back to sit beside her mother, and Wakefield had bowed and left, she didn't really mind when Lettie demanded again, "Tell me all about him. Did he just come over and introduce himself?"

Caroline gave the details of her encounter and while she was speaking, her father came in. At once informed by his wife of Caroline's new acquaintance, he said with some surprise, "Sir George Wakefield? I've heard of him—fine family, lots of money, I understand." Clearly pleased, he smiled at his wife.

Just then two men began to walk toward them.

"That's Sir Lionel Fairfax, our host," Barksdale said under his breath. "I don't know the fellow with him." When Fairfax reached them, he stopped and said, "I'd like you to meet Sir George Wakefield."

Caroline stared with shock at the man with Fairfax. He was over six feet tall and somewhat overweight with brown hair, brown eyes, and a squarish face. As soon as the introductions were made, he said, "May I have this dance, Miss Barksdale?"

"Certainly, sir."

Caroline moved out on the floor and discovered her present partner was far better at dancing than her previous one. He spoke cheerfully enough in a bluff, hearty manner, asking how she liked London and other light matters.

Finally Caroline said, "I danced twice with a gentleman whose name was Wakefield. Someone had mentioned George Wakefield, and I assumed it was you."

"Oh, that's my brother, Andrew," George Wakefield said and laughed aloud. "He'll be amused to find out you took him for me. No one ever did before."

"He's your younger brother, I take it?"

"Yes. Fine chap. He told you about going to Oxford?"

"No, he didn't mention it."

"Oh, yes. Going to be a clergyman, you know."

Though this came as a shock to Caroline, she found she was amused, too. "I didn't know that, either. He didn't mention it."

Again George Wakefield laughed. "The young scoundrel! I'll have to reprimand him. Nineteen-year-old parsons can't go around impersonating dancing masters. Look! There he is. Come along."

Caroline saw the man who had been her first partner standing alone watching them. When George Wakefield stopped in front of him, he said, "Hello again, Miss Barksdale."

Sir George Wakefield reached over and nudged his brother in the side. "Andrew, I'm surprised at you, sailing under false pretenses."

"I beg your pardon, George?"

"Now, don't give us that," George said, winking broadly at Caroline. "Miss Barksdale has told me how you romanced her, never mentioning you were a budding clergyman."

Andrew Wakefield looked uncomfortable. "I didn't mean to deceive you, Miss Barksdale. The subject just never came up."

Caroline saw the man was truly embarrassed and hastened to

reassure him. "Don't let your brother make a great thing of this. It was natural enough—and I did enjoy our dance. I never dreamed," she said, smiling roguishly, "that clergymen were such good dancers."

"I'm not actually a clergyman yet," Andrew commented. He shrugged, smiling at George. "There can be only one elder son in the family. Younger sons either have to go into the army or the church."

"I'm glad you chose the church," George said as Caroline stood listening to the two men. "A lot more dignity than getting your head blown off by a cannonball or some such rot!"

Later that evening, as Caroline danced a final time with Andrew Wakefield, he looked at her carefully. "I'm sorry for deceiving you, Miss Barksdale," he said engagingly. "I don't feel much like a clergyman. It takes so long—years, before anything ever comes of it. . . . May I call on you before I leave for Oxford?"

His question caught Caroline off guard but she at once replied, "Of course. My family will be glad to receive you."

❧

"You'll never guess what the young reverend here did at the ball," George said, smiling broadly at his family. It was the day after the ball and he and Andrew were having breakfast with their mother, Lady Ann Wakefield. Also present was Hope Wingate, a distant relative. As the daughter of Christopher and Angharad Wakefield and the widow of Darcy Wingate, this diminutive, white-haired woman was now dependent upon the Wakefields.

"What did he do, George?" Lady Ann Wakefield demanded. She was a short, plump woman with auburn hair and a strong face.

"He was romancing one of the most beautiful young women at the ball—and he didn't even tell her he was a parson. Disgraceful!"

Andrew flushed and shook his head. "It wasn't as bad as George makes it seem. Actually she's a very nice young woman."

"Who was she?" Lady Wakefield demanded and listened as Andrew gave the data on the Barksdale family. She shrugged then, saying, "She sounds like a nice young lady. Stop teasing him, George."

George laughed heartily. "He'd better get his romancing done before he goes to Oxford. I don't think they have time to do anything at that place but read books. But I will admit you have good taste, Andrew. Miss Barksdale is a pretty little thing."

Later, as Hope Wingate sat at the table alone with Andrew, she said, "Tell me about the young woman." Although Hope's health was not good and only traces of the great beauty that had been hers in her youth remained, she was still fiercely proud of her Welsh blood—and very fond of Andrew, and he of her. She sat there quietly, listening while he described the encounter, and then asked, "Did you really like her, Andrew?"

"Very much." Andrew gave her a direct look, his face serious. "I intend to see her again before I go to Oxford. She said I might call on her and I will." Andrew reached over and held Hope's frail hand gently. "I'll tell you all about it. It'll be better than reading a romance novel."

"It'll be your first romance." Hope smiled, enjoying the feel of his hand on hers. "You haven't been much for chasing young ladies."

Andrew Wakefield looked thoughtful. A sober young man, resigned to being a younger son, he was a good student, very intelligent, and not at all discontented with going into the church for he had long been active in religious things. Hope Wingate, whose hand he held, was a devout Christian who had helped him all along the way.

"No, I've not been much for romance," Andrew said, "and I'm probably not now. But I have to admit I've never been so taken with a young woman and I'll be happy to see her again."

Hope squeezed his strong hand, then laid her other hand on top of his and said quietly, "I hope she realizes what a fine young man will come calling on her."

Andrew smiled almost rashly, his white teeth gleaming. "I wish I were half the man you think I am, Aunt Hope."

He leaned over and kissed her cheek, then left the room. Hope Wingate sat there for a long time, thinking of the past and this young man who'd become quite dear to her. "I've prayed for you many a year, Andrew," she whispered. "And now I'll start praying God will give you just the right woman to be a companion."

ANDREW MEETS A HOLY MAN

"Your home is beautiful, Mr. Wakefield. I've never seen grounds more lovely."

Caroline Barksdale had been escorted by Andrew on a tour of both the Wakefield house and the expansive grounds. With the July sun a pale disk high in the sky, heat rose from the earth as Caroline gazed at the lush, well-tended estate. As they stood in the midst of a large rose garden, she bent over to smell a crimson blossom, then smiled up at Andrew. "You must be sad to leave this place and go to Oxford."

"Why, no, I don't believe I am," Andrew replied briefly. "I've been looking forward to my time at university for quite a while now." He looked at her, taking in her pink-and-white-striped silk dress with taffeta bows down the front and the hemline that barely dusted the ground. Around her shoulders Caroline wore a lace-edged gauze scarf and on her carefully arranged hair sat a white straw hat over a linen bonnet. As her reddish blonde hair caught the sun, Andrew admired her prettiness but said nothing.

The two had been together several times since their first meeting and now the Barksdales had come to Wakefield as a family for a visit.

"It must have been wonderful to spend your entire life here," Caroline mused as she walked slowly along the brick pathway that separated the rose beds. "I can't imagine living in a place this large." Glancing at Andrew, she noted he was neatly, though not expensively, dressed in brown knee breeches, white stockings, a short tan waistcoat, and a white shirt with a dark blue cravat. Even his soft leather shoes with flat heels and brass buckles were uncharacteristically plain and sensible for a man of his social stature.

"Do you know," Andrew said abruptly, taking her arm lightly and turning her toward him, "how many times we've been together?"

"Not very many."

"Four times," Andrew declared. "Dinner at your home. A ride in the park. Tea at the bishop's. And once at the races."

"You keep short accounts with your social life, Mr. Wakefield."

"Oh, don't call me that. We know each other well enough now for first names. Come along—I'll show you the rest of the estate."

He led her down the winding garden pathways until they came to a sunken ditch. "This is what they call a ha-ha."

"A ha-ha? Why do they call it that?" Caroline inquired, lifting her eyebrows. She looked down at the ditch curiously. "What's it for?"

"It's really sort of a sunken fence," Andrew replied, "to keep the cattle from getting across. That way we don't have to use an unsightly fence. There's just one drawback. You can't see it unless you're directly over it." His blue eyes filled with humor. "I broke my arm once, falling into the blasted thing."

"Oh my," Caroline teased. "I didn't know parsons swore like that! 'Blasted thing' indeed!" She laughed at the expression on Andrew's face, then quickly said, "I'm sorry. I was only teasing."

"I'm accustomed to it. My going into the ministry has been quite a joke to some."

"Well, it's not to me," Caroline insisted. She had been thinking of his earlier remarks and returned to the subject. "You must be keeping a journal of all of the times we've met. Someday you'll label it a biography and call it *My Misspent Life as a Clergyman.*" Humor lit her face as she teased him. One of the things she found troubling about Andrew was that he was too sober. It had taken some time before she could bring herself to tease him.

Andrew shrugged. "I hope my life won't be misspent. It's my intention to serve God as best I can." He earnestly searched her face. "Caroline—will you write me while I'm at Oxford?"

"Of course—if you'll write me first. I'm certain my parents would approve." Her lips turned upward. "You can give me pastoral counseling. Tell me all about the things young ladies should try to avoid." She took his arm. "Come along. It must be almost time to eat. I'm starved!"

They made their way back to the large manor house, which was set back from the smaller outbuildings, and entered through a massive oak door. Carlton, the butler, met them. "I was just coming to get you, sir. Dinner is ready."

Andrew was conscious of Caroline's light touch on his arm as they made their way down a long hallway and then turned off into the dining room.

"About time you got here!" George Wakefield exclaimed. He was wearing fawn-colored breeches, a double-breasted waistcoat with flap pockets, and a narrow bow cravat at his throat. His wig was straight on the top with a padded roll on either side. Drawing back a chair, he ordered, "Sit down right here, Miss Barksdale. I intend to tell you all the horrible stories of Andrew's wretched youth."

"I'm certain the list would be very short," Caroline said demurely. She took her seat on one side of the great oak table, between her parents. Andrew moved across from her to sit beside his mother, Lady Ann Wakefield.

George took his seat at the head of the table, nodding to the servant. "All right. Bring the food in, Justin."

Neither Caroline nor her parents were accustomed to the ornate servings that followed. Mrs. Barksdale seemed to be tabulating them, obviously making plans to emulate the nobility when it came her turn to serve. The meal consisted of thin filets of lamb served with vinegar and minced onions, venison pastry highly seasoned with butter, and stuffed, roasted pike that was richly spiced. Loaves of white Wheaten bread, fresh from the oven, filled two silver platters. Other silver bowls and servers contained boiled kidney beans, carrots, and turnips, all simmering in butter. The servants kept the silver goblets filled with ale, pale and strong. And after the main meal, a Banbury cake was brought in and Lady Wakefield explained it was her own recipe, made of currants buried in a rich sweet-spice dough. Chocolate was also served for those who cared for the rich, creamy drink but most everyone preferred tea.

The conversation turned to the family, and Barksdale nodded. "I think the second son should go into the church," he pronounced. "It gives dignity to the family."

"Well, it's costing enough," George said, shrugging heavily. "I hope to get my preaching free for the rest of my life after bearing the cost of your education, Andrew."

Andrew was accustomed to his brother's odd humor. "I'll do the best I can. Sermons are very reasonable, I believe, George."

"You must be proud of sending a son to Oxford," Caroline said to Lady Wakefield.

"Oh, I suppose so. George attended for a time."

"Yes, I did," George responded, nodding. "Waste of time." His words were darkened with a touch of contempt. "No romance about the place. Not a speck! I heard a rumor that some of the bishops were worried about *enthusiasm* rearing its ugly head there. No danger. They're not enthusiastic about anything, not even athletics. Never saw such a boring place in all my life!"

The Barksdales were slightly shocked at his peremptory words, and Caroline glanced, surprised, at Andrew. "Not a very encouraging report for you, Mr. Wakefield."

"I'm not going to Oxford for enthusiasm," Andrew said evenly. "I don't hold with that sort of thing."

This didn't really surprise Caroline. She knew *enthusiasm* was the term given to any so-called excesses of religion in England. Among the lower classes, primarily in Wales, there'd been cases of people in church or worship services shouting, falling to the ground, and behaving in ways the clergy considered unsuitable. Well she knew that the worst thing one could say about a man—in one sense—was that he was an *enthusiast*.

"I should hope you'd keep yourself free of such things," Lady Ann Wakefield said and sniffed. "It's enough that we attend services, take the sacraments, and support the church as is proper."

Andrew shifted uncomfortably in his seat. His mother's religion, he knew, was little more than a formality. His grandmother, who'd passed away three years earlier, had been a warmhearted Christian who had spent much time and effort trying to instill Christianity into the rest of the family. George and Lady Ann, however, had not taken to such things. George had once said of his grandmother, "She'd be an enthusiast herself if she had half a chance."

When the meal was over, the men went to another room to smoke and George and Mr. Barksdale had something a little stronger than ale. The women remained in the dining room, sipping tea and sustaining light, polite conversation. Caroline studied Lady Ann carefully for it was her belief that if one was curious as to what a child would be like when he or she grew older, it was a wise thing to study the parents. Since Andrew's father had passed away some years earlier, Caroline determined to study his mother.

Lady Ann Wakefield had been an attractive woman in her youth, no doubt, but the excess weight had thickened her figure and coarsened her face. There was a pride in her that could not be concealed and was evidenced by her ornate dress and the ostentatious diamond that glittered on her finger.

Caroline was unimpressed with Lady Ann and chose to say so when the Barksdales were in their carriage on their way back to London. "I think Lady Ann would be difficult to get along with."

"I don't know why you say that, Caroline," Mrs. Barksdale scolded. "She has an air of command about her but that's only proper for a lady of her stature."

"She wants her own way, *that* is certain," Caroline replied.

"And why shouldn't she have it?" her father insisted. "She has money, position, and a title. Such people will have their own way."

Caroline gave her father a sharp glance but said nothing.

Her mother said stiffly, "I'm shocked you paid so little attention to Sir George, Caroline. I think his feelings were hurt."

"Do you think so?" Caroline shrugged. "I didn't notice."

"He's got thirty thousand pounds a year," her father interjected. "I'd think it's only wise to pay attention to any man with that much money."

"I find Andrew much more interesting," Caroline remarked carelessly. "All Sir George can talk about is horses."

"A man with thirty thousand pounds a year," her father grandly announced, "is not required to be interesting."

Once again Caroline felt there was some flaw in this logic but knew her parents well enough not to argue. She had been impressed, naturally, by the Wakefield estate but somewhat disappointed in the family itself. Somehow she had expected more stimulating conversation from nobility but she had not heard anything particularly impressive from either Sir George or Lady Ann. *Andrew is an attractive young man but he's been under his brother's thumb so long I doubt he'll ever break free*, she reflected. *He'll probably make a good parson, though.* She looked out the window of the coach as it sped along the dusty road leading back to London and smiled to herself. *Andrew will have to learn to be a little more romantic. I shall insist upon that, anyway.*

———

Arriving at Oxford, fifty miles north of London, during the first week of June in 1731, Andrew Wakefield didn't find it to be as bad as his brother, George, had proclaimed. After being cordially welcomed by the master of Lincoln College, Andrew was pleased to find his lodgings pleasant enough. He was aware, of course, that the university was organized around colleges—each of which had a head known as president, dean, ward, or master—and that a governing body of "fellows" served as teachers. As he settled into the routine, Andrew soon found college life more or less to his liking. He dined "in hall" at five o'clock, along with other students, and was required to be back at his college by nine or he'd be fined. He'd already encountered the disciplinary personnel known as "bulldogs," who wandered the streets in search of rule-breaking undergraduates and had the right to search any house in town with only ten minutes' notice. Breaking the rules could result in confinement (which was known as being "gaited"), suspension, or expulsion (which was called "being sent down").

Class distinctions at Oxford were prevalent. The nobility wore distinctive clothing and their hats were adorned with special tassels or tufts. They also sat at special tables. Andrew was not particularly pleased at being included with this group for he quickly discovered they were not the most studious men at Oxford.

After two weeks passed, he was rather lonely. He had made few friends; most of those men studying for the clergy were either dull or not at all interested in religious matters. Many of them were forced to enter the clergy—to "take orders," as it was called—and they made no bones about stating their dissatisfaction with such a life.

Andrew Wakefield had come to Oxford to learn how to serve God. The dissolute manners and lifestyle of some of the prospective clergy disgusted him. However, he had heard of two particular fellows, Mr. John Wesley and his brother Charles, who had mixed reputations. Andrew listened carefully and found that the more frivolous students disliked both men tremendously. When he questioned one of his acquaintances, a student named Paul Simmons, the young man gave him a sour look. "Oh, you're speaking of 'The Holy Club.'"

"The Holy Club? What's that?"

"Why, it's that bunch of 'saints' led by John Wesley. Have nothing to do with them! They're nothing but a bunch of wild-eyed enthusiasts!"

Simmons's recommendation had little effect upon Andrew. *If Simmons dislikes the men,* Andrew reflected, *there must be something to them.*

So Andrew went out of his way to make the acquaintance of the younger brother, Charles Wesley. Charles, a handsome young man of average height, was charming, witty, and sociable. He at once took to Andrew. "We have a small group that meets once a week. You may have heard of it. Some call it 'The Holy Club,' although we don't call it that ourselves. It has quite a few names. Some call us 'Bible Moths,' 'Bible Bigots,' 'Sacramentarians.' And some call us 'Methodists.' But we simply call ourselves 'our company.'"

"I'd like very much to join you," Andrew said eagerly.

"Capital!" Wesley smiled. "We're meeting tonight in my brother John's room. I'll pick you up and introduce you to the rest of the group."

Andrew looked forward to the meeting. That night Charles Wesley came by his room. "Come along. I've told my brother you're coming and he's anxious to meet you."

He led Andrew to the quarters of John Wesley, and Charles

24

promptly introduced them. "Brother John, this is Andrew Wake-field. I propose him as a welcome member to our company."

John Wesley, a small man of perhaps five feet six inches but with an erect posture, had alert dark brown eyes and long auburn hair that brushed his shoulders. His face was full lipped, with a long, thin nose. "We're happy to make your acquaintance," John said, smiling slightly. "Allow me to introduce you to the rest of our company." The two other men present, Robert Kirkland and William Morgan, greeted Andrew warmly.

Morgan was a handsome man with the unmistakable accent of Wales in his voice. Andrew commented to him, "Some of my ancestors came from Wales. Their name was Morgan too."

William Morgan looked surprised. "Do you tell me that? Why, then, we may be distant cousins. I don't know much about my family tree but my father knows it all. I'll ask him if he knows of any Wakefields crossing our path. But here now, it looks that we're about to start."

The meeting was simple enough. John Wesley was obviously the leader. He led the group in several songs and Andrew joined in with a strong voice. After they'd finished the singing, John told Andrew, "My brother Charles writes songs. From the quality of your voice I wondered if perhaps you are a musician?"

"A very minor one," Andrew replied. "It'll be enough, I think, for me to learn to write sermons, much less hymns."

Charles Wesley seemed drawn to Andrew and smiled warmly at the younger man's rueful tone. "We'll have time to spend together. If I can be of any help with your sermon making, don't hesitate to call."

The meeting consisted almost entirely of songs, prayers, and the sharing of needs. Afterwards, as Charles and Andrew walked back toward their rooms, Charles inquired, "What did you think of our company?" He cocked one eyebrow slightly. "We have a rather bad reputation, I'm afraid."

"I thought the meeting was most amiable," Andrew said sturdily. "I hope to be invited back."

"Certainly! Consider yourself one of us, Andrew. We simply want to help each other as we find our way to God, and to learn to serve the Lord Jesus as best we can."

Pleased, Andrew resolved to become a member in good standing of this club. After he had attended several meetings, he was accosted by an upperclassman named Peter Jamison, who was frowning as he muttered, "Watch out for yourself, Wakefield."

"How so?" Andrew asked in surprise.

"The Holy Club," Jamison retorted. "You don't want to get too mixed up with those fellows."

Andrew was irritated. He knew nothing good of young Jamison and answered him rather sharply. "I find them to be committed to God. They've been most helpful to me in my spiritual life."

Jamison shot him a look of disgust. "Mind what I say. You'll get into trouble. They're enthusiasts, every one of them! Wild, fanciful notions!" He was growing angry. "I've tried to be a friend to you; you'd best mind what I say, Wakefield!" He turned and hurried away, his back stiff.

Andrew walked slowly along. *How can anyone as godly as these men be dangerous?* he wondered and then nodded firmly to himself. *We must earn our way to heaven—and I know of no better company to do it with than that of John Wesley and the Holy Club!*

Three

DISTANT RELATIVES

Andrew left Oxford with high expectations. He had watched the seasons change and now December had come. On the fifth day of the month, as snow was falling lightly, he left his quarters, climbed into a carriage that held several other students who were also headed toward London, and said good-bye to his college for a season.

As the carriage rolled along, snowflakes swirled, falling on the horses' backs, giving them a strange, glistening appearance. Bits of white began to appear on the brown dead leaves beside the road. The wind whistled as it lifted the snow into miniature whirlwinds. Soon the open carriage was coated with the delicate flakes, some as large as a shilling. Andrew huddled tightly in his wool coat, pulled his hat down over his ears, and occasionally beat his mittened hands together to bring the feeling back into them.

The driver gave him a cheerful wink and pulled a bottle out of his pocket. "Hev a bit o' this, sor? 'Twill warm ye bones!"

"No, thank you," Andrew said shortly.

The coachman grinned. "I guess you'd be one o' them holy men, eh? Too good to take a drink? I'm glad 'tisn't my case!" As he tilted the bottle back, his knobby Adam's apple moved up and down rapidly. His neck was skinny, and it was almost like watching a snake swallowing a series of small animals. Popping the bottle away from his lips, he grunted, "Ahhh," then hid the liquor back inside his pocket.

Andrew eyed him with disgust. He'd been ridiculed by his fellow students—and even by some of his masters—for his activities with the Holy Club. He had grown to dislike this name and, along with the other members of the group, referred to it as "our company." It had been a good time for him, he reflected as he settled back to endure the cold ride.

Andrew, along with some of the other members of the small fellowship, had been introduced by William Morgan to a prison ministry. The two Wesleys and Andrew had walked to Bocardo Prison, an old castle at the edge of the city. They had sung hymns and John Wesley had preached. Afterwards the three passed among the miserable prisoners, mostly debtors, and shared Scripture with them. It was the same prison where Cranmer, Ridley, and Latimer had lain before they were burned at the stake.

It had been Andrew's idea to begin a small fund for the purchase of medicines and books and sometimes to help a debtor gain discharge. The bishop had heard of their activities and had sent a message that he was greatly pleased with their undertakings.

The wheels of the carriage now made a hissing sound and snow swept across in diagonal lines as they rolled along. Weariness washed over Andrew in waves. John Wesley was, in Andrew's mind, a wonderful man, but he was also demanding. Wesley urged method and order on all his disciples; he insisted every hour of the day had its proper use, whether for study, devotion, exercise, or charity. He continually urged the group to "keep in their minds an awful sense of God's presence." Wesley had put together and published a small booklet called *A Collection of Forms of Prayer.* The teaching was that as students were at their studies, they could offer up short prayers of petition. Wesley liked to shoot up prayers on the first second of every hour and he encouraged this practice among the company.

The demanding studies, plus the method and stringent discipline of the Holy Club, had inevitably worn Andrew down. He was not displeased with this, however; he thought he was finding his way. Now, as he neared London, he felt a sense of satisfaction that he'd been faithful to God's commandments. Wesley had stressed this—that they *must* please God—and that in order to do this they must work, and work methodically.

Caroline raised her eyebrows as she looked across the table at Andrew. "You've lost weight. I didn't know it was such hungry work, learning to be a minister."

Andrew leaned back in the chair that graced the drawing room of the Barksdale parlor and smiled at Caroline. Her dress was simple, light blue with dark blue trim and white lace at the neckline and wrists. Her hair was done in a new way, he noted. With an effort he took his mind off her appearance and stifled the compliment he was about to pay her. Taking a sip of tea, he murmured, "It's hard work serving God, Caroline. I never knew how hard it really was."

Caroline had been surprised when Andrew had simply appeared at the door. But she had welcomed him, explaining that her parents were calling on friends. Servants were in the house, however, which made it proper enough for Andrew to be her guest for tea. Now she smoothed her silk skirt as she considered Andrew's weary words. "And is it difficult, being a student at Oxford?"

"Nothing is too hard to do for God," Andrew replied. He sounded a bit pompous and sanctimonious, even in his own ears, and he quickly added, "I've enjoyed it. But I've had enough to make me glad for a holiday. Now—tell me what you've been doing."

Caroline spoke of friends, social calls, acquaintances, and Andrew listened quietly. In a few minutes Mrs. Barksdale entered the room. "Why, it's Mr. Wakefield!" she exclaimed as Andrew rose to bow over her hand. "I thought you were at Oxford."

"Christmas holidays, Mrs. Barksdale," Andrew said smoothly. "I'm on my way home but I stopped to call and pay my respects."

Lettie Barksdale's eyes narrowed but she forced a smile. "I'm so happy you could come, Mr. Wakefield. I've been hoping to see your mother and brother again but unfortunately we haven't had the pleasure."

Andrew seized the opportunity. "I'm certain they'll be waiting for you to call during the Christmas season, ma'am. I shall tell Mother to expect you."

This pleased Mrs. Barksdale and she sat down firmly in the parlor. Andrew realized his private visit with Caroline was over. He endured Mrs. Barksdale's pointed questions—mostly about the ministry, a minister's financial expectations, and whether large churches with large livings were readily available—for fifteen minutes. Then he rose. "I truly must be going. My mother will be expecting me."

"I'll be waiting to hear from your family," Mrs. Barksdale reminded him loudly.

"I'll show you to the door," Caroline offered. The two made their way to the front door and Caroline took a step out to say good-bye.

"We didn't have much time to talk," Andrew muttered.

"No, but we'll have more since you're home for some time. I'll have Mother and Father invite you back for dinner."

Andrew took her hand and with uncharacteristic gallantry he leaned over and kissed it. She blushed and teased, "Andrew! They didn't teach you *that* at the minister's school, did they?"

Andrew laughed. "No. I'm having to learn a few things on my own. You'll be hearing from me, Caroline."

When she went back into the house, Caroline's mother was

waiting for her. "I do hope we'll be invited to Wakefield. I've heard such good things about Sir George; now *there's* a man who can do you some good, Daughter."

"Mother, he's as dull as dishwater," Caroline scoffed.

The remark offended Lettie Barksdale, so she immediately launched forth into a lecture about the advantages of marrying well. Caroline could not deter her mother or distract her, so Caroline finally simply left the room. As she went to her bedroom, she thought of the two Wakefield men. Plunking herself down on the bed, she muttered ungraciously, "I don't see why George couldn't be the preacher and Andrew be the lord of the manor!"

Bishop Alfred Crawley was happy enough to see young Wakefield. He knew the family quite well and had spoken several times with Andrew concerning his plans. Now he drew him into his study, which was a large room lined with floor-to-ceiling oak book-shelves. The hardwood floor was covered with a lush Persian carpet so luxuriant, so obviously extravagant, that it seemed out of place even for a bishop.

Crawley, a tall man with gray hair and beetled brows over dark gray eyes, was the most conservative bishop in all of England, many said. But he had a true fondness for young ministers and felt it was his duty to see they went right. He urged Andrew to draw close to the fire and questioned him about his studies. As Andrew spoke, Bishop Crawley listened avidly, his eyebrows going up and down in a regular cadence. As Andrew finished his tale, the bishop nodded approvingly. "It would seem, then, that you've settled down to your work like a true scholar."

"I've tried to do my best, Bishop."

Crawley leaned back in his chair, making a steeple of his long thin fingers. He studied them carefully, almost as if they were a text of Scripture. Underneath his shaggy brows his eyes were sharp and penetrating. "I've heard reports you've been associated with a certain element at Oxford, Mr. Wakefield."

Andrew's heart sank, though he had suspected this might come up. "I've tried to associate only with godly men, my lord."

"Ah, yes. Godly men. 'Tis not for me to say that a man is not godly—however, I must warn you, there are always those who are dissatisfied with the church."

"I don't understand. . . ."

"What I mean, Andrew, is that there are always some who feel the church is somehow not good enough. That they must be more holy."

Clasping his fingers together, the bishop turned his palms outward and with a sharp, quick motion, cracked the joints. Grunting with satisfaction, he rose and went to the warmth of the hearth, holding his hands out to the flames that rose high from the yellow oak logs. Bishop Crawley loved heat and hated cold and now, like a worshiper at a shrine, held his hands even closer to the flames, his eyes half-closed with pleasure. "I refer to Mr. John Wesley and his group—called, I believe, 'The Holy Club.' You're familiar with it."

There was little use denying it; obviously the bishop had heard something. Andrew replied mildly, "Yes, my lord. We have met from time to time to pray, sing hymns, and encourage one another. Also, as I mentioned in my letters to you, we have visited the prisons. And Mr. Wesley has started a school for children of the poor."

Bishop Crawley clasped his heads behind his back, hunched his shoulders, and leaned forward slightly, looking very much like a large bird, with his sharp features highlighted by the fire's uncertain light. "Very well to do such things. But these men are enthusiasts, Andrew. Steer clear of men such as this! I will say it as plainly as I can: Your future in the Church of England is bright. You have a gift. You have intelligence. You have appearance. You have breeding. I'm highly hopeful of placing you in a fine church as soon as your studies are over. But this will be impossible if you go the way of the Wesleys."

Andrew looked into the bishop's eyes. There was something of a carnivore before him, he thought, for even with all his kindness, generosity, and goodness, Bishop Alfred Crawley—like many others in the established church—did not fear the heathens of Africa or the warlike tribes of the Muslims so much as they feared enthusiasm in their own ranks. Andrew understood the bishop was waiting for some assurance but he found he could give him none. "I will be on my guard, my lord, but I must tell you I see nothing but dedication and devotion in the men of whom you speak."

The bishop examined the young man closely and his lips closed into a tight line. "Very well, Andrew. I shall be watching your progress. Now, tell me your plans."

Andrew had been welcomed at home by his mother, who was fond of him and was clearly glad to see him. George had taken him hunting twice and they had made the rounds of the neighbors for various business matters. But it was his Aunt Hope who most encouraged Andrew. He had little chance to talk to her for a week. During that time he saw Caroline only once, but arrangements were made for having the Barksdale family for a dinner and the Barksdales graciously reciprocated by inviting the Wakefields to join them for dinner.

On the Thursday afternoon after his return, Andrew found himself at home in his room and recalled he hadn't spent any appreciable time with his aunt. Tossing his book aside, he left his room, made his way down the hall, and knocked on one of the oak doors. When he heard his aunt's voice, he opened it and stepped inside. "Were you sleeping, Aunt Hope?"

Hope, who was sitting in a chair beside the window, was covered with a heavy woolen blanket and had a cap down over her ears. She smiled at Andrew. "No, I was just hoping you might come by. Come in and stir up the fire, Andrew. Then sit and tell me what you've been doing."

"It's very simple," Andrew replied wryly, as he stirred the coals and added another log. The fire's blaze leaped up anew, casting a cheerful glow in the room as Andrew told his aunt of his experiences at Oxford. It was a small room, but the one window was large enough to allow a good view of the estate. The walls were covered with faded but intricately designed tapestries that he had been told had belonged to Hope's ancestors in Wales. As he spoke he kept his back to the fire but finally he came to sit in a straight-backed chair across from his aunt. "So, you see," he concluded, shrugging, "it's all work at Oxford. If I'm not studying, I'm busy with some of the other young ministers, going to prisons or trying to help the poor. Not a very dramatic life."

Hope Wingate smiled at him. Although her hair was mostly covered by the cap, the wisps that escaped were a shining silvery white. "It's a fine work you're doing, Andrew. Tell me about the young men you've made friends with."

She sat quietly as Andrew spoke with enthusiasm of the members of his group and particularly of John and Charles Wesley. When Andrew told her of William Morgan and his Welsh background, she grew very interested.

"William told me one of his family members knows the family tree of the Morgans," Andrew told her. "He said he'd try to find out if we're related."

"I wouldn't be surprised." Hope's eyes grew thoughtful.

"Tell me again how the Welsh blood got into our line."

"You don't know what you're asking, my boy," Hope said, her clear gray eyes twinkling. "Sir Robert Wakefield had a son by a Welsh woman. Her name was Margred Morgan. The boy became

Sir Myles Wakefield and the line comes through him. But also of the line of Margred Morgan comes a woman called Angharad. She married Sir Christopher Wakefield—she was his second wife—and was my mother, of course. Since I had no children, that branch of the line stops with me. But the blood of Margred Morgan still flows in your veins, Andrew. Here, let me show you the family tree. Get the chart, over in that drawer, will you, my boy?"

Andrew rose to retrieve the chart, then pulled his chair close beside the frail woman. She moved her finger along, naming the Wakefield men: Robert—Myles—then his son William, who was burned at the stake at Smithfield; his son Robin, who fought against the Spanish Armada; then Christopher, who went with the group on the *Mayflower* to America but who didn't stay long; then Christopher's sons, Gavin and Amos. "Amos, as you know, was your grandfather. He married a young noblewoman, Orelia Hampton. Sadly, she died birthing their son, John, who was your father . . . and now, you, Andrew . . . but the Welsh blood is still there," she finished softly.

Andrew was interested in his family, and his Aunt Hope knew more than anyone else. They talked for over an hour, with Andrew mostly listening to her quiet voice telling him of his heritage. Finally he said, "I'm tiring you."

"No, indeed! It's better than food to me to talk about the family. And there's one matter I must discuss with you. It's good we have talked of the Welsh strain in the Wakefield line."

"Why's that?"

"Look at this." Hope produced the second parchment, with another genealogy drawn on it. "You see? Here is Margred Morgan, the mother of Myles. You see she had a brother named John? The line goes like this. . . ." She traced her finger down, pronouncing the strange Welsh names with a native lilt. "There is Gwilym, his son Kelwin, and his son Rhys; here,

Rhys had a son called Evan. I knew him well. He was a fine young man. He married a girl named Jenny, who was an actress for a time. Jenny and Evan had a son," she went on in a lecturing tone, "called Samuel. And Samuel had two children; a son called Gareth and a girl called Dorcas. And it's of these two that I must speak."

Andrew looked down and repeated the names thoughtfully. "Gareth and Dorcas. What of them, Aunt Hope?"

"I've kept in touch with them throughout the years. They've had a most difficult time. Evan went back to Wales and tried to raise his family there. He was a coal miner—as was his son, Samuel—and that's a cruel, hard life. The mines are playing out now but they've always been man-killers anyway."

The light filtered in through the thick glass and bathed the face of the old woman. Her skin was like old ivory and though there were lines on her face, there was strength there too, with a peace and joy Andrew had always admired. Hope had a strange expression in her eyes, almost as if she were dreaming while awake, and she murmured quietly, "I've wanted to do something for those two—Gareth and Dorcas. The mines are dangerous, but when they're shut down—as they are most of the time these days—then hunger becomes something to fear, too."

Andrew was somewhat puzzled. "What is it you want to do? Send money? I'm sure George would agree to that."

"No, that's what I've tried to do, but that's not their answer. They need to leave Wales and come here, to England."

Andrew leaned back and stared at his aunt. She had never spoken so passionately of anything, and now as the fire crackled and snapped in the silence, he wondered what was going on behind that placid expression of hers. "Then what is it, exactly, you want to do?"

"I think it's wonderful you've helped the poor and those who are in prison but I'd like to see you help these two, your kins-people. They're young and they have no future where they are."

"But what can I do?" Andrew asked, perplexed. "Isn't it George's place to see about the family?"

Hope hesitated. "I—I don't think George has a heart for helping people as you do, Andrew. Come here; come close." She waited until he had drawn even nearer; then she took his hands and stared deeply into his direct blue eyes. "I won't be long in this world and somehow I've thought so much of my mother, Angharad, lately. Such a kind, gentle woman she was, so strong, filled with courage . . . these are her people. These are my people—and yours, Andrew." She let the silence run on for a few moments, watching Andrew intently. "Help them, my boy. God will reward you for it."

Andrew Wakefield was not an impulsive man. But he loved this old woman; he was closer to Hope, in many ways, than he was to his own mother. The desire to please his aunt suddenly filled his mind and heart. "I will," he said firmly. "I don't know how I'll do it but I'll do the best I can for them."

Tears filled Hope Wingate's eyes and she squeezed his hands. Before he could stop her, she bent over and kissed them.

"Oh, you don't have to do that—"

"You're searching for God with all your heart," she interrupted softly, looking up at him again. "My prayer is that you will find him. And this may, in some way, be part of God's plan for you—and for the Wakefield line."

Four

"YOU'LL NEVER GET A HUSBAND!"

The November of 1733 was one of the coldest Dorcas Morgan could remember. Even the old people said Wales had never seen such a winter. Dorcas shivered as she opened the door to the little stone house and entered quickly, pulling it sharply behind her to keep out the wintry blasts. Straightening up and rubbing her numb hands together to bring feeling back to her fingers, she glanced darkly around the room.

Illuminated only by two tiny windows on either side of the door, the room was small and cheerless, the poorest of dwellings in the village. Dorcas Morgan had seen it every day of her life for she had been born in the bedroom off to her right. At eighteen, she'd never been as much as a night's journey away from the cottage. She'd decorated it as best she could, with miniature colored pictures on the walls and bright scraps of fabric woven or sewn together for doilies and trim. In summertime the room was always brilliant with wildflowers arranged in any container that might come to hand. Now, however, it was winter, so there were no flowers and Dorcas longed for the spring that seemed so far away.

Crossing the room, she removed her shabby overcoat but kept on her ancient gray wool tunic. Moving to the fireplace, she husbanded what wood she had, quickly and efficiently built a little fire, and gratefully warmed her hands. Since wood was scarce, it was almost like burning money, and Dorcas begrudged each stick that went up in smoke.

Then she straightened, stepped across the room to the single cabinet, and made preparations for a meager breakfast. There was little to be had except for oats and they were running dangerously low. A single piece of bacon remained and the slice she carved off was so thin she could almost see through it.

Ten minutes later she sat at the rough wooden table made by her father, chewing the food slowly, trying to absorb every morsel of energy from the scant portion. The wind whistled through the cracks under the door and around the windows but she ignored the desolate sound. Dorcas Morgan was no more than average height and when she went to the fireplace to put the kettle on for a cup of weak tea, the firelight outlined her slender figure even through the rough and bulky clothing she wore. Her face was long and she had large dark eyes and hair a mixture of brown and night black. Her features were strong and the expression in her eyes and full lips was determined and unafraid. She used her left hand to do her work, keeping her right hand tucked in a fold of her skirt. The fingers on her right hand were curved inward, permanently immobile except for her thumb. Although she had learned to use her maimed hand fairly well, even in the isolation of the room she unconsciously kept it down at her side, entwined in her full skirts, hidden from prying eyes. To her it was a mark of incompleteness, of fault, of flaw, that she could never completely erase from her mind.

"Well! Devil fly off!" she exclaimed as she moved back to the table and treated herself to her second cup of weak tea. "This won't get the work done!" Dorcas often spoke to herself for she was both lonely and mostly alone. The village was small and she knew everyone and had all of her life, but she had never formed close relationships easily. Now as she did the menial household tasks—Dorcas always kept their cottage spotless—she wondered if Gareth had another day's work. The mines opened and closed sporadically. Whispers and rumors had flowed through the village that a shutdown was coming. The thought disturbed her for times were terribly hard. Gareth's work at the coal mines was all that sustained them and in the weeks and months of the shutdowns, starvation stalked the village. No one actually died of starvation for they were all neighbors, and neighbors were careful to see to each other in such critical times. But faces grew gaunt, children cried for more milk, and anything other than the basic sustenance of life—bread and meat—was a far-off, almost forgotten dream. The perpetual threat of starvation hung over the entire land of Wales.

A knock sounded and Dorcas started. When she opened the door, a man in his mid-fifties smiled and bowed slightly. "Good morning, Dorcas! I've brought you some potatoes. Thought you and Gareth might find them tasty."

"Why, thank you, Mr. Ellis," Dorcas replied, rather reluctantly taking the knobby cloth-wrapped bundle the small man held out to her. Seeing he expected to be asked in, she stepped aside resignedly. "Won't you come in?"

"Believe I will." Like most miners, Rhys Ellis was well built and trim and he moved inside with a compact and quick economy. "A bit of weather, what?"

"Yes, it is."

"You'll be needing more wood. More bad weather a-coming," he said succinctly. "You send Gareth to me later and I'll put him in the way of cutting some of mine."

"It's kind you are, Mr. Ellis." Dorcas hesitated, then offered, "A cup of tea for you, is it?"

"There is kind you are," Ellis said. He nodded, pulled off his heavy greatcoat, seated himself at the table, and studied the cabin as Dorcas made tea and small talk. He was no longer a miner but owned a fairly large farm two miles north of the village. His face was narrow, with creases from nose to mouth, and his eyes were too close together. The smile he wore was a bit forced, for Rhys Ellis was not normally a cheerful man. Ellis had worn out two wives and had grown children, two of which—by his second wife—were still at home. His eyes wandered over Dorcas's figure as she bent over the fireplace to retrieve the kettle but as she came to the table he quickly shifted his gaze away. "Seems Gareth will still have work. At least for a time."

Dorcas sighed. "There has been talk of the mines closing again."

"Always talk such as that—and it's usually true, I'm guessing."

"It's hard times, Mr. Ellis."

"You should call me Rhys," Ellis said, his mouth working itself upward with an obvious effort. "I feel like the minister, you calling me that. But I'm no monk—not me!" This was true enough; Rhys Ellis, unlike most Welshmen, never showed his face in chapel. He had a reputation of being a stingy man. His children went about in rags, despite his relative prosperity.

Abruptly he frowned and asked Dorcas, "And what is it you two will do if the mine closes?"

"I—I—don't know." Dorcas simply could not bring herself to call him "Rhys." She was aware the man was well along the road in selecting his third wife; she was also aware he'd already been turned down by every young woman of marriageable age in the district. Even Mary Withers, who was in her late forties, freckled, and cross-eyed, had turned down Rhys Ellis.

And now it's to be my turn, Dorcas thought with a stab of anger. *He's gone through all the able-bodied women and now he's starting on the cripples!* Of course she said nothing of the sort aloud—he had, after all, brought the potatoes—so she sat down with him and determined to listen politely as he began to carry on a conversation that was much more like a monologue. Mostly he bragged about his farm, how well it was doing, and how next year was to be a great year for him.

Ellis kept slyly eyeing her as he spoke but he was unable to draw her into conversation beyond monosyllables. Finally he wound down. "I must be returning to the farm, for we're a-butchering a hog this e'en. I'm of a mind to bring you a nice ham."

Instantly Dorcas knew she could not accept this; it was gift on a larger scale and it would both obligate her to him and also encourage him. "No, no, we couldn't possibly pay for a whole ham," she said quickly. "But I'm thanking you, all the same."

"And who says aught about money, Dorcas?" he asked slyly. "A gift, 'twill be."

"It's very kind you are," Dorcas said carefully, "but it would not be fitting."

Ellis stood and when Dorcas rose he suddenly reached out to take her by the arms. He'd been a miner for many years and his grip was strong. Looking up, she protested, "No, please, Mr. Ellis—"

"No 'Mr. Ellis' to it!" he declared. "Look, girl! It's a plain man I am. You know I've lost my wife, and with two youngers at home, too! I need help with them. And cold weather such as this, a man needs a warm loving woman to warm his blood!" Having gone so far, he locked his arms around her back and kissed her. His breath was rank and the white stubble of whiskers he never seemed to shave closely enough stung her face. Dorcas struggled helplessly in his grasp for he was far stronger than she. He didn't let her go until he was ready.

She stepped back, her face pale, and rubbed her hand across her mouth. "You shouldna have done that, Mr. Ellis!" she said angrily.

"Why, you're a woman, aren't you? And here I'm a man asking you to be his wife!"

"Thank you, but I couldn't even think of it!" Dorcas flung back at him.

Ellis's eyes narrowed. "It's not exactly a herd of young men out there waiting to ask you, Dorcas!" He waited for her answer, but Dorcas merely stared defiantly at him, so he went on in a voice lowered with spite. "You're not likely to get an offer, Dorcas Morgan. There's them in the village what say you're not right—as a woman, it is."

Dorcas's face flushed but her voice was even. "They must say what they will. No one can shut the mouth of a gossip."

"Ah, but there's one way," he countered with another grimace of a grin, "to put the tongues to rest. When you marry me, we'll soon show them whether it's a true woman you are. I'm not so old and I don't mind having another younger or two in the house!"

Sternly Dorcas repressed a shiver of repulsion and found she could not frame proper words to speak.

Ellis grew impatient. "A woman needs a man, Dorcas! I'm not as young as once I was but it's a tight, neat little house I have, a good farm—not a penny owing on it! You'll never starve." He waited a moment, then added, "And this may be your last chance, Dorcas Morgan. You think on it. I'll return tomorrow for your answer."

Dorcas's throat seemed to be closing. She nodded weakly and croaked, "Thank you for the potatoes—but you have my answer now, Mr. Ellis."

"I'll have another one," he said smugly as he pulled on his coat and set his cap firmly on his head. He looked her up and down, considering kissing her again. Dorcas stood straight, her head held high, her eyes direct. Finally he turned without speaking and left the cottage.

Dorcas stood motionless, staring at the door as it closed sharply behind him. She had known this scene was coming and she had tried to think of how to prevent it, but no escape had been possible. And it had been worse than she had anticipated.

It was true enough she had no suitors. Her right hand had been

44

injured when she was three and had never healed properly, so she'd been set apart from other girls who were "whole." Her own mother, before she died, had done her best to convince Dorcas she was the same as other girls. But Dorcas had felt shame and embarrassment all her life, as if she had done something wrong. A few boys had chased her when she was coming into her teens but she had not known how to handle them and had put up a wall between herself and them that would have baffled any young man. *Dorcas doesn't like boys,* the whisperers said. She had learned to be, and live, alone.

Now she thought of Rhys Ellis's hard words: *It's not exactly a herd of young men out there waiting to ask you, Dorcas!* Slowly she sat and stared unseeing at the hewn surface of the table. She looked into the future and saw nothing but poverty and a life barren of the simplest of joys other women had.

<hr>

Dorcas looked up as she was setting the table for supper. "Gareth! What's wrong? How did your face get all bruised?"

Gareth Morgan, at sixteen, was a full six feet in height and weighed 180 pounds. He was strongly built, both by blood inheritance and by three years of coal mining. His hair was as black as the coal he dug from the cold ground and it had a crisp curl to it that defied even the choke hold of coal dust. The eyes in his wedge-shaped, handsome face were so dark blue they seemed almost black. The only extravagance about Gareth's face was his thick, lustrous eyelashes, the envy of every girl and woman who met him. This embarrassed him, which in turn angered him and he often was obliged to engage in man cracking over any remarks made by other young fellows.

"Gareth? What is it you've got yourself into?" she insisted.

Throwing himself clumsily into a chair, he glowered at her. He'd obviously been drinking. "They're closing the mines!"

"Oh, no!"

"Oh, yes," he mocked her. Staring down blankly at the plates that contained a small portion of bacon and a few of Ellis's potatoes, he grunted, "As soon as we eat this, it's starving we'll be!"

Dorcas rested her left hand on his broad shoulder and whispered, "We'll get by."

"We'll bloody well starve!" The tone of his voice was cold and cruel, which was unusual for Gareth. Except for his quick flashes of temper, he was normally cheerful and generous to a fault, well liked by all. But the hardness of life was weighing on him. Others in the village generally learned to live with it but Gareth couldn't seem to accept it. As the years had gone by and Gareth had been obliged to become a man, he'd seen there was little chance his life—or indeed, any miner's life in Wales—would ever get better. The owners of the mines lived in England and cared nothing for those who worked like animals, groping in the dark bowels of the earth for the coal. What did they care about the black lung disease that killed healthy, strong men before they were thirty? What did they care about the mine cave-ins that crushed men like bugs, far beneath the surface of the earth? What did they care about the hungry and hopeless widows and orphans of these men who died scrabbling for the black rock? Political organizations did exist and they worked to force the owners to make conditions better for the miners. But Gareth had long since decided such organizations were worthless and cursed them under his breath. Welshmen kept mining—and dying.

He looked up to Dorcas and saw her face was white with strain. Standing again, he patted her shoulder awkwardly. "Ah, none of this caterwauling helps, does it? I'll be washing up and then we'll have a bite of supper."

He washed his face and hands as well as he could, using what little water could be heated on the small fire. Staring down at his hands, which never really came clean, he saw the coal dust thickly engrained in the creases, scars, and calluses. Suddenly it seemed to him that hands were the mirror of life: One's soul got scarred and calloused and neither would a man's spirit come clean. He let the thought run through his mind and the taste of bitterness, strong and rank and wild, mixed with the eternal grit of coal dust in his mouth. Then, glancing at Dorcas as she waited anxiously for him, he turned and put his futile anger away. "Now, let's sit and eat! And what's this? Where have you gotten potatoes, now?"

"Just eat, Gareth," Dorcas said wearily. "No—a blessing first."

Gareth bowed his head rebelliously and muttered a semblance of a blessing. With his knife he opened up one of the potatoes, which Dorcas had cooked in their reddish jackets. The firm, fresh, white meat steamed up, fragrant in his nostrils, and he lavished a slab of white butter and salt and pepper on it. Hungrily he began to eat. "Naught such as potatoes!" he said, grinning at her. "Come, now! Where'd you get such fine treats?"

Dorcas knew he'd have it out of her, so she replied carelessly, "Mr. Ellis stopped by. He left us four of them."

"Ellis, eh?" Gareth stopped chewing and frowned at his sister. "And I'm thinking he asked you to marry him?"

Dorcas looked up, her eyes dark with misery. "Yes, that he did."

"And are you going to?"

"No! How could you think such a thing, Gareth?"

Gareth shrugged. "He's older than you, but 'tis not unheard of. Minnie Satterfield was only seventeen when she married Tom Gifford, and him at least sixty."

"I'm not Minnie Satterfield and I'll not have him!"

Gareth smiled at the sudden flash in Dorcas's dark eyes. "Good! It'd be like marrying a—a—a porcupine!"

"You've never seen a porcupine, now, have you? Just pictures of them!" Dorcas teased.

"I know," he said with equanimity, "but that's the worst thing I could think of." Gareth had an imaginative mind and his eyes grew far seeing. "I wonder what it'd be like, being a porcupine?" he mumbled.

Dorcas looked puzzled. "You think of the oddest things, Gareth!"

"Hmm? No, I mean—I mean—how do they kiss each other? How do they make love? Seems to me they'd be saying 'Ow!' quite a bit!"

Dorcas couldn't contain her laughter. "Oh, you are a fool! Here, now, eat your supper before it's as cold as the snow!"

After supper, Dorcas washed up and then read to Gareth from a history book that had been a favorite of their father's. The two had been orphaned after his death for they had no other kin. Because of this, they'd always been close. As Gareth listened to Dorcas's voice but not the words, he thought bitterly, *I see now how we two are lining up. . . . I'll be a drunk and you'll be an old maid!*

❦

The day after Rhys Ellis had delivered Dorcas his potatoes and his offer, he appeared again at the door of the Morgans' cottage. This time Gareth was home and Dorcas had begged him not to leave her alone with Ellis when he called again. Obviously Gareth's presence irritated Ellis but the young man merely grinned at him and whittled at a piece of wood. Finally Ellis snorted, shot up out of the chair, and announced angrily, "I'll come back, Dorcas!"

Dorcas replied, "Oh, no, don't bother yourself, Mr. Ellis. I've given you your answer, sir."

He glowered at her, his face flushed with heat. "You'll be getting no other offers! Not a cripple like you!"

Gareth Morgan moved quicker than one could imagine a man could move. One moment the young man was sitting with his chair tilted back against the wall, an insolent smile on his face, whittling aimlessly at the stick. The next he towered over Rhys

48

Ellis, one strong hand wrapped around his throat. "You'll speak respectfully to my sister or I'll break your scrawny neck, Ellis!"

Ellis squealed piggishly but Gareth ignored it. He dragged Ellis across the room, pulled the door open, and shoved him out, adding a hearty kick to the rear for good measure. Then he plucked Ellis's coat and hat off the pegs by the door and threw them out after him. "Don't bother to call again!" he shouted and slammed the door.

Dorcas's hand was at her throat, and her eyes were wide. "You shouldn't have done that, Gareth," she whispered.

"No, I should have broken his nose! Maybe he wouldn't be so quick to be lookin' down it then!"

"He'll make trouble. . . ."

Gareth went to her, put his hands on her shoulders, and stared down at her. "Here we are, no work, no food, no prospects—and you think that old stringy rooster is trouble?" He turned abruptly and went back to his whittling.

All that day the brother and sister were quiet. Gareth whittling in moody silence, and Dorcas going about her housework.

That afternoon another knock sounded at the door. Gareth frowned. "Probably Ellis. Maybe this time I'll take care of his nose!"

Ignoring Dorcas's protests, Gareth went to the door and opened it, already visualizing the range from his fists to Ellis's nose.

But it was a stranger who stood on the Morgans' stoop. A man, shorter than Gareth and slightly older, looked up at him. "Yes, sir?"

"I'm looking for Gareth and Dorcas Morgan." The stranger's accent was unmistakably English and his tone undoubtedly cultured.

"I'm Gareth Morgan. Come in out of the cold." Gareth stepped back and motioned to Dorcas. "This is my sister, Dorcas." He eyed the smaller man curiously. "And how may we be of service to you, sir?" Gareth felt obliged to call him "sir," for the man was obviously of the gentry. His clothing was well cut, his coat new and made of thick, luxuriant wool, and his boots were finely made. The man removed his hat, revealing dark blond hair, and his blue eyes were clear and direct as he eyed Gareth and Dorcas.

"My name is Andrew Wakefield." He hesitated, watching Gareth and Dorcas carefully. "I thought you might have heard the name. . . ?"

"Why, surely, sir," Dorcas said eagerly. "We get letters from a distant relative who lives with a family named Wakefield."

"That would be my aunt, Hope Wingate," Andrew said, nodding.

An awkward silence filled the room. At length Dorcas stirred and said, "Please sit down, won't you, Mr. Wakefield?"

"Yes, I believe I will," Andrew said gratefully, pulling off his coat. Dorcas took it from him. As she hung it on the wooden pegboard, he saw her right hand was maimed and he averted his eyes. But Dorcas had seen his glance. Smoothly Andrew went on, "I'm sorry to come without giving you some notice of my visit, but it was rather a quick trip. I didn't know too much in advance that I was coming myself."

As soon as Andrew had left the coach, he had immediately taken in the poverty and drabness of the village. Like most other Welsh villages, it was bleak looking: small hovels huddled together, and very little richness or warmth about it, especially in midwinter, when the mines were usually shut down. He had inquired at the local church, where the minister, Griffin, had spoken highly of Gareth and Dorcas Morgan. Griffin had spent an hour with Wakefield after he had found out his errand.

"Sad thing, sad thing," Griffin had told Andrew. "Lost their parents within a year of each other, with no other kin in the world. Gareth works in the mine—when there is work—and

Dorcas keeps the house. Gareth's only sixteen but he does a full man's work. Not for a man's wages, though." Bitterness creased the minister's lips. "The mine owners see to that. Until a boy is past sixteen, he can't get a man's wage."

"That hardly seems fair," Andrew commented.

"Fair! And when did a mine owner ever decide to be fair?" Griffin retorted angrily, then recovered and glanced up at Andrew. "I'm sorry, sir. I didn't mean to get into that. Now, about Gareth and Dorcas. They're not as godly as their parents, I must say. Dorcas comes to church, but Gareth—never! I've tried to talk to him— and he will listen—but he'll have nothing at all to do with religion."

"Is he an honest young man?"

"Oh, yes, I should say so!"

Andrew listened as the minister gave a description of Gareth's life and activities and then he asked about Dorcas.

"Yes—well—it's a little strange," Griffin said with some diffi- culty. "She's not a bad-looking woman—not beautiful, you see, but not at all ill-favored. Other girls far less attractive than Dorcas have gotten married. She's eighteen now and as far as I know she's never been interested in a man. I do think, though, that it's her own fault."

"How so?"

Griffin made a careless gesture. "She has a bad hand; it was crushed when she was a child. A horse stepped on her. The hand never healed correctly. Her right hand, it is. She feels—different— unworthy, I would think. I worry about her." He eyed Andrew cautiously. "You are a relation, sir?"

"Yes, some of my ancestors are Welsh." Andrew explained the connection and finished by saying, "I came to visit them. Will you tell me, Reverend, where I can find their cottage?"

Griffin gave Andrew directions and ended their conversation by saying, "Anything you can do to help them, Mr. Wakefield, anything, would be a godsend. There's not much hope in this place for them."

Now, as Andrew studied Gareth and Dorcas and their small cottage, he reflected that Reverend Griffin had been right. Pulling an envelope out of his pocket, he said, "I have a letter here for you two, from Aunt Hope."

"Oh, wonderful!" Dorcas exclaimed. "She's so kind and always sends us a little money—" Suddenly she cut off the words, as if she had said something shameful. Hesitantly she took the envelope, then offered it to Gareth.

"No, you read it," he said, shaking his head.

Dorcas scanned the letter quickly, then looked at Andrew thoughtfully. "She speaks very highly of you, Reverend Wakefield."

"She's my favorite relative," Andrew said, smiling. "I've always felt that way about her. You'd like her very much, Miss Morgan."

"I should like to meet her but that hardly seems likely."

Andrew hesitated, searching first Dorcas's face, then Gareth's, and then made his decision. Normally Andrew was not a man of hasty decisions but he felt he had acted as conscientiously as he could. He had found out all he could about the character of the two Morgans. He'd measured them personally and been impressed with them, and looking at the poverty evident in the small cottage, he felt he truly had no other choice.

"I didn't come just to visit, Miss Morgan, Mr. Morgan," he said slowly, his eyes on Dorcas Morgan's face. She was younger than he was, he judged, but perhaps only a year or two. Her face was rather plain and because of her rough clothing, it was difficult to tell about her figure. But he thought that his Aunt Hope could do—something—for the girl. After all, her features were even and her dark brown hair showed promise. Then he studied Gareth Morgan and saw he was strong, with a man's body and hands that showed that he worked hard.

"Then what is it you've come for?" Gareth was asking curiously. "We don't get many visitors, you know."

"No, I'm sure you don't," Andrew said dryly. "I'm here, you see, at the insistence of my Aunt Hope. She's very concerned about you. She says times are hard here."

"Yes, sir. You can see that for yourself," Gareth said, waving his hand in an all-encompassing motion.

"The mines are shut down?"

"Yes, they're shut down," Gareth replied forcefully, "and when they're not shut down, they don't pay enough to keep a man's body and soul together."

"I take it it's not likely to get any better."

"No, sir," Dorcas said quietly. "It's always been this way and I believe it always will be. Many have left the village but it's no better in the big cities. There's not work to be had there, either."

Andrew took a deep breath. "I hope you won't think me presumptuous, but actually I've come here to make you an offer." He could see they were riveted by his words and he went on quietly. "Not a very great offer, I'm afraid, but perhaps you'd be interested."

"What kind of offer, sir?" Gareth demanded.

"I think something better might be found for you in England," Andrew answered.

Dorcas stared at him as if he'd said something quite impossible. "In—England? You mean—you want us to come to—England?"

"It's up to you and your brother, of course, Miss Morgan," Andrew said smoothly. "But I think you should know my aunt is not in good health and she needs someone to care for her as she gets older. I believe you would find that within your powers, would you not, Miss Morgan?"

"Why, of course!" Gareth answered eagerly for Dorcas. "She takes care of every sick thing in the village! But what about me?"

"The minister tells me you were quite a scholar in school—although he says you don't go to church."

53

Gareth flushed. He had no answer, for Andrew spoke the truth. It sounded boastful to say he was a scholar—and he couldn't deny he hadn't gone to church since his parents had died. Andrew smiled at his confusion. "Churchgoing is not a requirement for what I have in mind, Mr. Morgan, but it's something a young fellow like you should consider." The smile faded and he became serious. "Do you know what a *servitor* is?"

"No, sir, I don't."

"A servitor, at Oxford," Andrew explained, "is a rather strange convention. It's a young man who comes to Oxford and works— at whatever there is to be done. Building fires, valeting for the students, blacking their boots, and so on."

"A servant?" Gareth's tone was edgy.

"I'm afraid so. But the servitors are actually students at the college. So yes, they do these services, but they also can get an education."

"Oh, that would be wonderful!" Dorcas exclaimed. Her large blue eyes lit up and Andrew thought she was almost pretty at that moment. She moved to stand beside Gareth and took his hand. "Oh, Gareth! You were so good in school! If you just had a chance to get a good education . . ."

Gareth frowned, struggling with the vision of this sudden life change. "I've never actually been a servant before, sir."

"Oh, yes you have," Dorcas argued. "You're a servant of the men who own the mines! I see no difference in blacking some- one's boots and digging coal out of the ground—for someone else!"

Gareth suddenly grinned. "I believe you're right, Sister." He turned back to Andrew. "Please tell me some more, sir."

Andrew spoke with the brother and sister who were almost breathless and in shock as Andrew expounded on his plans for them. The means to help Gareth and Dorcas Morgan had come to him as an inspiration. Hope certainly needed someone to care for her, and Dorcas seemed to be fit for this. As for Gareth, if the young boy had any brains at all, being a servitor at Oxford would certainly be a good chance to get himself out of these awful coal mines. Finally Andrew said, "The minister offered me a room in the parsonage for the night. I'll let you two talk this over. I shall need to leave tomorrow, so if you can't make your minds up right away, perhaps you can write me."

"Thank you, sir," Dorcas said gratefully. She moved to him as he rose, and held out her left hand to Andrew, which he took with ill-concealed surprise. Gareth also was surprised, for this was unlike Dorcas. "Thank you very much, sir," she said again in a low voice.

Andrew returned to Reverend Griffin's house and the two men sat up talking for some time. When he explained what he had done, Reverend Griffin slapped the table with exuberance. "Just the thing for the boy!" he declared. "He's a real scholar! A mite hot-tempered, you understand, but that's not such a bad thing for a young man. Needs a little spice in him, to my mind. With a little help, he'll be a fine young man."

The next morning, after he had breakfast with the minister, Andrew walked back to the Morgans' cottage. Both of them had dark circles under their eyes and they looked rather wan. *I'll bet they didn't sleep a moment,* Andrew reflected. Dorcas made tea and the three sat down at the rough table and enjoyed the hot, steaming brew, although it was rather weak, Andrew thought.

Abruptly Gareth interrupted the small talk. "Sir, we've been up all night, talking."

"I suppose this isn't a thing to be easily decided," Andrew said.

"We'd like to go with you," Dorcas said softly.

"Are you sure? This is your home, I know, and it's never easy to leave a place you've been all your life."

Gareth shook his head. "It can't be harder than staying here, sir."

Andrew nodded. "I must ask you one thing, Mr. Morgan. As I

55

mentioned, you'll be required to serve the other students, and likely you'll have a hard time of it—especially the first year. Some of the older chaps—well, let's just say they aren't the gentlemen they should be. Some of them can be sharp and harsh, unkind. I'm sorry to have to say it but there it is."

Gareth met his eyes. "You want to know if I can keep my temper."

"That's it. It'll be necessary, you see."

"I don't set myself up for an even-tempered man," Gareth said slowly. "But I want to learn, I want an education. I believe I'd do just about anything honorable to get one, sir."

Andrew was pleased. "That's a fine answer. I'll hold you to it, as your word."

"Certainly, sir."

The three talked for a while longer; then Andrew rose to leave. "My stage leaves in an hour and I must return to the parsonage to get my things." Dorcas fetched his coat and hat and he looked down at her with a kindly expression. "I think we're going to make my aunt very happy."

"She's been so kind to us and I'm so anxious to meet her," Dorcas said.

"I don't know how long this might go on, Miss Morgan. As long as Aunt Hope lives, I suppose. As long as you wish to stay. But you might marry," he added offhandedly.

Dorcas looked up at him and they were silent for a moment. "No, sir," she said evenly. "I will never marry. I will work."

Her directness startled Andrew Wakefield. He had rarely seen such forthrightness, not even in most men. As he returned to the parsonage, he thought, *Now there is a pair for you. . . . I wonder how they'll do in England?*

Five

AN OPEN DOOR

orcas blinked nervously as she entered the enormous wooden doorway, wishing for a brief moment she had remained in Wales. Leaving their home had been a traumatic experience, both for her and for Gareth, as they'd left behind not only a cottage but also their country, the people they had known since their birth, and a way of life. Coming to England had been as alien to Dorcas Morgan as crossing the ocean and landing in Africa.

They had gone first to Oxford, where Andrew had made the arrangements for Gareth to enter into his new life there. Dorcas had clung to Gareth when they'd parted. He'd whispered to her, "Don't worry, Sister. It'll be all right."

She'd wished desperately there were some way the two of them could remain together. But she knew this was impossible, so she'd obediently continued her journey with Andrew Wakefield.

Andrew was sensitive enough to realize the fears the young woman was enduring. All during the daylong rides from Wales he'd attempted to encourage both Dorcas and Gareth in their new endeavors. Andrew was, ordinarily, rather good at this sort of thing. But he'd never faced this exact situation of throwing two young people into a completely different life. Each day he'd watched as Dorcas grew more and more withdrawn and apprehensive and finally he'd felt a pang of apprehension as the girl clung to her brother so desperately at Oxford.

Maybe I've made a mistake, he'd thought nervously. *It's a dangerous thing to do, tinkering with people's lives. . . .* Then he'd comforted himself by thinking how much help Dorcas would be to his Aunt Hope.

"Welcome home, Mr. Andrew," Baxter said warmly. The steward's honest face was wreathed in smiles. He'd known Andrew since boyhood and shook his hand heartily.

"It's good to be home," Andrew said. "This is Miss Dorcas Morgan, a young woman you'll be seeing a great deal of. She's to be a companion to my aunt. Dorcas, this is James Baxter, our steward. James, I'll take Dorcas and introduce her to my brother. Is he here?"

"No, sir, he's not," Baxter answered. "He should be back tomorrow. Your mother is at home, of course."

"Very well, we shall see her," Andrew said rather wearily.

"Fine, sir," Baxter said, nodding.

Dorcas was encouraged by the steward's friendly smile but her heart began to beat rapidly as she followed Andrew Wakefield down the long hallway. The walls were adorned with portraits the like of which she had never seen. She wondered if they were all Wakefield ancestors and determined to find out more about the stern men and beautiful women later. Turning to the right, Andrew led her down a shorter hallway, paused before a door, and knocked quietly. A voice answered and he opened the door.

"Mother, I'd like you to meet Dorcas Morgan. Dorcas, this is my mother, Lady Ann Wakefield."

Dorcas had no idea how to behave with nobility. She'd had no training at all and certainly no experience. In her nervousness she could only manage to bob her head.

"Come closer," Lady Ann ordered rather loudly. When the girl took three steps and halted, Lady Ann looked her over carefully, then nodded. "I hope you had a good journey. Your brother is with you?"

"No, we left him at Oxford," Andrew explained. "He's to be a servitor there."

"Oh yes, I'd forgotten. I'm glad you've come, Dorcas. Your mistress will be Mrs. Wingate. You'll be a great help to her, I'm sure."

"Yes, ma'am. I'll do my very best."

"Take her to Hope, Andrew," Lady Ann said imperiously. "Then return to me. I have some matters to discuss with you."

"Of course, Mother."

Andrew turned and held the door for Dorcas, who hurried out of the room. She was breathing rapidly and her thoughts were scattered. How would she ever learn to meet, and live with, such great persons as Lady Ann Wakefield?

"My mother is rather a formal person," Andrew said in a kindly tone. "But she'll grow fond of you as time goes on. Now, let's go see my aunt."

As they moved down more hallways and made turns, Dorcas stared wide-eyed at the rich tapestries that adorned the wall, at the golden urns and vases that graced carved, ornate walnut and rosewood sideboards and pedestals. It occurred to her that a single one of the heavy silver candlesticks—there were many of them— would have fed her and Gareth for weeks back in Wales. But she had little time for such thoughts, for Andrew had stopped before another door and knocked lightly. A faint voice answered and he opened the door and stepped aside to let Dorcas go before him.

Inside the room, a woman sat in a chair beside a window, huddled against the cold with a multicolored woolen throw over her lap. Dorcas could see she had fine, delicate, aristocratic features and a kindly face, though it was thin and pinched looking. And though she looked tired, her gray eyes were alight and alert.

"Here she is, Aunt Hope," Andrew said lightly by way of

introduction. He smiled and nodded at Dorcas. "This is your kinswoman, all the way from Wales, Dorcas Morgan."

"Please, come closer, my dear," the tiny woman said softly.

Just the use of the words "my dear" were encouraging to Dorcas. The kindness and warmth in the woman's face and the obvious pleasure with which she greeted Dorcas had taken away most of the fears that had cloaked the young girl since she walked through the massive front door of Wakefield. Dorcas moved forward and when the woman put her hand out, Dorcas clasped it tightly. Although the hand was small and the bones seemed almost as fragile as glass, the woman's grip was much firmer than Dorcas had supposed it could be.

"I'm so glad you're here, Dorcas," Hope said, smiling.

Dorcas swallowed hard. "Mrs. Wingate, I must thank you again, in person, for the help you've been to me and my brother. You'll never know how great a hope you've been in our lives." Dorcas thought again how many times the small gifts of money had come just when it seemed there was no possible way for the two Morgans to survive. She returned Hope's smile with a shy one of her own. "We can never thank you enough for all your kindnesses."

Hope accepted this with a wave of her free hand. "'Twas nothing at all, dear. Come and sit beside me. I want to know all about you, and I know you'll want to know all about my mother, Angharad Morgan."

Andrew said politely, "Now I'll leave you two while I go speak to Mother." He bowed in the direction of the two women but his eyes were on Dorcas. "I leave you in good hands, Dorcas. Later I'll introduce you to the other servants and our housekeeper, Mrs. Beard. She'll see about a place for you. Aunt Hope, it's good to see you looking so well."

"Come back when you can," Hope called as he left the room. "I want to hear about everything." After he closed the door behind him she turned to Dorcas. "Now, tell me all about yourself. . . ."

Dorcas untied her cloak and hung it on the peg by the front door, then hurried down the hallway toward the kitchen. Her eyes were bright and her cheeks rosy from the cold. A pleased smile played upon her lips as she entered the kitchen where Naomi Beard, the housekeeper, was speaking with Bertha, Lady Ann's maid. Mrs. Beard greeted Dorcas by smiling and saying, "Your face is red, Dorcas! Are you frozen to ice?"

"Oh no, ma'am," Dorcas said, smiling. "Look what I've found!" She held out a basket with her left hand. Pulling back the linen cloth with the thumb of her maimed hand to display the speckled eggs nested inside the cloth, she went on excitedly, "I found eight! Cecile is laying again. Two of them are hers."

"Cecile, indeed," Mrs. Beard said, sniffing. "You treat those chickens as if they were children!" She was a tall, strong-boned woman with iron-gray hair, thin lips, and a rather prominent chin and jaw. Although a stern taskmaster to the servants, male and female, she was not unkind. In fact, Mrs. Beard had grown quite fond of the young Dorcas Morgan. "And will you be making Mrs. Wingate one of your famous egg dishes?"

"Yes, indeed. But it will only take two eggs—perhaps I could make something Lady Ann would like, as well?"

"Hmm" was all Mrs. Beard deigned to reply, and then she imperiously dismissed Bertha. When the young maid was gone she turned back to Dorcas, and her eyes sparkled. "And save one of them for you and one for me, Dorcas. After all, we're deserving, aren't we? For locating those hens and scouting out their hiding places!"

"Oh, it's such fun!" Dorcas breathed a happy sigh. "I've always wanted chickens to take care of but we could never afford them. Seems that back in Wales we always ate them before they could lay."

"Aye, when you're hungry, a hen on the table's better than

eggs in the henhouse in a fortnight," Mrs. Beard agreed philo-
sophically. "And I'm thinking these hens would have been eaten
by now if you hadna found them and protected them." The
chickens had been running wild about the estate; it had been
Dorcas's idea and delight to gather them, pen them up, feed
them, and gather eggs. She'd thought it strange no one had
thought to do this before, since it was almost impossible to find
the eggs. The hens laid them in secret places, which they
changed as soon as they were found out. It had been Dorcas's
delight to get permission to gather the hens and pen them up.
With the help of Silas, the coachman, and Jeremiah, the gardener, she'd built a fence and a small shed where the chickens
could take shelter in the cold weather. Over the few weeks
Dorcas had been at Wakefield the little flock had increased and
several chicks now were growing rapidly. She loved each
chicken and named them all.

"I'll just make these dishes for Miss Hope and Lady Ann," she
said cheerfully. "And it looks like we'll have two eggs left over."

"And don't you be forgetting! You'll be expected to bring
Mrs. Wingate down for the tea this afternoon," Mrs. Beard
reminded her.

"Hmm . . . I have nothing to wear," Dorcas mumbled, mostly
to herself.

"The blue dress will do," Mrs. Beard decided. "The Quality
don't particularly care to have their attendants well dressed, you
know. They don't want them in rags, mind you, but modest and
ladylike."

Dorcas saw the truth in this and replied humbly, "Yes, ma'am.
I'll see Miss Hope is ready."

Quickly Dorcas prepared her precious eggs and a short time
later left the kitchen with a tray holding two silver platters with
two heavy silver covers. First she went to Lady Ann's room, where
she found the mistress of Wakefield reading a thick, leather-bound

book. "I found some eggs, ma'am," she said shyly. "I thought you might like this recipe."

Lady Ann looked up from her book. "Very well, set it down here." Dorcas set one of the platters down, removed the cover, then stepped back. Lady Ann took a tiny taste and nodded. "What's in it?"

"Oh, just eggs and cheese, a few spices, a little ham," Dorcas replied carelessly. "I'm glad you like it, Lady Ann. I made another for Miss Hope."

"It's very good. Take Hope's to her, Dorcas."

Dorcas went to the apartment where Hope Wingate lived. She'd also brought a small pot of tea and she set the heavy tray on a tea table in Hope's room. "I've brought you something you'll like very much, Miss Hope."

Hope looked up and smiled. "What is it this time?"

Dorcas had proven to be an excellent cook and was expert at making special dishes to tempt the woman's birdlike appetite. Hope hobbled over to the tea table and looked down at the silver platter.

"Something good, Miss Hope," Dorcas answered. "Sit down and I'll pour your tea."

When Hope tasted the egg dish, her eyes opened wide with surprise. "This is very good! Wherever did you get the eggs? I thought the chickens had stopped laying or were gone or something."

"Oh, I've got them all penned up now. Don't you remember, I told you all about our adventures—me and Silas and Jeremiah on a hen hunt and making the pen and shed? Drink your tea now, while it's hot."

Hope nibbled at the eggs and took delicate sips of the tea. She watched Dorcas, who was moving about the apartment, straightening her bedcovers, fussing with the pillows, running her fingers over the surfaces of the bedstead and tables to check for dust. *How much comfort she's been to me since she came,* Hope reflected. Then she asked, "Did you keep one of the eggs for yourself?"

Dorcas smiled. "Yes, and one for Mrs. Beard, too. I hope to raise a big enough flock so everyone can have eggs most of the time."

She sat down by Hope as she spoke. Her eyes were bright and her expression peaceful. Dorcas was quite different from when she first arrived. *She was like a frightened young bird then,* Hope thought. *All eyes, and beak tightly clamped together, not saying a word . . . but a little kindness can work miracles.*

"I think having you here is the nicest thing that's happened to me in a long time, Dorcas," Hope said softly.

Dorcas blushed. She was unaccustomed to compliments, although she'd found Hope Wingate was more generous with them than anyone she'd ever known. "It's been so good to be here, Miss Hope! I've never had so much to eat!"

"A fat little piglet you'll be if you keep on!" Hope teased. "Or perhaps you think the young men like plump young women?" She saw her careless remark disturbed Dorcas. "Hmm, what's this? What's the matter, Dorcas?"

"Oh, nothing, Miss Hope." Dorcas got up to fuss at the tea tray and changed the subject abruptly. "Mrs. Beard says I'm to take you down to tea at two o'clock."

"Why, yes," Hope said thoughtfully. "I believe I do feel well enough to go down for tea."

"Who's to be here?" Dorcas asked.

"It'll be mostly the Barksdales. They're a wealthy family from London."

"You must wear that lovely wine-colored dress, Miss Hope," Dorcas said firmly.

Hope laughed. "It doesn't matter much what I wear. Everyone will be looking at Caroline Barksdale, as always."

"Caroline Barksdale?"

"Yes, she's the daughter. An attractive young woman—one of

those that men can't seem to look away from." Hope smiled slightly. "Andrew won't be paying much attention to anyone else."

"Oh," Dorcas mumbled. "Is he to marry her, then?"

"I fear he's going to try," Hope answered stiffly, "though I hope I'm wrong."

Dorcas was startled. She'd poured herself a cup of tea and tasted it cautiously as she considered Hope's words. Quietly she asked, "Don't you like Miss Barksdale, Miss Hope?"

"Oh, she's a fine girl, I suppose. But I'm afraid she's not suited for Andrew." Suddenly Hope felt vaguely disloyal for making this judgment aloud and went on quickly, "Please don't repeat what I've said to anyone, Dorcas."

"Oh, no, ma'am, I wouldn't." But Dorcas was extremely curious and she thought hard about Andrew Wakefield. She couldn't resist asking, "And so he cares for her, you think?"

"He gives all the evidences young men give when they're interested in young women," Hope replied formally. Dorcas thought her mistress was no longer willing to speak of the matter, so she dismissed it.

"Well, we'll dress you up so you'll put this young woman to shame," Dorcas said with a smile.

When they left Hope's apartment at two o'clock, Dorcas was pleased at how well Hope looked. She moved slowly, clinging to Dorcas's arm with one hand and leaning heavily on a cane with her other. But she did look very nice in the wine-colored velvet dress. Dorcas had arranged her shining silver-white hair prettily and Hope wore a gold necklace with square red stones.

"This necklace was given to me by my father," Hope told Dorcas.

Dorcas had learned the Wakefield family tree. "Sir Christopher?"

"Yes, indeed. I wish you could have known him, Dorcas! What a fine-looking man he was! And so kind!"

The two entered the large parlor where more than a dozen people were gathered. Andrew was standing at the far end of the room, talking to a young woman Dorcas knew at once must be Caroline Barksdale. He turned as they entered and hurried to Hope's side. "Why, Aunt! Look at you!" His eyes shone with admiration and pleased surprise. "I haven't seen you looking so pretty since—since—"

"Don't commit yourself, Andrew," Hope teased. Looking pointedly at Caroline, who had followed Andrew, she remarked, "You look beautiful, Miss Barksdale."

"As do you, Mrs. Wingate," Caroline replied gracefully. "Where did you get such a beautiful necklace?"

Dorcas listened as the two women exchanged pleasantries and suddenly she was aware of Caroline Barksdale's lively brown eyes resting on her. She held the woman's gaze for a moment, then dropped her head.

"This is my Aunt Hope's kinswoman, Dorcas Morgan, from Wales. She's come to be a companion to her," Andrew explained.

Caroline Barksdale said politely, "I know you must be a comfort to Mrs. Wingate." Her eyes grazed Dorcas Morgan's right hand; then she glanced up to see the girl was embarrassed.

Later, when Caroline spoke to Andrew, he told her of his trip to Wales, and of Dorcas and Gareth Morgan.

"Oh, is the young man a servant here?" Caroline inquired.

"No, he's at Oxford."

"She's rather a pitiful little thing, is she not?" Caroline commented. "What crippled her?"

Andrew answered shortly, "A childhood accident, I believe. It doesn't affect her work though."

"Oh, yes, some cripples do adjust marvelously, don't they?" Caroline said carelessly. "I'm sure she's grateful. Times are hard in Wales, I believe?"

"Very hard," Andrew said, his jawline tense. He glanced over to where Dorcas stood by his aunt's chair. "She's been a great help to Aunt Hope. I'm grateful to her."

"I'm sure."

Dorcas stayed close to her mistress and mentally filed away everything that went on for future consideration. She noted that Sir George Wakefield was a man who must dominate the room at all times, while Andrew kept in the background. Idly she wondered why George Wakefield had not married and determined to ask Hope later.

When Dorcas was getting Hope ready for bed that night she asked, "Why hasn't Sir George married?"

"Oh, silly young man. He's been interested in several young women but none of them seems to have suited him. What did you think of the Barksdales?"

Actually Dorcas didn't care too much for any of the Barksdales. The older couple had barely glanced at her and then had ignored her entirely and Dorcas felt Caroline Barksdale's attitude to her had been quite condescending. *There's no good reason for me to be hurt,* she scolded herself. *I'm just a servant, after all, and I'm not supposed to be noticed.* . . . Still, Dorcas could clearly see that the simple kindness such as her mistress had was lacking in the Barksdales.

Dorcas retired to her room, which was much nicer than her cottage in Wales. She sat upon her small bed and thought about the Wakefields and the life she had now. Suddenly she felt discouraged. There was no reason for it; she had more to eat, better clothes, a better place to live.

But Dorcas was lonely. She longed to see Gareth. She'd heard from him only once, in a letter Andrew had brought when he returned to Wakefield from Oxford. It had been a gloomy letter. Gareth had said he was working hard, that he had to learn to adjust to his circumstances, and that he hoped she was well.

Dorcas snuggled down into her bed and pulled the warm

covers up around her. She tried to sleep but she couldn't. She kept wishing she could talk to Gareth, if only for a moment.

⟡

At approximately the same time his sister was studying the Barksdales, Gareth was sitting in his room, staring down at a pile of shoes. He picked up one of them, stared at it balefully, then began to rub it with the gummy blacking from a pot beside him. He was angry and sullen and when he finished blacking the shoe, he held it up and aimed it carefully at the door. It would have given Gareth great pleasure to throw the shoe, for somehow he found blacking the shoes of upperclassmen most degrading. He was still holding the shoe when a small young man with light-colored hair that hung down to his shoulders in an untidy wave came through the door. His deep blue eyes opened wide when he saw Gareth's threatening posture.

"Wait! Don't hit me, Gareth!" he called out, squinting his right eye.

Gareth sheepishly tossed the shoe down and picked up another one. "Come in, George." Resigned, he picked up another shoe and began to black it. "This is the worst job I've ever had," he muttered. "I'd rather be back digging coal."

George Whitefield was a servitor himself. He had blacked shoes and done all the other disagreeable and menial tasks laid upon him. But there was a cheerfulness in him that Gareth Morgan lacked. Now Whitefield sat down, picked up another shoe, and began helping Gareth with his task.

"I don't know," Whitefield said mildly. "I don't think blacking shoes is all that bad." For a stripling, he had a marvelous resonant voice, somehow uplifting to the hearer. One had the feeling that if he raised his voice, he could shake the very rafters. Whitefield had been at Oxford longer than Gareth and he'd made friends with Gareth the day he arrived. There was a total lack of guile in

George Whitefield. He was one of the few at Oxford totally committed to his religious convictions. Even the ministerial candidates, Gareth had seen, were mostly lacking in conviction.

As usual, Whitefield began speaking of the Scriptures. "I had a wonderful time yesterday at the prison. I was able to speak to four men about their souls. One of them gave his life to the Lord in response to the gospel." As the two men blacked shoes, Whitefield talked and Gareth listened. At length Whitefield asked, "Have you heard about the Wesleys' father?"

"No, I haven't. What about him?"

"He's been very ill. John and Charles left to be with him. I don't think he's expected to live." Whitefield studied the shoe he was working on with a critical eye, gave it another touch of blacking, and went on, "He's a wonderful Christian man, Mr. Wesley. Quite exemplary. He'll be happy to meet with God. That will be wonderful, won't it? Going to meet God?"

Gareth raised his eyebrows and replied wryly, "I don't think I'd like it so much. Not just now."

"But wouldn't you?" Whitefield said earnestly. "Think of all the pain and difficulties of this life! Think how wonderful it would be to see the Lord Jesus!"

"Oh, shut up, George," Gareth retorted rudely. "Ever since I've been here you've been so blooming happy, blacking shoes and being a servant! I can't stand it! I'd rather dig coal, I tell you!"

Whitefield apologized. "I didn't mean to force my views upon you, Gareth. But I'm just so happy! For years I tried to work my way into God's good graces. Just recently I found myself so helpless and sick and worn out. . . . Then I discovered the secret!"

Gareth sighed. "Yes, yes, what secret?"

"The secret!" Whitefield said softly, his normally pale face radiant. His voice lifted as he intoned reverently, "That Jesus is all we need! Grace, just grace! He's already paid the price—all we must do is accept his gift! Isn't that wonderful?"

"Wonderful," Gareth repeated woodenly. He knew of White-field's reputation: He'd fasted until he'd almost become a shadow; he'd refused to sleep, standing up to pray all night; he'd done other men's work in addition to his own, such as he was doing for Gareth right now; and George Whitefield was not a strong man. The students ridiculed him—all except the members of the Holy Club. But Whitefield had persisted and had had an experience he couldn't really explain. Although he seemed mystical and slightly dangerous, Gareth found himself fascinated by the slight young man.

Finally Gareth finished the last shoe in the pile. "Well, I go to service and take communion. As long as I do that, I suppose I'm all right."

Whitefield stood up and glanced down at Gareth. Compassion fired his eyes as he said quietly, "It takes more than that, Gareth. It takes the blood of Jesus Christ, which we can have only by faith." Whitefield saw Gareth's expression grow rebellious and went on, "Don't be angry with me, Gareth. I'll not preach anymore now. Come with me. Let's go see if there's aught left to eat."

John Wesley would later say that few things were as beautiful and triumphant as the passing of his father from this world to the next. He described it as "going out of life in a comfortable manner."

He stood beside his father's bed, along with his brother Charles and other members of the family. His father blessed each one, then all heard him say plainly, "Think of heaven, talk of heaven, all time is lost when we are not talking of heaven."

John Wesley, in the presence of death, saw a victory in his father. For years John had struggled to find peace with God; no man had ever sought God harder. He had forged ahead, embracing every difficult religious duty with a determination and a dedication most men never possess. Now, as he saw his father passing from this world, a great restlessness grew inside him.

The body of Samuel Wesley was buried in the churchyard at Epworth. The old home was broken up and John and Charles's mother, Susanna, went to live with Emelia, her daughter, who lived in Kingsborough. The two sons set about finishing their father's last project, a massive book on Job.

Shortly after this, as John Wesley was preparing to return to Oxford, he was introduced to General Oglethorpe, who was attempting to establish the gospel in Georgia, one of the American colonies. John's visit happened to coincide with the meeting of the trustees from Savannah. They were looking for a qualified Anglican clergyman to give pastoral care to the Savannah settlers and perhaps serve as a missionary to the Indians.

To John Wesley's surprise, General Oglethorpe approached him as a possible candidate. John had just declined the offer of the Epworth parish, for he was unwilling to relinquish his fellowship at Oxford. But the Savannah project, he learned, could be accomplished simply by taking a leave of absence. It was a difficult decision for John Wesley—to cross the ocean and leave all that he knew so well. But he decided to go.

On September the eighteenth he went to his mother, Susanna, half fearful she'd be opposed. But that gallant lady, so recently bereft of her husband, said, "Had I twenty sons, I should rejoice that they were all so employed, though I should never see them more!"

John Wesley, a man who tried to be honest in all his ways, wrote to a friend, "My chief motive, to the which all the rest are subordinate, is the hope of saving my own soul. I hope to learn the true sense of the gospel by preaching it to the heathen."

He returned to Oxford and began making his preparations to leave. As in everything else, he did this effectively and methodically.

* * *

"Well, my boy!" Bishop Crawley said with a pleased smile. "I believe I have the best possible news for you!"

Andrew had been called to the office of the bishop and had no idea why the bishop seemed so happy. "Yes, my lord?"

Although Bishop Alfred Crawley was a rather pompous man, he had a measure of kindness and a special liking for Andrew Wakefield. Wakefield reminded him of himself as a young man—earnest, anxious to serve, properly humble. The bishop had worked diligently to find Wakefield a place. Such placement always involved a certain amount of political manipulation in the ecclesiastical world and no man became a bishop without being expert in such politics. As a matter of fact, Bishop Crawley would have been an excellent politician had his life been turned in that direction. He knew who had power and he was shrewd enough to perceive how such men might be swayed. He was constantly moving about the world of bishops, directors, and churches, and now he'd accomplished what he viewed as a very tidy bit of business.

"I'm pleased to say you'll be asked to serve at Saint Mark's Church," he told Andrew. This was a fairly large church in the suburbs of London, one that would ordinarily be served by a much older man. Although the bishop had experienced some small difficulties in shouldering another candidate aside, that was now done. His eyes sparkled as he went on, "By Saint George, I wish someone had given me such an opportunity when I was your age! Ordinarily you'd be pottering about in some small village for five, perhaps ten more years!"

"Why, Bishop," Andrew stammered, "I—I—can hardly think of what to say!"

"We'll have plenty of time for you to say whatever it is that you can't say!" Bishop Crawley declared. Slapping Andrew's shoulder, he continued, "I'm so happy for you, my boy! I see a bright future for you. I'll see to it you are ordained at once."

"Yes, yes, of course."

For some time the two men talked and made plans. After

Andrew's ordination date was set, the bishop said, "I trust you've taken my advice."

"Your advice, my lord?" Andrew asked in confusion.

"Yes, about those Wesleys and that Holy Club. All of that."

"Oh! I'm not too alarmed at Mr. Wesley and his brother," Andrew said easily. "They have very little influence—as you know."

"They have enough to cause some trouble," the bishop rumbled. "But in any case, you'll be out of it as soon as you go to Saint Mark's. I suppose you'll be wanting to hurry home and tell Lady Ann and Sir George the good news?"

"Yes, indeed." Andrew thanked the bishop profusely, then hurried to his rooms. But it was not his mother or his brother he was thinking about. He was thinking, *Wait until Caroline hears this! Now we can afford to be married!*

WHEN THE SKY FALLS

W hen Andrew entered Gareth's room, the young man was lying flat on his back on his narrow bed, staring at the ceiling. "I must talk to you," Andrew said, squinting a little in the dark room as he searched Gareth's face. "What are you doing in bed? Are you sick?"

"No."

"Then light a candle," Andrew demanded impatiently.

At first he thought the young man didn't intend to respond. But Gareth sat up slowly and lit one of the stubby candles from a coal in the fireplace until it threw a feeble gleam about the room. Then he set the candle down with a defiant thump on the rough table by his bedside. "What is it, Mr. Wakefield?" he asked sullenly.

Andrew stared at Gareth. "I think you know what it is. You're not attending to your duties and you're neglecting your studies. You really must do better."

Gareth ran his hand through the dark, thick locks that hung untidily below his neck. He needed a haircut. Andrew had requested more than once that Gareth attend to his grooming more carefully but Gareth simply ignored the advice. His clothes were rumpled, his shoes ill polished. "And I suppose the master's been complaining again," he grumbled.

"And why shouldn't he?" Andrew countered. "After all, you haven't done your work."

Gareth shrugged carelessly. "I've done as much as some of the others."

"That's not good enough."

"It's the best I can say," Gareth snapped. He straightened his shoulders, taking satisfaction in his superior height. Looking down on the smaller man he challenged him, "Did you come to throw me out?"

"Oh, don't be absurd, man! I've come to help you! Can't you see you're well along to getting thrown out on your own? There's nothing I can do to save you unless you straighten up."

"Let them toss me out! See if I care!" Even to Gareth's own ears he sounded petulant and childish and his shoulders slumped with depression. "I'm sorry. I don't seem to be able to make myself fit in here. I'm just a rough coal miner and that's all I'll ever be."

Angry words leaped to Andrew's lips but he managed to stay them as he saw the depth of the unhappiness in Gareth's mind and spirit. *I should have spent more time with him,* he thought regretfully, *but it's too late for that now.* Aloud Andrew said, "I've received some good news."

"Yes? And what is it?"

"I'll be leaving Oxford. I'm to be ordained and I'm going to be the rector of a large church in London."

Gareth was dismayed. It had been difficult at Oxford and in spite of his careless words, he knew Andrew Wakefield had saved him more than once from expulsion. Now he foresaw even more difficulty in making his way in this place so foreign to him. Nevertheless, Gareth Morgan had a generous heart, so he said warmly, "I'm happy for you, sir."

"Thank you, Gareth. But you do understand this means I'll be leaving and you must get along without me. I know you can do it."

"When are you leaving?"

"I'm going home, right away, to tell my family."

"Take me with you, sir! I want to see Dorcas!" Gareth said almost pleadingly.

"Gareth," Andrew said with surprise, "you can't leave Oxford! You have your duties, your studies!"

Gareth longed to see Dorcas but because he had a lot of pride, he stifled the urge to beg Andrew. "Very well," he said curtly.

"I'll try to arrange a vacation for you," Andrew assured him. "Perhaps sooner than you think. I'll say good-bye now. Behave yourself."

Andrew paused and tried to think of something more encouraging to say. Gareth had been almost impossible. The young Welshman had a fiery temper, an independent spirit, and much pride. Rebellion seemed to be an integral part of his personality. He hadn't actually done harm to anyone. But one of the upperclassmen had told Andrew, "By Saint George, when Morgan's eyes start to burn, I think I see a wild animal inside him! Someday he's going to break loose, mark my words!"

Now, thinking of that, Andrew added, "Try to be patient. As soon as I get into my parish I'll be able to do more for you. Perhaps I might even be able to arrange it so you won't have to be a servitor any longer."

"That's—that's kind of you, Mr. Wakefield," Gareth said dully. Again he pulled himself straight and said more firmly, "But then you've done more than enough already for both Dorcas and me, and I thank you now."

Andrew spoke with Gareth a little longer, then left the room. He had mostly been thinking of Caroline Barksdale but as he was in the coach that headed toward Wakefield, he thought more and more of Gareth. *I hope Gareth finds his way. . . . It would break Dorcas's heart if he gets expelled from Oxford.*

He made the trip home and gave the news to his mother, who

was pleased, though not ecstatically happy. George was not at home, so Andrew immediately went to speak with Dorcas. He found her outside, feeding her beloved chickens, calling them by name, scolding the naughty ones. They were a numerous flock now, fine, fat, and contented. Though the weather was nippy, Dorcas wore only a thin shawl, knotted carelessly at her breast, and a blue bonnet to cover her head from the cold gusts of wind that lifted her dark hair. She turned in surprise from the chickens, who seemed to blossom like noisy flowers around her feet, clucking and nudging her skirts.

"There now, that's quite enough!" she called with mock sternness, making shooing motions with her good hand. "You all go away! Yes, you too, Cecile, you naughty girl!" She threw the remainder of the feed she held to the winds and turned to Andrew with a smile. "Mr. Wakefield! It's so good to see you again!" She came to stand close to him. There was a freshness in her smile, and her face was almost pretty. "Did Gareth come with you?"

"No. I'm sorry, he was unable to leave his duties and his studies." He looked around at the chickens and asked idly, "How many do you have now?"

"Forty-two," she said proudly. "Yesterday we got seventeen eggs! Perhaps you'd like some for supper tonight? I'll be glad to prepare them for you."

"That's kind of you, Dorcas." He saw she was pleased with what she'd accomplished. It actually took little to please her, as his aunt had told him. The triumph with the chickens had obviously been good for her. She'd been, according to all accounts, an excellent addition to the staff at Wakefield. Her primary duty, of course, had been to take care of Hope but she had done far more than that. She was eager to work, he could easily see, and she never let her handicap hold her back . . . in that way, at least.

Now that he was thinking of it, he noticed she always held her right hand slightly behind her, always hidden in the folds of her skirt—a habit, he supposed, from childhood. "I have some news," he remarked as they walked back toward the house.

"Yes, sir?"

"I'll be leaving Oxford. I'm going to be rector of a fine church in London."

She turned to him and smiled. He noticed her teeth were unusually fine: white and even and strong. Her gladness obviously genuine, she exclaimed, "Oh, I'm so glad for you, Mr. Wakefield. You'll be a fine minister. I wish I could be there to hear you preach!"

"I'm quite inexperienced for such a position," Andrew said deprecatingly. "I hope they'll be kind to me."

"They'd better be," Dorcas retorted. "If they aren't—"

Andrew turned to her and laughed. "Yes? If they aren't, what will you do? Take a switch to them?"

"Oh, no, sir, don't be foolish. But I'd do something. I'd write a letter to the bishop."

"And then he could take a switch to them, eh? He could do it, too, but let's give my poor parishioners a chance. We must hope they'll be kind and understanding to a young minister."

As they walked he spoke with excitement of his new appointment, then said abruptly, "I'm hoping to have other news soon, too, about—" He broke off and seemed confused.

"About Miss Barksdale," Dorcas said for him.

Andrew stared at her. "You're a quick girl," he admitted. "I shouldn't even have implied anything about this, of course. But how long have you known?"

"Since the first time I saw you look at her," Dorcas replied promptly. "Have you asked her yet?"

"No. I couldn't ask her until I had a place. Fellows at Oxford can't be married, you see. But a rector can, of course."

"I wish you the greatest of happiness, sir," Dorcas said in a low voice. "You and Miss Barksdale. She's a beautiful young woman."

"Thank you, Dorcas. You have a kind spirit. You know, I find you're a great deal like my Aunt Hope. She's one of the kindest women I've ever known and you have that same warmth and caring in you."

Dorcas bowed her head. "I wish I were beautiful like her," she whispered.

Andrew thought this remark very odd and it brought him up short. He studied her carefully as he decided what to say. Andrew had not thought of Dorcas much, being so busy with his own affairs. Now he remembered what she'd said when they'd spoken that last day in Wales. "Dorcas . . . you didn't mean what you said, did you?" he asked uncertainly. "About never getting married?"

"Did I not?" she flung back at him. "I shall never marry!"

"I think you shouldn't say that, Dorcas," he said quietly.

"It's the way I feel."

She made an impatient movement and quickened her step, which told Andrew she wished to change the subject. But he was not yet satisfied, so he asked, "Is it because of your hand?" As pain shadowed her face he added hastily, "I know you're sensitive about your—your—handicap. But it really means nothing. You look better than most women with two hands. It shouldn't be a difficulty for you, Dorcas."

"I—don't think of it."

Andrew reached out, put his hand on her shoulder, and stopped her quick stride. "Dorcas—that's the first time you've ever told an untruth to me. Of course you think of it! What woman wouldn't? What man, either?"

"Please, sir, I'd rather not talk about this anymore," Dorcas said firmly, her face reddened. "I'll never marry and there's no point in discussing my hand. I'm happy here with Miss Hope, and taking care of her is all I want to do."

"But she can't live forever," Andrew said insistently. "As bad as I hate to think of it, sooner or later she'll die. You need to think about a husband and a home of your own." Seeing his words troubled her, he knew he'd bothered her enough—for now. But he'd speak more of it later. "Never mind, Dorcas," he said kindly, "you'll never want for a home. After I'm married, no doubt we'll need domestic help. You can come—and wait on me. I know what a good cook you are and I take lots of care, you know!"

She looked up and Andrew was surprised to see her eyes fill with tears. Dorcas was unused to such kindness; in her life she'd seen it only from her brother and, lately, from Hope Wingate. Now her lips trembled as she murmured, "There's kind you are, sir." Turning, she hurried toward the house, her head and shoulders bent against the cold wind, leaving Andrew behind.

Dorcas fled to her room, threw herself on her bed, and let the tears flow. All the time she wondered why, exactly, she was so overwrought. Dorcas was not a young woman given easily to tears, for hardship had toughened her. But Andrew Wakefield's kindness had touched her. Finally she dashed the tears impatiently away. "She's not good enough for you!" she muttered, "but then—I don't know who would be!"

⟡

Andrew had hoped to find Caroline Barksdale but had been disappointed. After an exasperating interrogation of the Barksdale servant, he'd learned that Caroline was on an extended visit with a friend and that Mr. and Mrs. Barksdale weren't home either. So he'd been obliged to return to Oxford. As soon as he arrived he wrote letters to Caroline and then was forced to wait for her reply.

Andrew was disappointed to find that Gareth Morgan hadn't improved much, but he saw him only occasionally and said very little to the boy. He spent some time with George Whitefield, who was perhaps the most cheerful and personable young man at Oxford. He proclaimed his conversion experience—his "new birth," as he termed it—to everyone.

Whitefield's joy came as a shock to his fellow students, as most of them went through the form of religion and such talk of "new birth" hinted of enthusiasm.

"I wish you wouldn't be so outspoken about this new birth," Andrew cautioned him sternly. He fell into step with young Whitefield as they walked through an Oxford quadrangle. "The bishop says those men here who are affected with that are doomed either to be put out of the church or to go nowhere in the church world."

"Ah, but I'm going somewhere in another world," Whitefield said happily. "Now that you're going to be in a large church, Mr. Wakefield, you'll have an opportunity to proclaim the riches of the Lord Jesus. How I envy you! I wish I could go with Mr. Wesley to America. Or with you, to begin proclaiming the gospel. How happy you must be!"

Andrew felt uncomfortable with this sort of talk. For some reason, he believed it slightly unseemly to be as happy as George Whitefield apparently was. He tried to tell himself it was just Whitefield's manner—but in truth there was nothing at all unseemly about the young man and Andrew Wakefield knew it. He'd seen George Whitefield come into the Holy Club as a shy young man, presented to the group by Charles Wesley. Young Whitefield had enthusiastically embraced the discipline of the group—so enthusiastically, perhaps, that it was unnerving. He'd practically starved himself fasting until finally John Wesley himself ventured to rebuke him mildly. Whitefield had respectfully countered with, "Nothing is too great to find the riches of God." Since John Wesley had encouraged such beliefs, he could make no argument.

Now, as the two young men walked and Whitefield spoke continually of the riches of God's grace, the glories of heaven, and the love of Jesus, Andrew thought uneasily, *It's as if Whitefield is truly in another world. I feel none of this joy, none of this excitement that flows so genuinely from him.* As Andrew reflected on this, he told himself sternly, *I must try harder. I must work harder for God so I might be acceptable!*

❦

Two days later, a letter came. Andrew was passing by the great tower when George Whitefield hurried up to him. "This letter came for you, Mr. Wakefield. The master asked me to bring it to you."

"Thank you, George." Eagerly Andrew tore open the letter for he recognized Caroline Barksdale's flowing, elaborate hand. He couldn't even wait to get to his room and as he opened the single sheet, he was aware that George Whitefield was still standing, waiting to speak more with him. But Andrew was too eager so he rudely ignored Whitefield and began to read.

The letter was brief and Andrew read it quickly, his face seeming to freeze. He felt a strange sensation, as if his heart had stopped. Then he vaguely realized he could hear the thudding of his heart, though the sound was strangely faraway. His stomach felt empty and his head too light.

> Dear Andrew,
>
> I'm sorry to write this letter but it must be done. I shouldn't have allowed our relationship to become as serious as, apparently, you believe it has. I wish to be totally honest with you. I admire you greatly and think you're a fine man.
>
> I realize you couldn't speak of marriage while you were at Oxford. I understand from what you've written that you'll be leaving there and will be able to marry. Andrew, you have given indications, I believe, that you have an affection for me. I'm honored by this but I must tell you that I could never accept an offer of marriage from you. Suffice it to say that no matter how much

affection I might have for you I am totally unfit to be the wife of an Anglican minister. Please forgive me for not making this clear sooner. I trust you won't be badly hurt.

Perhaps I've misunderstood you and you are shocked at my presumption. I sincerely hope this is so. In any event, when we meet again, let us meet as friends.

With affection,

Caroline Barksdale

"I say, Andrew, are you all right?"

Whitefield's voice seemed to come from worlds away, and Andrew, with an effort, looked up and focused on his pale features. His lips felt incredibly stiff and unlifelike and he wasn't certain for a moment what Whitefield had said. "What?" he mumbled, then swallowed hard. "Oh . . . yes, I'm quite all right, George."

George Whitefield knew this was not so, for Andrew Wakefield was clearly a stricken man. He was pale and even his lips had gone bloodless. Whitefield watched as Andrew moved away, walking woodenly and mechanically. *He's been badly hurt,* Whitefield thought compassionately. *I wish I could comfort him . . . but he obviously wants to be alone.*

For two days Andrew moved along the paths of Oxford and among the men of Oxford in much the same way he had left George Whitefield that afternoon: like a man in a dream, without much conscious thought to what and where he was. He hardly slept and circles darkened his eyes. As the time grew closer for Andrew to leave for his post, only George Whitefield seemed to realize Andrew's soul was in agony. Finally Whitefield spoke to him. "You know, Andrew, if I could ever be of any help to you, I'd be honored to be asked. I don't know your troubles but I know God is able to answer all our needs."

Andrew thanked him weakly and returned to his quarters. Another letter arrived the next morning, this time from his brother.

Because Andrew had never received a letter from George before, he couldn't imagine what had prompted it. Vague panic set in when he saw the large, clumsy, childlike handwriting. He ripped the letter open and was almost struck dumb by what he read.

> Dear Andrew,
>
> You'll be surprised to hear from me since I don't care for letter writing. And you'll be even more surprised at what I have to say.
>
> I've thought for some time that Caroline Barksdale was in love with you. But she assures me she isn't. I'm not a very astute man in such matters. However, now that I've ascertained there is no impediment, I propose to ask her to marry me.
>
> I hope there are no hard feelings. Caroline assures me there is no possibility she could be the wife of a minister. I hope this isn't too much of a shock, Brother. Come home when you can.

It was signed simply "George Wakefield," without any other closing.

Andrew Wakefield felt as if he'd been shot through the heart. For two more days he performed his duties and finished his studies but he was emotionally crippled. It was almost time for him to leave Oxford, and with a jolt he realized he couldn't live in London. Desperate and hopeless, he walked the streets for hours, alone, trying unsuccessfully to think clearly and to pick up the tattered remnants of his life.

Finally an idea took form. He didn't accept it at once but helplessly sought God in prayer. It seemed his prayers fell on deaf ears, yet still he persisted. One afternoon he went to John Wesley's quarters.

Although Wesley was aware of Andrew's depression of late, he didn't know the cause. "Good to see you," Wesley said, greeting Andrew at the door. "Please come in. What can I do for you?"

"Something has happened, Mr. Wesley. May I tell you about it?"

"Of course," John Wesley said kindly, "sit down." The two men made themselves comfortable and Wesley listened as Andrew spilled out his difficulties, with pain and tension evident in his face and voice.

"This was a hard thing to be so disappointed," Wesley said as gently as he could. "But if you give your heart completely to God, he'll surely make it up to you. Look on it as another discipline."

"I can't go to Saint Mark's," Andrew said almost violently. "I must do something else."

"What else would you do?"

"Take me with you to America!"

"Why—why—I never thought you'd considered such a thing."

"I hadn't," Andrew admitted, "but I can see now I must do more for God. I want to throw myself into his service. I'll never marry now." His tone was filled with bitterness. "Take me with you, Mr. Wesley!"

This was but the beginning. Wesley at first refused. But after two days, during which he sought God about it a great deal and had several discussions with Wakefield, they made an agreement.

"Very well, Andrew. You shall go with me to Georgia. We will go together and there will be plenty of God's work for both of us." Wesley was actually glad Wakefield was going; it seemed a way to continue at least a fragment of his beloved Holy Club there. "We'll be leaving soon. Can you wind up your affairs?" he asked.

"Indeed," Andrew replied.

Dorcas Morgan had been shocked to discover Caroline Barksdale was to marry George Wakefield. Hard upon this had followed the further unwelcome news that Andrew was going to

America with John Wesley. Dorcas had not been greatly surprised. She had spoken of it to Hope Wingate.

"It's not the worst thing in the world," Hope said comfortingly. "That young woman was not at all suited for Andrew. Perhaps on the mission field Andrew will be able to find himself."

Then Andrew had come home to say good-bye to his family. He'd been hard put to keep from showing his feelings to George but he'd managed it, congratulating him on his engagement. To his Aunt Hope he'd been more open.

"I can't help being hurt," he told her. "I don't think George was fair."

Hope's eyes were filled with pain for she suffered with Andrew, who was so dear to her heart. "I know how you must feel. But you must be strong. God is with us. You'll see!"

"I hope so," Andrew replied. "I intend to give myself completely to God."

Somehow his set, determined jaw almost frightened his aunt and she said cautiously, "You know, Andrew, you can't wrest salvation from God. It's his gift, freely given."

"And we must be faithful," Andrew said sternly. "I intend to be the most faithful of all as his servant. Mr. Wesley will help me. I've never known a man so dedicated to giving himself to the Lord. He knows how to organize and I'll be beside him, to learn."

Hope wished to say more, for she hoped to see more softness, more joy, in Andrew. But she saw he was filled with disappointment and in danger of becoming bitter. So she did her best to encourage him, to lift him up, promising to pray faithfully for him.

"I may not be here when you get back," she said with an odd lightness, "but if I'm not in this world, I shall see you in the next. We'll meet at the feet of Jesus, Nephew."

Touched by Hope's words, Andrew kissed her cheek as he rose to leave. Turning at the door, he said, "Bless you, dear Aunt Hope. You've been a great blessing to me."

Next he went to Dorcas's room and knocked. When she opened the door he said simply, "I've come to say good-bye."

"Come in," she said quickly.

He took one step inside. "I've done my best for Gareth. I hope he'll make his way. I wish I could be there to help but I must go."

She reached for him with her left hand and he took it. Squeezing his hand hard, she whispered, "How kind you've been! How can I ever thank you for all you've done?"

"It was nothing." Suddenly it was harder than he'd thought to leave. Then, resolutely, he put all thoughts of Wakefield and England aside. "I'll write to you."

"And I'll write back," she said eagerly.

He stared at her, hard, for long moments. "You know, you're right about marriage, Dorcas."

"About marriage?" she repeated in bewilderment.

"Yes." Andrew was still holding her hand. He looked down at it; it was a woman's hand, soft but strongly muscled. Abruptly he let go and went on almost harshly, "Yes, you were right. This is best—just friendship. We'll always be the best of friends, won't we, Dorcas?"

Dorcas hesitated for a moment. There was a softness in her lips and a vulnerability in her clear eyes as she lifted her gaze to him. "Yes, sir," she whispered. "Always the best of friends."

He turned and left.

She reached out as if to touch him, to stop him. But he was gone.

Dorcas stood at the door, and heaviness fell on her as she heard his footsteps fading away. There seemed to be a finality about it, as though he were walking not just out of Wakefield or out of England but out of that place he had in Dorcas Morgan's heart. Aside from Hope, he was the kindest person she'd ever known.

"Good-bye," she said, though it was to an empty doorway. "Good-bye, Andrew."

On October 14, a small group of ministers stood on the deck of the *Simmons*. As England faded into the mists, they stood solemnly beside the rail and looked west. Andrew Wakefield felt a poignant emptiness in his soul and he couldn't explain it. The pain of losing Caroline had faded somewhat but was still a dull reminder of failure. He did not, however, regret turning his back on the affluent church in London. Now he turned to walk to the prow of the ship. Standing there alone he looked ahead, as though he might be able to see across the hundreds of miles of ocean to Savannah. He thought of the Indians there, who had never heard of the gospel, and the settlers who needed a minister. He stood alone for a long time. Finally he said quietly, "God, I'll do the best I can. I'll work for you until I die." :

He waited for some answer, for the Inner Voice others spoke of to speak to his own heart. He thought of George Whitefield's joy and longed for such an experience. Yet it had never come. Perhaps it never would. Perhaps he'd always be a man who would trudge forward in his religious duties without the joy others seemed to have.

Wind bit at his face, and the sails flapped noisily over the sibilant hissing of water as they caught the breeze. As the ship swept forward, Andrew Wakefield held to the rail tightly, his knuckles white with strain. "I *will* find God," he said. "I will if it kills me. . . !"

END OF PART ONE

Storms in

Part

TWO

the Heart

Seven

STORM AT SEA

Andrew Wakefield had never been in any ship larger than a small rowboat and as the *Simmons,* far out in the Atlantic, dipped into the troughs of the pitching waves then rose to the tops of the crests, he grasped the rail. *I hope I don't get seasick,* he thought desperately. *I'd hate to make a spectacle of myself at the beginning of our mission.*

Looking up, he saw the sky had turned a dead slate color and was punctuated by a flight of gulls. Even as he watched, they disappeared into a nebulous cloud bank that resembled mountains of soiled cotton. Taking a deep breath, Andrew felt the salty air fill his chest. He was not yet accustomed to the tangy smell of the sea and as he looked nervously back in the wake of the ship, for one moment he wished desperately he was back in England, safe on dry land.

It wasn't the first time Andrew had been struck by this thought, for despite his resolution in joining Wesley, doubts haunted him—especially at night. Even now, as he left his place on the rail and moved slowly around the deck, he wondered how he could face the trials that lay ahead of him. Something about the emptiness and the forlorn cadence of the rolling sea, which stretched out for miles and miles without a house or a tree or a hill to be seen, seemed to quell his spirit and accentuate his loneliness. Desperately he wrenched his thoughts away.

"I *must* do better than this," he muttered almost grimly. "I'm going to serve God. That ought to be enough!"

The thought should have cheered him but he experienced no joy—only a rock-hard determination to give his entire life to preaching the gospel to the Indians of the New World. He hadn't the faintest idea how this would take place but trusted he'd be taught by the Spirit. Now, however, a poignant memory came of England, with all its summery greenness in the spring, and of Oxford, with the fellowship of the Holy Club. . . . Caught by this vision, Andrew once again stopped at the rail to stare down at the green waters that churned along the side of the ship.

"Looking ahead to the New World, are you?"

Startled, Andrew turned to find John Wesley, wearing a rather soggy greatcoat and a floppy brimmed hat, standing beside him at the rail. Wesley's penetrating brown eyes were lit up with excitement and he nodded toward the invisible shore. "It's out there somewhere, my brother. Soon we'll be in Georgia, bringing the great gospel to the heathen."

Feeling compelled to join in Wesley's spirit, Andrew forced a smile. "It's a glorious thought, isn't it?"

"It is indeed." Wesley stood there, his active mind running over future possibilities as he zealously shared them with Andrew. Finally he said, "The captain assured me that the weather will clear up soon, but meanwhile we'll have our meeting below. I'll be preaching on the subject 'Christ the Glory of the Father.' Come along, Andrew. We'll need your help with the singing."

Andrew followed John Wesley down to the lower deck, hoping the fellowship would lift his spirits. As they moved down the narrow ladders, he was assailed by the odors of the ship, which could not be masked by the tangy sea air. So many people grouped together could not fail to leave their mark, and a feculent stench struck him forcefully as he moved into the largest room below the deck, the mess hall. The tables had been moved back and every inch was filled with people standing, waiting for John Wesley to arrive.

"Well, sir, we're ready if you are." The speaker was Captain Abraham Patton, a strong-bodied man of fifty with cropped white whiskers and skin the texture of leather. His pale blue eyes were surrounded by creases brought on by long years of peering into sunlit waves and bright skies. An ardent Christian, he delighted in the fellowship of the ministers who had taken his ship for this particular voyage.

"Thank you, Captain," Wesley said pleasantly. "Suppose we have a time of singing?" He nodded toward Charles, who at once began a hymn. As the ship rose and fell, Andrew had to balance himself. He noticed that Charles Wesley and the other two companions who had joined their little group, Benjamin Ingram, a tall blond, and Charles Delamotte, slightly over twenty, were far more comfortable than he was. The small group of five composed the force that had left England—all of them having been members of the Holy Club.

The singing went on for twenty-five or thirty minutes; then John Wesley, wearing a cassock, as was his custom, began to speak powerfully. His clear and strong voice, combined with years of study, gave him a manner of assurance—some called it arrogance but this really wasn't the case. As Wesley spoke, Andrew thought with a sense of longing, *Oh, if I had the gifts of John Wesley!* He listened as the speaker moved from the New Testament to the Old as easily as men moved from one room in their house to another. Wesley was a formidable Bible scholar, an expert in Greek and Hebrew, and he had a prodigious memory. Whenever anyone needed to know where a verse was, all he needed to do was quote the first few words and Wesley could at once cite the chapter.

The room was crowded with a group of German passengers, some of whom Andrew had met. These were Moravians, members of the Church of the United Brethren and direct descendants of the pre-Reformation martyr John Hus. Although the group had almost passed with others into oblivion, it had been revived by young Count Zinzendorf. They were becoming widely known as a missionary-minded group, and the passengers on this ship were to become settlers who would plant the seeds of the gospel in Georgia.

Andrew was favorably impressed with the Moravians. They were always cheerful and willing to take on the tasks that some of the English emigrants were too proud or too lazy to perform. They never returned evil for evil and when the crewmen or passengers abused them or made fun of them, they inevitably turned the other cheek, smiling and quoting Scripture.

Something about this particular service and the Moravians' participation disturbed Andrew. Their faces and singing reflected a deep-down freedom. Their music was so joyful, it made the Church of England's metrical hymns sound almost stilted in contrast.

After the sermon was over and the group was dismissed, most of the passengers left the mess hall. John and Charles Wesley remained to speak with a few who gathered around them, and Andrew stayed close beside John. He intended to learn as much as he could about the two Wesleys for he trusted their vision more than he did his own.

John Wesley was speaking with Mrs. Hawkins, a short, striking-looking woman and the wife of the surgeon. She'd been to every service and now she drew close to John, turning her rather sharp brown eyes on him. There was something about her that caught Andrew's attention. Perhaps it was the royal blue gown that was more expensive and fashionable than those of the other women on ship—and which set off her curvaceous figure in an obvious fashion. Or it might have been her thick black hair, provocative face, and especially full lower lip. All in all, Mrs. Hawkins was a pretty woman. "Oh, Mr. Wesley," Mrs. Hawkins said as Andrew listened carefully, "I thought your sermon was *divinely* inspired!"

John Wesley turned his intelligent eyes upon the woman. "Why, thank you, Mrs. Hawkins," he said. "I'm pleased at the compliment. I'm glad to see the Spirit of God is among us as we hold our communion."

"I can't wait until we get to Savannah. I'll be one of your flock, you know." Mrs. Hawkins arched her eyebrows and a dimple appeared in her right cheek. "I'll hope you'll allow me to introduce you to our people."

"Why, of course. That would be delightful," Wesley said. He hesitated, then smiled at her. "It would be most convenient to have you serve in this capacity."

The conversation between Wesley and Mrs. Hawkins went on for some time. Andrew moved away with Charles and was surprised when the young man said, "I wish Jack would stay away from that woman." Although those close to Wesley often called him "Jack," Andrew would never be so familiar.

"Why do you say that, Charles?"

"The woman's obviously not what she seems to be." Charles was quick-witted and rather astute in judging people. "Jack is a brilliant scholar but sometimes he's not very clever when it comes to seeing inside people." He turned and cocked his eyebrow at Andrew. "I hope you saw through her."

Andrew cleared his throat uncertainly. "She's a little over-dressed perhaps—and I suppose she gushes a little."

"It's more than that," Charles said almost bitterly. His mouth turned downward and he shook his head in short motions. "I've seen so many of her kind. They hang around preachers; they're drawn to them somehow. They *talk* a lot about religion but they're shallow. That woman means trouble for us."

"Have you told Mr. Wesley about this?"

"I've tried but Jack doesn't always listen to me." Charles smiled suddenly and clapped Andrew on the back. "You'll have to help me convince him that the Hawkins woman is a danger to him. Preachers have to be careful of women—but I suppose you're aware of that."

For one instant Andrew hesitated, then he shrugged and said, "That won't be a bother to me. I've decided never to marry."

"Never to marry? Why, that won't do!" Charles exclaimed. He stopped abruptly and faced Andrew. "A minister needs a wife in the rectory. There are some things he can't do for his people, like making his home hospitable." Then he added, "A bishop must be given to hospitality as the Scripture says."

Andrew still hurt from Caroline Barksdale's betrayal. Although he'd desperately tried to forget, he knew the struggle was one he might never completely win. Now he shook his head, his lips pulled together stubbornly. "I'll furnish whatever hospitality is needed in my parish."

There was such unusual stubbornness in Andrew Wakefield's face that Charles Wesley was surprised. He'd found Andrew to be amiable and full of potential, although he seemed a little uncertain and somewhat glum. "What made you decide this?" he inquired.

"I'd rather not talk about it," Andrew said shortly. Then, seeing Charles's eyes narrow, he stumbled on. "Well—I—I might as well tell you. I've been rejected by the one woman I could ever love. Therefore, I'll be a bachelor." He straightened his shoulders and forced a smile. "After all, that'll be a help where we're going. I can give all my time to serving God. That's what Paul suggested, isn't it?"

Charles Wesley shook his head. "I think you'll have problems. All of us young fellows must go through certain phases." There was sympathy in his warm brown eyes and he put his hand lightly on Andrew's shoulder. "Things will look different when we get to Savannah. Once we get involved in our work there, you'll feel different. Wait and see. . . ."

Three months had passed since the *Simmons* had left England. Andrew and his group had settled down into the sometimes dreary affair of getting from one continent to another. All five struggled with the rigid routine John Wesley had laid out for them. He'd been seriously influenced by the book *Holy Living and Holy Dying* by Jeremy Taylor and it had made Wesley move in a direction that would stay with him all his life—the keeping of diaries and journals. Later they would become a treasure-house of facts, invaluable to those who study the lives of the Methodist workers in England. Early in his life Wesley kept, in a red notebook, some of his principals. One of them was a list, in shorthand code, of his temptations:

A. too much addicting myself to a light behavior at all time
B. listening too much to idle talk and reading vain plays and books
C. idleness
D. want of due consideration in whose presence I am

This habit of list keeping, along with his determination to discipline his heart, his mind, and his body, had molded John Wesley into a ferocious disciplinarian. He had led the young ministers to pledge themselves to continue their own introspective diaries, continuing the rigorous Oxford Methodist system of prayers, readings, fasts, and good works.

Andrew soon discovered, to his surprise, that the Moravians weren't impressed with this tremendous discipline. One of them, Bishop David Nitschman, commented to him, "Spiritual things cannot be achieved by routine. It would be more helpful if you were to spend your time studying the doctrines of grace as set forth in the Scripture."

Neither John Wesley nor any of the others seemed to under-stand what Nitschman was saying, and as the days passed they threw themselves into tight discipline. It wasn't until the pitching of the ship made them aware that a storm had overtaken them in the middle of the night that they were shaken out of their habit and routine.

For days the storm grew worse and at midnight John Wesley wrote in his diary, "Stormy still and I am afraid." He went on to admit his lifelong problem: that he was afraid to die. Wesley didn't share this thought with his fellows. But because fear is a difficult thing to hide and it flashes out when one least expects it, Andrew saw it in him one Sunday afternoon. As Wesley was standing at the rail hanging on, the ship took a tremendous roll to starboard, and down—down—down it went until it seemed the ship would turn turtle. Andrew glimpsed Wesley's face and saw it was con-torted with fear. Andrew himself was almost paralyzed but he couldn't conceive of John Wesley's knowing such a weakness. The two hung on to the rail desperately and Wesley gained control of himself. That one glimpse of Wesley's human weakness, however, remained fixed in Andrew's memory.

Later that day the ship was rolling so much that walking was almost impossible. Wesley and Andrew joined the twenty-six Moravians below the deck. It came as a real shock to Andrew that even as the ship groaned, the timbers creaked, and the wind howled like a thousand wolves outside, the Moravians sat calmly, singing one of their magnificent hymns.

Wesley and the other fledgling missionaries were all taken aback. Andrew watched the faces of the Germans carefully, thinking, *They can't be as calm as they seem to be—or as filled with joy. It's impossible!*

Just then a great wave struck the ship, split the mainsail, and water poured in between the decks. The wind was a shrill crescendo and terror swept the ship. Cries went up from some of the crew and a terrible screaming among the English. Fear came to Andrew Wakefield then—paralyzing him! He stared wildly at John Wesley and saw his mentor was in the same condition.

Fear was almost a nausea in Andrew as he backed against the bulkhead of the ship. His hands were trembling and his legs would scarcely hold him up. He knew death was a real possibility. With stark disbelief, he watched as the Moravians joyfully continued their singing as calmly as if they were in a church built of rock!

Finally the winds grew somewhat calmer and the ship ceased its alarming rolling. When the singing was over, Bishop Nitschman came over and spoke to John Wesley pleasantly. Wesley's face was pale and his lips tight as he asked, "Were you not afraid?"

"I thank God, nein!" Nitschman said, somewhat in surprise.

Wesley looked at the women and children. "But were not your women and children afraid?"

Nitschman turned his gaze on the young English missionaries and felt a moment's compassion for them. A man of infinite love, he was strong and stocky at fifty-six, balding, but with a full brown beard and piercing blue eyes that sometimes seemed to turn darker. Although his English wasn't good, it was good enough as he said, "Nein, our women und kinder, dey are not afraid to die."

Something about the bishop's remark seemed to penetrate John Wesley's usual calm manner. He stared at the Moravian with an odd light of alarm in his eyes, then wheeled abruptly and walked away, clinging to the sides of the ship as it pitched from side to side.

Andrew would have followed but Nitschman turned to say, "Your leader needs grace in his soul."

Surprised by this remark, Andrew said, "Why would you say that, Bishop? Mr. Wesley is a most accomplished minister. He knows the Scripture better than any man I've ever known."

"Ya, he knows the Scripture. But it is better, I tink, to know the God who wrote the Scripture." He stared at Andrew after uttering this cryptic remark, adding, "I trust you and your friends vill learn to know the Lord Jesus in your own spirits."

His words frightened Andrew. He'd spent years studying the Scripture, and now being told it wasn't enough was a distinct shock. And it was even more disturbing that John Wesley had been shaken by the Moravian's words too.

Andrew spent the rest of the voyage thinking about this storm at sea, and once, as he stood looking out into the gray waters of the deep, he thought, *There are two kinds of storms. One is the physical storm that may lead to death, but the other is the storm inside a man's soul, and this is the worst of all!*

On February 4, the *Simmons* anchored in the Savannah River. The ship rail was lined, for every passenger had come to see the new land—the rows of pines, palms, and cedars that stretched along the shore beneath a cloudless sky. Andrew noticed Mrs. Hawkins had wedged herself firmly between the two Wesley brothers and was looking up into John Wesley's face saying something. Even as she spoke, Charles Wesley turned and caught Andrew's eye. There was a frown on his face and he shook his head in disapproval. *He's worried about his brother,* Andrew thought. The two of them had spoken more than once about the strange inability of John Wesley to see the shallowness of the woman but apparently if he had a weakness, this was it.

The gangplank fell to the ground and the passengers eagerly jostled one another, anxious to leave the ship. After weeks without real bathing and no way to wash clothes, they were a rumpled, smelly bunch. But no one cared. As soon as they were on shore, Oglethorpe led them across to a rise in the ground where they knelt down in thanksgiving. Afterwards, Oglethorpe took the boat for Savannah, first telling the Oxford group, "I'll return tomorrow and we'll make our plans."

After Oglethorpe left, Andrew joined Wesley and the others in a service under the cedars, where they were sheltered from the sun and the wind. Walking around afterwards on the sandy shore, Andrew smelled the rich, loamy earth and enjoyed the sense of solid ground under his feet. That night the group slept in a small hut and they rose the next morning to prepare a good breakfast.

When Oglethorpe returned that afternoon and met with them, he said at once, "I will ask you, Mr. Charles Wesley, to be my secretary."

"But, sir, I came to preach the gospel to the Indians, not to scribble!"

Oglethorpe smiled indulgently. "Such scribbling is necessary; you'll have your chance." A sharp tone came to his voice as he said, "There are plenty of heathens to go around, sir. You'll soon discover that." Then he turned to John. "Mr. Wesley, the Georgia trustees have appointed you as rector of Savannah in succession to Mr. Quincy."

"But, I too, sir, came to preach to the Indians."

"Mr. Quincy wants to return north to Boston. There are Indians in the area, so you'll have your opportunity to preach to them."

Later that day the five said their farewells as Charles Delamotte and Benjamin Ingram were assigned to an area north of Savannah.

The next morning Andrew and John Wesley were surprised by a visit from General Oglethorpe, who brought with him August Spangenberg, the leader of the original Moravian settlers. "Mr. Spangenberg has a great deal of experience in this country," Oglethorpe said. "He'll be able to assist you." Spangenberg, a tall, thin man with reddish blond hair and chin whiskers and mustache of the same shade, had a tremendous bass voice, surprising in one so thin.

After Oglethorpe left, Wesley turned to the missionary. "I'd be grateful for your advice, sir. As you've been told, we are mere novices in wilderness experience."

Spangenberg stared at the two men thoughtfully, then finally said, "May I ask some questions, Mr. Wesley?"

"Of course."

"Do you know yourself?" Spangenberg asked. "Does the Spirit of God bear witness in your spirit if you are a child of God?"

Both Wesley and Wakefield were shocked by the tenor of these questions. After all, they were missionaries who'd given their lives to God! "Why, yes, I think I may say so!" Wesley answered.

Spangenberg then asked directly, "Do you know Jesus Christ?"

Silence filled the room. Andrew was shocked at the basic simplicity of it. Was this not to be taken for granted? Wesley, too, was taken aback and replied lamely, "I know he is the Saviour of the world."

"True," said the other, "but do you know he has saved *you?*" Again the silence seemed thick—almost palpable. Andrew could clearly hear the merry sound of birds singing and children playing outside the small hut. . . . At length Wesley, obviously uncomfortable, said in a low voice, "I hope he has died to save me."

Spangenberg asked again quietly, "Do you know yourself?"

Wesley swallowed hard and nodded slightly. "I do," he replied, but later he wrote in his journal, "I fear they were vain words."

Spangenberg studied the pair, started to say something, then thought better of it and instead began offering various practical suggestions about Georgia. Soon he left to go with General Oglethorpe.

It had been a disturbing interview and it was etched into Andrew's mind. He and Wesley spoke of it briefly and Andrew asked, "What do you suppose he meant by such strange questions?"

"I suppose he asks the same questions of all new missionaries," was Wesley's reply.

After that the two spoke no more of this event and soon made their way into Savannah and began their work. They lodged at first with the Moravians until the rector left, and then settled into the parsonage. They unpacked their books and threw themselves into the work of pastor to Savannah and the scattered settlements of ex-debtors and Scottish Highlanders.

The weeks passed and Andrew served Wesley as well as he could, assisting him with pastoral duties and the secretarial work for the colonies. He found time to walk the forest paths and even go on short canoe trips. Twice he stayed out in the pine forest, sleeping wrapped in an Indian blanket. He found this part of his work most enjoyable.

As for the colonists, they found themselves somewhat taken aback by their new pastor. They listened to his sermons with what seemed to be a deep affection but they seemed wary.

Andrew also noticed, with some displeasure, that Mrs. Hawkins was always on the front row and that she often came to Wesley for "counsel," as she called it. Once Andrew said, "Perhaps I could help you, Mrs. Hawkins." The woman had looked at him with her dark eyes, smiled, and said, "Thank you, Reverend, but I'd prefer to speak with the rector himself."

The two men immersed themselves in their duties with the same sense of discipline they'd undergone at Oxford. Although the colonists admired their energy and willingness to work long hours, visiting the sick, some of Wesley's habits disturbed them. They weren't pleased with the formal services or his insistence on dipping babies at baptism instead of sprinkling them. They were also shocked to discover he expected his flock to fast as well.

When Charles Wesley wrote from his post with Oglethorpe that he was unhappy, Andrew penned a note back, describing their work. A few weeks later, he was shocked to hear that Mrs. Hawkins had gone to Charles, confessing an adulterous affair with Oglethorpe.

John Wesley promptly investigated the matter and interrogated Mrs. Hawkins. After he returned, he called Andrew in and said with an air of relief, "There's nothing to the rumors we've heard about Mrs. Hawkins."

There was a silence then and Andrew said, "I think it would be well, sir, to keep yourself clear of this woman's affairs."

"Nonsense!" Wesley replied sharply. "She's one of my flock. She simply wants counsel." Abruptly he turned and left, with Andrew staring after him.

Tossing and turning that night, Andrew had a strange dream that he was back on board the *Simmons*. The ship was being turned upside down and the wild wind was beating out a terrible cadence of doom. Startled, he awoke in a sweat. He gasped with relief as he realized it was but a dream. As he tried to go back to sleep, he thought, *That storm at sea wasn't as bad as some of the storms taking place in my own heart*. Again he longed for England and thought of the heartache that had shaken him so badly. Upon giving his life to God as a missionary, he'd expected that things would go well, that his heart would know peace. But that was not so. Suddenly he remembered the Moravians' peace as they faced the storm. *How had they faced death with such calmness?* "When will I ever find that kind of assurance in my own heart?" he whispered aloud, then rolled over and again sought the sleep that wouldn't come.

"I Didn't Know Scholars Were So Romantic!"

O h, Miss Hope, I have a letter from Andrew—!"
Hope Wingate had been dozing in her uphol-
stered chair by the fireplace with a lap rug over her
legs. She opened her eyes at once, smiling faintly to see an
excited flush on the face of the woman who'd burst into her
room.

"Sit down, Dorcas, and read it." The winter had weakened
Hope Wingate considerably but she made no complaints. Now
as the young woman pulled up a stool and began to read the
letter, she noted that good food had done a great deal for Dorcas
Morgan. The girl had been thin and her face pinched with
hunger when she first arrived at Wakefield. Now her cheeks
were filled out and rosy and the plain brown dress she wore
revealed the lithesome curves of her body. Dorcas had the
freshness of youth, and her coming had pleased the old woman
very much.

Holding the paper up to the firelight, Dorcas shook her
head. "So strange this has come all the way across the ocean,"
she marveled. "Think of it, Miss Hope—it's almost like
magic!" She held the envelope, rubbing it with her fingers and
enjoying the texture of the paper. Then, at Hope's urging, she
began to read.

Dear Friend Dorcas,

This letter, I trust, will find you in good health. It is my prayer that God has blessed you in your stay at Wakefield. I received the letters from you and Aunt Hope just yesterday and they were very welcome to me! They made me realize how far away from home and hearth I am and, to tell the truth, made me somewhat sad. To pull a man out of his native ground and make an attempt to transplant him in foreign soil is a difficult task. Our gardener tried this several times with various plants, I remember, and many times the transported plants simply withered and died.

But do not fear this will happen to me. It's a difficult life but this is a most pleasant place. The weather is warmer, I think, than in England and we haven't suffered intensive cold. Of course, the worst of winter is yet to come, and it may be I shall have chills soon enough. But the food is good, and the rectory better than Reverend Wesley and I expected.

The letter continued for some time, recounting the work in Savannah and detailing the visits he and John Wesley had made to the prisons and the homes of the poverty stricken. Andrew had apparently been so influenced by John Wesley's meticulous record keeping that he even included the number of prisoners they had borne witness to on various dates. Then he continued,

It seems to me, my dear friend, that those in prison are more ready to hear the gospel than those who are outside. Perhaps it's because they have no other hope and no other arm on which to lean. We remember, of course, that the Lord Jesus came to set the prisoners free. While I'm sure this was meant in the Scripture as

108

a metaphor, yet surely we have seen many in their hearts turn to the Lord Jesus and receive salvation. I must confess, however, that our ministry outside the prison has been less successful than we might have thought.

We have, however, been disappointed in our attempt to convert the heathen. One of the Indians, dressed in English clothes, we did bear witness to. He was an aged man, believing himself to be nearly one hundred. His name was Chief Tomo-Chachi and he wore a large blanket, beads in his hair, and a scarlet feather behind one ear.

He seemed to be receptive to the gospel but when we returned for a second visit, the wigwams were empty. Mr. Wesley has importuned General Oglethorpe to go into the deeper forest to preach to the Indians but the general has refused. He says we might be captured by the French or the Spanish and embroil the colony in war.

I'm sorry to report that Mr. Charles Wesley has given up on our mission venture. He sought to compel everyone to lay down their tools and come to church four times today at the beat of a drum. The people simply rebelled at this and at other disciplines he imposed on them. He is making plans now for his return to England.

I must confess that our people here in Savannah are not as receptive of discipline as we had hoped. Mr. Wesley and I had expected they would submit to somewhat of the same discipline that we ourselves have taken, but there is, I regret to tell you, much complaining. It disturbs me that the people have not discovered that the road to heaven is steep and heavy and difficult, and religious duties and exercises must be assumed if they are to be true Christians.

Dorcas glanced up at Hope, who had been listening carefully, and said tentatively, "I'm afraid Andrew isn't too happy in his work."

A flicker of doubt flashed across Hope's face. She sat there silently for a moment, as if in prayer, then shook her head slightly. "Andrew has missed out on the joy of Christian life, Dorcas. He always was that kind of youngster—even as a boy. He threw himself into whatever came before him with all of his might. Why, even in games he seemed to get more pleasure out of the discipline of them than he did from the actual game itself. Does he say anything else?"

> Mr. John Wesley has given considerable time to Sophy Hopkey, a young woman in the group. She's very pretty and the niece of the chief magistrate of Savannah. Mr. Wesley feels she needs special pastoral care and her aunt has already hinted that she might make a good housewife. Mr. Wesley, however, is persuaded that it's better to remain unmarried, which agrees exactly with my own views.
>
> My best regards to all, especially my dear aunt and to you, Dorcas. I am writing a letter to Gareth. I trust it may be some help in his situation.

Dorcas frowned, saying, "I hope a few words from Andrew will help Gareth. He's not happy at Oxford."

The two women sat there talking for a while about Andrew, so far away and in such a strange place. Finally Dorcas looked out the window as if she could see all the way to the Colonies and, with a mild yet strained voice, said, "I pray that God will keep Andrew safe—and that he'll find more joy in the Lord."

After a moment of silence, Hope nodded. "Yes, I pray so too." Then she said hesitantly, "Dorcas, I think we'd best invite Gareth for a visit. His last letter troubled me. I fear he is very unhappy."

At once Dorcas's eyes lit up. "Oh, could we do that? I'd so love to see him!"

"Get your pen and paper and write the letter. Tell him I long to see him." While Dorcas scurried around the room getting writing materials, Hope sat quietly. When Dorcas had finished writing the letter, Hope said, "Now, go give it to George and ask him to mail it for you." Dorcas jumped up and ran from the room. As she watched Dorcas leave, Hope's thoughts were with Andrew, the pride and hope of her heart, and with Gareth, who needed a deeper work done in his own heart.

Gareth opened the letter almost feverishly. He was sick not only of his studies at Oxford but also of the service he had to pay to upperclassmen. The strong pride that ran deep in his Welsh blood resisted polishing shoes and doing menial tasks for others. When one of the upperclassmen had thrown a pair of shoes at him and cursed him for not getting them done quickly, he'd felt a flash of anger. It had taken all his willpower to keep from smashing the pale face of the upperclassman. But he had swallowed his pride, knowing there was no other way for him to turn.

Tearing the envelope open, he stared at it for a moment, then closed his eyes with relief and muttered, "Thank God, I can get away from this place for a while!"

At once Gareth began making preparations. He had to get the headmaster's permission, which was difficult. He was insistent, however, and at last left the headmaster's office with a smile. He went to his room, packed his few things, and noted that a letter from George Whitefield had come for him. Whitefield related that he'd left for Gloucester to recover from overwork and that he'd been blessed by God in his efforts there. He also said he'd started what he called a *society*—a group of believers who gathered to encourage each other and pray for one another. Whitefield, no doubt, had the Holy Club in mind as a model and he encouraged Gareth to find fellowship for himself.

As Gareth traveled toward Wakefield, it seemed the very air was fresher away from the confines of Oxford, with all of its disadvantages. But a sense of shame ran through Gareth's mind as he rattled along in the carriage to the small village that touched on the Wakefield property. *I ought to be ashamed,* he thought. *Back in Wales I'd be starving to death—or else grubbing coal out far underground. At least I don't have to do that.* He tried to feel grateful but somehow found it very difficult.

When the carriage stopped in the village, he got out and retrieved his one small piece of luggage—a leather case Andrew had given him. As Gareth walked along the road that led out of the village, his face grew numb with the chilling wind. The snow that had fallen a few days earlier had mostly melted away, but the white patches still striped the fields and clung to the tops of a few of the larger oak trees. But since Gareth had never been troubled by physical hardship, the cold didn't bother him. Away from Oxford and about to see Dorcas and Hope, he began to whistle cheerfully.

When he arrived at Wakefield's back door, he found Naomi Beard, the housekeeper, instructing the cook on the evening meal. Her eyes grew large as she saw him. "Mr. Morgan? I recognized you from your sister's description. I'm happy to see you! I'm Mrs. Beard, the housekeeper."

"How are you, Mrs. Beard?" Gareth stepped into the kitchen, enjoying the smell of bread baking and a roast that was turning on a spit in the fireplace. He winked at Olive Maddox, the cook. "And you must be Olive. I'm looking forward to your cooking. Dorcas told me that nobody at Oxford can cook like you can."

Olive, a robust woman with red cheeks and heavy hands, flushed slightly at the compliment. "You wait," she promised. "I'm making a mince pie. I remember from Dorcas you like it."

"Is my Aunt Hope here—and Dorcas?"

"Of course. Do they know you're coming?"

"Yes, they're expecting me, I think. I'll go right up." Having been directed by Mrs. Beard, he nodded and left the warmth of the kitchen. His feet echoed on the stone floor as he traced his way down the hall, then ran up the steps two at a time. When he stopped at Hope's door he knocked loudly. "Open up in there!" he called cheerfully.

He heard footsteps and then the door opened and he was swarmed by Dorcas. She threw her arms around him and he staggered backwards. "Wait," he cried, "don't eat me alive!"

"Oh, Gareth, it's so good to see you!" Dorcas hugged him for a moment, the tears stinging her eyes. "Come in," she said, drawing him inside and clinging to his hand as she'd done when they were children.

Gareth moved with her at once to where Hope was sitting in a chair, smiling up at him. He knelt by her side and took her hand with his free one. "Aunt Hope, it's good to finally meet you," he said, smiling. Although they were not related in this way, Gareth called her "Aunt," as was common in Wales.

Hope felt the strength that ran through his hand and saw the glow of health in his face. "Why, Nephew," Aunt Hope said quickly, responding in kind, pleased that he would call her such, "you're looking very well. Here—sit beside me and tell us everything."

The three talked rapidly. Pleased, Gareth noted Dorcas's appearance. She was wearing a pale blue dress with white lace at the neck and wrists. But even now she kept her maimed hand out of sight whenever possible. "You're looking well, Dorcas," he said. He reached over and ran his hand along her cheek. "You've fattened up some. You keep on eating like that and you'll be as big as Olive."

Dorcas smiled with pleasure at his teasing, "You wait," she promised, "I'm going to stuff you like a suckling pig. Do you

113

know I've got the chickens all confined now? I'll make you some eggs for supper, as many as you like."

"How many do you have? I'll have all the eggs we can find."

Hope listened as the two sat closely together, talking. *She's missed him,* Hope thought. *She's been lonely here and I'm not much company for a young woman. I'm glad he came.* Aloud she said, "How are your studies going, Gareth?"

A scowl replaced the smile on Gareth's broad lips. He wrinkled his forehead and shut his eyes. "Not worth discussing," he groaned. "I think I have wood up here instead of brains."

"That's not so," Dorcas protested. "You've always been smarter than any of your friends."

"Well, I'm not smarter than anybody at Oxford." Gareth started to tell them how he hated being a servant, then hesitated. *That will do no good,* he rebuked himself sternly. *Put a good face on the thing.* "Well," he said, "I suppose I'm doing well enough. Greek is the hardest subject."

"Can you speak Greek?" Dorcas asked.

"Oh, I can read some of it. I brought a New Testament with me. That's to keep up with my studies."

"Let me hear some of it," Dorcas pleaded. "I've never heard Greek before."

When Hope joined in Dorcas's pleas, Gareth opened his bag, pulled out the portion of the Greek New Testament he was working on, the book of First John, and began to read aloud. He had a clear voice and had studied the pronunciation well. When he looked up and shut the book, the two were staring at him, almost in awe. "Well, that's enough of that."

"You do it so well, Gareth," Dorcas said. "I'll bet you do it better than any of the others."

"I'm glad you think so, though that's not exactly true," Gareth admitted. He looked at the two women and exclaimed, "It's good to be here. I've wanted to see you both!"

"We have longed to see you too, Nephew," Hope said quietly. She was feeling rather tired but didn't want to show it. "Now," she said as brightly as she could, "we'll have supper here in my apartment in your honor tonight. Just the three of us."

It was a fine supper. Olive had outdone herself, and Dorcas did some cooking of her own. That night as the fire crackled cheerfully in the fireplace, the three of them sat around the table and Gareth ate heartily. They talked for a long time and laughed often and harder than any of them had laughed for a considerable time. After they had finished their meal and were drinking tea, Hope asked, "Did you hear from Andrew?"

"Yes, I've had two letters. Both rather short. I suppose he's very busy. Missionaries are, I understand." He saw the concern in her eyes and managed a laugh. "I suppose I might as well confess; Mr. Wakefield's worried about me. He knows I'm impatient and somewhat hot tempered."

Hope said at once, "Andrew is fond of you, Gareth, as I am. We want you to prosper in the Lord." Then she asked, "Are the sermons good at Oxford?"

"Dull as dishwater."

"You don't mean it!" Dorcas exclaimed. "With all the great ministers, teachers, and professors there?"

"Dry as dust." Gareth threw up his hands in disgust. "Our pastor back home, in our little church in Wales, could preach circles around any of them. He's got fire and life in him. These fellows—all they do is stay in their dusty studies and write dusty sermons. Faugh! I need to take a bucket of water with me into the service, so dry they are!"

"That's a shame," Hope commented, shaking her head. "The Word of God is exciting."

"Not the way they preach it," Gareth said, shrugging. "Most of those fellows have forgotten what it's like to serve a living God. I miss Mr. Wakefield—and George Whitefield. Now there's a fellow who isn't dull! Mark my words, the world will hear from him." He spoke for a while about George Whitefield's conversion and finally Dorcas asked about this phenomenon.

"He says a man must be born again—and that he never was until recently. Since that happened, he goes around talking about grace, saying God cannot be reached by ritual or good works. I must admit he's very convincing. He doesn't look like much with one eye out of kilter. The fellows make fun of him there for his bad eye but I think a great deal of him."

The two young people saw that Hope was tired, so they kissed her good-night and exited, taking the dishes with them. When they had deposited the dishes and were sitting in the kitchen alone, Gareth turned to his sister and studied her for a moment. "Are you happy here, Dorcas?"

"Oh yes. Miss Hope is such a dear." She looked at her brother carefully, then asked cautiously, "What about you, Gareth?"

"I'm all right," he said quickly.

But Dorcas knew him well. She reached out her good hand and took his. "I can tell you're not happy. What's wrong? Do they mistreat you at Oxford?"

"No more than the other servitors," he confessed. "I'm just not cut out to be a bootblack, I suppose—but I'll not complain. It beats starving to death in Wales, doesn't it, Sister?" He sat there and went to some trouble to turn the conversation to more cheerful things. He wanted to enjoy these few days away from his prison. "Can we go into the village tomorrow? I have a few coins—maybe we can buy you a few ribbons or something."

They did go into the village the next day and Gareth was amazed. Dorcas knew almost everyone. "You've made so many acquaintances since you've been here," he commented.

"Oh, they're nice—like our villagers back home," Dorcas said. "They're all impressed I have a brother who's a scholar." She led him through the small shops and they spent some of the few coins he had before returning home. As they approached the house, George Wakefield rode up, dismounted heavily, and said at once, "Hello, young fellow. I'm George Wakefield. I've been looking for you."

"How are you, Mr. Wakefield?"

"Very fine. Are you on a vacation?"

"Yes, sir, I have a few days. It's kind of you to let me visit my sister."

"Not at all, not at all!" George said expansively as the servant took his horse away. "I have an invitation for you."

"An invitation, sir?"

"Yes, my bride-to-be is giving a ball here at Wakefield." He laughed loudly. "I've started giving her a free hand."

"I'd be happy to come, sir, but I don't have any fancy clothes."

"Oh, I have a few I could wear when I was a stripling like yourself. They're no good to me now," he said, patting his stomach with a grin. "Come along and we'll see what we can find. Then we'll get Mrs. Beard to cut them down if we need to." As the two stepped inside the house, Dorcas left and went back to Hope's room.

"Sir George has invited Gareth to the ball," Dorcas excitedly told Hope, "and he's having some of his clothes fitted for him. Isn't that nice?"

"Why, yes. Of course, you will go as well."

"Oh, no. I have nothing to wear."

"Nonsense. You'll have to see your brother. We'll put on our best clothes and celebrate with the new bride-to-be."

<hr />

Sarah Lancaster, a tall and shapely woman with a tiny waist that emphasized her curves, examined her new dress with a critical eye. "I hate this!" she exclaimed pettishly.

Agnes, Sarah's maid, who'd been arranging the dress, looked up with surprise. "It's a beautiful dress, Miss Sarah. Sir Talbot must have paid a fortune for it. Why don't you like it?"

"I hate these side *panniers!*" Sarah emphasized. She was standing in the middle of the room, wearing the undergarments Agnes had just fastened and glaring at the whalebone-and-tape affair tied to her waist. A *pannier* served the purpose of spreading skirts to the sides and it supported the weight of layers of material. More than anything else, it resembled a couple of baskets turned upside down.

"I like the old farthingales better." Sarah referred to the old Spanish *farthingale,* which had been in vogue in France for many years. It consisted of a round framework that held the skirt out from the waist.

Sarah swung her hips from side to side so the whalebone affair swung with her. "Isn't that ridiculous? The dressmaker told me the word *pannier* comes from the Spanish word *basket*—baskets that donkeys wear. That's what I feel like—a donkey!"

"Oh, no," Agnes protested. "When you walk with these skirts—" she used her hands in an expressive French way—"it lends a lilting gentle motion to the skirt—flowing, feminine, and provocative."

Sarah gave her maid a disgusted look. "I feel like an idiot. What's wrong with a skirt that simply falls to the top of the shoe? That would be good enough for me." Sarah was a lively girl, sometimes *too* lively. Her father and mother often rebuked her for shocking people.

"I'd like to go to the ball without looking like a donkey," she muttered, but she knew she was trapped into the styles of the day. "Well, help me get the dress on," she said impatiently.

"Good," Agnes said. "You'll be the most beautiful lady at the ball." The dark velvet gown was trimmed with gray fur. The pink taffeta underskirt had a dark lace band that peeked out from beneath the skirt. As soon as the dress was in place, Agnes stepped back and said admiringly, "You look wonderful, my lady!"

Accustomed to such compliments, Sarah shrugged and said, "Well, let's see if we can do something with my hair. Then I'm off to the ball."

Agnes was a fine hairdresser and soon Sarah's blonde hair was arranged to suit her. "Now for your bosom bottle," the maid said. Quickly she slipped the small glass cylinder, filled with water, into a pocket at the top of the gown. Then she darted to the table, returning with a fresh flower, which she inserted into the bottle. "This will last until the dance is over, I'm sure."

Sarah smiled and said, "Thank you, Agnes; you've done a good job." She slapped the *panniers,* which stuck out a foot on either side of her hips, and laughed ruefully. "Now I'll have to turn sideways to get through the door, but that's all right. You didn't invent these awful things."

She descended the stairs and found her parents waiting. "You look beautiful, Mother," she said dutifully. Her mother, Lady Jane Lancaster, was also a tall blonde woman, but she didn't have her daughter's beauty. Lady Jane also wore an ornamental dress styled with *panniers.*

Sir Talbot Lancaster stared at his wife and daughter. "You'll have to sit on opposite sides of the carriage with the things you've got on those hips," he observed, then turned and led the way to the carriage. When they were on their way he said, "Have you met the young woman George is going to marry?"

"No, I haven't," Lady Jane said. "It will be quite a catch for her, I suppose. She comes from a poor family, so I understand."

Sir Talbot pondered this and shook his head. "George could have done better." He turned to Sarah. "Why didn't you trap him, Daughter?"

"He's too fat," Sarah said calmly.

"But he has money, and better a fat man with money than a skinny one with none."

Sarah smiled at her forty-seven-year-old father. "That may be well enough for you, but you don't have to sleep with the man I marry—*I* do."

Lady Jane gasped. "Sarah! Don't speak of such things!"

"Why not? It's true, isn't it?"

"It's not well to speak of such things, true or not," her mother admonished her. "I'm always worried you're going to break out and say something like that in polite company."

"I'm sure worse things than that are said when the men leave the table to go to their smoking room; isn't that true, Father?"

"That's men," Talbot said bluntly. "Men are rougher creatures than women. We expect ladies to be more dainty."

Sarah was amused. "You might be shocked at some of the things young women say when they're alone."

Sir Talbot's eyes flew open. "I trust I would *not* be shocked." Then curiosity got the better of him and he studied his daughter closely. "What sort of things are you talking about?"

"You tell me what the men say," Sarah said, smiling, "then I'll tell you what the ladies say."

"Neither one of you will tell such dreadful things," Lady Jane pronounced. She turned the conversation to other things at once and Sarah winked at her father and whispered, "I'll tell you later."

When they reached Wakefield and passed into the ballroom, Sarah looked at the massive walls of stone that held up the fanned arching of the ceiling. On each side huge fireplaces blazed, six of them, and each had logs up to eight feet long. The flickering flames, aided by a great many candles, threw light up among the shadows. A flash of gilt was everywhere. The dancing had already started and men and women moved across the room, the colors of their costumes almost dazzling the eye. Red, green, yellow, all mingled and flashed as the dancers wove intricate patterns in the ever-changing firelight. Soon they were met by Sir George Wakefield and his bride-to-be. "Well, here she is," George said proudly, "the future Lady Wakefield." He watched their faces carefully and saw they were impressed with Caroline Barksdale's appearance. Then he took Sir Talbot off at once to the billiard room, where the other gentlemen were meeting.

The ladies moved around the floor, watching the dance, and Sarah made it her business to become acquainted with the future Lady Wakefield. She found her to be quick-witted, much like herself, and the two got on rather well. Later Caroline was pulled away into the dance by an elderly gentleman. Almost at once Sarah was approached by a tall officer in uniform. "Well, Miss Sarah," he said, "I'm delighted to see you. May I have this dance?"

"Yes, of course. How are you, Major Crenshaw?"

Sarah stepped to the floor with the major and was swept into the dance. Ian Crenshaw was a huge man in every way. Six feet three inches tall, he had the bulk of a wrestler, with a thick neck and hands like hams. Although Sarah liked him well enough to dance with, she'd never considered him a suitable prospect although he'd been a suitor of hers for some time. "How are things with the regiment? Are there any wars to be fought, Ian?"

"No, not at the moment. I'd rather be here dancing with you. Your gown is beautiful and so are you."

"Which is more beautiful, me or the gown? You named the gown first," she said, teasing him. "Do you always notice clothes before the woman?"

"No, that I don't!" Crenshaw, a rather cocky man who had enjoyed success with women, was handsome in a rough way. Now his arms tightened around her waist imperiously. "I'd think you were beautiful even without the gown," he said.

Sarah lifted her eyebrows and said, "Why, Major! What a shocking thing to say!"

"I meant in a less expensive gown," Crenshaw said, smiling. He knew Sarah was a witty woman who sometimes spoke daringly.

And since his charm hadn't worked well with her in the past, he set himself to improving that matter.

The dance went on for some time and Sarah enjoyed herself. She danced twice with Major Crenshaw, then seated herself beside the wall to speak with a friend from London. Suddenly a young man seemed to materialize out of nowhere and asked in a low, husky voice, "May I have this dance?"

Sarah looked up. She had never seen this tall, strongly built man before. He had coal black, curly hair and his eyes were such a dark shade of blue that they seemed almost black. He had a wedge-shaped face, handsome features, and eyelashes so thick she envied them for a moment.

"I believe you may." Sarah rose and went out on the floor with the young man. Because he was even taller than she thought, at least six feet, she had to tilt her head back to look at him. "I don't believe I know your name, sir."

"Gareth Morgan."

"Ah, Mr. Morgan, are you new in this county?"

"Yes, I am, Miss Lancaster."

Sarah raised her eyebrows. "Oh, you know my name?"

"Indeed," Gareth said, lifting one of his eyebrows. "I saw you and asked Sir George."

"Sir George Wakefield?"

"Yes, and he said I had exquisite taste in ladies." Again Gareth smiled and Sarah was more impressed by his attractiveness than she liked to admit.

"You're a better dancer than I am," he said. "You've had more practice, I suppose."

"And what have you had to practice at, Mr. Morgan?"

"Things much more earthy than dancing. So earthy you'd be bored to hear about them. Now dancing—I find that exercise most dangerous."

"Dangerous, sir?"

Gareth tightened his grip on Sarah's waist. "Such things can cause an explosion. When a man and a woman are fused in such an intimate manner—who knows what will happen?"

"Then you need not hold me so tightly, sir!" His evasion puzzled Sarah but she was enjoying the dance. *He has an accent I can't quite place,* she thought. *Not quite English . . . Irish perhaps?* She took a chance. "Morgan—is that an Irish name?"

"Welsh, Lady Sarah."

Sarah was adept at picking men out and seeing behind the obvious but she couldn't pinpoint what was so different about this man. He was not in the army, she felt sure of that. She had never seen a lawyer so handsome—besides he was rather young, not over eighteen or nineteen she would guess, about her own age. And his dancing wasn't smooth enough for him to have had a great deal of practice . . . therefore, what was he?

Gareth knew this beautiful woman was puzzled and he delighted in what he was doing. He'd seen her when she entered, and upon finding out her name had thrust himself upon her. He'd scarcely expected she'd dance with him, a stranger. But he saw at once that she was a woman who liked challenges. As they danced together she probed, trying to identify a station. He was pleased his Oxford time had smoothed out some of the roughness of his grammar so that she made no headway at all.

Then the dance was over and he led her back to the chairs along the wall. They were met by a displeased Major Ian Crenshaw. "I thought we had this dance, Miss Sarah."

"Oh, I'm sorry, Major. I forgot. This is Mr. Morgan and this is Major Ian Crenshaw."

Crenshaw did not extend his hand. His nod was perfunctory and there was an edge to his voice when he said to Sarah, "I believe you owe me the next dance."

"I'm sorry. I promised it to Mr. Morgan." Sarah deliberately invented this and turned her head sideways, noting that Gareth

123

Morgan took the hint without blinking an eye. "Maybe later on, Major." Crenshaw looked angry; he shook his head, glared at Gareth, then turned and stalked away.

"You bruised his feelings, I'm afraid," Gareth observed.

"He's big enough to endure a few hurt feelings."

"Is he a suitor of yours?"

"Of a sort—but I wouldn't like to be married to a soldier," Sarah said, then asked straightforwardly, "What is it you do, Mr. Morgan?"

"I'm at Oxford. A poor anchorite, nothing more."

"What is that?"

"A hermit, Miss Lancaster, one who renounces such pleasure as this for a life of study."

"Indeed! Studying for the law?"

"I'm not sure. I suppose you might say I'm studying to endure my time there."

"Is it so dull a place?" Sarah said, interested.

"I find it so. Come, the music is starting again. This is my dance, the Major's loss."

For Sarah it was a strange time. She'd never seen a young man quite as handsome as Gareth Morgan—and with such sharp wit. She was not able to draw any more information out of him about what he intended to do, but as the dance went on she found he was able to make her laugh, something she admired in a man.

When he finally bowed and left her, she went at once to Sir George, who was talking with his bride-to-be, and asked, "Who is that gentleman?"

"That," George said, looking in the direction she nodded, "is a young dependent of mine. His name is Morgan."

"A dependent? Of what nature, Sir George?"

"He's a young coal miner from Wales. My brother Andrew picked him up out of it. Actually, they are some relation to our family. The young woman is nursing my aunt, and I've put young

Morgan there into Oxford. I suppose he'll make a minister like my brother."

"Oh, that's very kind of you, I'm sure."

As the evening came to a close, Gareth came once again to stand before Lady Sarah. "I wanted to say good night." The two were standing in a private alcove, away from the main ballroom. "I must tell you, you made my evening quite pleasant." He put out his hand and, surprised, she gave it to him. He bent over and kissed it but didn't release it. "You're a lovely young woman, Miss Lancaster. I've never seen a lovelier in all my life."

Sarah was accustomed to compliments, but the dark blue eyes and unusual, husky voice caught her and held her fast. She was very much aware he was holding her hand firmly. "Thank you, Mr. Morgan," she responded. "It's been most pleasant to meet you." She hesitated, then said, smiling, "I didn't know scholars were so romantic."

"People think that—but they're mistaken."

Gareth had intended to drop her hand but there was a playful look in the young woman's blue-gray eyes—almost a challenge. Without thinking, he stepped forward and pulled her into his arms. He kissed her and suddenly his nerves tingled with excitement. She didn't resist him as he held her close. Her lips were soft under his firm ones and she smelled of violets.

Sarah Lancaster was somewhat shocked at her own behavior. She'd been kissed before, but not with such suddenness. For one moment she allowed herself to enjoy the touch of the kiss; then she stepped back and said sternly, "You are presumptuous, Mr. Morgan!"

"Yes, I am. I ask your pardon, Miss Lancaster." But he did not look in the least downcast. Rather, his dark eyes were glowing and his lips were turned up slightly in a smile. "The fault was mine," he added. "I beg you will forgive me." He hesitated, saying, "I hope to see you again." Then he turned and left the room.

As Sarah watched him go, she asked herself, *What am I thinking of . . . to let a man kiss me like that?* Yet, as Gareth moved through the guests, she realized, *I've never seen a man who could stir me quite like that young Oxford scholar.* When she rejoined her parents, she listened to them talk for a while. But inside she was still wondering, *Why in the world did I let a stranger kiss me like that. . . ?*

Nine

GARETH HEARS THE
TRUE GOSPEL

M y dear fellow, what in the world has happened to you?"
George Whitefield had returned in June to Oxford. He'd been ordained and had preached his first
sermon, and found great success in Bristol. But now, as he stood
staring at his friend Gareth Morgan, concern was written on his
plain features. He'd found Gareth sitting in his room late one
afternoon, staring blankly at the wall. Now he walked over, sat
down, and said in a kindly voice, "Tell me what's happened to
you. You've buried yourself in this room as if it were a tomb. Out
with it!"

Gareth pulled himself out of his reverie, looked at George Whitefield, and finally said, "It's probably something you wouldn't care to
hear."

"I think a friend always wants to share in the problems of
others. Now, what is it?"

"I've fallen in love." Quickly lifting his hand, Gareth continued,
"Don't laugh at me, George. I know you care little for the charms
of young women but I'm different from you."

It was true enough that George Whitefield seemed to care for
nothing but the things of God. He'd never had a sweetheart—
indeed, had never courted a woman. Truthfully, he was lacking
in sympathy for Gareth because, for him, serving God was

everything. He lived moment by moment in the Scriptures and he was always involved in ministry. Still, he was most kind-hearted and he put his hand, in a friendly fashion, on Gareth's shoulder. "It's true enough I'm not romantic but I've seen young men suffer the woes of love. So of course I can sympathize. Who is she?"

"Sarah Lancaster." Since the ball, Gareth had thought of little else but the beautiful features of Sarah. He didn't need a painting, for it seemed all he had to do was turn his thoughts on her and her lovely face leaped into his mind full blown. He had managed to see her twice during his visit at Wakefield but both times were brief and unsatisfying. "She's so far above me I can't even *think* of her without being depressed," he muttered. "She's the daughter of a wealthy family and can marry anyone she chooses. Why should she look at a poor servitor like me, a drudge of a scholar, and not much of one at that?"

Whitefield sat quietly listening, watching the despair in the Welshman's dark eyes as he unburdened himself. When Gareth ran down, Whitefield began to encourage him. "God does strange things. Who knows but what he might put this young woman in your way for a future wife? Stranger things have happened." He spoke in this vein for a while, then tentatively said, "I've been praying you'd find Christ to be all sufficient. You know the Scriptures say, 'Seek ye first the kingdom of God, and his righteousness; and all these things shall be added unto you.'"

Gareth grinned almost sardonically, his white teeth flashing against the tanned cheeks. "You mean if I seek the kingdom of God, Sarah might be added unto me?"

"Oh no, no, dear boy! I wouldn't put it like that *at all!* That would be *using* God to get something you want. We must seek God because we want him and long for him more than anything else in the world. He's the pearl of great price, and if we would have him, we must sell all we have to purchase that pearl."

Gareth was in no mood to be preached to. Truthfully, he was wallowing in his own misery. He had poured out his grief in a long letter to Dorcas, had pondered over the wisdom of mailing it, and finally had torn it up, thinking, *What good would it do to burden her with my problems? She can't make me rich and an eligible suitor for Sarah's hand.* He also felt somewhat ridiculous: Having seen a woman three times was not enough for falling into a lover's swoon!

Finally he said, "Let's talk of something else."

"I think that might be best." Whitefield was glad to see Morgan turn his thoughts away from the young woman. *He'll probably forget her if he puts his mind on other things.* Aloud he said, "Come along, I've come to fetch you."

"To do what?"

"Charles Wesley is back."

"Back in Oxford?"

"Not to stay—just a visit. He sent me up to fetch you. He's in my room."

Eagerly Gareth accompanied Whitefield to his room. As they entered, Charles Wesley was writing at a desk. He rose at once and shook Gareth's hand warmly. "Morgan, it's wonderful to see you. I've missed you, dear fellow!"

"I've missed you too, Mr. Wesley," Gareth responded. "I want to hear all about your missionary experience."

A spasm of anger crossed Charles Wesley's aristocratic features. "I wouldn't go so far as to call it that," he said sharply and took several paces around the room. "Sit down, sit down; we'll have tea, and I'll give you my report."

Whitefield and Morgan sat down and as tea was brought by one of the servitors, Wesley, obviously distraught, quickly gave his report. "It's all been a horrible miscarriage of a mission. Nothing—absolutely *nothing* has gone right! As far as the Indians were concerned, they are not the 'unspoiled children of nature'—as some would have us to believe. They are sinners like the rest of men. And the church in the colony, why, it's ridden with scandal and intrigue! I'm glad to be out of it. I was a complete misfit, to tell the truth. I tried my best to compel everyone to obey the gospel but they're a hard-hearted lot."

"What about your brother?" Gareth inquired.

Charles hesitated. "I fear for brother Jack. He's tried his best to impose discipline on the church there but he's made some serious errors."

"What sort of errors?" Gareth asked quickly.

"Well, he became too sympathetic to a woman we met on the ship—a Mrs. Hawkins. Andrew and I saw through her at once." Charles shook his head. "But Jack seemed to be impervious to her real character. She'll be trouble, you mind what I say!" He paused, his face stormy with grief and anger, then continued. "I also have been troubled with Jack's interest in an eighteen-year-old woman named Sophy Hopkey. I think he is making a mistake."

"You think he's serious about her, Charles?" Whitefield inquired with consternation. This was the first he'd heard of this development.

"I fear so. Jack isn't romantic, but it's a minister's responsibility to take a wife. From what he has told me, he is considering asking this young woman to marry him. I trust he will have more wisdom."

Whitefield considered this carefully, then said, "I've had a letter from Mr. Wesley, asking for help."

"Help?" Charles said, staring at him. "In what manner?"

"He wants me to serve with him as a missionary in Georgia."

"Do not do it, sir! Do not do it!" Charles became excited and for some time spoke of the impossibilities of the situation in America. He concluded, "It would be the ruin of you. You are doing so well with your ministry here—I beg you keep it up, sir. Do not *think* of going to Georgia!"

Although in the end Whitefield wouldn't comment on his intentions, the three enjoyed a fine visit together. But neither

Whitefield nor his two friends could have foreseen the next development in his life.

Despite Charles Wesley's apprehensions, George Whitefield made one of the most far-reaching decisions of his whole career. He decided to become a missionary in Georgia. But no sooner was this decision made than he began to be besieged with invitations to preach. In his detailed journal he wrote:

> I embrace the invitations, and so many came that some-times we were obliged to consecrate fresh elements two or three times, and stewards found it somewhat difficult to carry the offerings to the communion table.
>
> Congregations continually increased, and generally I preached four times on the Lord's day to very large and effective congregations. For the past three months there is no end of people flocking to hear the Word of God. I sometimes have more than a dozen names of different churches where I have promised to preach. The sight of the congregations was awful. Thousands went away from the largest churches for want of room. They were all attention and heard like people headed for eternity.

London, a city of about six hundred thousand inhabitants, suddenly became stirred by the young minister. Why did they flood into the churches? Doubtless, many of them were drawn by deep spiritual hunger. It's also true that they'd sought in vain for help from the churches and looked upon the clergy of that day with bitter contempt. Bishop Ryle himself says of the general clergy,

> The vast majority of them were sunk in worldliness, and neither knew or cared anything about their profession.

They hunted, they shot, they farmed, they swore, they drank, they gambled. They seemed determined to know everything except Jesus Christ and him crucified.

When Londoners discovered George Whitefield, scores of them began filling the churches. Whitefield spoke with the firmest of convictions and his sermons were such that all could understand. He preached nothing but the basic doctrines of the Church of England. And, in glowing contrast to the majority of the clergy, his life was marked by personal holiness—he seemed ablaze with zeal. Thus it was that multitudes followed George Whitefield. Many followed him from church to church, vigorously endeavoring to be present every time he preached.

When this explosion, as it might be called, took place, Gareth was shocked—as was most of Oxford. "How can this be?" he muttered when hearing of the fame of his friend. "It's just plain George Whitefield! No older than I am. I don't believe there's anything to it—it's just a fad!"

Others at Oxford said worse, and the term *enthusiast* began to be used even more frequently. The masters at Oxford, instead of being proud of their successful young graduate, glowered darkly, saying, "It's not healthy—this running to hear a mere man. Why can't they come to hear their own pastors in this fashion?"

Gareth went about his duties unhappily, thinking about Sarah Lancaster. His future seemed dark; he wondered if he would ever finish the course at Oxford. He had no vocation nor any desire for one. "I spend my life blacking boots for men who are unfit to be here," he muttered to himself on more than one occasion. There was a confusion in his spirit, almost like a storm. Night after night he'd sit in his room staring at the wall and berating his conditions. Once, he became so desperate he almost considered going back to Wales—but he knew that was foolish.

The weeks rolled on and the glowing reports of George

Whitefield's success came more often. Finally Gareth was struck with an idea. He mentioned it to his headmaster. "I'd like to go to London and hear Mr. Whitefield preach. Do you suppose you might spare me for a couple days?"

The headmaster, a short, rotund man with thinning gray hair, grunted unenthusiastically. "If you want to waste your time, go on," he said, then added, "see what the fellow's up to. Nothing but enthusiasm, I'm sure. People are getting their emotions in an uproar. It'll all blow over—but I'd like to have your judgment on it, Morgan. You're a sharp young fellow. Give me a report when you come back."

"Aye, sir, I'll do that."

On the next Saturday Gareth left Oxford. He was fortunate enough to procure a ride with one of the instructors, who owned his own carriage and was also making the trip. As they made their way toward the city, Gareth wondered if he could find a way within his short holiday to see Sarah, since George Wakefield had mentioned that the Lancaster family house was in London.

As soon as they reached London, Gareth at once made it his business to seek out Sarah. The Lancaster house was a tall, three-story brick in one of the more pleasant neighborhoods. Straightening his back, he walked up to the door and knocked loudly.

A butler with cool gray eyes studied him for a moment, then said, "May I assist you?"

"I would like to see Miss Sarah Lancaster."

"I'm sorry, Miss Lancaster is not at home, sir. If you'd care to leave your card—"

Gareth had no card but he went through the charade of fumbling through his pockets. Finally he muttered, "I seem to have misplaced my cards. Just tell her Gareth Morgan called, will you?"

"Yes, sir, I'll do that." The butler suppressed a smirk and Gareth was well aware he had failed to pass muster. Angrily he turned and spent the rest of the day walking the streets of London to find a cheap room. The next morning, he had no money for breakfast so he did without. The sun was bright in the sky as he made his way toward a large, imposing church, Saint Ann's, where he was jostled by a growing crowd. Everyone seemed excited and he heard someone say, "There's nothing like him, this Whitefield. The hand of God is on him, I tell you!"

Gareth had risen early, for he had heard the churches were always packed. As it was, when he came to the door, one of the deacons was attempting to close it. "Sorry, sir, there's just no more room," he said plaintively.

Without arguing, Gareth simply shoved his way through the tiny crack. He didn't think the deacon would enter into a wrestling match to keep him out and he was correct. The door closed and all around him he heard half-angry voices from the crowd who hadn't been able to find seating.

Gareth didn't find a seat, but standing room was available along the walls. The mumble of voices sounded like the hum of a mighty beehive and Gareth looked around with interest. He'd never seen a church packed like this—every seat filled to capacity and more. The worshipers were packed like sardines on the pews, and the space around the walls was filled.

Although he didn't speak to anyone, Gareth wrestled, wondering, *Why would people pack a church like this to hear George?* He'd never heard Whitefield speak and knew him only as a pleasant young man who wanted to be helpful. His puzzlement grew as he saw the worshipers were not from the poor section of London, for many were well dressed. Some of the women sported expensive jewelry and the most fashionable dresses.

The service began and Gareth endured the preliminaries. He hadn't come to worship but to satisfy his curiosity about the phenomenon of George Whitefield. He expected sensationalism:

perhaps far-fetched interpretations, rhetorical fireworks, or emotional stories. Somehow George Whitefield had stirred practically the entire nation—certainly all of London. There *had* to be more to it than he'd seen in Whitefield up until this time.

Finally the moment came when George stepped into the pulpit, which was suspended ten feet over the congregation. He looked no different, wearing the cassock of an Anglican minister. His face was pale, but he was perfectly calm as he began to read the Scripture in even tones. It was his voice that first caught Gareth's attention. He'd never heard Whitefield speak in more than conversational tones, but what he heard now was an organ—rich and full and effortless, filling the vast height and airy reaches of the church with glorious sound. With a shock, Gareth realized Whitefield wasn't even raising his voice and he knew, suddenly, that if George had the inclination, he could increase the volume until the very stones would reverberate!

After reading the Scripture, Whitefield began to preach—and it was not a sermon such as Gareth had expected. There were no rhetorical fireworks, but Whitefield was aglow with holy fervor, his whole being conscious that he was the messenger of God to the people.

The subject of his sermon was self-denial. He began by speaking of the futility of finding satisfaction in the things of the world. The voice, glorious and full, rose and fell, and the people in the church swayed like heads of grain in a slight breeze as Whitefield's voice thundered, then fell to almost a whisper. There was vitality, strength, and health in his words, too. Whitefield wasn't even halfway through the message when he began to speak of the necessity of the new birth and knowing Jesus Christ. He showed the futility of outward religion to satisfy the longing of the heart.

Although Gareth had attended church in the past, his attendance had only been dutiful, not heartfelt. Now, for the first time in his life, a strange thing was taking place. He was experiencing

a strange sort of fear connected with the name of Jesus—for when
Whitefield used that name an unusual pang smote him. As the
sermon went on, perspiration broke out on Gareth's brow. Then
Whitefield began to speak of hell:

> Think of the pains of Hell. Consider whether it is not
> better to cut off a right hand or foot and pluck out a
> right eye if they cause us to sin rather than to be cast
> into Hell, into the fire that never shall be quenched.
> Think how many thousands there are now reserved in
> chains of darkness, under the judgment of the great day,
> for not complying with this text. Do you think they
> now imagine these lost ones that Jesus Christ is a hard
> master; or, rather do you not think that they would give
> ten thousand times, ten thousand worlds could they but
> return to life again and take Christ's easy yoke upon them?
> And can *we* dwell with the everlasting burning more
> than they if we cannot bear this precept, how can we
> bear the irrevocable sentence, depart from me ye cursed
> into everlasting fire prepared for the devil and his angels.

Gareth had always had great physical courage but the fear he
faced now was not a natural thing. It wasn't as if a wild animal
suddenly prepared to spring on him and tear his life from his
throat. It was different from those times when he'd fought against
larger, stronger men and knew he'd be physically harmed. This
fear came from outside himself. It gripped his heart. For the first
time in his entire life Gareth Morgan was conscious that hell is a
reality. He stood with one foot on the brink of a precipice and he
could step off at any moment into that burning place where he'd
never know any peace or goodness or life!

Just then Whitefield paused and looked over the congregation,
seeing the anguish in many faces. In a loving voice that throbbed

with emotion, he said, "That is hell—but now think of the joys of heaven. Think with what unspeakable glory those happy souls are now encircled." He paused and looked up toward the ceiling. "Hark! Methinks I hear them chanting their everlasting hallelujahs and spending an eternal day in echoing triumphant songs of joy. And do you not long, my brethren, to join this heavenly choir? Do not your hearts burn within you as the heart panteth after the water brooks; do not your souls so long after the blessed company of these sons of God?" He extended his arms wide and cried out, "Behold, then, a heavenly ladder reaches down to you by which you may climb to this holy hill. If any man will come after them let him deny himself and follow them. Come and join this heavenly throne. Come to Jesus and be converted."

A storm swept through Gareth Morgan's spirit and soul. Despite himself, his body trembled and his knees felt so weak he was afraid of falling to the floor. Desperately he shut his eyes and leaned back, clasping his hands together to stop their trembling. Still the fear that had been born in him swept through his soul, and to his shock, tears began to run down his cheeks.

And then as Whitefield spoke of Jesus Christ, it was as though Gareth were alone with the preacher. When he looked through tear-glazed eyes, Whitefield, arms extended, eyes glowing with love, cried out again, "Come to Jesus that he may give you life!"

Suddenly Gareth Morgan knew God was in this.

O God, he prayed, *I'm lost. I have no hope. I deserve hell.* He began to berate himself and confess his sins until, as Whitefield cried out the name *Jesus,* without knowing it Gareth echoed, "Oh, Jesus, save me by your precious blood!"

Gareth Morgan never forgot the next few moments, for the moment he cried out, the presence of the Lord God came into his soul. It was like nothing he'd ever known. He realized he'd never known peace but was instead tossed by his own desires and wrongheaded notions. Now, however, these all seemed to flow away and he began to weep. For Gareth, it was the new birth, although he didn't know to call it that. But there inside the packed church, Gareth Morgan, filled with joy, dropped to his knees, oblivious to the stares of those around him, and received the Lord God.

He didn't know how long he stayed there but when he felt hands on his shoulders and looked up, he saw through his tears the face of George Whitefield. Whitefield, an emotional man, was weeping also. As he pulled Gareth to his feet, he threw his arms around him. "My dear brother, you have found the Lord Jesus! Glory to God in the highest!"

Gareth Morgan clung to his friend. Joy surged through him and finally he was able to say, "Oh, George, this is heaven, this is heaven. I have found him—the Lord Jesus Christ!"

Dorcas took one look at Gareth, who'd burst into the room where she and Hope sat, and gave a small cry. But she had no chance to say more, for Gareth fell on his knees before Hope, taking her hands and saying, "I have found the Lord. I am saved by his blood."

The two women cried aloud with joy and both of them began to weep. There was something in Gareth's face that hadn't been there before. He'd always been a handsome man but now he was transformed entirely by light and joy and strength.

"Sit down. I must tell you," Gareth insisted. And with a broken voice and victorious eyes, he told how he'd come to London out of curiosity about George Whitefield but God had struck him to his knees.

When he was finished, Hope reached out and he came into her arms. As tears ran down her withered cheeks, she held him and whispered, "How Angharad Morgan must rejoice in heaven now that her kinsman is in the family of God."

Ten

SOPHY OF SAVANNAH

After the scorching Georgia summer, the fall of 1737 was a welcome relief for Andrew Wakefield. Returning from a pastoral visit to a small village east of Savannah, Wakefield passed under one of the large live-oak forests—something that never failed to capture his attention. As he walked between the massive trunks of the magnificent trees, he looked up and saw the live moss draped across the spreading foliage. Some of the bunches were small, like birds' nests, while others were scattered across the branches like straw. He was fascinated by the lower branches, some of them as large as good-sized trees. The enormous weight of the limbs, spread out horizontally from the massive trunk, dragged them down so the tips of the branches touched the ground. Since there was nothing like this in England, Andrew stopped and leaned his hand against one of the trees that had been pulled by gravity to the moist earth.

Overhead a sharp staccato sound rattled the afternoon stillness. He looked up to see a bird he'd never seen—a woodpecker of sorts, but a giant one. This bird, at least fifteen inches long, with a flaming red crest and gray-black feathers, cast a glassy yellow eye on Andrew, then rose in the air, his flight a swift trajectory as his wings beat with sureness and power.

The sound echoed in the stillness of the late afternoon and

Andrew watched until the bird was out of sight, then continued his walk toward the village, his eye on the ground. He was fascinated by the abundant variety of wildflowers that dotted the ground in Georgia. He had learned the names of a few, including the large plant with heart-shaped, purple flowers he now saw. "Skunk cabbage," he murmured aloud and smiled at the ugly name of the rather attractive little plant. But its unpleasant odor accounted for its name. Stopping, he nudged one shell-like leaf that curled about the tiny flowers and looked rather like a great snail when it lifts itself above a muddy bed. Moving along, he identified another flower, a dull, fuzzy, purplish-brown plant with kidney-shaped leaves. This, he knew, was wild ginger. He loved the smell of it and broke off several stems, cramming them into his pocket as he continued his walk. The most common plant was the palmetto, with its bayonet-like leaves forming fan-shaped branches. The natives of the place liked to weave them into small baskets or make small badges of them which they sometimes painted and pinned to their clothing.

By the time Andrew reached the outskirts of Savannah, he was weary. He'd walked more than twenty miles, a feat he couldn't have accomplished during the hot summer months. But now October, with its snappy breezes, was in the air.

Looking out into a field that adjoined the village, he saw men at work, moving slowly. Thin and black as ebony, they were naked to the waist, even in the airish breeze. He shook his head, for he had seen the brutal effects of slavery. Many of the poor victims were driven by a slave driver's whip, like oxen, from dawn to last light, six days a week. Their endless backbreaking labor, poor diets, and wretched living conditions made their lives terrible and warped them physically and psychologically. Many, he noted as he passed by, were bent and crippled, and one old man, with white grizzled hair, looked at him with eyes that had long since lost their light.

Then he passed into the town of Savannah, which was actually little more than a clearing in the woods. There were no more than one hundred houses, many of them primitive cabins. The population didn't exceed more than five hundred. It certainly wasn't the Edenic paradise Andrew had imagined while he was back in England.

As wood fires sent up thin spirals of smoke that scrawled across the iron-colored sky and were twisted into serpentine forms by the wind, Andrew suddenly longed for the sight of England. He pushed this feeling away quickly. His jaw hardened as he moved toward the rectory, one of the houses built from sawed lumber and whitewashed recently so that it stood out among the darker, weather-stained houses like a banner. It was a two-story house with a steeply pitched shake roof pierced by several gable windows. Andrew had never seen shakes before, but he'd been told it was the best roof available in the Colonies.

As he entered the house he called out, "Mr. Wesley, are you here?"

"Yes, Andrew, in the library."

Following the sound of the voice, Andrew made his way down a short hall, then turned and entered a moderate-sized room where John Wesley sat at a walnut desk with his Bible and several books laid out before him. As usual, Wesley was dressed in an almost fastidious manner.

Throwing himself into a chair, Andrew shook his head wearily. "I'm afraid I have little good news to report, Mr. Wesley." He still called his companion "Mr. Wesley," for there was an innate dignity in the smaller man that seemed to demand it.

Leaning back in his chair, Wesley examined his young assistant. "What's the trouble?"

"The services were poorly attended. I can't think why there's so little interest in building up the congregation. You'd think they'd see the need for it. It's a godforsaken little village and all they have is a church. But they'd rather drink and play cards, I suppose." There was a bitterness in Andrew Wakefield's voice that had become almost chronic. He sat hopelessly slumped in the chair, a dejected look etched across his face. His dark blond hair was long and needed trimming and the weariness in his blue eyes and tightness in his lips revealed an inward tension.

Wesley said quickly, "You mustn't blame yourself. These are not Englishmen here, but colonists. We can't expect the sort of discipline we had back home."

"Most of them are English—or the offspring of Englishmen."

"I know, but there's something about living in the wilderness that enervates the spiritual life. You mustn't be too hard on yourself." An unexpected scowl touched Wesley's countenance and he tapped the desk impatiently with the fingers of his right hand. "I'm unhappy with the church here in Savannah. It's not a faithful congregation."

Wesley spoke the truth, although it was grudingly pulled from him. Looking up quickly, Andrew saw what he had noticed some weeks earlier—that Wesley was looking tired and almost gaunt. "Are you discouraged, Mr. Wesley?"

"I try not to be—but it is difficult," Wesley said, changing the subject abruptly. "I'm troubled about Mrs. Hawkins."

"What's she done now?" Andrew asked in disgust.

"She's still spreading rumors about General Oglethorpe—and about us, I'm afraid."

"What can she possibly say about us?" Andrew demanded.

"I'm afraid some of it comes from her husband. As I understand it, he has a disreputable religious background and he lets the woman do as she pleases."

"She does that, all right. I wish the man would take a firm hand with her."

Wesley waved his hand in the air and said, "We'll have to be on our guard and not give any occassion for gossip." He hesitated, then said, "I made it my policy when we left England to have no intimacy with any woman in America."

Andrew stared at Wesley. He longed to ask, "But what about Sophy?" He had been troubled about Wesley's interest in Sophy Hopkey. The young woman was in Communion service every Sunday and saint's day, and Wesley felt it his duty to speak privately with every communicant every week. He was always careful, Andrew noticed, to choose times when Sophy and he were in the open air. But there was something in Wesley's demeanor when he was with this particular young woman that was lacking when he talked with other female members of the congregation.

As if reading Wakefield's mind, Wesley looked up and said in an apologetic tone, "I have felt it necessary to invite Sophy Hopkey and another young lady to the parsonage for devotional instruction."

"I'm not sure that's wise, sir," Wakefield replied. "As you just said, we need to be very careful."

"Oh, yes, I intend to be careful. You may depend on that. You look tired, Andrew. We'll have an early supper; then we'll have our prayers and get to bed early."

But apparently John Wesley was unable to keep the young woman out of his mind. Later that month he recorded in his journal a walk he took with her. He also added, "I took her by the hand and before we parted I kissed her. And from this time I fear there was a mixture in my intention, though I was not soon sensible of it."

Wesley was somewhat relieved of the responsibility of Sophy when she went for a visit to Frederica. During this time, Wesley visited with five Chickasaw Indian braves from up-country, eagerly asking them about their beliefs.

"Do you believe in One above who is over all things?" he asked.

"We believe there are four beloved things above: the clouds, the sun, the clear sky, and he that lives in the clear sky."

"Do you believe there is but one who lives in the clear sky?"

"We believe there are two with him, three in all."

From this conference Wesley convinced himself that the Indians, with their strange mixture of religious ideas, were ripe for conversion. He wrote out an account of this conference and mailed it to *Gentlemen's Magazine* in London.

Truthfully, Wesley's health was breaking under the strain of the tropical climate—but even more so under the pressures of his failure as a minister. He was restless and unhappy, though he concealed it from most. But Andrew knew it and was rather surprised when Wesley said to him one day, "We will make a visit to Frederica. I fear Miss Sophy has been bothered by the attentions of a young man named Mellichamp. All of her relations want her to accept him, but I know him to be a villain and Sophy does not want him. And I need to rebuke Mrs. Hawkins for her gossiping."

The next day, with some apprehension, Andrew accompanied Wesley on horseback to Frederica. When they arrived at the Hawkinses' house, Mrs. Hawkins interrupted Wesley as he spoke. Her sharp brown eyes seemed to throw off sparks as she screamed at him, "You come to correct me? You with your loose ways among the young women of our congregation?" She began to scream and her husband, who stood nearby, made no attempt to pacify her.

Andrew was shocked when the woman threatened to shoot Wesley. He was even more shocked when she jerked a pair of scissors out of her pocket and ran toward him. Wesley lifted his hands to defend himself, but before he could resist, Mrs. Hawkins grabbed his hair and cut off huge hunks from one side of his head. She swore at him, tearing his cassock, and finally the servants came rushing into the room. In the end the constable came to the house and Wesley and Andrew left. The adventure of "the little parson," as he was called, was soon all over the colony.

When Wesley returned to Savannah, he made rather a comic sight with his hair so long on one side and so short on the other. One critic said, "Well, those long, fine locks, which he takes such infinite pains to have in the most exact order, are not so attractive right now!"

Wesley and Andrew never spoke of the incident to one another. It was not forgotten by the colonists, however, and they ridiculed John Wesley behind his back—for his lopsided appearance and the fact that he'd been attacked by a mere woman.

During this period, Andrew received letters rather frequently from Dorcas. They were always warmhearted and encouraging. She wrote in a fine hand, finer than his own, and though she was not highly educated, there was a simplicity and directness in her words that encouraged him. In one letter she'd said,

> You must not grow discouraged, Mr. Wakefield. Your work for God is so important and I know that the difficulties are great. To be far away from home among strangers is difficult, but you may rest assured that the God who marks the sparrow's fall is observing the glorious work you are doing for him. I trust you take time to have your own devotional time with God. It would be so easy—or so I would think—to become so burdened with your responsibilites as a pastor that you forget to seek the sweetness and goodness of God for your own life. I urge you to seek him so he can pour his sweet Spirit into you.

This pleased Andrew—yet troubled him at the same time. Truthfully, his own devotional life was almost dead. He performed his religious duties faithfully, slogging through the swampy low-lands and driving rainstorms, enduring mosquitoes and ticks and other vermin stoically. But as far as his own soul, there was none of the sweet Spirit of God Dorcas spoke of. He wrote her back, thanking her for her concern and asking her to pray for him. As he closed he said:

> Pray for Mr. Wesley. I fear he is in danger of making an improper marital alliance with one of the young women here. She is not an immoral young woman, I am sure— but she wouldn't make a proper wife for a minister of Mr. Wesley's stature. I wouldn't have thought it would come to this. Of all the men in the world to be taken by the disease of romantic love, Mr. Wesley should have been the last in my judgment. Pray he will come to his senses and see that, if he does take a wife, it should not be a romantic attachment but an agreement between two sensible people.

In Georgia, the darkness sometimes falls swiftly. John Wesley, sailing from Frederica to Savannah late in October with no other passenger except Sophy, landed on an uninhabited island. They were alone except for his volunteer servant, a young boy named Jemmy, and a boat crew who respectfully kept their distance. Wesley had returned to Frederica on Oglethorpe's orders, to baptize, marry, and discipline an erring flock who failed to live up to the high standards Wesley demanded unless their parson was among them. He'd found Sophy unhappy and her violent suitor in prison for a minor offense. Her uncle had virtually given her to Wesley—if he would have her—since Wesley had visited her frequently in that village. Yet Wesley had always kept their visits on an exalted plane.

Now as they made a fire on the island, Wesley waited until supper was finished and then read prayers. The crew had rigged up the sail on four stakes to keep out the bitter wind and to separate their sleeping quarters: the sailors on one side and Sophy, Wesley, and Jemmy on the other.

That night, before they retired, Wesley took Sophy aside and they sat down beside a little thicket. Wesley talked about Christian perfection, about holiness. Abruptly he asked, "Miss Sophy, are you engaged to Mr. Mellichamp?"

"I have promised to either marry him or no one at all."

John Wesley looked at the girl's pretty features and said, almost as if the words were forced from him, "I should think myself happy if I was to spend the rest of my life with you."

Instantly Sophy broke into tears. "I'm so unhappy. I won't have Tommy, for he's a bad man, and I can have none else."

Most women, especially attractive young ones such as Sophy, can touch even a strong man's heart through weeping. Wesley found himself having done all but actually propose. When they returned to Savannah, he secured an arrangement from the Caustons, Sophy's uncle and niece, whereby Sophy would sleep at their house but breakfast at his so that she might join in the devotions and sing the hymns. The arrangement continued all winter. Wesley disregarded gossip about his relations with Sophy. He wrote in his journal, "I find that I cannot take fire into my bosom and not be burnt." It was obvious to Andrew that John Wesley was in love and would sooner or later take the young woman for his wife.

Eleven

"WOMEN ARE WEAK!"

Savannah, like all small towns, was susceptible to gossip in any form. Cut off from the wider world, the inhabitants tended to turn their eyes inward so that the slightest folly of any of the colonists tended to be magnified and spread abroad.

If this were true of ordinary citizens, how much more the "courtship" of Sophy Hopkey by the pastor of the church spread like wildfire! But John Wesley, for all his intelligence, seemed to be almost oblivious to this aspect of life. Andrew Wakefield, however, was not unaware of the spreading gossip. More than once he tried to warn his superior of the danger he was courting but Wesley seemed to have closed his ears to all counsel.

The arrangements for Sophy to meet in the rectory with the pastor continued all winter. From time to time Wesley would record in his journal that he allowed himself a kiss. He also wrestled with the problem of celibacy but could not seem to arrive at any firm decision.

Early in the spring, he revisited Frederica. The colonists had rejected the heavy religious yoke he'd placed on their shoulders and he returned saying, "I have beaten the air in that unhappy place. My utter despair of doing good there made me content with the thought of seeing it no more."

From that point on, his feelings toward Sophy resembled a

pendulum, swinging wildly this way, then that. He'd decide to give up all thoughts of the young woman, then almost immediately would find himself wavering. On February 3, he mentioned in his diary that he had dropped a broad hint about marriage and said that "had Sophy responded he would have proposed at once, but she said it was the best for both of them never to marry." Upon reflection, Wesley considered this, in his own words, "a very narrow escape." Finally, after consulting with the Moravian pastor, John Toeltschig, a man older than himself, he decided to seek solitude. Leaving Savannah, he made his way to the country and reached a state almost of despair, for he recorded in a plaintive tone, "My heart was with Sophy all the time."

Returning to Savannah, he was overcome by the young woman's presence. "Her words, her eyes, her hair, her every motion and gesture were full of such a softness and sweetness." Wesley took her by the hand and once again nearly proposed, restraining himself only by force of will.

Andrew suffered through this crisis with the man he admired so much. He, too, was despondent, for as far as he could tell the ministry was an utter failure. The more he drove himself into spiritual discipline, the more it seemed his public ministry failed. He simply couldn't understand why the colonists found the strict discipline of the Christian life so impossible to maintain. Neither could he understand why they seemed to resent his insistence on those things.

Exhausted physically and spiritually, Andrew was sitting in the small study of the rectory. For over an hour he'd tried to write a letter to Dorcas but could not settle his thoughts. They flew through him wildly and he could only gather them with an effort. He dipped his quill in the ink bottle and was about to begin anew when the door opened and John Wesley walked in. When Andrew saw his face, he asked impulsively, "What's wrong, Mr. Wesley?"

"I cannot bear this uncertainty any longer," Wesley burst out. "I must settle it once and for all!"

"You mean this matter of Miss Sophy?"

"Exactly." Wesley paced feverishly up and down the floor. Finally he turned and said, "I have decided to settle the matter right now—immediately."

"Settle it how, sir?"

"We will let the thing be decided by the lot."

Andrew was instantly disturbed. This tendency of Wesley didn't seem to fit in with the spiritual side of the man. By the "lot" he meant going back to a habit of the Moravians, based on an incident in the book of Acts. When the apostles needed to fill the vacancy left by the death of Judas, they settled it by lots. This didn't seem wise to Andrew but he knew Wesley was adamant in the matter. He'd used it before and had great confidence in it.

Wesley moved over to the desk, took a sheet of paper, and tore it into three sections. Andrew watched as he wrote in his careful script on the first one *Marry;* on the second he wrote, *Think not of it this year,* and picking up the third, he carefully etched, *Think of it no more.* Wesley folded the sheets, carefully shifted them around, then lay them on the table.

"Let us pray, my dear brother," Wesley said urgently. He then prayed quickly, asking God to lead him to the right decision by this means.

Andrew watched as he picked up a paper and studied it. When Wesley handed it to him, he saw that the paper said, "Think of it no more."

"Now," Wesley said with relief, "we can put this behind us."

"I'm happy for your decision, Mr. Wesley," Andrew said. "I think it's the wisest choice."

"I'm happy the Lord has spoken."

When Wesley left the room, Andrew still sat there, feeling an immense relief. At once he began writing his letter to Dorcas. He spoke of Wesley's decision but ended the letter on a rather plaintive note: "It seems to be the first thing that has gone right for Mr. Wesley and me since we came to Georgia!"

<hr />

No one could have read John Wesley's mind, for he went about his duties as always. But apparently, while the use of the lot had settled his problem, it hadn't ended his anxiety. Although Andrew observed him carefully, he could see no trace of regret. However, on March 8, on a visit to the Caustons, Sophy's relatives, he found Sophy and her aunt quarreling. The quarrel was so fiery that Mrs. Causton cried out, "Mr. Wesley, I wish you would take her away with you!" Sophy wept and Wesley, feeling helpless, returned and repeated the details of the scene to Andrew.

"She's an unhappy young woman, Andrew."

"I'm certain she is, sir, but there seems to be little you can do, aside from prayer."

Wesley didn't answer. He looked at the floor and finally muttered, "I have heaviness of spirit for the young woman's suffering."

The next day Wesley was strangely silent. He stayed in his study but Andrew was aware he was disturbed. Finally at noon Wesley put on his hat and coat and turned to say, "I'm confused about this matter. I must go see what dear Sophy is feeling."

Andrew said nothing but felt that it was unwise. *Nothing good can come of it. I wish he had never seen the woman,* he thought after Wesley left.

It was approximately three-thirty when John Wesley reentered the rectory with a strange expression on his face. He paused, staring at Andrew. His lips were drawn together in a white line, and he'd clasped his hands behind him—a sign of tension.

"What is it, sir?" Andrew inquired.

Wesley remained silent for a moment. Then his words came out like chipped stones: "Miss Sophy is marrying a man named Williamson."

Andrew was so surprised, he couldn't speak for a moment. There'd been a rumor of a young adventurer named William Williamson being interested in Sophy. But according to Wesley she'd denied it and assured him she'd take no steps without his advice.

"I can't believe it," Andrew murmured, his heart filled with compassion. He saw that John Wesley was shocked, perhaps as shocked as he'd ever been in his life. Only at that moment did Andrew realize how deep were Wesley's feelings for the young woman. "I'm sorry, sir."

Wesley didn't reply. He simply stood there looking at Andrew with a strange, blank expression. He looked, Andrew thought, like a man who'd been wounded in battle and did not comprehend the severity of his wounds.

Finally Wesley murmured, "I must get about my work." He put his hat carefully on the table, sat down, and began to write. Andrew watched him for a moment, then left. His one thought was, *Well, at least he's rid of the problem now. If she's marrying another man, it's all over.*

He was mistaken, for the affair wasn't over. Four days later, Sophy married Williamson in South Carolina, without banns. True, without this announcement from the clergy that they would wed, this was an irregular marriage—but it was never challenged.

Rumors flew like birds across the colony, and from what Andrew could make of them, he discovered Sophy had been dallying with Williamson for at least two weeks before their sudden engagement.

Wesley's spirit was wounded but he rallied as best he could. The Moravians welcomed him, as usual, but their quiet faith and stirring hymns merely highlighted his sense of failure.

In June, Wesley wrote to his sister Kezia, suggesting she come to Georgia to keep house. But as soon as the letter was sent, he said, "I doubt the wisdom of this. This is no place for my sister."

"No, sir, I think not," Andrew said. He wanted to ask Wesley a more intimate question about his own feelings but felt it would be out of place.

One month after the wedding, Wesley wrote Sophy a letter he thought was mild and noncondemnatory. But to her it seemed abrupt and offensive.

At that point John Wesley made his most serious mistake since coming to Georgia: When Sophy came to church, he publicly refused to administer the sacrament.

"On what basis, sir?" Sophy's husband demanded.

Since Wesley could not accuse her of being an open and notoriously evil woman, he said, "It's necessary that the communicant give prior notice to the minister."

This was a feeble reason at best and Sophy's humiliation infuriated her husband. Williamson secured a warrant for Wesley's arrest, claiming one thousand pounds for defamation. Wesley was arraigned before the bailiff and was summoned to appear at the next court. Throughout all this, Andrew suffered with Wesley. More than ever he realized the failure of their ministry and felt even more strongly the sense of futility that had been weighing on him for months. After the arraignment, he and Wesley met and sat silently in the quiet evening. Wesley seemed to be drained and Andrew said as cheerfully as possible, "Never fear, Mr. Wesley. We will weather this storm."

Ordinarily Wesley responded well to encouragement, but now as he looked up, the lamp showed marks of strain on his face. He'd been humiliated by being dragged before the bailiff and he knew worse things lay ahead. "I fear things will not be better," he said. "Mr. Causton, the chief magistrate, is no friend of ours. He dislikes me intensely. I fear when I think of what the trial will be."

"Surely it will not come to trial!"

"You do not understand the malice of Mr. Causton," Wesley replied wearily. He leaned forward and put his head in his hands. There was such vulnerability in the minister that if Wesley had been his brother Charles, Andrew would have gone at once and put an arm around him. But he could not do this with John Wesley for there was some sort of barrier between this man and most of the world. It had not been so in his home, for the Wesleys were a close family. But since the death of his father and since Wesley had assumed the position of elder son, it had made him more diginified and perhaps more reserved.

The small clock ticked monotonously as time ran on, and the two men still sat there quietly. Desolation filled Andrew and he could think of no comfort to give. At length the two men rose and went to their separate rooms. As Andrew lay awake that night, his heart torn with grief over what John Wesley was suffering, and darkened by a sense of forboding, he tried to cry out to God—but it seemed God wasn't listening. Or if he *was* listening, he'd chosen not to answer. The night passed on leaden feet, the hours dragging by, and still Andrew could not sleep. As dawn lightened the east, he arose, weary and heartsick. Even dressing himself was a chore. *This is not what God intended for his servants to be. Where is the joy that is promised?* he thought. But he found no answer, either in the world or in his own heart.

Twelve

RETREAT FROM GEORGIA

The iron skies of November hung like lead over Savannah. The winter was cold and bit like frozen metal into Andrew as he passed through the open field. He pulled his greatcoat about him, shivering, and for the moment the memory of England came, warm and green and lovely. He knew that winter in England could be cold and wet and uncomfortable too, but during recent weeks his thoughts had turned more and more to Wakefield and home.

Overhead a red-tailed hawk circled silently. Looking up, Andrew watched the great bird suddenly fold its wings and drop like a plummet. It hit a rabbit that had looked up at the last moment and bounded too late to escape the steely needle-sharp claws. Andrew watched the brief life-and-death struggle, fascinated by it, and then the hawk's beak rose and struck four times and the rabbit lay still. The hawk held on for a moment, then raised his wings and seemed to beat the air in a symbol of victory. Reaching down, he opened his beak and tore a patch of fur out of the rabbit's neck.

Andrew continued his walk, not wishing to see the bloody feast of the hawk. His feet struck the ground numbly and he thought, *I must wear an extra pair of socks; my feet are like ice.* He passed through the open fields and encountered the beginnings of the settlement, where icicles hung from the eaves of houses like daggers, glittering in the pale, feeble light of the sun that seemed bled dry of all its vitality, like everything else he saw. Even the sun seemed to be slowed and numbed by the cold that wracked the earth. He had not known the American South could bring such weather! The natives all said it was unusual, that they'd never seen such a winter. But one of them had said, "I seen the fuzz on caterpillars was thick last fall—and the acorn's hide was thick. I know'd it was going to be a hard, bitter time this year."

An old woman, out gathering firewood, appeared on his left and he turned to say, "Good morning, Mrs. Finn."

Betty Finn turned a pinched blue face toward him. "Good morning, Parson. It be cold today."

"Yes, too cold for my liking. Let me help you carry that load."

Andrew reached out and took the wood from the woman. She shivered and he saw her hands were marked with handling the rough wood. She blew on them, then asked, her small black eyes peering at him, "How be Mr. Wesley today?"

"Very well, Mrs. Finn."

"I hear the law has him."

"It's hardly that serious. He has to appear in court to answer a charge."

"Aye, so I heerd." The old woman seemed to be wearing all the clothes she had. Yellowish-tinged linsey-woolsey showed from under her heavy ancient wool coat; her feet were encased in men's boots, and underneath, several layers of dark wool stockings bulged around her ankles and knees. As she clumped along, she inquired, turning to look at him with the eye of a busy bright bird, "Will he go to the prison, do you think, Parson?"

"Oh no, nothing like that!" Andrew protested. "You mustn't say things like that, Mrs. Finn. It's a civil matter."

"Civil matter, is it? Not very civil for a man of God to go to court. Don't the Scripture say something about that?"

"Well, we aren't to bring charges against fellow believers," Andrew admitted, then quickly said, "but Mr. Wesley isn't bringing the charges; they're being brought against him."

As they moved along, a huge shaggy dog came out from one of the houses, his fangs bared, growling horribly. Andrew reached down, picked up a stone with his free hand, and sent it flying. He'd always had a good aim and the stone struck the dog in the throat. The animal did a backflip and ran away yelping, with his tail between his legs.

"That be good enough for the varmint!" Mrs. Finn said with satisfaction. "There be some two-legged varmints I'd like to see you put a stone to!"

"Now, Sister," Andrew said, smiling at her, knowing she was a lonely woman with few friends. "We must be charitable." He talked with her as cheerfully as he could until they reached her one-room house. He carried the wood inside, placed it down beside her fireplace, then said, "We have some wood split, good red oak. I'll bring you a load of it when I can get the use of the cart."

"That'd be good of you, Parson," the old woman responded. Hungry for talk, she insisted he sit down. Building a small fire, she quickly brewed sassafras tea. As he sat there at the rude table drinking it, she drank in all that he had to say. When he thanked her and finally rose to leave, she said, "Poor Mr. Wesley. He didn't get a wife, did he now?"

"No," Andrew said softly, "he didn't get a wife. . . . Good-bye, Sister—I'll see you in services day after tomorrow."

He continued his solitary walk, noting that most people were inside, braced against the freezing cold.

When he reached the parsonage he stepped inside at once and went to the study. A cheerful fire was kindled so he knew Wesley was somewhere in the house. He pulled off his coat, tossed it across a bench, and removed his mittens. Holding his hands out, he soaked up the warmth from the fire, put on another log, then pulled a chair up and sat down to pull off his boots. He had gotten his feet wet and as he pulled off his sodden woolen stockings he gave a sigh of relief. Carefully he held his bare feet out toward the fire and soon feeling began to return. When he was thoroughly warmed, he went to his own room, changed clothes, and returned. Going to the small desk beside the window, he saw a letter propped against the inkwell. He picked it up and recognized the handwriting at once. "Dorcas!" he murmured. Sitting down, he opened the envelope. It had taken weeks to reach Georgia during this time of the year since shipping was slow. Eagerly he began, but he'd read no more than the first few lines when he stiffened.

> My dear Mr. Wakefield,
> I'm grieved to bring you sad news. Last night your Aunt Hope passed away in her sleep. She'd been ill for some time—worse than usual. I was with her the night before she died and she was very weak, but she talked for some time about you. Mostly she told me how proud she was that she had a man of her blood serving God. She was so proud of you, Mr. Wakefield—so very, very proud!

Andrew felt the tears rise in his eyes. As a rule, he was not a crying man but his spirits had been dampened by the long months in a strange land, the seeming futility of the work, and the problems Wesley had encountered. "A godly woman," he whispered, and his mind went back to his boyhood. Now that Aunt Hope was gone he realized clearly what an influence she'd been in his life. His own parents had often been too busy to pay attention to a small boy, and it had been his aunt who sat and read to him and played the games boys love to play. She'd been a younger woman then and he remembered times she'd gone with him to the fields surrounding Wakefield and had taken him fishing, for he loved to fish.

"She, above all I've known, loved God," he said aloud. As the sound of his voice stirred the air, grief rose sharply in him like a fresh wound. He held the letter up again and continued to read.

> As I brought her medicine that final night, the last thing we did was have a prayer. Oh, what a prayer it was! Lovely it was, Mr. Wakefield! Miss Hope prayed God would send his angels down with sharp swords to protect you from all harm. I have never felt so in my life! It would not have surprised me, indeed not, to have seen one of those angels suddenly appear over her head, so close to God she was!
>
> I have grieved for her, as you must, and I have shed my tears, but we have the comfort of knowing she is with the God she so adored. I have never known another human being who loved God the way this woman did. You have a godly heritage, Mr. Wakefield, and though we will miss her, still one day we will go to her.
>
> I remain your dutiful servant, Dorcas Morgan.

Wakefield thought of Dorcas and of her large, dark blue eyes. He could almost hear her speak the words aloud, and a great longing came over him to hear her speak in person. *She could give me comfort,* he thought. *She is a comforting woman, aye, that she is!*

But there was nothing to be done. The funeral was over and his aunt had gone to be with God. "If I could have just seen her one time . . . ," he whispered. But that was past and he folded the letter carefully. For a long time he sat, staring out at the frozen ground that surrounded the rectory.

As chief magistrate, Causton had packed a grand jury who could be relied on to find a true bill against Wesley, who would then go to trial. Forty-three men, one-fifth of the adult males in Savannah, sat for two days. They found Wesley guilty on ten counts, although some of the jurors brought to Wesley a minority report that rejected most of the charges against him. But in Oglethorpe's absence, Causton had civil power and Wesley knew the case was hopeless.

He also knew the colony itself was split, with part of the people abusing Wesley, the other half abusing Causton and the Williamsons. John Wesley and Andrew Wakefield sorrowed to see so thin an audience at church. The congregation had been whittled away by the strife that had torn the church, as well as the colony.

Wesley's work was in ruins and he knew it. He said as much to Andrew on November 22, when they were walking toward the city hall. "I've decided to leave the colony, Andrew."

Although this wasn't unexpected, Andrew Wakefield was still shocked. "I'm sorry to hear it, sir—but perhaps it's best at this time."

Sunk in his own depression, Wesley didn't answer. When the two reached the city he pinned the notice up on the outside of the building.

The next day Williamson pinned up his own notice to remind the public of his pending claim for one thousand pounds damages. The note threatened to prosecute, with utmost vigor, any who helped Wesley escape before his trial.

When December 2 came, Wesley asked Mr. Christy, the recorder, "Will the court stop me if I try to leave the colony?"

"I must put you under a bond of fifty pounds, sir."

"I have sought trials seven times," Wesley retorted. "I refuse to give the bond."

The matter proceeded quickly. The magistrates ordered all constables and sheriffs to prevent John Wesley from leaving the colony, in effect making him a prisoner in a land where he had come to preach the gospel of Jesus.

"What shall we do, sir?" Andrew asked as the two met for a brief conference in the rectory.

"I have decided we will leave this place."

"What about the magistrates, Mr. Wesley?"

"We will have to avoid them. There's no other way, Andrew." For a moment Wesley looked at the younger man and said, "I'm sorry to have dragged you into this unsavory affair, my dear fellow." It was the closest thing to sympathy Wesley had ever offered to Andrew and it moved the younger man.

"I came of my own free will," Andrew responded. He wanted to add, *This trouble isn't of your own making,* but in his heart he was well aware that much of the trouble Wesley found himself in was, indeed, of his own making. Still, he loved the man and revered him. "We'll do better another time, sir."

<hr/>

After prayers that very evening, Wesley and Wakefield slipped out into the night. Catching a favorable tide, they crossed into South Carolina with three others—a constable, a tithing man, and a barber, who also wished to leave the colony. All three, some said, were men of ill repute.

When they landed in South Carolina they headed at once for Port Royal on foot. Snow fell lightly and the earth was frozen in an iron band. They entered the swamps, where they struggled along a forest path marked by blazes chipped in the barks of the trees. Finally they came to a fork and followed through an almost impassable thicket. The briars scratched their skins and ripped their clothes.

When the blazes stopped, Wesley looked blankly into the primeval forest. "We're lost, I'm afraid."

"I fear we are," Andrew whispered. "What shall we do?"

John Wesley might have made his mistakes with people but he knew what to do in this case. "We must pray to God to direct us," he said calmly. He bowed his head and Wakefield listened as John Wesley prayed to God. It was a short prayer, simple and unaffected. Andrew thought, *I wish Mr. Wesley were as plain and simple and direct with people as he is with God.* He joined in the prayer, adding his own, and then the two forged on into the forest. They found other blazes from time to time but these were rare. At last they came across a wagon track with freshly marked ruts.

"Thank God," Andrew said. "I don't know where this road goes but it surely leads somewhere."

Later that night they reached Port Royal, exhausted, and found shelter with a local clergyman. They shared the same room that night and as they knelt and had a prayer, it was Wesley who seemed to be totally exhausted. He could only mumble a few words. Then, after the amens rose, he looked across at his friend and assistant with bleary eyes. "All has been in vain, Andrew," he whispered. "The devil has had his way."

Andrew, drained himself, said, "We will have another day, sir. Never fear."

<hr />

John Wesley and Andrew Wakefield boarded the *Samuel,* a merchant ship bound for England. The weather was mild for that time of year, and Wesley, exhausted from his labors in Georgia, slept more than he ever had.

Andrew, on the other hand, was troubled. Day after day as the *Samuel* dipped its prow into the gray waters, he walked the decks and studied the wake of the ship. Once he saw what he thought was a mighty whale—a leviathan—churning the waters! He had never seen such and couldn't be sure but it occupied his mind momentarily until he went on with his tedious thoughts.

For over a week this went on. Andrew felt the defeat in Georgia as much as John Wesley did. The two didn't speak of it now but both had been scarred by the experience. Neither would be the man he was before. For better or worse, they had thrown themselves into a missionary endeavor—and they had not tasted the anticipated joys of harvest. Indeed, they'd both drunk the bitter medicine of defeat.

They passed through a storm. Although it was nothing like the one they'd endured on their journey to Georgia, it tossed the ship for twenty-four hours. During that period, as Andrew clung to the rail and watched the waves roll toward the *Samuel* and lift it like a chip, he was struck by a thought. He didn't mention what was on his mind to Wesley or to any of the other passengers but gave himself to fasting and prayer. Having made one catastrophic decision, he wanted to make no further mistakes.

Day after day he read his Bible and prayed and fasted and sought God.

Finally on January 24, as he was on deck, the mate came by to say, "We're only 160 leagues from England—from Land's End, sir."

The news that they were close to England galvanized Andrew Wakefield, and the thought he'd been nurturing for days seemed to glow within him. He felt God had given him an answer and he went over it again in his mind. No one was on deck save the mate, who had gone back to the stern of the ship.

Standing alone on the prow, looking through the murky distance toward his homeland, he didn't fear being overheard so he spoke aloud. "I've seen what romance can do to a man, especially to a preacher. I've seen it take the strongest man of God I've ever seen and make a wreck of his ministry. Poor Mr. Wesley. I pray he'll recover from it but I doubt he ever will. I must learn a lesson from all of this. Perhaps that's the good that will come out of the wreckage."

He paused and watched as a group of gulls sailed across the sky, their white breasts making vivid dots against the grayness of the heavens. They circled around and followed after the ship, making their eerie calls.

"I must never let such a thing happen to me," Andrew whispered. "I will marry—but I will do so in a *logical* fashion. I will not be thrown into the throes of romantic notions. The woman I marry must understand that marriage to me is a duty—nothing more than that. It is an—an *arrangement* that must be made like all sensible arrangements. A clergyman needs a wife: someone to take care of his home, to greet visitors, and to entertain, for a bishop must have hospitality. God has said we are to replenish the earth, and there must be children to be brought up in the nurture of God. But no romance."

All day he thought about his plan and the more Andrew thought of it, the wiser it seemed. It was not only John Wesley and the disaster that had overtaken his courtship; he'd had obvious and plentiful evidence from others who were almost destroyed by this thing called "romance" too. Now that he'd made up his mind, he wanted nothing to do with it. The next step was almost logical.

He was walking along the deck, satisfied with his plan, when he stopped abruptly. "Dorcas!" he said aloud.

Instantly it all seemed clear. "Of course!" he exclaimed loudly, attracting the gaze of a seaman who was passing by. Abashedly he clamped his lips together and strode hurriedly away, his mind full of the plan. *Dorcas is the most sensible young woman of my experience and she will never have a husband—not in the usual sense of the word. Why, she has said many times she will never marry! No romantic nonsense about Dorcas Morgan!*

This seemed to confirm all that had come to him and he grew suddenly happy and content. *I can give Dorcas my name*

166

and a home—which is more than she ever thought to have. Before continuing down the deck, Andrew looked up at the heavens and felt a moment's thankfulness, glad that he had found his way at last!

END OF PART TWO

Revival

1 7 3 8   **Part** — **THREE**   1 7 3 9

Thirteen

STRANGE PROPOSAL

The new year of 1738 brought little cheer to John Wesley. He had sailed from Charleston on Christmas Eve. He was a deserter, having left Georgia without permission of the trustees. Although he'd jumped his bail, he reckoned it never should have been set.

Most of all, he'd failed as a missionary. As he stood peering over the rail at the coast of England, he realized he'd lost the basis of his hope. He had carefully constructed his manner of living and structured it into a methodical way of life. But now it seemed that, like the great seas that had broken over the ship on which he left England, his entire philosophy and the foundation of his faith were being bludgeoned by doubt and even fear.

As he leaned against the rail, his face numbed by the cold wind, he thought of the lines he had written in his journal the night before:

> I went to America to convert the Indians; but oh, who will convert me? Who? What is it that will deliver me from this evil heart of unbelief? I have a fair summer religion. I can talk well: nay, and believe myself, when no danger is near. But let death look me in the face and my spirit is troubled. I am continually doubting, and never out of perplexities and entanglements.

Later, a fair wind veered and held the ship back, then changed and took her through the Strait of Dover into the North Sea until finally a calm wind brought them safely into the Downs. Unknown to Wesley, the wind that had carried him into harbor had carried George Whitefield out of anchorage on board a ship called the *Whitaker*. Whitefield was bound for Savannah, eager to join John Wesley, whom he supposed still to be there. But the wind dropped and Whitefield's ship lay in the Downs and waited. Informed that his revered friend and mentor had arrived, Whitefield sent his servant ashore to arrange a meeting, instructing him, "Tell Mr. Wesley I will meet with him willingly at any place he might choose to appoint."

Andrew packed his few belongings carefully and joined Wesley as they left the ship. They made their way to the home of a pastor of the local church—an old friend of Wesley's named Donald Cameron. A tall and bulky Scotch gentleman, Cameron was delighted, though shocked, with Wesley's unexpected arrival.

"My dear Mr. Wesley," the Scot exclaimed, "I had no idea! Come in and let me make you welcome."

"We don't want to impose," Wesley said quickly, "but I'd like to find out from you, sir, what has been happening in England since I've been gone."

Cameron bustled about calling his housekeeper, who fixed tea and cakes—then a full meal. The two voyagers, who had grown weary of the food on ship, sat down and ate heartily. The roast beef, fresh and succulent, was delicious, as were the fresh bread with creamy butter, and glasses of sweet milk.

Cameron asked eagerly about the mission and work in Georgia. He was an astute man, a fine student of human nature, and though Wesley said little, the pastor sensed Wesley and Andrew's feelings of failure.

Wesley, unwilling to speak much of the past, for he still smarted from his defeat in Georgia, turned the conversation to affairs in

London. "The news is all of your friend George Whitefield!" Cameron exclaimed. "God has poured out his Spirit upon that young man. The whole nation is in an uproar!"

"Can it be so?" Andrew exclaimed. He tried to think of how the mild-mannered, seemingly callow, youth he remembered could have been the instrument of such fervor. "Tell us. How is he received?"

"Why, the whole world has gone out after him, sir! But you've heard, I suppose, that he is on his way to Georgia?"

"Georgia!" Wesley stared at the pastor. "No, I hadn't heard such a thing."

"Why, sir, you are his motivation. Mr. Whitefield told me so himself." Cameron's voice grew warm as he spoke of how Whitefield had chosen to turn his back on the most successful ministry in Great Britain to go to the savages in the New World. "But, sir, I know you have done the same." Wesley sat there, stunned. He exchanged glances with Andrew and finally said, "I wish I could have spoken to Mr. Whitefield before he left."

Strangely enough, he got his wish. Whitefield's servant, Griffith Jones, who'd gone to Wesley's ship, the *Samuel*, had been disappointed. However, he'd been directed to the rectory in Deal, and two hours after Wesley and Wakefield arrived at Cameron's, Whitefield's servant arrived at the pastor's door. Cameron brought the servant into the rectory and introduced him to Wesley.

"Mr. Wesley, I have a message from your good friend, Mr. Whitefield." Jones handed Wesley a letter that Whitefield had quickly sketched off.

Wesley scanned the letter, then asked, "Would you, sir, give my associate and me time to think of this?"

"Of course, Mr. Wesley. Mr. Whitefield is anxious to have your counsel."

After Jones and the pastor had left the room, Wesley turned at once to Andrew. "This is dreadful," he said, his voice tinged with doubt. "Whitefield needs to be warned about Georgia."

"I agree. It would be dreadful if he buried himself in the swamps of Savannah," Andrew said. "With such a ministry as he has in this country it would be a deprivation to waste him in that place."

Wesley paced the floor, his face strained and pale. He was a man accustomed to making decisions but this one seemed to have no proper answer. He had no control over George Whitefield, of course, except for the power of a friend's advice. Still, it grieved him to think of the young man, of whom he was very fond, making a serious mistake—such as he himself had made.

"We must rely on the lot, Andrew."

"The lot, sir?"

"If we had time we could wait in prayer—but there is no time. Here, let me make out the slips."

Andrew watched, somewhat appalled, as Wesley tore a sheet of paper into several strips. Quickly he wrote the various possibilities for Whitefield's future on them, folded them, and put them into a box. "You shuffle them, Andrew," Wesley said almost grimly. "I want no mistake about this. I must not rely on my own wisdom— God must speak."

Andrew shuffled the slips of paper, handed the box back, and Wesley drew one. He opened it, stared at it for one moment, then smiled. "It says, 'Let him return to London.' There," he said with an air of relief, "now let me write him a quick letter."

<hr>

George Whitefield, on board the *Whitaker,* paced back and forth on deck. His eye was on the small dory that was being rowed, with all possible speed, over the choppy gray waters. The wind was quickening and Whitefield knew the *Whitaker* would quickly set sail for Georgia.

Finally the boat reached the ship and Griffith Jones scrambled aboard. "Here is Mr. Wesley's answer, sir."

Eagerly Whitefield grasped the paper, opened the envelope, and read the message. He stared with disbelief as Wesley explained that, in his judgment, it was imperative Whitefield give up his journey to Savannah and return at once to London.

The note was brief and Whitefield found it difficult to believe. He was amazed at Wesley's action but he knew there was no possibility of following Wesley's advice. At once he went down to his cabin and penned his response:

> I received the news of your arrival with composure
> and sent a servant to you. Your kind letter reached me
> and I thank you for it. I think many reasons may be
> urged against my coming to London. First, it cannot be,
> for if I come there the enemies of the Lord will think
> I am turning back, and so blaspheme that Holy name
> wherewith I am called. Secondly, I cannot leave the
> flock committed to my care on shipboard and perhaps
> while I'm in London the ship may sail. Thirdly, I see
> no cause for my not going forward to Georgia. Your
> coming rather disannuls my call. It is not fit that the
> colony should be left without a shepherd; and though
> they are a stiff-necked and rebellious people, yet, as
> God hath given me the affections of all where I have
> been, why should I despair of finding his presence in a
> foreign land.

Whitefield was upset and the next day as his ship sailed for America, his heart was heavy over the difference between himself and John Wesley. He also distrusted the use of the lot. What he didn't know was that in days to come, Wesley's treatment of him in this case would influence both their lives.

After supposedly settling the matter with Whitefield, Andrew and Wesley left Deal the next day and made their way to London. Everywhere the two men went, whether in the carriage that carried them or as they walked the streets, they heard of the mighty, powerful preaching of George Whitefield.

As they arrived in London, Andrew said, shaking his head, "I can't actually believe George Whitefield has become so famous!"

Wesley was as mystified as his companion. "God uses whom he will." He looked out as they passed over London Bridge and said, "There's glory in the preaching of the gospel when it's followed by such results. Mr. Whitefield is a most unusual young man." He turned to Andrew, studying the face of his assistant. Andrew had lost weight, he saw, and his face was thinner, giving him almost a hungry look. Thinking back, Wesley remembered that young Wakefield had been a cheerful young man when they'd left London nearly two years ago. Now he realized he hadn't seen Andrew laugh in some time and said suddenly, "You're very tired, Andrew. It has been a hard and difficult trial for you."

"No harder than for yourself, Mr. Wesley."

"What will you do now?"

Andrew hesitated. He'd wanted to share his views on marriage with John Wesley but it had been a rather sensitive area. He said quickly, "I intend to remain in this country—and I intend to marry."

Wesley's eyes blinked with surprise. After a moment's silence, he said, "I hadn't known you were engaged, Andrew."

"Neither am I, sir, but it's a clergyman's duty to marry—especially one who is a pastor. A wife is necessary for certain duties in the church. The people have need of such. I have been praying and have decided I shall find a woman who wants to serve God in this way." Quickly he described his views, that marriage should be more a business arrangement than a romantic interlude. When he finished speaking he asked eagerly, "What do you think of it, Mr. Wesley?"

Wesley nodded slightly. His affair with Sophy had seared him more than he would admit to any living soul. "If a man would marry—especially a minister—I think your plan is best and I commend you for it."

Relief washed over Andrew Wakefield. He admired and re-spected and trusted John Wesley as he did no other man. Despite Wesley's obvious blind spots in certain areas, he was a man learned and wise, in Andrew's judgment. He leaned back in the coach and thought, *Dorcas will have a home and a place to call her own and I'll have someone to fulfill the needs of a minister. It's enough.*

Wesley directed the carriage to the house where his brother Charles was staying in Westminster. As he got out of the carriage, he shook hands warmly with his friend. "God give you wisdom, Andrew. Let me hear from you as soon as you are settled."

"Thank you, Mr. Wesley. I shall certainly do so."

As the carriage pulled away, Andrew leaned out and gave directions to the driver. It was not far to the bishop's rectory and as he gazed out the window at the familiar settings, he felt a certain security in being back in his own world again. The carriage proceeded from Grafton Street to Albany Street. The wind was cold and once the carriage stopped along with all the other traffic. Andrew looked out to see a funeral going slowly north, toward the Union Road. The hearse was drawn by four black horses with black plumes and through the glass he could see the coffin covered with many pounds' worth of flowers. Andrew could imagine the perfume of them and the care that had gone into raising them at this time of the year.

Behind the hearse were three other carriages packed with mourners, all in black. No expense had been spared. Judging from the neighborhood, Andrew knew the flowers had cost money that should have been spent for food and there would be cold hearths and empty tables to pay for this funeral. "Death," he said softly, "must have its due, and the neighborhood must not be let down by a poor show." He thought it strange that poverty must be concealed at all cost. That mourning had its place in the system of London's world—and perhaps all systems everywhere.

After the funeral procession had passed, the carriage moved on through the river of traffic. A brewer's dray passed by him. Great shire horses with braided manes gleamed in the sun, decked in shining harnesses, and behind them were landaus and the ever present hansoms.

The carriage crossed the road, turned right on Albany Street, which ran parallel to the park, and pulled up in front of the bishop's house. Getting out, Andrew paid the man, noting that he had little money left and realizing this would be his last carriage ride for some time.

He moved up the steps, knocked on the door, and was admitted at once by James, the elderly servant of Bishop Crawley. "Ah, sir, it's been a long time."

"Yes, indeed, James. I'm surprised you haven't forgotten me."

James shook his head firmly. "I would not do that, Mr. Wakefield, never on any account." He took Andrew's coat and hat, hung them up, and said, "The bishop is free now. I know he'll be wanting to see you. He spoke of you just the other day."

"Did he now?" Andrew inquired anxiously. "How was that, James?"

"Why, he keeps closer track than you think, sir, of his favorites—and you were always a favorite of his."

A warmth flooded through Andrew. Although he hadn't admitted it, even to himself, dark thoughts of his future had hovered over him ever since the decision to return. He had no connections to speak of in England. His best hope had been that he might become a curate for some influential pastor. Such a thing had weighed upon him for it was a life of poverty—thankless and without color or excitement. He'd had enough of that in Georgia.

"My lord, an old friend of yours—Mr. Wakefield."

Bishop Alfred Crawley had been sitting before a blazing fireplace, dressed in a wine-colored wool robe. Welcome leaped into his face as he looked up to see his visitor. "Wakefield! My dear fellow—!" The bishop rose at once, tall and stooped, his gray hair unkempt, and he brushed it back as he gave Andrew a warm handshake. "I am so happy to see you, my dear boy! Come and sit down. James, we must celebrate. We'll have some of that wine Mr. Daily sent over."

"I'm sorry to come without notice—"

"Nonsense! Nonsense!" The bishop busied himself getting Andrew seated, then said, "Now, let's get caught up on our visiting. You know pretty well what I do, but tell me all about your experiences with the savages."

Andrew began at once. The fire crackled and snapped and the two men both enjoyed a glass of the wine James brought in. The bishop raised his glass saying, "Here's to you, sir, and to your return to your home."

Andrew drank the toast, then carefully continued speaking of his experiences in Georgia. He was aware that the truth would soon come out and was quite frank with Bishop Crawley. He explained that Mr. Wesley had entangled himself with some of the church members—most unwisely, perhaps, with a young woman—and they had returned disappointed over their mission.

Crawley made a steeple out of his fingers and stared over them as he listened. As bishop, it was his job to place men—and Bishop Crawley was a highly intelligent leader. He knew every church in his area and exactly what sort of man would be needed. As he watched young Andrew Wakefield, studying his face carefully, his mind was running rampantly over possibilities. *How can this young man be used most effectively?* he questioned, and when Andrew had finished his story the bishop said quickly, "Ah—well, there it is! Our plans do not always work as well as we would like. But you must not be discouraged, my boy. You're young and it will be a valuable experience for you."

"I feel it will be that, my lord." Andrew grew more grim as he said, "I have, indeed, learned much."

Crawley leaned back in his chair. The fire was hot and he drew the chair back slightly, then said, "I have great confidence in you, Andrew. Except for your ties with the Methodists, I think there is no young man of my knowledge of whom I have more hope."

"You speak of the matter of the enthusiasts."

"I do." Crawley's face grew stern. "I know you are a friend of Mr. Wesley, as your sacrifice proves. I must tell you, sir, that I do not share your admiration. Mr. Wesley is a scholar, a man of ability—but this Methodist movement means nothing but trouble for the Church of England!" The bishop spoke for some time about the Holy Club and then mentioned George Whitefield.

"I understand the people are quite taken with Mr. Whitefield," Andrew questioned. "What is your feeling about him, my lord?"

"Mr. Whitefield stirs the emotion, and people like to have their emotions stirred. Why, there have been stories of people falling down, rolling on the ground under the effect of his preaching. Nonsense! That is not preaching. That is sensationalism!"

Andrew listened as the bishop continued to speak adamantly against the movement that gathered around George Whitefield. And finally the bishop said what Andrew knew was coming.

"I must tell you plainly, Andrew, that although I have great confidence in your ability, I cannot in good conscience recommend you to any of our ministries as long as you are a part of that movement."

Suddenly Andrew remembered once having been lost in the

woods. He had floundered through a forest, his face scratched with briars, and at last came to a road he didn't know. He'd followed it for a short time and then abruptly it divided into a *Y*. As he sat before the bishop, he remembered how confused he'd been then, knowing he must choose one or the other. It had been a frightening moment for a child and now some of that fear came back to him as he sat looking at the cranelike visage of Bishop Alfred Crawley.

If I make the wrong decision here, he thought desperately, *my life will be ruined*. He knew what the bishop was asking. It was not a complicated matter at all, for a chasm was developing within the Church of England. It was the old story, of course, the old power against the new movement that always arose at any structure. Men like Whitefield, Wesley, and Howell Harris in Wales represented a threat to men like Bishop Crawley, who saw it as their function to keep the standards that had been handed to them. He saw the church as a walled city where no one must be allowed to breach the walls, where things must go on as they always had. He had a deep respect for order and the past and any challenge was met at once with all the force in Crawley's heart.

Slowly Andrew began to speak, knowing what he said now could turn his life. "Bishop," he said quietly, "while I was at Oxford I was very impressed with the real hunger for God that I saw in Mr. Wesley and his group. I'm convinced these are not evil men but good men— "Andrew hesitated, then blurted out—"but they are, I fear, misled men." He saw at once a smile come to the bishop's lips and knew he'd said the right thing. "I cannot condemn them, for the Scripture teaches that I must not. However, my own view is that the Church of England is a bulwark. We have a proud heritage and we must maintain that heritage. No doubt there will be other movements such as this. For myself, I am content to glory in the church as it has been built through the years of our history. It is this church—the Church of England—that I am giving my life to serve."

Crawley slapped his thin legs with both hands. "Excellent, my dear Wakefield! Just the sort of thing I've been praying you would come to!" Delight danced in the old man's eyes, for he was extremely fond of Andrew Wakefield. "Now then, something can be done!"

Before Andrew left, he discovered what that something was, and it was more than he'd dreamed. The bishop spoke for some time of the need for a pastor at Redeemer Church. "It's a fine church, not as large as some, but with a good man such as yourself, it will grow—oh yes, it will flower under your hand, Andrew." He went on to describe the rectory and Andrew was delighted. "The one thing it lacks is a woman's hand," the bishop commented, cocking his head and peering at Andrew.

Andrew flushed and cleared his throat. "You speak prophetically, Bishop."

"Ah, is that the way of it?" The bishop again was delighted. "I hadn't heard, but no doubt you have returned with a young woman in mind."

"Indeed I have. A very modest, humble young woman I think will please you."

At this, the bishop's delight could know no bounds and when Andrew finally was allowed to leave the parsonage, Crawley slapped him on the shoulder. "I think God is in all this. Redeemer Church needs a pastor—you need a church. I will expect to be asked to perform the ceremony when you and your young woman work out all the details."

Andrew left the bishop's house elated—as if, for the first time since his dreary experience in Georgia, the sun had come out.

Then he thought of the Holy Club and John Wesley and for one moment the sunlight seemed to grow dim. "Mr. Wesley will have to go his own way," he whispered to himself. "As for me, I have chosen my destiny. . . ."

Dorcas Morgan loved the kitchen at Wakefield more than any other room. She knew it as she knew no other part, even the succession of annexed outbuildings that unfolded as kitchen, buttery, sink room, laundry, wood house, carriage house, and privy. Since Hope had died, Dorcas had spent most of her time here helping Olive cook, and her help was well received.

Now, standing before the tall window that let the pale sunlight fall on the tiled floor, Dorcas was happily aware of her surroundings. After the small cheerless cottage in Wales, this was a kingdom! It was a store place for all kinds of things: Hooks or nails had been driven into the beams to hold bundles of dried herbs, strings of red peppers, dried apples, various tools, bags of all sorts and sizes, golden ears of corn, bilas of physics and nostrums for man and beast, bits of cord and twines, skeins of yarn and brown thread, just spun. A stag's horns were nailed near the ceiling for hanging various items on, such as bonnets and hats.

A great fireplace dominated the room at one end, obliging as cookstove, lighting device, and furnace. This fireplace was outfitted with a crane from which hung a kettle, a pot, and perhaps an additional large water kettle with a spigot so hot water might always be at hand for cooking and cleaning. All of these could be raised or lowered to suit the heat.

Dorcas looked over her equipment, feeling greedy. In the old cottage in Wales, there'd been no more than two or three worn pots. But here there was a wealth of equipment! Universal utensils of iron, brass, copper, or tin. There were chafing dishes, a dipping pan, frying pan, kettles, saucepans, pattypans, skillets, skimmers, a stew pan and toaster. It was early in the afternoon and Dorcas was making sausage, a dish she dearly loved. She'd been working for some time, making a paste of lean and fat pork duly pounded and richly seasoned. Cheerfully she began stuffing the filling into the scrubbed casings, made from the intestines of pigs. To help her fill the casings compactly she used a funnel, a special hollow implement, wide at the top and narrow at the bottom, which was called a tin fill-bowl. When she had carefully measured off six inches for each link and tied each section with heavy thread, she stood looking down at the sausages with satisfaction. When she wanted to serve them, she would boil them in water, adding salt, sometimes adding currants. They would come out tender; then she would add a little wine, butter, and sugar. At Wakefield she had tried using almost every meat, including fish, rabbits, oysters, and mutton. The family had expressed its approval and now she was satisfied with what she had done.

As she moved around the kitchen, cleaning up after her messy task, she paused a moment and walked over to the window to look out at the gray sky, thinking of how much she missed her benefactress, Hope Wingate.

Life had not been the same since Hope's death. It had had a purpose as long as she was nursing the woman, but now she was—nothing. She wasn't a relative—at least in the eyes of the Wakefields—and she wasn't a hired servant, although it was possible she would be taken on if she asked. She felt an emptiness she couldn't define.

She thought suddenly of Andrew and the time he'd come to their cottage in Wales. She remembered every moment of it, as time and again she'd dwelt on that almost magical event. To be lifted out of poverty and hunger and fear and brought to this place where there was plenty! It had been a thing from God, she felt sure. Even now as she saw the brown and lifeless fields, she was unable to keep back the grief that lately seemed to fill her. She had no close intimate friends, no one to share her fears with. Gareth was back at Oxford—happy with his newfound walk with God. Although she rejoiced in that, it didn't help her loneliness.

She spent the rest of the afternoon in her room reading and

finally, in desperation, put on her heavy wool cloak, a bonnet that came down over her cheeks, wool stockings, and shoes. Then she left the house and walked through the woods. The fresh cold air brought a flush to her cheeks and she made her way over the estate, stopping by the creek to watch the icy waters flow over the rounded stones. Overhead, rooks marred the quietness of the afternoon with their raucous cries as they wheeled and darted. When they landed nearby, they strutted with arrogance, their pale yellow eyes fixed on her as if they were angry she'd invaded their domain.

"Go away, birds," she said, waving her arms. They broke from the earth, wildly fluttering their wings.

Finally she returned to the house. Her feet, face, and ears numb, she slipped in through the side door and made her way down the hall toward the servants' quarters, where she intended to help Olive with the evening meal. As she passed by the drawing room, she heard two voices and knew it was Sir George and his mother. She turned and would have moved away but heard her name mentioned. She stopped still and despite her abhorrence of eavesdropping, she was curious. Lady Ann was speaking: ". . . and I cannot think but what the young man will take care of his sister."

"Gareth? I'm sure he will, when he gets a place." George's voice was heavy and complacent. There was a silence and then he said, "Are you unhappy with Dorcas?"

"Why no, she's helpful enough. But we really have no need for her as a servant. We have plenty of help already."

"I suppose that's true."

Dorcas's heart fell within her and her breath grew short. It was almost as if she'd heard she had a lingering, dangerous illness. Suddenly she was aware that she was in a strange country with no place to go and no one to protect her. Gareth was helpless— almost as helpless as she. She knew his poverty and as she stood there in the hallway listening, a hand seemed to close coldly around her heart.

"I'll speak to the girl," Lady Wakefield said. She was a strong-willed woman, rather cold, and George was a great deal like her; Dorcas had always known that. Andrew was different and she had long ago decided he must have taken his warmhearted ways from his father.

She turned and tiptoed silently away, making her way to her room. Once inside, she shut the door and sat down on the bed, staring at her hands and trying to think. Her mind seemed paralyzed and she couldn't come to any conclusion. Then, as always, she began to pray, "Oh God, show me what to do. . . . I can't stay in this place—where shall I go? How will I live?"

Outside, the shadows darkened as night came on. Dorcas sat there so long that total darkness fell in the room but she wasn't aware of it. Downstairs she could hear the faint sounds of people talking and knew the meal was being served. But she had no heart to go down. Finally she got up and made her way to the window. The air was bitterly cold and touched her face with an icy hand that made her shiver deep inside. Fearful, she once again cried out, "Oh God, help me. You are my only hope."

<hr />

For the next two days Dorcas went about her work. She was more quiet than usual and Olive asked once, with concern on her broad face, "Are you sick, girl? You haven't said two words for days now."

"No, I'm fine, Olive."

But if she was not sick in body, she was troubled in spirit. She had read that the Bible said, "Pray without ceasing," and she had never been able to understand what this meant. She had asked herself, How can anyone pray all the time? Now she knew what this meant. She was so troubled that no matter whether she was working, reading, or simply walking through the woods, her heart

never ceased crying out for guidance and some light in the
darkness that seemed to grow around her. Nothing came and she
grew almost desperate. Finally, on a Wednesday morning as she'd
just finished helping with the breakfast, Mrs. Beard, the housekeeper, came to say, "Dorcas, you're wanted in the study."

"Is it Sir George?"

"No, it's Mr. Andrew. He's come back."

At once Dorcas brightened and took off her apron. "He's just
come back from far places," Mrs. Beard called after her, smiling
at the haste the girl made. "We'll have to put some meat on his
bones!"

Dorcas hurried to the study where she found Andrew standing
beside the rosewood desk that sat in the center of the room. "Mr.
Wakefield," she said, "I'm so glad you're back!"

Andrew moved toward the girl and put out his hand. She took
it and he squeezed it gently. "Yes, I'm back, Dorcas. You're looking
very well."

"Well—thank you, sir." Dorcas was thinking Andrew *didn't*
look well. He was thin, and strain showed on his fine features. His
dark blond hair was long and needed trimming and she noticed
he was nervous.

Andrew was indeed more nervous than he could ever remember. He spoke for some time as they sat in front of the fire, telling
her of his experiences in Georgia, and finally said, "Would you
take a walk with me, Dorcas?"

"Let me get my cloak."

Dorcas put on her heavy cloak and when she met him at the
door he held it open for her. She passed outside and noticed that
the sun was shining, though feebly, through scattered clouds. "The
sun's trying to shine, Mr. Wakefield," she said.

"Look here, Dorcas—can't you call me Andrew? I'm not old
enough to be your grandfather."

"Why, if you like—Andrew."

187

"That's better. Come now, show me what you've been doing. I've heard great tales of these chickens of yours."

It was a task Dorcas willingly obeyed. She was proud of her flock and showed him the house she'd built, the runs for the chickens and how she stored their feed in special bins.

Andrew listened to all of this, noticing Dorcas's prettiness. Her large dark eyes were filled with excitement as she spoke of her beloved chickens and he noted again what striking features she had: her mouth, determined chin, and the clearest complexion he'd ever seen on a woman, flawless and smooth.

They left the chickens and walked through the grounds. When they reached the creek where Andrew had fished so often as a boy, Andrew knew he couldn't put this matter off any longer. Turning to Dorcas he said, "I have a very serious matter to discuss with you."

"Yes, sir?"

"I—have been—thinking a great deal of my future." There was a hesitancy in Andrew's voice and Dorcas asked, "Are you having trouble?"

"No, not trouble, but my plans concern you."

Hope suddenly sprang in Dorcas and she had a vision of being a servant to Andrew Wakefield. She'd always hoped he would get a church and she could be a housekeeper for him. Now she said, "Tell me, please."

He looked down into her eager face and somehow what he had planned to say did not seem quite suitable. But Andrew Wakefield was a stubborn man. Once he made up his mind he never changed. "I have been assigned to a fine church in London, Dorcas. It's a great opportunity for me. Bishop Crawley has always favored me, you know, and he's given me an opportunity." He began to speak of Redeemer Church and his eyes grew warm with excitement as he described the possibilities.

"I'm glad for you, Andrew! No man deserves it more," Dorcas said, pleased.

Andrew swallowed hard and then said, "It would be well for a minister . . . not to be single."

Dorcas's eyes showed surprise and she asked, "Well, sir. What then?" Her first thought was that he'd become engaged to a woman from Georgia.

"That's—that's what I have come to say to you." Andrew clamped his lips together for a moment and marshaled his thoughts. He'd made up his mind and now he was determined to say what he needed to, simply and in the most businesslike fashion he could put it. Planting his feet firmly, he faced her and said, "Dorcas, you've said many times you would never marry. I've doubted that, but you're always so firm. I have thought the same. I've seen what romance can do to people."

"Romance?"

"Yes, you know what I mean. Falling in love—kissing and that sort of thing."

"I'm surprised to hear you say such things."

"I've seen what that foolishness can do to people!" Andrew's tone grew very firm then, almost hard, and his eyes narrowed. "There's no romance in you, Dorcas; neither is there in me." He took a deep breath and said almost desperately, "What I'm saying, Dorcas, is that I would like to marry. I need a companion. I'm not at all emotional or romantic. I want none of that—and I assume you feel the same." He waited for Dorcas to reply but she merely looked puzzled. "I'd like you and me to be married, Dorcas."

Shock ran along Dorcas's nerves. She'd expected anything but this! She turned away from him, unable to control her expression. Marriage was something she'd put out of her mind long ago and now Andrew was asking her to be his wife!

Andrew saw her confusion. Putting his hands out, he turned her around and saw that her eyes were wide with shock. "I know this is difficult for you. I didn't know any other way to tell you," he said, making his voice gentle. He hesitated, then said, "Dorcas,

I need a wife and you need a home. You're sensitive about your hand but it has made you close the doors to ideas about marriage. We are not romantic; therefore, we need not be disturbed by that sort of thing." He waited for her to speak, but she didn't. Finally he said, "But perhaps you find me—repulsive."

"Oh no, sir, not that," Dorcas cried out. She put her hand on his chest without thinking and let it rest there. "It's just that—I never thought of being married."

"I know, but I think you should. You can serve God this way, Dorcas. You and I together. It will be—a *sensible* arrangement. There's so much good that we can do." He paused, hoping for her reply, and when she still hesitated, he said, "Will you think on it?"

"Yes, I will think on it—Andrew."

Dorcas turned and made her way, almost blindly, back toward the house. Her thoughts were tumultuous and she couldn't make them be still. She repeated when she reached the house, "I will think on it, Andrew. . . ."

Fourteen

WHEN GOD SAYS
NOTHING

Since the Wesleys' departure from Oxford, the Holy Club had continued but Gareth Morgan soon discovered that things were greatly changed. On his return to the university, he'd thrown himself into his studies with a vigor and excitement that had been lacking. He was also astonished to find his new walk with God carried over into every part of his existence. The menial tasks he'd been forced to perform for the upperclassmen had previously been abhorrent to him. Now he found he was able to carry out these duties with a cheerfulness that mystified his fellow students—especially the upperclassmen.

Charles Vaney, a tall, cadaverous upperclassman who had made Gareth's life miserable, finally asked Gareth directly what had changed him so greatly. He was leaning back in his straight chair, reading from a Greek New Testament, when Gareth brought his boots back gleaming.

"There you are, Mr. Vaney," Gareth said, with a smile on his lips. "Is there anything else you'd be wanting?"

Vaney lowered the Bible and stared at the young servitor. He asked querulously, "What's got into you, Morgan? You never used to be happy about having to polish my boots."

Gareth set the boots down carefully, gave them an admiring look, then turned and responded, "Mr. Vaney, I suppose I just discovered we can serve God in small ways as well as in great ones."

"What's *that* supposed to mean?"

"Well, I once had the idea that a man had to shake the world in mighty ways." Gareth put his dark blue eyes on the older man as he added, "But now, I have discovered I can black boots to the glory of God just as well as win an empire."

Staring at him with a mystified expression, Vaney grumbled, "I suppose this is all part of that new birth you keep harping on." Shaking his head, he said sourly, "Well, if it gets my boots polished, I suppose you can hold to that enthusiast theology if you please. Have you heard what's happening to John Wesley?"

"No, sir, I haven't."

A satisfied look crept across Vaney's gaunt features. "Well, he's finding out what it's like to go against the establishment."

"How is that, Mr. Vaney?"

"Why, when he got back from the Colonies the people wanted to hear about the mission work there, but Wesley declined to speak of his experiences." Vaney smirked and brushed his thin hair back in a careless gesture. "It's all out, of course, that his work there was all a washout. I knew it would be." He went on to tell the rumors that had followed John Wesley from Georgia and added, "He was mixed up with a woman. I suppose this will bring John down to earth with the rest of us now. He was too heavenly minded to be any earthly good around here. Anyway, the doors of the churches are closing."

Although Gareth had been better informed by Charles Wesley, who'd been back to Oxford for a brief visit and had explained the situation as he had it from John, Gareth knew this was no time to argue with Vaney. So he took his leave and went about his duties with a gladness of heart. If Gareth had had any doubts about walking close to God, they'd disappeared after his conversion experience. Life, which had been a prison for him at Oxford, suddenly had become a thing of joy. He'd thrown himself into the study of the Scripture, amazed that what had been almost a dead book now blazed with light. He seemed to hear the voice of God in his spirit as he poured over the New Testament. The person of Jesus Christ, who had been vague and dim, was now in a very real sense his constant companion. "I know what it means," he whispered more than once in his devotional, "when the apostle says that it is 'Christ in you, the hope of glory.'"

Early the next morning after his encounter with Vaney, he left Oxford and made his way once again to London. He had an appointment to meet with the Wesleys and eagerly looked forward to it. He had also made his plans to return by way of Wakefield Manor, for he longed to see Dorcas. Her letters had been puzzling to him. She was usually such a cheerful young woman, but he sensed there was a heaviness in her spirit and he wished to go find out the cause and comfort her.

He arrived in London in midafternoon, the day before his meeting with the Wesleys. For some time he wandered the street, grieved at the conditions that greeted him on every hand. He was always brought up short by the fog of London. In his native Wales, there'd been no such thing, for the air was clean and pure. But the London fog, a great yellowness, reigned everywhere and the streetlamps were lit even during the day. As he walked, he had a painful sensation in his lungs and knew that part of the fog was the smoke from coal stoves. Looking over the city, he saw that the sky was literally black from thousands of coal fires. There were problems underfoot as well, as he picked his way along. The streets were loaded each day with tons of manure and the city itself smelled like a stable yard. When a crossing sweeper swept the streets before him on Crawford Street, he gave him a penny.

He passed by the Thames and stared down at the murky waters. It was impossible for fish to live in this stream. He'd gone once on a short tour and was aware that factories along the riverbank constantly dumped pollutants into the water. London Sewage, he'd been told, dumped three hundred thousand tons daily. The smell sickened him and he turned back. Determined to turn his mind from the unpleasantness, he finally gave in to the thought of Sarah. He'd been fighting his awareness of her all day, but now, as he walked along under a dull afternoon sky, he determined to pay her a visit. She'd been somewhat out of his thoughts during his time of spiritual renewal, but never completely. Although he knew it was a foolish dream to think of any permanent relationship with a woman of her station, he still recalled her features and the sound of her voice.

"I'll see her! There's no harm in that," he said aloud and turned to make his way along the streets, conscious of the incessant sound of wheels and horses' hooves clacking over the pavement. He heard the cry of street peddlers who sold dolls, matches, knives, rat poison, eggs, and china. Once, he passed by a German band that drowned out everything else with their loud playing, and after this, children added their din to the noise. Many of them were street arabs, or "mud larks," as they were called, who scavenged the bed of the Thames. They were all playing in the streets, crying their wares, holding horses for gentlemen, fetching cabs for theatergoers on rainy days. There was no school for these children, indeed not much hope, and Gareth's heart went out to them as he passed along the busy streets.

He arrived at the Lancaster residence and, marching up to the door, he knocked loudly. When a maid answered he said, "Mr. Gareth Morgan calling on Miss Sarah Lancaster."

The maid gave him a quick inspection, her sharp eyes noting the plainness of his clothes. Gareth understood he was being classified as "not top drawer," but it didn't trouble him.

Finally the maid said, "If you'll step in, sir, I'll see if Miss Lancaster is available."

"Thank you very much." Gareth stepped inside the house and

was, as always, interested in his surroundings. As he was taken to a large sitting room, he took in the heavy gold picture frames that adorned the wall, the graceful furniture carved by masters and tastefully ornamented with silk bolsters, and the chairbacks protected by embroidered covers. The high ceiling was coffered in deep squares, giving the room a classical appearance. A stuffed weasel stared out at him from under a glass dome, its bright artificial eyes seemingly fixed on Gareth. He walked over, put his hand on the glass dome, and smiled. "Well, you look like my teacher back in Wales—no, you have a much kinder look than that dear lady."

He went over to stand beside the fireplace, admiring the tall slender candlesticks on the mantel shelf. And on the Sheraton table by the window, there was an arrangement of flowers, mostly coppery birch leaves with dark purple-red buds, in an enameled gravy boat.

"Why, Mr. Morgan . . . !" Sarah entered the room and he thought she filled it with her presence. She was wearing a purple gown, trimmed with black, obviously the latest fashion, and he admired her narrow waist, pleated bodice, and floral trimmings. She looked both voluptuous and fragile with her blue-gray eyes and beautifully textured skin. She'd obviously been outdoors, for she also wore a cloak of dark purple and a bonnet that perched rakishly on her blonde hair, making her look absolutely dashing. Once again Gareth sensed her vitality.

"I come without invitation but I wanted to see you," he said.

"Come outside and see my garden," Sarah replied. As she smiled at him, he noticed her mouth was wider than most women's and her lips were very red—but as far as he knew, it was a natural color, not obtained from a bottle. Her face was a mirror, Gareth noticed, that changed often. He saw laughter in her eyes, and pride, and somehow her coming brought a turbulence to his spirit.

"It's good to see you," she said as she walked rapidly out of the house. "What have you been doing?" He followed her outside and she led him at once to a small garden. When they went inside a small hothouse he finally answered, "I've been tending to my studies." He looked around and remarked, "You tend to all of these during the winter? I never saw anything like it."

"I love flowers," Sarah said, smiling. "Let me show you what I managed to keep alive during the winter." She moved over to touch tiny purple plants, wild violets, she informed him, and then pointed out several others. He didn't know most of those she mentioned but she was a beautiful sight to his eyes. Finally she turned and said, "Now, tell me what you've been doing."

"I wrote you. Did you get my letter?"

"I did." She touched her cheek tentatively with one hand and cocked her head to one side. "I didn't understand a great deal of it. Especially about the religious turn your life has taken."

"May I tell you about it, Sarah?"

"Why, certainly, but let's go back in the house. I just wanted you to see my flowers."

When they returned and were back in the sitting room, he began to tell her what had happened in his life. She listened quietly, interest flickering in her eyes, and didn't interrupt.

Gareth explained that Christ had transformed him and at last said apologetically, "This sounds, perhaps, like a sermon. I didn't mean for it to be so, but it's been such a wonderful thing for me."

Sarah thoughtfully sipped the tea that the maid had brought and studied the young man before her. *He doesn't know how good-looking he is. That's a good thing, I suppose.* His curly hair was long and needed trimming, but she admired again the thick eyelashes and the eyes so dark blue they seemed almost black. Slowly she said, "You mentioned the 'new birth' several times. I don't understand that and frankly, Gareth, it troubles me. You seem to be saying you were not a Christian at all until whatever this was took place."

"I don't think I was."

"But you went to church all your life—you told me that."

"Yes, I did, but going to church doesn't make a man a Christian any more than putting him in a stable makes him a carriage, does it?"

Sarah smiled at his choice of words, then shook her head. "I'm afraid you are into some sort of mystical thing and I'm not a mystic, you know. I have, I think, a fair imagination, but the words you use, I must admit, trouble me."

Gareth hesitated, the words coming to his mind, *the natural man receiveth not the things of the Spirit of God.* He wanted to speak to Sarah but knew from his experience at Oxford that many were offended when they heard the gospel as he now perceived it. He said carefully, "I don't want to be self-righteous and I'm certainly no judge of anyone, but there's a possibility of walking with God in the Spirit and it comes only when we have been born again. The Spirit of God must come into us. Only the Holy Spirit can interpret the Scripture to us."

His words disturbed Sarah and she said rather sharply, "Gareth, I'm a member in good standing of the Church of England. I take Communion, I try to be kind to others, I never killed anyone, I don't hate anybody." She stopped abruptly, then shook her head. "I think that's all I want in my religious life."

Immediately Gareth saw that there was, despite Sarah's beauty and breeding, a hardness in the spiritual side of her character. He'd noticed often that when he spoke the name of Jesus some people reacted rather violently. They didn't do so when he mentioned Mohammed or Buddha, but somehow there was a power in the name of Jesus Christ that aroused people. He saw it now in Sarah. It was not much, but she straightened her back, narrowed her eyes, and her lips grew slightly tense when he tried to speak of what Jesus meant to him. Finally he said, "I didn't mean to preach."

Sarah relaxed. "Perhaps it's better we don't talk about such things."

Gareth said quietly, "I'm afraid I'll always have to talk about such things, but there's one topic of conversation you may desire even less than talk of religion."

"I can't imagine what that would be."

Gareth had thought about this for a long time. He knew that in speaking out he was probably barring the door to all access to this beautiful woman, but he was a bold young man and now said fervently, "Sarah, the first time I ever saw you, I fell in love with you."

Sarah blinked with shock, then laughed. "Why, Gareth, that's impossible! People don't fall in love like that."

"I don't think they do, not very often," Gareth admitted. "What drew me first, naturally, was your beauty. I've never seen a more beautiful woman. But that's not why I loved you. Why, I'd love you if you lost your beauty!"

"Would you really?" Sarah had never considered this. She thought he was talking foolishly and knew she should stop him, but she was fascinated by the young Welshman and said only, "I don't think you love me at all, Gareth."

Gareth leaned forward, his dark blue eyes intense. It was the young man's intensity that drew Sarah to him and set him apart from others. Most young men she knew were indolent, whereas a fire seemed to burn in Gareth Morgan that from time to time leapt out of his direct eyes and revealed itself in the quick movements of his body. Now this intensity was obvious as he said, "I believe marriages are made in heaven."

"Made in heaven? What does that mean?"

"I think God puts people together if they listen to him."

Sarah stared at him with amazement. "You mean God decides who people will choose for their husband or wife?"

"I think so. Why would he not be interested in this?" Gareth demanded. "If God is interested in us at all then he's interested in all of us." He went on speaking of how he felt about marriage and realized she'd grown very quiet. "You don't believe any of this, do you, Sarah?"

"Not really." She knew it was time to stop their conversation. "I'm glad you came to see me, but I must ask that you not return."

A heaviness settled over Gareth's spirit. He knew the old Gareth would have lashed out in anger. Now he simply said, "I'm sorry to hear you say that." He rose and she rose with him. As he moved to the door, he took his hat and coat and put them on. Settling the hat on his head, he said quietly, "I love you, Sarah Lancaster. You may not believe that. I may never see you again. It may be that I will marry another. But I want you to know this, it's you who I'll love, always."

Sarah couldn't answer for a moment, for his words were so plain, so simple, and obviously so honest as he spoke them. Then he turned and walked away without another word. She watched him go, standing at the door until he disappeared down the street. Closing the door, she leaned back against it, much disturbed by this scene—more so than she'd been in a long time. She headed for her room and as she sat by the window, she remembered every word he said.

"He can't be right," she whispered. "It's impossible! God doesn't take that much notice of any of us." She thought again of what he'd said: *"Marriages are made in heaven"* and of his final words, *"I may marry another, but it's you who I'll love, always;"* No matter how hard she tried to wipe these words from her memory, Sarah knew she'd think about them for a long time. Finally she said aloud, "It's impossible! He's an attractive young man—but we're far too different."

"Why, Dorcas—I can't think what to say!"

Gareth was so rattled by the news Dorcas gave him that he stood to his feet at once. He had come to Wakefield and noticed instantly that Dorcas was behaving most peculiarly. She'd always been calm—even as a child—so her restlessness drew his attention at once. She'd taken him outside, where they had sat down on one of the low stone walls bordering a meadow. The wind was brisk, but spring lay in the offing and the skies were light blue, dotted with fleecy pink clouds. A loamy smell was in the air as the fecund earth began to release her treasures. The mild setting was welcome to both of them, but after they had talked awhile, Gareth asked his sister, "What's wrong, Dorcas? I can see you're troubled."

Dorcas indeed *was* troubled. She'd slept poorly since Andrew Wakefield had made his astonishing proposal. Her appetite had fled and, having no one to confide in, she had turned inward and then upward to God in her thoughts. She'd prayed during long vigils in her room at night, kneeling beside her bed, begging God to reveal his will.

"I know it comes as a shock to you, Gareth." A strange smile pulled at her lips as she said, "Sad it is when a woman is driven, almost distracted, by a proposal of marriage, but—there it is! I'm like an old mule, I suppose—stubborn. But oh, Gareth, I've prayed and God is silent as a tomb. I don't know what to do!"

Gareth overcame his shock and, reaching out, he put his arm around Dorcas and drew her close. "There," he said fiercely, "only a little shocked I was—but now tell me all about it."

Dorcas was glad to feel his strong arm about her and she leaned against him. As she related the content of Andrew's proposal, he listened carefully. Finally she said, almost in despair, "Why would he want to marry me, Gareth? Why?"

Gareth shook her almost angrily. "Are you a rat with green teeth then? You're a lovely woman, full of spirit. Any man would be lucky to have you."

"Even with this?"

Gareth glanced at her maimed hand, then took it with his free one. "That's nothing," he protested. "He wants the woman inside you."

Dorcas couldn't keep the tears from forming in her eyes, so glad she was to have him there, to have his comfort. With diamonds in her eyes she whispered, "There's a comfort you are, old man! I always went to you with my bruises and my hurts, didn't I?" She retrieved her hand, dashed the tears from her eyes, then said, "But it's not like you think. It's not a proper marriage he wants."

Gareth was somewhat taken aback. "Not a proper marriage? What does that mean?"

"He doesn't want—" Dorcas hesitated. She was a modest young woman and didn't know how to put the thing into words. "He doesn't want—love," she whispered.

Gareth could make nothing out of this and asked bluntly, "Well, what in heaven's name *does* he want?"

"He wants someone to keep house. A minister, he says, needs a wife to be hospitable, to see to the things in the parish."

"Well, there's no one who would do better than yourself." He saw, however, that his assurance didn't calm her and said gently, "What is it, Dorcas? Tell me now—out with it."

"He doesn't want *romance*," she said. "That means he doesn't want love. He's not interested in a woman in his heart . . . or his bed." Her face flushed scarlet and she turned away quickly.

All of this was incomprehensible to Gareth and he slowly let it revolve in his mind. "Don't be ashamed, Sister," he said. "Tell me what you mean by that."

With difficulty Dorcas explained Andrew Wakefield's theory. "It would be," she whispered, "more of an arrangement than anything else."

Gareth was silent. Ten feet from where they sat, a flock of sparrows lit on the ground and began fighting over a morsel of food, fluttering in the dust, chirping loudly. Then the losers took wing and flew away while the victors enjoyed the spoil. Gareth watched them for a moment, then said, "What will you do, Dorcas?"

"I don't know—I just don't know, Gareth! I thought and thought and prayed and I have no answer!" She turned to him and in desperation pleaded, "Tell me what to do."

"I can't do that!"

"You must. I've got to know whether it's God's will or not. Tell me, what do you do when you pray and God doesn't say a word?"

Here was a problem Gareth himself had encountered more than once and he had no ready answer. At last he said, "Sometimes when those things come we have time to wait. If we do, then I say do nothing."

"But I can't wait! Andrew wants an answer."

"Those are the hard times, when you have to make a decision. What does your own heart say, Dorcas? Do you care for the man at all—as a woman for a man, I mean?"

Bowing her head, Dorcas nodded silently. Her heart was full and she could only whisper, "I think I do, Gareth."

A great sorrow then rose in Gareth, for he saw how things were. A sharp anger rose in him as he focused on Andrew Wakefield. He let it break out and said, "When he made you such a terrible proposition, did you give him a good kick?"

"Oh, no!" Dorcas protested, staring up at him.

"I should have been there!" He saw then that his words hurt her and said, "Never mind me—I'm just upset. I want you to have what other women have. I've always wanted that for you. You always said you'd never marry because of your infirmity, but now this may be of God."

"How can it be of God when he doesn't love me? At least—at least—" She couldn't finish her sentence. She was confused. Dorcas was a woman who needed love more than most. The austerity of her early years and the loneliness of her girlhood had branded her. She needed to be touched, to be told she was pretty. She needed to be cared for in the way every woman longs to be cared for, by a man who is strong and loves her. Yet although this proposal seemed almost hideously wrong, she couldn't put it out of her mind.

Gareth said slowly, "Why do you suppose he feels like this, Dorcas?"

"It has something to do with Mr. Wesley. I know that much." She related what she knew of Wesley's bad experience with the young woman in Georgia while Gareth listened.

"Yes, his brother Charles told me some of these things. I think Mr. Wesley behaved foolishly—but young men have done that before." He looked at Dorcas, studying her face. She had vitality and imagination—and a temper, though it was rarely exposed. Gareth fully believed his sister could, if necessary, shoot a man down and not go to pieces afterward. And she had pride, too; he had seen it sweep her violently at times. He looked at her then, for the first time in years, not as a brother but as a man. Studying her womanly qualities, he noted that she was in that first maturity that followed girlhood. Now he longed for wisdom, for the answer that would bring peace to her, but he couldn't find it. Finally he said carefully, "Often in Wales, when the marriage is arranged between a young man and woman by the parents, things don't go well at first."

Dorcas received this statement with some degree of surprise. "That's true!" she murmured. "Remember Allen Richards? He hated Faith Bradshaw when they first married but afterward they became very loving. I remember that now."

"Yes, that's true, and there are others," Gareth said with more assurance. "It may be that Andrew Wakefield is a man who's wrong-headed about this thing of marriage—but with a woman to give him love, real love, he could change."

For the first time since Andrew had proposed, Dorcas felt a streak of hope. She looked at Gareth and her lips parted slightly as the thought ran through her. Quick to express her thoughts, her laughter and love of life seemed to be waiting for release. "Maybe it's so," she said, and as the future came to her in a flash,

Gareth saw the hint of will and pride in the corners of her eyes. "Maybe it's so," she whispered again.

The two rose and walked for some time and when he brought her back to the house he asked, "What will you say when he comes for an answer?"

Now self-possessed, Dorcas made a sudden gesture with her shoulders that told him that her mind was made up. "I will marry him, Gareth!"

Despite all attempts to keep himself calm, Andrew Wakefield was undergoing inward turmoil. As he walked down the hall toward Dorcas's room, he felt a moment of panic and thought agonizingly, *What if I'm all wrong about this? I can't afford to make a mistake.* But he forced himself to approach her door. When he knocked and she opened, he saw she was calmer than she'd been the last time. "Are you ready to go down to supper, Dorcas?"

Dorcas had made up her mind and now she asked, "Andrew, do you still want to marry me?"

Her directness came as a shock to Andrew. She'd been uncertain and almost fearful since he had proposed. Now, however, he noted her composure and—without meaning to—grew aware of her slender beauty and femininity, her smooth form in the simple dress. An almost beguiling womanliness slid through the armor of his self-sufficiency and he felt suddenly muddled. "Why, of course," he said quickly, hoping against hope she didn't realize the effect she was having on him.

"Then I will marry you, Andrew."

He felt her eyes upon him and knew she was waiting with expectation. Meeting her glance, he saw in her eyes a shadow and shape of something odd that he couldn't analyze. She was breathing quickly and color suddenly ran across her cheeks in spite of her coolness.

Andrew bowed slightly and said, "I'm honored at your decision, Dorcas." Still, she seemed to be waiting for something and
he felt more awkward and callow than he had in all his life. He
swallowed and said, "We will have a good life, you and I. There's
much we can do together to serve God."

"I will be the best wife I can to you, Andrew—in every way."

Wakefield thought he heard an odd intonation in the final
syllables of her speech and stood there trying to fathom the
difference he seemed to see in her. His mind was made up to build
a life for himself, and this seemed best. But something in Dorcas
Morgan troubled him, though he could not determine why that
should be.

"We will make our announcement at once. It will come as a
surprise to many, I fear."

"For a man in your position to marry a servant is always
shocking."

"You mean my family? You needn't worry about that. They will
accept you as my wife; I feel sure of it."

Dorcas didn't answer but she knew that it wouldn't be as simple
as Andrew hoped. She knew enough of the world to know that
whenever a girl marries above her station, there are always those
who will mock. However, she'd crossed all her bridges and thrown
herself into what she felt was the will of God. Almost timidly she
put out her hand and he took it with surprise. "I'm honored you
would ask me to be your wife," she said, her voice soft.

Andrew felt a moment's confusion, then put aside her strangeness
and said, "Come, we will go down and tell the family our news."

⁂

Sir George Wakefield was surprised to hear of Andrew's news but
said only, "Are you certain, Andrew? You can do much better, I'm
sure—that is, there are more prominent women."

"The wife of a pastor must have certain qualities, George.

Among them humility. I've never known a more humble woman than Dorcas."

"Well, then," George said heartily, slapping his brother on the back, "more power to you. I will give you a fine wedding. We'll dress her up in the most beautiful dress a bride ever had." George was actually feeling relieved, for he'd always liked Dorcas. Now he nudged Andrew and said, "Let's go break the news to Mother." He grimaced slightly, saying, "She may not be as amiable as you would like but she'll come through. Never fear."

Lady Ann Wakefield was not happy over Andrew's decision but, seeing that his mind was made up, she agreed and threw herself, to some degree, into the mechanics of getting her younger son married off.

Dorcas understood very well her future mother-in-law's feelings but said nothing to Andrew. She knew she'd have to change. It was a tremendous leap for a poor, young Welsh girl to even think of becoming the wife of a preacher, much less a pastor of a prominent church in London. She knew she'd have to move in a level of society she had not known except for the Wakefields. Fervently she thanked the Lord for the time she'd spent with Hope. Her manners, she knew, had been refined and she'd been exposed to the gentry—and even to nobility—so she could calmly face what was to come.

Two weeks after Dorcas accepted Andrew's proposal, he took her to the home of Mr. and Mrs. Rawdon Sylvester. He'd told her, "Mr. Sylvester is a real leader in Redeemer Church. He's been very generous with his time and money. The former vicar was a favorite of his and he misses him. But I'll win him over in time." Alarm bells had gone off in Dorcas's mind as she heard this but she'd said nothing.

When they arrived at the Sylvesters' ornate and expensive home, she gave little heed to the fine furniture or the expensive settings but studied the host, who greeted them at the door. "Well, it's the pastor with his bride-to-be. Come in and let me meet the lady."

Rawdon Sylvester was forty-eight years old. He was a short, muscular man with a ruddy face, pale blue eyes, and side whiskers. He bowed shortly to Dorcas and began at once to exert what he thought was charm. But Dorcas was at once aware there was an arrogance below the surface of the man's manners, and from the look in his eyes she also knew she had not passed inspection. Mrs. Elizabeth Sylvester was a moderately pretty woman with dark brown hair and brown eyes. She was wearing an expensive steel-gray dress, and a pair of large diamonds dangled from her ears. "My dear Miss Morgan," she said languidly upon meeting Dorcas, "we are happy to receive you. This is my daughter, Emmajean."

Emmajean Sylvester was a petite girl with blue eyes and light blonde hair. She was shy and nervous, Dorcas saw instantly, and could only murmur her greetings.

The dinner that followed was very informative for Dorcas. She understood, before she'd been in the house half an hour, that the Sylvesters were displeased with their pastor's choice of a wife. She innately understood also what *would* have pleased them: a wedding with their own daughter, Emmajean, marrying the new parson.

The meal was like the mistress of the house, overdone and far too exotic. There was soup, fish, a cutlet, a roast fowl, and some game. She sampled the delicate soup, then a turbot with lobster and Dutch sauces carved by an able butler. This was followed by a portion of red mullet with cardinal sauce. Later on there were meringues à la creme, a maraschino jelly, and chocolate cream.

Dorcas was seated next to a young woman who introduced herself as Sally Bradwell. On her far side was Sally's husband, George, a cheerful and rather overweight young man.

Sally was full of marriage, being a new bride herself. The two young women found themselves alone in a corner and Sally at once said, "You must be absolutely beside yourself with excitement, Miss Morgan. I know exactly how you feel, for I've only been married a little over a month myself."

As a matter of fact, Dorcas didn't feel tremendously excited but she was encouraged by the young woman's manner. She sat there, smiling and nodding encouragement as Sally told of the glories of her husband.

Sally asked about her family and when she discovered Dorcas had none to speak of, only one brother, she bit her lip. "Why— that's rather sad! A girl needs women around when she's going into marriage." She leaned forward and nodded confidently, her bright blue eyes sparkling. "There are things you need to know, aren't there, Miss Morgan?"

"Just call me Dorcas, please." She understood at once what the young woman was saying and her face took on a rosy hue. She could not, for the life of her, come up with an answer. She knew very little of what was expected of a wife—at least in a physical way—and this bothered her.

"And you call me Sally. You must let me help you. It's a very important part of marriage. I'm sure you want your marriage to be perfect."

The conversation went on and when the party was over Sally said, "We must visit, and I'll help you all I can."

Dorcas left the party and on the way home she looked at her husband-to-be, realizing, *How can I ever really love Andrew when we think so differently?* The troubling thought plagued her all the way back to Wakefield.

Fifteen

ANDREW WAKEFIELD'S BRIDE

C an't you be still just for a moment, Dorcas?" Sally Bradwell had been working to adjust Dorcas's wedding dress but had paused to speak rather sharply. "We've got to go out in just a moment. Here, let me look at you." She turned Dorcas around, then stepped back, examining her friend with a critical eye. The two had become close friends since their first meeting and Sally had taken over the affairs of the wedding almost as if she were Dorcas's mother. Now she studied the gown, which she herself had been influential in selecting.

Dorcas's gown was the fashionable *sacque* style made of patterned silk. The basic color was deep rose and embroidered over the extensive bodice and skirt were tiny, exquisite flowers and blossoms in a rich green. Frills of chiffon and lace adorned the dress, and the short, tight sleeves ended with a lace band and flounces just above the elbow. It was a delicate and beautiful dress, with a wide, square-neck décolletage with a chiffon handkerchief fastened at the bosom.

"You look beautiful, Dorcas—just beautiful!"

Dorcas's face was pale but she was encouraged by Sally's words. "I couldn't have done this without you, Sally," she said in a low voice. When she looked up, her eyes were wide and there was a tenseness around her mouth. "Sally, I'm afraid," she said simply.

At once Sally Bradwell went to Dorcas and put her arm around her. As she held her close, she whispered, "Don't worry, everything will be all right." She hesitated then, for Dorcas had told her a little of Andrew Wakefield's strange concept of marriage. It had been repugnant to Sally Bradwell, who was romantic to the bone, but she had constantly given assurance. "Your Andrew will love you, you'll see. You'll be very happy."

A gentle knock sounded on the door and Sally said, "Come, it's time," and left the room. Dorcas followed her and soon found herself walking down the aisle of Redeemer Church. The church was filled and she felt the weight of eyes on her as she made her way down the aisle. She managed to block out the nervousness, concentrating only on the face of the bishop who stood at the front of the church with Andrew.

"He'll be my husband," she said over to herself, repeating the words as an incantation. "He'll love me." She studied Andrew as she approached the front of the church. His brother, George, had taken him to the finest tailors and the coat he wore was a deep, rich blue. It was close fitting and waisted, with a fully flared skirt reaching to just below his knees. The coat was without a collar and cut rather low in front. The sleeves had enormous cuffs that ended well above the wrist and were turned back and studded with what seemed to be gold buttons. The breeches were gathered into a waistband, with the leg narrowing downward, finishing just below the knee that was tied with bright green ribbons. And as she dropped her eyes, she even noticed his shoes: block square toes with square high heels and silver buckles.

Then she had no time to look at him further, for Bishop Alfred Crawley stood before them and began to speak. His voice resonated in the high-ceilinged room and she could only grasp a part of his words. She heard her own voice responding, promising to love the man who stood beside her. Then she listened as

Andrew said the ancient words and Dorcas clung to them as he promised to love and cherish her as long as he lived.

She kept her maimed hand hidden under a specially designed bouquet of flowers and was grateful for the subterfuge. When Andrew took her left hand, she noticed his own trembled slightly. She turned her head upward and saw that his face was pale and his lips were tight with strain. *Why,* she thought with shock, *he's as afraid as I am! I didn't think that would be the case.* When he slipped the ring on her finger and said, "With this ring I thee wed," she saw something in his eyes she couldn't read. Later she thought, *I'll be able to remember all this.*

And then it was over. She took his arm and they made their way down the aisle. Again she felt the weight of a thousand eyes and wished there was no reception—that she and Andrew could leave and go somewhere far away. But that was not to be.

The reception was loud and noisy, with raw jests from some of the younger men. The fact that Andrew was a minister didn't make him immune, and although Dorcas didn't understand the nature of the jokes, she saw Andrew's face flush and wondered at his embarrassment.

The bishop stood aside, speaking to those who passed. Rawdon Sylvester came to stand beside him. "They make a fine couple, eh, Mr. Sylvester?"

"Very proper, I'm sure." Sylvester's voice was clipped and he didn't seem pleased. He said, "I'm hoping she'll be a fitting wife for the man of God."

"Do you doubt it, sir?" Crawley said, surprised.

"She's a raw girl, not accustomed to much beyond a homely cabin in Wales, so I understand."

"She's very quick. I'm sure she'll learn to handle the duties that will be laid upon her."

The bishop's answer didn't satisfy Sylvester but he said no more. He and his wife had quarreled bitterly concerning their own daughter just before the wedding and he was not in an amiable mood. "I hope he's got all this Wesley sensationalism out of his head," he grumbled.

"Oh, I think you need not fear that," said the bishop. "He went through a phase. Most young men do if they're worth their salt. You should've heard some of the ideas I had when I was Reverend Wakefield's age." He smiled crookedly and watched the couple. At first, he, too, had been apprehensive about Wakefield's choice of a bride and had gently tried to intimate he could do better. But seeing that Wakefield's mind was made up, he'd paid careful attention to the woman. He found her to be godly, simple, and humble, and that satisfied him. "They're going to Bath for a week's honeymoon," he said. "Then he'll be back and they'll begin their married life."

The trip to Bath allowed Dorcas to regain her composure. There had been no wedding night, as such, in London. The two had gotten into a carriage and traveled hard and they'd arrived in Bath weary from the strain of the wedding plus the journey.

"We'll be staying at a cottage that belongs to a friend of the bishop. It's a fine place, I understand," Andrew had told her. When they arrived they discovered the cottage was, indeed, a fine place. It was adjacent to the famous warm baths and not as crowded during the spring season as it would be during winter.

Andrew directed the coachman to bring their luggage inside and tipped him handsomely before he left. Turning to Dorcas, he felt a strange hesitancy. "What do you think of the house?" he asked, to gain time.

"Come, let's look at it," Dorcas said. They went through the rooms, examining the exotic oriental wallpaper that the owner favored. It had three bedrooms, one much larger than the other, and Dorcas gave an almost frightened look at the huge bed that boasted at least three feather beds—or so it seemed.

"I suppose this will be ours," Andrew said. "Perhaps you'd care to arrange your things."

"Yes, I will."

She took her time unpacking the small trunk that Sally Bradwell had accumulated. When she pulled out the sheer pink silk nightdress that Sally had insisted on giving her for a wedding present, her cheeks flushed. She had never worn a garment so expensive and she doubted the wisdom of it. But Sally had been adamant. "You'll look beautiful in it," she'd said and then leaned over and whispered in Dorcas's ear something that made her face turn fiery red. Sally had laughed at her and said, *"You* may not like it but I guarantee your husband will!"

It seemed to Dorcas that the sun was plummeting, so quickly did night come on. She was glad there was no servant in the house so she could busy herself with making a simple meal. It was something to do—something that she did well.

When the meal was on the table, Andrew sat down across from her and looked over the table settings and the spotless damask tablecloth. Candles set at each end gleamed and the food was on silver platters. "You've done well, Dorcas," he said. He bowed his head, asked the blessing over the food, and they began to eat.

"You're a fine cook," he said, "but you won't have to do much of that when we get to the rectory."

"Oh, I hope I can make some of the things you like best. You'll have to tell me what they are."

"Yes, of course. It will be as you please."

They managed to keep the conversation going but both were strained and words did not come easily. He insisted on helping her clean up after the meal and when there was no more to do they went out for a walk. Bath was beautiful in April but truthfully Dorcas did no more than glance at those who promenaded back and forth on the broad streets. She was thinking about *that huge bed in that large bedroom.*

Finally they went back to the house, and Andrew said, in almost a strangled voice as they stood uncertainly in the middle of the hall, "Dorcas, perhaps neither of us knows a great deal about marriage."

"No, Andrew, we don't."

"You will never know meanness from me," he said; then he hesitated. When he continued, his voice was low and strained. "Some things I cannot give you. You know my views. But I do think . . . I hope God has made . . . has decreed certain parts of marriage as right and good—" He stopped abruptly, looking away from her. She could tell he was caught in a struggle that threatened to overwhelm him, and wished she could help him. But she knew she could not.

At last he sighed and said, "I have a little work to do. Perhaps you'd like to retire for the evening."

Dorcas blinked in confusion, then realized with a pang that this was her new husband's way of telling her to prepare herself for her wedding night. She took one look at his face and saw a reluctance there that was not encouraging. *Lord, is this what you intended?* she prayed desperately. Her answer was an odd calm that came over her and she was able to meet Andrew's eyes with earnestness. "Yes," she said, "I think I shall." She started to turn, then paused and looked back at him. He stood there, watching her, his expression bleak. She managed a small smile, hoping to ease his struggle. "God created us for this, Andrew. Man and woman, to be together, part of each other, following him as best we can." He didn't respond and she gentled her voice as though speaking to a small, frightened animal. "I believe you are right in your thoughts. God did decree, and bless, the marriage union. We are in his care and in his will."

The expression in his eyes told her he wanted to believe her but his only response was a slight nod. She would have to be satisfied with that. For now.

214

She went at once to the bedroom, took off her dress, hung it up carefully, then stood in her shift, wishing she were anywhere in the world but in this room. For all her words of encouragement to Andrew, she now felt the apprehension sweep over her. *O Lord our God,* she prayed, *help us.*

She shivered, although the air was warm; she knew it was not a matter of temperature. Going to the chest, she opened it and took out the sheer silk gown. Her hands trembled as she laid it on the bed. She undressed, taking off her underclothes, and put on the gown. She glanced in the mirror and was shocked by what she saw. The silk clung to the curves of her youthful figure and there was a sensuous quality in the garment that disturbed her. She almost removed it and put on the simple cotton shift, but she heard again the words of Sally Bradwell, "You must make him love you!"

She moved to the bed and pulled the covers back. When she got into it, it sank beneath her weight. She lay there, as tense as a stick of wood, her mind racing. Truthfully, she had no knowledge of the marriage bed. She'd heard a few things but now she was frightened. "Let him be loving," she whispered, "and I'll ask for nothing else."

After what seemed a long time, the door opened and Andrew entered. Dorcas immediately closed her eyes and lay still. She heard his movements in the room and listened as he blew out the candles.

For some time there was only silence. Then she felt the bed give and was stirred as he got in beside her. His arm brushed against hers and she felt the shock of it. She lay there unable to think clearly—and then she felt him turn toward her. . . .

⌦⌫

At breakfast the next morning, both were silent. Andrew spoke as cheerfully as he could, saying, "We'll see some of the town today. Some of the houses go back several hundred years. You might be interested in them."

2 1 5

"Yes, of course."

There was a quality in her voice that drew a sharp gaze from Andrew. When he looked at her, her eyes met his—and the emotion he saw there stirred him. For a moment he felt an odd warmth, a sense of closeness and intimacy—then he flushed as if he'd done something shameful. *Keep your mind on what's right!* he scolded himself, then said, "Perhaps we'll get a servant to help with the housekeeping."

"That won't be necessary. I'd rather do it myself." Dorcas tried to make her voice agreeable, but when she met his eyes she saw that he flinched. She remembered the previous night and was filled with disappointment. There'd been nothing of love—no gentleness. He had used her as a man might use a tool—and even with her lack of experience, she'd known this was not what love meant. After he had turned from her, she'd waited until his breathing told her he was asleep and then tears had flowed down her cheeks. She had cried silently, without sobs, and now as she looked at him she wondered what he was feeling. She knew they could never talk about such things and she also had a feeling of despair. What Sally Bradwell had described to her was not what she'd found in her own marriage.

When they went out that afternoon, she took an interest and made herself as agreeable as she could. Andrew was courteous and she saw in him a goodness. But there still was a hollowness in her that she couldn't escape.

The week passed quickly. If she'd hoped to find something warm in their relationship, she was disappointed. Andrew seemed to hold himself back; except for those brief moments when he'd touch her in the stillness of the night, he never showed his affection by a kiss or a caress. There was a formality in him, and Dorcas felt he was fighting against his own instincts. *It's as if,* she thought, *he's afraid of women. Afraid to let himself love me.*

They returned to London after a week and she made her entrance into the world she supposed she would inhabit for the rest of her life.

The rectory, located on Mary Street, was close to the church. It was a narrow house that sat on a narrow lot. Because of the density of London's population, houses tended to be organized vertically instead of sprawling outwardly as in the country. London dwellings were, more or less, stacked or jammed into narrow spaces and the rectory was no exception. She'd been at the rectory before but as soon as they arrived Andrew appeared anxious to take her on a more thorough tour. He started at the kitchen, which was in the basement. It was a large room with a huge fireplace flanked by two great coal-fired ovens. It was filled with oak tables and solid chairs, for the servants took their meals there. She studied the floor, which was painted a saffron color, and Andrew said, "In the winter a rag rug is put here, except for around the stove." Off the kitchen was a smaller room with all sorts of devices to keep a house running: mousetraps and rat-traps; cleaning supplies, dustpans, brooms, pails and mops; clean and ready-to-be-used chamber pots; candle molds and candles and snuffers; and linens stuffed in large chifforobes.

"I love the kitchen! I'll be spending a lot of time here," she said.

Andrew laughed. "You'll be spending more time on the ground floor." He led her upstairs, which was composed of the dining room, the drawing room, and a large study. The dining room was a high-ceilinged affair with an old mahogany dinner table rubbed with a brush and beeswax. "You can see your face in it!" Andrew pointed out. "These are fine chairs," he said proudly. They were leather, covered with horsehair and protected from spills by slipcovers. Over to one side, he showed her the huge sideboard with its deep cupboards and breakfront style. It was packed with extra plates and served as a table where the cold meats and salads for supper were kept. The parlor, which served as a reception room, was expansive. The furniture was rich and delicate and the walls papered with cheerful light yellow colors. The carpet was nailed tightly to the floor to prevent it from bunching as the furniture was moved about. Chairs were constantly being rearranged, as was the other furniture.

Andrew said, "We'll entertain our guests in this room. Do you like it, Dorcas?"

"It's a beautiful room," she said sincerely. She ran her hand over the polished mahogany surface of one of the chairs and looked at him with a smile. "It's a beautiful house."

"Come and see my study," he said eagerly. "The former rector left me many of his books." He led her into a room some twelve feet square. The walls lined with shelves had many gaps and empty spaces but he said, "I'll get those filled, soon enough." He showed her the huge rosewood desk with two sets of drawers and somehow looked almost boyish as he said, "Isn't this fine?"

She took in the eagerness of his face and was glad he was pleased. "It's wonderful. I'm sure you'll produce the most wonderful sermons in England at this very desk."

"I'm not at all certain of that."

"Well, I am." Dorcas came over, impulsively taking his arm and squeezing it. "You'll see, my husband will be the best preacher in London."

Andrew was pleased at her words but somehow her touch made him nervous. Hastily he said, "Come now, let me show you the rest of the house."

Dorcas was hurt as he pulled away from her but she said nothing. The floor above the drawing room and the dining room contained three bedrooms: the master bedroom and two smaller rooms. "One of these," he said offhandedly, "was used for a nursery once."

The room he indicated was not large but there was still a cradle there and a chest and table that were smaller than usual. Dorcas looked around and said, "It's a fine place for a nursery. One could raise babies here very easily."

Her words seemed to rake against Andrew's nerves and he said quickly, "Come. We'll meet the servants now. Their rooms are on the top floor, but they'll be downstairs."

When they went downstairs, they were greeted at once by Mrs. Lesley, the housekeeper. Dorcas had met her—and found her to be a cheerless woman. Tall and gaunt, she curtsied slightly as Andrew said, "Remember, you two will be spending a great deal of time together."

Mrs. Lesley said at once in a tight voice, "I'm sure Mrs. Wakefield will have other duties than housekeeping."

"Oh, no, I want to help all I can," Dorcas said.

Clearly this didn't sit well with the housekeeper, who said, "The wife of the former rector left all the arrangements to me." This may have sounded harsh to her own ears, for she said quickly, "I want to make things as pleasant for you as possible."

Dorcas realized, instinctively, the woman was resentful, though she did well to mask it from the pastor. "Of course, we'll work it out, Mrs. Lesley," Dorcas said quietly, realizing she'd found an enemy. Later she discovered Mrs. Lesley had been almost obsessively devoted to the former rector's wife and learned it would be impossible to please the woman.

She found a friend, however, in Beth Buchanan, the cook, who stood slightly aside from Mrs. Lesley. Beth was a short woman, rather heavyset with reddish hair, a round face, and startling green eyes. "It's good to have you here, ma'am, and it's doing the best I can to please you, I will."

Something about the pattern of her speech made Dorcas look at her more closely. "Are you from Wales, Beth?" she asked.

"Yes, I am." She named her hometown and Dorcas exclaimed

at once, "Why, I've been there! It's not too far from my own village!"

"Do you tell me that!" the cook exclaimed and a smile lit her homely face. "Well, now, perhaps we can work together on some good Welsh dishes for the reverend."

Dorcas felt good at once about this woman. She saw the disapproving light in Mrs. Lesley's eyes and said to herself, *Well, we'll see who'll run the kitchen, Mrs. Lesley.* Then she turned to the other woman, who was introduced as Lilly, the housemaid. Lilly was a mousy girl with brown hair and brown eyes and appeared to be very timid. "I hope I'll please you, ma'am, and welcome to the rectory," she said softly.

"I'm glad to meet you, Lilly," Dorcas said, and thought for one moment, *I'm glad there's a person in this house more insecure than I am.* Dorcas noticed that Lilly kept watching Mrs. Lesley. *Why, she's terrified of the old dragon,* Dorcas realized. Dorcas gave the house- keeper that name on the spot, and in her own mind never called her anything else.

"I'm sure you'll all be doing your best to make Mrs. Wakefield feel at home," Andrew said. "Now come along, and we'll look forward to our first meal together tonight."

Sally Bradwell came three days after the return of the newlyweds. She practically quivered with curiosity, and as soon as she got Dorcas to one side began to pry the details out of her. Dorcas put her off for a while, speaking of the household staff. "The old dragon, that's what I call Mrs. Lesley—is a Tartar, but sooner or later there's going to be an explosion."

"Let her know who's the mistress here," Sally said. Then she leaned forward and said, "Tell me all about your honeymoon."

Dorcas knew there'd be no peace until she shared some of her thoughts and experiences with Sally, and in truth she was yearning to talk. She began to speak mostly of the details of the wedding trip but soon found herself bogged down, for she had reached the subject of the wedding night and the wedding bed.

Sally sensed her evasion. "Tell me—was it bad?"

Dorcas had determined to keep her own council but the sympathy in Sally's eyes softened her. "It was very bad," she said slowly. "He's not a rough man or cruel, but there's no—gentleness in him. The time—the times when he touches me, it's as if it is out of duty and nothing more."

Sally Bradwell was young but she had a certain innate feminine wisdom. She drew Dorcas out for some time, then finally said, "You must make him love you, as a man loves a woman."

"But how?" Dorcas cried out in despair. "How can I do that?"

Sally was filled with ideas. "You must make yourself attractive for him." She began to enumerate some of the tactics she'd used with her own husband, such as the use of scent and things to say that would please a man. She concluded with, "Make him *want* you, Dorcas."

"He never will. He doesn't love me—not as a man should love a woman—and he never will."

Sally saw that Dorcas was close to tears. She put her arms around her and whispered, "He will love you; we'll see to that." But there was a heaviness in her spirit and she thought of Andrew Wakefield in a way and in terms that would have shocked even her loving husband. When it came time for her to leave, she hugged Dorcas and kissed her on the cheek. "It's going to be all right . . . you'll see."

Dorcas smiled but when Sally was gone she felt worse than ever. She stood in the middle of the rectory, looked around, and shook her head in despair. She had been poor and almost destitute in Wales but this was almost as bad. She had plenty to eat, fine clothes to wear, and a fine house to live in—but she knew now she didn't have the one thing she craved most—a man to love her with all of his heart!

"MY HEART WAS STRANGELY WARMED"

The pale, feeble bar of wintry sunshine fell over the journal on John Wesley's desk. He'd been staring at it for some time and now read again the words he'd written there in his firm, even hand:

> This, then, have I learned in the ends of the earth—that I am fallen short of the Glory of God: that my whole heart is altogether corrupt and abominable, that I am a child of wrath and an heir of Hell.

Wesley leaned forward, closed his eyes, and put his face in his hands. Since his arrival in London he'd sunk into a dreadful period of doubt and despair. As sensitive as he was to success, the difference between himself and George Whitefield was glaringly obvious—and painful. Whitefield had concluded his work in London only five weeks earlier, but the fruits of his labor were clear—the thronged Societies, the published sermons, the awakened souls, and the reports of his immense congregations. Added to this was Wesley's own sense of failing in his missionary endeavors. For a long time he sat bent over the journal, the clock ticking, and finally, with a weariness that was unusual, he closed the journal, rose, and put on his coat and hat.

Leaving the house, he made his way to the lodgings of a man called Hutton, where his brother Charles was staying. When he arrived there, he was met by the Reverend William Hutton, who shook his head and remarked, "Good day, Mr. Wesley."

"Good day, sir, and how is my brother this morning?"

"Not well, not well." Hutton's eyes were doubtful. "I think he's very ill, Mr. Wesley, very ill indeed!"

Wesley followed the minister into a bedroom on the second floor and found Charles in bed, his face pale and his eyes lackluster. "Why, what is this, Charles?" John said quickly. "I expected to find you better today."

"I fear not, Jack. I have no strength, it seems."

Wesley sat down beside his brother. The two attempted to carry on a conversation. They were both men who did not do things by halfway measures and now their most intense efforts had failed. "I'm very sorrowful, Jack. I can't read, nor meditate, nor sing, nor pray." Charles Wesley threw his arm over his eyes, blocking out the light of the lamp, and soon sank into unconsciousness.

John Wesley felt in need of prayer himself but began to pray for his brother. When he finished he heard a door close and turned to find Reverend Hutton standing there with another man.

"This is Reverend Peter Bohler, who's on his way to be a missionary in South Carolina."

"I'm happy to know you, sir," John Wesley said. He studied the young man carefully. Bohler, a young, strongly built young man of twenty-six, with blue eyes and blond hair, smiled and attempted to speak to Wesley, but his English was frightful. However, when Wesley inquired if he knew Latin, Bohler's eyes lit up and he nodded, speaking fluently in that language to Wesley. The two men conversed in Latin easily and Bohler said in that language, "I am anxious to have your impressions of the mission work to be done."

John Wesley felt not at all like sharing his experiences with this enthusiastic young man and he said doubtfully, "I fear they would be of little use to you, Mr. Bohler. It was not a successful endeavor."

Peter Bohler had been born in Frankfurt and educated at the University of Jena. He had joined the Moravian brethren and been ordained by Count Zinzendorf. He said, "I'm sure it was difficult but perhaps I could benefit."

Wesley hesitated, then said, "Sit down, sir. I need to sit with my brother for a time."

The two men sat down and after a time Wesley, who was impressed with the young man's sincerity, asked, "What do you consider is the result of a true faith in Christ?"

At once Bohler said, "Dominion over sin, constant peace from a sense of forgiveness."

John Wesley stared at him. He turned to glance at Charles, who was now awake, and saw that his brother was as astonished as himself.

"I do not think many Christians have this assurance, Mr. Bohler."

"Then they have either followed a false gospel and mistaken their conversion—or else they have not availed themselves of the grace of God." Bohler went on speaking enthusiastically and with great assurance about the possibility of living a life free from the bondage of sin, and of the complete and utter peace that could come upon the children of God.

John Wesley might have failed as a missionary but in the matter of the Scripture he felt himself equal to any man. He continued disputing Bohler with all his might. He liked the young man immensely but found he had met the man who knew the Scripture almost as well as he did. Finally he lowered his head and admitted with some difficulty, "I haven't achieved this state, Mr. Bohler. I'm groaning under a heavy load." He looked up then, his eyes filled with pain as he added, "But the more I labor to be holy, the more sin seems present with me!"

Bohler replied frankly, "Believe and you will be saved. Believe in the Lord Jesus with all your heart and nothing shall be impossible to you. This faith to live with the peace of God is like the salvation that you found in Christ—it is the free gift of God. Seek and you will find!"

As Bohler spoke for some time on the possibility of living a victorious life, Wesley knew he was echoing the advice of the Moravians of Georgia. "Strip yourself naked of your own good works and your own righteousness," said Bohler, "and go naked to him! For everyone that comes to him, he will in no wise cast out."

Wesley found it difficult to accept this concept of grace. He'd struggled all of his life to discipline himself and somehow he felt there was no other way.

Charles agreed and cried out, "What, Jack, have we then nothing to do? I cannot accept it! We must work for God."

But John Wesley had been tremendously impressed by the young German. During the days that followed, he sought Bohler out and invited him to travel with him and Charles to Oxford.

At Oxford they found the Methodists waiting to receive them. They found, also, that they were mocked. However, Bohler assured them he took no offense: "My brother, it does not stick to our clothes!"

Throughout their days together at every opportunity Wesley continued his argument with Bohler. Finally Bohler said to him plainly, "My brother, that philosophy of yours must be purged away!"

Whenever Bohler pointed to a passage of Scripture that supported his concept of grace, Wesley construed it differently. On Sunday, March 5, while he and Bohler were reading the Greek New Testament together and Bohler was expounding on the Scripture "Believe on the Lord Jesus Christ, and thou shalt be saved," Wesley turned to Bohler and said, "How can I preach to others when I, myself, don't have faith. Shall I leave all preaching?"

"By no means," said Bohler.

"But what can I preach?"

"Preach faith *till* you have it. And then, *because* you have it, preach faith."

John Wesley said in despair, "I cannot understand it, Mr. Bohler. From what you tell me, you believe that conversion is instantaneous."

"Exactly—it can take place in one moment of time."

John Wesley had always zealously denied the possibility of a deathbed repentance. If he accepted Bohler's position on salvation by faith, this would have to go—along with other doctrines to which he held firmly.

From this point on, Wesley began a thorough study of his Greek New Testament. He'd always been a student, but now, night and day, almost every waking hour, he pored over his Bible. His heart grew more and more hungry and yet he knew that to accept Bohler's teachings would change his whole life.

Bohler had written to Zinzendorf:

> The elder, John, is a goodly-natured man. He knows he does not believe on the Savior and is willing to be taught. His brother is, at present, very much distressed in his mind but does not know how he shall begin to be acquainted with the Savior.

The two Wesleys struggled with their doubts and fears but nothing seemed to help. Finally, late in March, Wesley was asked to minister to some condemned prisoners. He took Kinchin, a friend, to visit a prisoner named Clifford who was to be hanged that day. As they sat in the cold, cheerless cell, despair and misery were etched on the thin face of Clifford.

Kinchin sat silently and John Wesley found words stuck in his throat as he looked at the man on whom the frost of death already lay. He searched desperately for words of comfort—but found none. What could he say to this man who would be thrown into a shallow grave and would be in the presence of God in a few hours?

After several fruitless attempts, Wesley suddenly seemed to hear the words of Peter Bohler echoing in his mind: *Strip yourself naked of your own good works and your own righteousness and go naked to him! For everyone who comes to him, he will in no wise cast out.*

Almost timidly, Wesley began to say these words and to read the Scriptures that Bohler had drummed into him in the past weeks. Finally he took a deep breath and said, "Clifford, my friend, you must throw yourself on the mercies of Jesus Christ."

Clifford, a frail man in his early thirties, looked at him with disbelief. "I killed a man," he whispered.

"Yet, come to Jesus. He will forgive all your sins."

"I don't know how."

Wesley glanced at Kinchin and said, "We will pray. My friend and I will pray for you—and you call upon God in the name of Jesus Christ."

"What good will that do?"

"You will be forgiven of your sins." Wesley had little faith himself but he desperately said, "Come, let us kneel and pray. Trust in Jesus."

They began to pray and Wesley broke with his Anglican custom of praying set prayers and prayed extemporaneously. He knew that if his brother Charles ever heard of it he'd be dismayed, but some of Clifford's desperation had entered into him. As they knelt there, he suddenly became aware that Clifford was weeping and calling out to God. This so encouraged him that he, too, began to pray fervently.

At last Wesley looked up and as he rose from his knees, Clifford

rose with him. His face was wet with tears but there was a light of
hope in his eyes as he whispered, "I am now ready to die. I know
Christ has taken away my sins; there is no condemnation for me."

Kinchin and Wesley were shocked beyond measure. They'd
never seen a man transformed instantaneously and although some
skepticism remained in Wesley, Kinchin had no doubts.

When the jailer and sheriff came to take Clifford to the gallows,
Wesley and Kinchin went in the cart with him. Wesley didn't say
a word but he watched the face of the prisoner carefully. There
was not a sign of fear—indeed, there was joy. And as they put the
rope around Clifford's neck, he said loudly, "Christ Jesus has
forgiven my sins. I have a perfect peace in my heart."

Wesley turned away as the trap was sprung. He heard the solid
clunk as the body of the condemned man hit the end of the rope.

As they left the prison, John Wesley knew he'd seen a miracle.
He said to Kinchin, "That man went out to meet God a
believer—and it happened in one instant of time!"

On May 21, Pentecost Sunday, Charles Wesley was still suffering
from poor health; he'd been shut up in his bedroom for four days.
He recorded in his diary,

> I received the sacrament but not Christ. I looked for
> him all night with prayers and signs and unceasing
> desires but I have nothing but dejection.

On Sunday morning, he resorted to the practice of opening
the Bible at random and accepted the first verse his eye lighted
upon as the message of the Lord to him. This was the Moravian
practice that had not always proved successful. However, on this
particular morning he found himself moved and touched by an
unusual sense of the presence of God.

John Wesley had walked westward to the baroque church St. Mary-Le-Strand to help the rector administer Holy Communion. When he came out of the church, three friends surrounded him.

"What is it?" he asked quickly. "Is Charles worse?"

"No, he has found Christ. He's at peace with God," they said, and rejoicing, they led John Wesley to where Charles was, now up and fully dressed. There was an excitement in the younger brother's eyes and he said at once, "Jack, I have found Christ. I have put a full reliance on the blood of Christ which was shed for *me.*"

"Why, God bless you, dear Charles!" Wesley exclaimed. He sat down and listened as Charles talked about what had happened. "I had always thought," Charles said, "that I must be holy before I could be saved. Now I know I deserve nothing but wrath. All my works, my righteousness, my prayers, they are nothing. My mouth is stopped. I have nothing to plead. God is holy; I am unholy."

"Tell me again," John said, a pleading note in his voice, for he saw in his younger brother the same assurance he'd seen in Peter Bohler and the Moravians. He longed for it himself and listened as Charles spoke of how he'd finally cast aside his good works and thrown himself only on Christ.

The group in that small room sang together and gave praises to God. And it was a victorious night.

But John Wesley was no different and as he left Charles's quarters he lapsed into misery. Again he began fasting and seeking God. But it seemed that God had forsaken him.

───────

Early on Wednesday morning, May 24, 1738, John Wesley was reading his Greek New Testament as usual. His eyes were red with strain and all day long he studied the Scripture. That afternoon he accompanied a friend to Evensong at Saint Paul's Cathedral. The choir sang Purcell's anthem "Out of the Deep Have I Called unto Thee, O Lord." Every line of the hymn encouraged him, and finally the choir sang, "O Israel, trust in the Lord, for with the Lord there is mercy, and with him plenteous redemption. And he shall redeem Israel from all his sins."

Wesley seemed to hear an echo in his spirit as the choir sang these words. As he left the church, he continued to pray. That evening he agreed to accompany James Hutton, his host, to a Moravian meeting. As they moved through the slums of London, they passed men and women lying drunk from cheap gin. More than once they waved away harlots. Wesley kept an eye out for pickpockets and thieves—the very outcasts who, until lately, John Wesley had believed could never be saved instantly.

The meeting was held in Aldersgate Street, a few yards from Charter House. They turned into Nettleton Court and as the service began, a minister read Luther's *Preface to the Epistle of St. Paul to the Romans.* Wesley listened, and the darkness thickened about him. But he began to feel the presence of God as he'd never felt it before. He began to pray at once, and later he described the experience in what would become a famous passage.

> In the evening I went very unwillingly to a society in Aldersgate Street, where one was reading Luther's Preface to the Epistle to the Romans. About a quarter to nine, while he was describing the change which God works in the heart through faith in Christ, I felt my heart strangely warmed. I felt I did trust in Christ, Christ alone for salvation; and an assurance was given to me that he had taken away *my* sins, even *mine,* and saved *me* from the law of sin and death.

As John Wesley stood listening to the words of the minister, something happened inside his heart. He knew he'd found Jesus Christ—the object of his search. Life would never be the same again for now he *knew* he was under the blood of Jesus!

Seventeen

THE DOORS CLOSE

O ne of the more unpleasant aspects of being pastor of
Redeemer Church was dealing with Mr. Rawdon
Sylvester. Mr. Sylvester was convinced he—not the
new rector—was the best fitted to make decisions for the congregation. He often said to Andrew, with heavy-handed humor,
"You young ministers must learn to rely on us older fellows. We
are put here to be certain you don't get off into some half-baked
scheme." These remarks would always be punctuated by a sly look
and a laugh.

Andrew had learned to bear with the arrogance of his chief
deacon, but one Thursday afternoon after his visit with Mr.
Sylvester, Mrs. Sylvester apprehended him in the vestibule of their
massive and ornate house. "One moment, Reverend," she said.
And when Andrew turned to her with some surprise, she said,
"May I have a word with you, sir?"

"Why, certainly, Mrs. Sylvester." Andrew followed her into the
smaller of the two drawing rooms, thinking wryly that "small" is
a relative term. It was simply less enormous than the main
drawing room. As they entered, he glanced around at the paintings
by Hogarth and Hamilton and at the exquisitely wrought mahogany furniture—the work of Woster—and he wished fervently
that his chief deacon had less money and a better spirit.

"Now, Mr. Wesley"—Elizabeth Sylvester turned to Andrew, an unsmiling look on her face. She'd been a great beauty in her youth and spent a great deal of money even now perpetuating it. The gown she wore cost enough, Andrew supposed, to feed a dozen families in the London slums for a month. Bracing himself, he saw her lips were drawn tightly together in a frown of disapproval. "Far be it from me to interfere with my pastor's private life," Mrs. Sylvester said grimly, "but there is a matter you need to consider."

"And what is that, Mrs. Sylvester?" This was not the first time the woman had called Andrew aside. Like her husband, she felt eminently qualified to run everybody's business in the parish—especially that of the pastor!

"Since you're still a newly married man, it might not have come to your attention that your wife has turned her attention in what I feel is the wrong direction."

Andrew stiffened. "In what way, Mrs. Sylvester?"

"It's quite natural, of course, that she should do so; after all, she's a young woman and comes from rather disadvantaged circumstances. I have attempted to offer my advice but like most of the younger women, she prefers to go her own way."

Andrew stared at Mrs. Sylvester. He was well aware Dorcas was having difficulty fitting into her new life. He blamed himself partly for this, for they had not been able to talk as he'd hoped. More than once he'd wished fervently he could guide Dorcas into what he felt was a wise attitude toward the ladies of the parish, but so far he had not been able to do so. "What exactly is the problem?" he asked quietly.

"Why, I'm sure you understand that the pastor's wife has a certain responsibility to the *established* members of the congregation."

By *established* Andrew understood, at once, that she meant the women who were wealthy. He'd been somewhat shocked to realize that the parish life at Redeemer Church was no less stratified and severely organized than the hierarchy of England. At the top of the pyramid Mr. and Mrs. Rawdon Sylvester reigned supreme. Beneath them was a very small group of some four or five powerful and wealthy individuals, and below them a group of respectable but rather humble individuals. The pyramid built steadily until on the bottom were the rank and file—who had absolutely nothing to say about the affairs of Redeemer Church.

"Please explain yourself, Mrs. Sylvester. Do you feel my wife has neglected you?"

"Well, far be it from me to complain, but I feel Mrs. Wakefield spends far too much time with her charity work. No one desires more than I to see the poor helped, as I'm sure you realize, but I'm afraid your dear wife has gone into that sort of thing excessively."

For one moment, Andrew was tempted to blurt out, *Woman, if you'd spend more time with the poor and less on your personal appearance, God would be more satisfied with you!* But he bit his tongue and said, "Mrs. Wakefield is concerned about the poor but I shall speak to her."

"Of course, my dear Mr. Wakefield. *Balance,* that is what's necessary." Mrs. Sylvester continued to speak for some time, in essence saying she'd expect Dorcas Wakefield to pay more attention to her and to the top of the pyramid than to the waifs who roamed the streets of London. Finally she forced a brittle smile and added, "I'm sure you'll be able to give proper guidance to Mrs. Wakefield. If you would like me to talk to her, I'll be happy to do so."

"I don't feel that will be necessary but I thank you for your concern."

Andrew left the Sylvester house angry and dissatisfied with his visit. *I'll have to talk to Dorcas,* he thought grimly. *We can't afford to offend the leadership of the church. It's difficult enough to keep their minds turned on spiritual things without deliberately creating a worse situation.*

———❦———

Mrs. Irene Lesley was angry to the bone. She drew herself up rigidly before Dorcas Wakefield and said, "I'm certain you mean well, Mrs. Wakefield, but you must realize I have far more experience in these matters than you."

Dorcas had been bracing herself for this moment. Gareth had come earlier in the day and she'd determined to give him the best bedroom and to oversee the evening meal. Ever since coming to the rectory, Mrs. Lesley had kept an iron lock on her authority. The former pastor and his wife, a Mr. and Mrs. Milton, had allowed her full authority over all things inside the house. She had planned the meals, assigned visitors to whichever bedrooms she felt would be suitable, and had ruled unchallenged in every area of daily life.

Dorcas had meekly accepted Mrs. Lesley's "suggestions"—but she had wished to do her very best for Gareth. She had called Mrs. Lesley into the parlor and said as gently as possible, "Mrs. Lesley, you put my brother in that small room at the end. I would rather he stayed in the blue room."

"That room is reserved for dignitaries, Mrs. Wakefield. It's always been that way. Mrs. Milton and I decided that would be best."

Dorcas stiffened. "I'm sure you and Mrs. Milton had reasons for doing that but Mrs. Milton is no longer here. My brother will be in the blue room." There was a finality in her voice and she met the gaze of the tall woman before her, noting the active dislike in the slate gray eyes. "And I will choose the menu for dinner tonight."

"Mrs. Wakefield, that would not be at all fitting! As house-keeper, I feel responsible for all that goes on in this house—I will speak with the cook. As a matter of fact, I've already done so. I'm sure you'll like what I've decided."

"It isn't likely I'll know what you decided, Mrs. Lesley, because we won't be having it. I have decided what the meal will be and will not require your advice or your services."

"Perhaps you don't realize how dangerous it is for young women with no experience to do these things. Perhaps it wouldn't matter so much with your brother but it would set a precedent. When important visitors come, it's critical they be treated with a certain skill."

Dorcas's anger flared up. "My brother *is* an important visitor, Mrs. Lesley." She'd endured the sour-faced woman ever since coming to Redeemer Church, and now her anger boiled over and she said clearly, "From now on, *I* will make the decisions about meals, about linens, about cleaning, and *I* will rebuke the servants when it is necessary. If you feel you cannot live under this sort of arrangement, perhaps you had better seek other employment, Mrs. Lesley."

"I will speak to your husband about this!"

"You may speak to the archbishop of Canterbury about this. That's as you please." Dorcas's face was pale but the stubbornness that lurked beneath her meek exterior had suddenly been struck. It gave off a spark and she said, "I think you might be happier with another employer. One you can bully as you please."

Mrs. Irene Lesley turned pale at once. Her lips drew into a thin white line as she said, "The bishop is a friend of mine—a personal friend."

"Fine," Dorcas said, realizing the threat. She knew there would be trouble over this but she didn't care. "Perhaps the bishop can use a housekeeper. I'm sorry I cannot recommend you. You may feel free to leave as soon as you can collect your things."

At that point, Mrs. Lesley realized that the young woman who had been so meek and obliging and yielding to her wishes had a streak of hidden iron. Mrs. Lesley knew she had an excellent position and the thought of being thrust out became intolerable.

Swallowing hard, she held her hands together to conceal their trembling and said in an unsteady voice, "Mrs. Wakefield—I—I wish to say that I have been hasty. . . ." Perhaps for the first time in her life, Mrs. Lesley gave an abject apology. She wound up by saying almost pleadingly, "I would appreciate another chance, Mrs. Wakefield."

Dorcas knew this woman would not bring happiness into the rectory. She'd be bitter and would hold a grudge, but for the moment Dorcas had won the victory. "Very well, Mrs. Lesley. We'll say no more of it. From now on, we will meet in the morning and discuss the affairs of the rectory. That will be all for now."

"Yes, Mrs. Wakefield."

As soon as Mrs. Lesley was gone, Dorcas found that she was trembling and wondered at her own audacity. Nevertheless, looking over at the bust of Plato on the pedestal, she smiled and said, "Before I give in to that woman again, look for me on the floor!"

Then she laughed. For the first time since coming into the rectory, she felt a sense of freedom. She hadn't realized how completely the tyranny of Mrs. Irene Lesley had put a bondage on her spirit. Running her hand over her hair, she went at once to the kitchen and found Beth Buchanan busily stirring flour in a huge bowl. "Well, Cook," she said, "I think we should talk about dinner."

Beth Buchanan gave her a startled look. "Mrs. Lesley has already given me the menu."

"You may forget that. I know my brother better than anyone else, and you and I will fix up a Welsh supper for him, fit for a king."

"But Mrs. Lesley—"

"Never mind Mrs. Lesley. From now on you and I will decide on the menu, Beth."

Beth looked at her mistress, open-eyed with shock. "Well, devil throw smoke!" she exclaimed. "What's happened?" There was an audacious streak in this woman. Since her husband was an invalid, hurt in a coal-mining accident, she supported him and their two children. She'd despised Mrs. Lesley from the day she saw her. Now when she examined Dorcas Wakefield's face, she saw something there that made her ask, "Have the two of you come to an understanding?"

"The understanding is that I am mistress of this rectory. If Mrs. Lesley troubles you, come to me with it, Cook."

"Well, glory to God!" A smile lit Beth's round face. "Now then, let's get on with making this house a happy place."

As the two worked on the menu, Dorcas knew she'd found a friend. And when she left the kitchen and went up to knock on Gareth's door she was pleased with herself. When his voice bid her enter, she opened the door and stepped inside.

"Now," she said, with a happy expression, "I've been planning your dinner for the evening, but for now I want to hear all you've been doing."

Gareth came to her at once, a calmness and a peace in his expression, and she whispered, "You're happy, aren't you, Gareth?"

"It's more than happiness, Dorcas," Gareth said. His fine eyes examined her and he said suddenly, "I wish you had as much contentment as I have."

Dorcas dropped her eyes, for she understood that this brother of hers knew her well. She could not hide her unhappiness from him but she refused to talk about it. Taking his arms, she pulled him over to the settee and said, "Sit down now and tell me what you've been doing. I want to hear everything."

"Why, I've been learning how to wait on God," he said, "and learning how to preach."

"Tell me about Howell Harris."

She sat there quietly listening as Gareth told her about the Welsh evangelist who'd been in Bristol for a series of meetings that Gareth had attended. Now, as Gareth spoke of the multitudes that followed Harris in the open fields, his eyes burned with fervor. "I never saw anything like it—never! They come by the thousands to stand, sometimes even in the rain. Every time Mr. Harris preaches, the Spirit of God moves mightily."

"Isn't it strange, having a service out-of-doors?"

"Very strange indeed! But I imagine the Lord Jesus would approve. After all, the Sermon on the Mount wasn't held in a church, was it, Sister?"

"No, indeed. Tell me more."

The two sat there for over an hour, Dorcas soaking up her brother's words. She was spiritually hungry, for there was little life and no excitement at all in Redeemer Church. Everything was done according to order, and the rituals were well performed. The singers were well trained so they never sang a note off-key but there was little, if any, of the spiritual excitement Dorcas had known back in Wales. Their little church there had been poor and the preacher had been not nearly so well educated as Andrew, but he'd had a fiery love in his heart for God that communicated itself to the people. She spoke of this now to Gareth. "I think sometimes," she said wistfully, "of the days back in our little church and the good Reverend Griffith. Oh, how I would love to hear him again."

"So would I and so we shall. We must go back, you and I, on a visit."

Instinctively Dorcas knew this wasn't likely. She put the matter away and rose saying, "Andrew will be anxious to hear about Mr. Harris's meeting. You must tell him all about it."

At dinner that night Gareth found that Andrew Wakefield was not receptive to hearing of his recent experiences. The dinner was very fine—roast beef, potatoes, fish, and fresh bread with creamy bowls of butter to spread on it. He expressed his thanks to Dorcas but when he spoke of the outdoor meetings, a frown touched Andrew's face.

"I don't think," Andrew said, "it's fitting to hold services out-of-doors."

"But these people, many of them, never go inside a church. Many of them are coal miners, the very poorest of the poor," Gareth said. "I know what it's like, sir," he added grimly, "and the Spirit of God is mighty."

Andrew had been glad to see Gareth but now he was troubled. He looked over at the young man and said, "Have you heard what's happened to John Wesley?"

"Why, just that he's back from Georgia."

"He's gone to Germany to visit the Moravians." Andrew's eyes flickered with distrust. "I've warned him to stay away from those people. You'd think he'd seen enough of them in Georgia. They're all enthusiasts—all of them."

Andrew shot a glance at Dorcas, who seemed to disagree, from her expression, but said nothing. Gareth said mildly, "I've met a few of the followers of Count Zinzendorf and they seemed to be sincere, godly men."

"They are that, of course, but they are misled," Andrew said. "They're given to mysticism. Why, you're aware they taught Mr. Wesley to decide spiritual matters by drawing lots, or what they call 'consulting the oracle.'"

"Consulting the oracle, sir?"

"Oh yes, that simply means that when they want a word from God they hold a Bible and let it fall open." Andrew shook his head in disgust. "What a way to run your life, by chance. In any case," he added quickly, "the churches don't want John Wesley. He's had some kind of an experience."

"I've heard of this," Gareth said, nodding. "I understand he's preaching free grace."

"Yes, he learned that from the Moravians too—and from George Whitefield, I suppose. I'm surprised Wesley has let himself get involved in this."

241

Gareth wanted to argue the point but felt it would be improper. So instead he said, "I have something to say that may not please you, Mr. Wakefield."

Andrew looked over at his young guest doubtfully. "And what is that, Gareth?"

Carefully Gareth said, "I have taken a leave from Oxford for a time, sir. Our vacation is coming up, in any case."

Alarm ran through Andrew.

"I'm going to accompany Mr. Harris to Wales on a preaching tour."

Instantly Andrew said, "That wouldn't be wise, Gareth." He leaned forward and glanced at Dorcas, who met his eyes evenly. "It's not fitting for you to be with these people. You'll become an enthusiast like George Whitefield."

Gareth met Andrew Wakefield's eyes steadily. "I would that I would become so good a man, sir."

Anger washed through Andrew and he began speaking earnestly, trying to persuade Gareth not to go. He made no headway and for the next two days of Gareth's visit there was a bridge between the two men. Finally, when Gareth left, he said simply, "You have done so much for me, Mr. Wakefield. My heart knows such gratitude to you, but I must do as God bids me do and he bids me now to sit under this man of God for a time. I trust you will not be angry with me."

Andrew shook his head. "I fear for you, Gareth. You have great potential and this is a wrong way you are choosing." After Gareth left there was a strain between Dorcas and Andrew, even greater than before, for she defended her brother's choice.

Andrew said grimly, "He will come to no good if he follows those Methodists!"

⚬⚬⚬⚬⚬

John Wesley was, indeed, in ill favor, even as Andrew Wakefield had mentioned to Gareth. He had gone to church after church and preached his message of grace and after the sermon had been told by the pastor that he wouldn't be invited back.

Wesley himself, however, had undergone a tremendous change in his heart. There were times when he suffered from heaviness but amidst such struggles he testified to a new victory. His brother Charles began to declare salvation by faith to every soul he could reach and the two men suddenly found they were being heard in a way they'd never been received before. Charles was a man of rich, spiritual emotions and vehement zeal. He prayed continually, prayed anywhere, and prayed with strength. He spoke the gospel with boldness and power wherever he was and to everyone he met. He would not be held by forms of prayers and written sermons but his life was filled with spiritual activity as he'd break forth into joyous proclamation of the gospel.

John Wesley moved somewhat slower in his newly received faith. He was essentially an intellectual and when he asked himself what it was that really happened at Aldersgate, he spent days and weeks examining his transformation. He had gone to meet with the Moravians at Herrnhut, the Moravian Head-quarters in Germany. He found much to like in the earnestness of those people and in his journal said, "I would gladly have spent my life there."

His visit affected him strongly. He became convinced that a second Christian experience was possible—an experience that would bring him a larger victory than he possessed. With total sincerity he recorded his inward journey in his journal, speaking quite frankly of the faults he still saw in himself. Finally, he made an incredible statement:

> My friends affirm that I'm mad because I said I was not
> a Christian a year ago. I affirm I am not a Christian now.
> Indeed, what I might have been I know not, had I been

> faithful to the grace then given, when expecting
> nothing less I received such a sense of forgiveness of sins
> as till then I never knew.

Aldersgate was the occasion of his conversion but there was still some confusion in his mind. He was moving forward in his spiritual life, steadily and with a fresh certainty, but something was yet to come.

Whitefield returned in November. He met with the group of believers who had moved into a large room on Fetter Lane and called themselves the "Fetter Lane Society." These fifty-six men and eight women had divided themselves into bands of seven in order to support each other with prayer and in every way possible. It was the return of Whitefield that brought something new into John Wesley's life. Whitefield was cheerful and quick to laugh, whereas Wesley was graver by nature and still seemed to lack some of the younger man's joy. They spent many hours together praying and singing and as the new year began on January 1, 1739, the two Wesleys met with a small group that included Whitefield. The men met often and Whitefield eventually suggested to the Wesleys that they should break all precedent and preach outdoors to reach the outcasts, harlots, publicans, and thieves.

John Wesley said privately to Charles, "That is a mad notion indeed! Preaching out-of-doors. It would be unbecoming to a clergyman of the established church."

However, after Mr. Whitefield returned to Bristol, Wesley thought much about what the young evangelist had said. He received a letter from Whitefield saying that he had taken what he called "the mad step" and preached in the open air to coal miners as they left the pits in Kingswood, Bristol. Whitefield told how he'd been nervous as he stood on Hanham Mount to preach but that the gospel had had its effect.

"I saw white gutters, made by their tears, run down their black cheeks," he said in his letter to Wesley. "Blessed be God, I have broken the ice. There is a glorious door open among the miners. You must come and water what God has enabled me to plant." Then, later in March, he wrote, "I am but a novice. You're acquainted with the great things of God. Come, I beseech you. Come quickly! I have promised not to leave this people until you or somebody come to supply my place."

Wesley didn't wish to leave London. He felt his health wouldn't endure it, but on March 28 he put the question to the Fetter Lane Society as to whether he should go to preach in the open air in Bristol.

Charles could scarcely bear to hear of it, and others were equally opposed. Some, however, felt it was of God and finally Wesley resorted again to the lot. In this case the lot said, "Go preach in Bristol."

Sally Bradwell looked at her friend Dorcas Wakefield and saw the marks of strain. Sally was troubled about Dorcas. Leaning forward, she put her hand on Dorcas's arm and asked, "And how are things between you and your husband?"

It was a question Dorcas didn't want to answer. But she knew Sally loved her and longed for Dorcas to be happy in her married life. Being an honest young woman Dorcas lifted eyes filled with misery to say, "They're no better, I'm afraid."

Sally shook her head. "I'm sorry to hear it. Tell me about it." She listened as Dorcas spoke simply and painfully of how she and Andrew were strangers to one another. There was no bitterness in her voice but a tremendous sadness. Finally Sally said, "I wish I had an answer for you, but I don't. All I know is that Andrew Wakefield is a *man,* and sooner or later men find the women with whom they live day in and day out desirable." She smiled briefly. "Especially when you treat them lovingly. Giving love the way

God has instructed us results in receiving love. I am sure of that. I have seen it happen between me and George."

"But you and George were in love to begin with. Andrew doesn't believe in that sort of love."

"But you do. And your belief will sway him one day. It must! You can't go through life like this."

When Sally left, Dorcas went upstairs to her bedroom and sat down at the desk. She had begun keeping a journal, hiding it carefully. As she began to write she allowed herself to say the things in ink that she'd never say with her voice:

> What am I to do with my life? I've been told all my life that I must submit to my husband. The man chases the woman, who allows herself to be caught. But Andrew has never shown any intention of letting his love for me—if indeed there is any!—come forth.
>
> If he only knew how little it would take to please me! If he would just one time put his hand on mine and say, "Dorcas, I love you." Oh, how wonderful that would be.
>
> I do love Andrew. Before God, I love him! And somehow, behind that wall that he's built between us, I know that he cares for me, too.

She slammed the book shut and hid it in her chest beside the window. Then she stood there, looking out, and made up her mind that she'd try one more time to talk to her husband about their relationship.

She waited until that night when the two were ready to retire. She had undressed and was wearing a robe when he entered the room and he looked at her with some surprise. "Not in bed?" he said. He had stayed up to work late and expected she'd be asleep.

"No, I wanted to wait for you."

As he looked at Dorcas, so small in the plain white cotton

gown, with her dark brown hair sleek and glowing in the candlelight, he was suddenly troubled by something he saw in her. He began to undress, feeling embarrassed, for she had never allowed herself to be a witness to his nighttime preparations. Always she would be in bed first and now he hardly knew what to say. He'd removed his coat and opened his shirt when suddenly he turned to her. "Is something wrong, Dorcas?"

"No," she said hesitantly. She lifted her gaze and saw he was as tense as she was. She got into bed and lay there, trying to find some way to break the awkward strangeness that existed between them.

When he lay beside her, she whispered, "Andrew, do you not love me?"

Instantly he grew rigid. "Love you? What do you mean?"

"The question isn't difficult to understand," Dorcas said. She turned over to face him, and the full moon bathed the room in its pale light. She saw that his eyes were wide, that somehow she'd shocked him. "Is it wrong for a wife to ask a husband that?" She had gone too far now to back out and said, "You never touch me except . . . in this bed. And even then only when you feel you must."

Andrew felt a sense of shame wash over him but he didn't know why. It was true that he never offered her a caress. And the times he came to her were rare. Though they were married in God's eyes, he never ceased feeling a strange sense of guilt after each of their physical encounters. He had labored often over this, struggling to understand his feelings and reactions. But he had found no answers. So instead he had pulled even further away from Dorcas, hoping to still the warmth and longing that often filled him when he was near her. Surely God could not honor such feelings in a man who was supposedly wholly devoted to him?

And yet . . . was it honoring God to create such evident pain in his wife?

"I trust you know you are appreciated," he offered, hoping this would give her some safe measure of his feelings for her.

"Appreciated!" Dorcas stiffened and her voice became more intense. "Do you think a woman is nothing but a—a servant? When we are together you are nothing but a man doing a chore! You come to me as you do everything else, like winding the clock!"

"Dorcas!"

She had gone too far; she knew it. But she could not hold back the words any longer. "A woman needs love, Andrew. She needs to be touched, she needs to be told—nice things. Just gentle little things."

"You're talking foolishness!"

"Foolishness! To seek love, you think that's foolishness?"

"Dorcas, be quiet! What you speak of is not love! It is mere physical pleasure, carnal knowledge. Nothing more." She stiffened and made to move away and he reached out to stop her.

She shook his hand off and fixed him with a searing, pain-filled stare. "You don't love me at all, do you?"

Andrew threw the cover back and stepped out of bed. He pulled on a robe, saying, "Dorcas, I told you at the beginning there would be no romance between us."

Something about the way he said *romance* grated on her. "And, indeed, you've kept that vow, Andrew." Dorcas sat up in bed, her eyes angry. "But you're not a man. A man would love his wife. Truly. As God commands it. As Christ loves the church. He would seek to honor and please her. Not pretend she does not exist!"

Suddenly Andrew Wakefield knew he'd made a terrible mistake. *I never should have married her!* he said in his heart. Pulling his robe about him he said aloud, "I won't trouble you any longer, Dorcas, in—this way. I'll take another room. You can tell the servants I snore. Tell them anything you please—!" He broke off, wracked with confusion and anger, torn between a longing for peace and the warmth of Dorcas's smile and the determination not to fall prey to the influences that had undermined so many in their ministry. He made a frustrated motion with his hand and unable to bear the conversation any longer, stormed from the room.

Dorcas sat stiffly and watched him leave. When the door shut, she turned over and buried her face in the bedclothing. Great sobs tore her and she couldn't contain them.

Finally she said softly, "He doesn't love me—and he never will!" This seemed to be the death knell of all her hopes and the few dreams she'd had of a marriage that was real. She lay back, her eyes shut, tears coursing down her cheeks. She'd never have any more than this, she knew, and she said it aloud, "I'll never have love—not ever!"

Eighteen

"I SUBMITTED TO BE MORE VILE. . . ."

Bishop Alfred Crawley was not a man to disguise his ill humor. At the age of sixty-two he'd been a bishop for many years—and bishops have few acquaintances before whom they must dissemble. Perhaps the only two human beings Crawley found any need of hiding his true feelings from were the royal sovereign and the archbishop of Canterbury. Now, however, neither of these two were in the room where he sat at his desk, looking across at the young man who'd been listening to him for nearly an hour. Raising his voice to a growl, Crawley said, "I'm sick to death of these Methodists! They are bringing a spiritual plague upon the entire land. If I had my way, I'd lock them all up in prison until they came to their senses!"

"I hardly think that would answer, my lord," Andrew Wakefield said calmly. He'd patiently listened to the bishop's harangue once again. During the months Andrew had put in as rector at Redeemer Church, he'd become a sounding board for the bishop's thoughts. "I don't think the movement will last long," Andrew said carefully. "Emotionalism is like a hayfield on fire. It blazes up and makes a large showing at first but then it's gone."

Crawley stared at his young friend. "Yes," he said, nodding grimly, "and what do you have when the fire is over? Nothing but a blackened field, worth nothing." Standing to his feet abruptly, he stalked to the windows and stared outside, engrossed in thought. When he finally pivoted to face Andrew, he said, "I have an assignment for you."

"For me, sir?"

"Yes, a rather unusual one."

"I'm ready to serve you in any way possible, my lord."

Crawley stared at Andrew owlishly, then shook his head. "My lord—what a thing to call a man—especially a man of God!"

"It's the accepted title for bishops in the Church of England," Andrew remarked, wondering at the old man's irrationality and voice. "What else should we call you?"

"You could call me Alf, I suppose." Humor was such a rare thing in Crawley that Andrew couldn't believe what he'd heard. Noting the disbelief in Wakefield's eyes, Crawley plumped himself down in his seat and let the moment pass. He was, in essence, a lonely man, his wife having been dead for over ten years. His exalted position left him without many intimate friends and he'd formed an especially close relationship to Andrew Wakefield. Perhaps it was because he'd lost a son who would have been Andrew's age. Now he leaned back in his chair and studied Andrew carefully.

The large clock that rested on the mantel over the fireplace ticked a smooth cadence in the silence of the room. The leather backs of hundreds of books that lined the walls gave off a dull sheen, reflecting the light that streamed in through the windows of the study. The bishop let his eyes pass over the books, then turned to face Andrew.

"All these books! I've spent my life reading," he commented in a low tone. Dissatisfaction scored his face and, almost angrily, he continued, "Books are not men. *Men* must be our business, Andrew."

"Yes, sir, of course. But scholarship is necessary."

"Sometimes I wonder. When John the Baptist came preaching

in the wilderness, he'd enough education to call the hypocrites who faced him 'snakes.'"

Andrew smiled suddenly. "I hardly think that would do in this day and age."

"Perhaps not, but it's men—living, breathing men—we have to deal with." The old man leaned forward, locked his fingers together, and squeezed them. His eyes narrowed and he lowered his voice as though he were revealing a secret. "I want you to go to John Wesley, Andrew."

"Me, sir?" Astonishment flashed across Andrew's face. His eyes wide, he asked, "But why would you have me do that?"

"Because I need to know what's inside the man."

"But you know him well, my lord. You've known him for years."

"I thought I did but there's something in the air—something I cannot pin down. I don't understand this—this thing they call 'evangelism.' I don't understand a man like John Wesley—a graduate of Oxford—throwing his life away."

"Do you feel it's that serious? I mean, after all, Mr. Wesley is still in the Church of England."

"Is he? His papers are in order, but what about his heart? He's dabbling at dangerous doctrine, Andrew, and I would to God that he'd cut himself free from these winds that seem to be buffeting the true church."

Andrew sat there while the bishop spoke again of the Methodist movement. He could tell the old man was greatly disturbed and Andrew felt much the same. Crawley had grown up in an England where all was stable. The church might have been on a low spiritual plane but it was steadfast. Men knew where they were within its structures.

"Who knows where this will stop unless something happens," Bishop Crawley said. "Go to Wesley—you know him well. You were a protégé of his, more or less, at Oxford. Take some time off, visit some of their meetings, see what you can find out."

Shifting nervously in his chair, Andrew hesitated. "It sounds very much like being a——" He searched for a better word, not finding any, and said bluntly, "A spy, my lord."

"Call it what you will. We must find out what is happening in this country. Will you do it?"

Andrew thought hard, then nodded slowly. "Yes, my lord. I'll go to Mr. Wesley." Then he looked Crawley straight in the eye. "I love the man and respect him firmly, Bishop Crawley, and desire to see him find his way. On those grounds, I will accept your assignment."

The bishop's face seemed to relax and he leaned forward with a kindly light in his faded eyes. "That's well, my boy," he said. "Very well indeed."

"I'll be away for a few days, Dorcas," Andrew said quietly. He'd come into the drawing room where Dorcas was sewing, and when she looked up, he added, "I should be back within a week."

Dorcas was surprised, for it was the first time since they'd been married that Andrew had left. "Where are you going?" she asked.

"To Bristol."

"Is it something to do with the church?"

"Not really." Andrew walked over to the desk and seated himself but he turned to face Dorcas. "The bishop called me in to talk with him a few days ago."

Instantly Dorcas was alert. "Is he unhappy? Have some of the church leaders been complaining?"

"Probably so," Andrew said evenly, "but this was about a different matter." He was aware that although he and Dorcas had maintained a smooth relationship outwardly, they were further apart than ever before in spirit. Ever since the night she'd broken forth in anger and told him she was unhappy with their marriage, it was as though a wall had separated them. He'd kept to the spare bedroom, ignoring the questioning looks and eyes of the servants. The physical side of their marriage had terminated and the spiritual had been demolished during that same instant of time. Andrew hadn't realized a marriage was such a fragile thing. To him it had been logical enough to think one could agree with a wife as one would agree with the butcher. There were certain things that needed to be done, certain regulations that needed to be adhered to—and once these things were done, the association should function well.

Looking over at Dorcas, he was uneasy. She was wearing a simple, light green gown and he thought involuntarily, *She's not a beautiful woman, but she's attractive.* The lines of her figure were outlined by the satin dress and he felt his face flush as he remembered the moments of intimacy they'd once had—and experienced a pang of regret that they had lost whatever closeness they'd shared. Quickly he cleared his throat and said, "It might be well that I speak with you about it. In a way, it concerns you."

"Concerns me?"

"The bishop wants me to speak with Mr. Wesley. He's concerned about the Methodist movement. Since Gareth is apparently throwing himself into it, I think it's a matter we might discuss."

"I see." Dorcas was somewhat surprised her husband had been asked to speak to John Wesley. "Why did the bishop ask you to talk to Mr. Wesley?"

"Because I know him well and spent such a long time with him on the mission field, he thinks I might have some influence. He's wrong about that, of course, but he does want to try to understand what this thing is about."

"You're not sympathetic, are you, Andrew?"

"No, I'm not. You've always known that. I was caught up with it when I was at Oxford, but you see what's happened, don't you? The men who were in the Holy Club are all suspect now. Most of them have been put out of the churches. Why, there's scarcely a church in London that would welcome John Wesley. If he had regained his senses, he could have had his choice of almost any pulpit in England."

"Perhaps he sees something more than a large church." Dorcas put her sewing down and stuck the needle into a pincushion. Leaning forward, she said quietly, "I don't know about Mr. Wesley but Gareth has found great peace and joy in his new service for the Lord Jesus."

Shifting uneasily, Andrew replied, "Couldn't he just as well serve the Lord within the church? Does he have to go outside?" This is the issue that troubled him the most. He, too, had been envious of the confidence and assurance of the Moravians but he felt their fanaticism outweighed this quality.

"I think our personal relationship with Jesus Christ must come before anything else," Dorcas said simply. "Don't you remember how wonderful it was when we'd sit with your aunt? Hope had such a wonderful spirit. I think if she'd lived and she'd been able, she would have been a Methodist."

The idea shocked Andrew. He ran his hand through his hair and shifted on the chair before saying, "I don't know about that. But I do know there is trouble ahead for everyone connected with Whitefield or Wesley or others in this movement. And if you have any interest in Gareth's well-being, you will do your best to dissuade him from having a part in it."

"I can't do that, Andrew," Dorcas said plainly. Her chin lifted as she added, "He is being obedient to what God is telling him to do. No man can do more than that—and no man should interfere with that."

"I won't argue the point." Andrew rose, sadness filling him. Even in this they seemed opposed. "Do you have enough money to run the house while I'm gone?"

"Yes, everything will be well." Dorcas moved to stand beside him. "Andrew," she said, "be gentle, will you?"

Her request startled Andrew and he flushed slightly. "I'm sorry if you think I'm harsh but I have my duty to do." A sudden impulse swept him to reach out for her, to hold her close, feel her warmth, and seek some assurance. But he steeled himself against the urge and the moment passed. "I'll leave early in the morning," he said quietly.

Dorcas watched him go, a sadness permeating her spirit. She sat down again and tried to think of some way to reconcile herself to what Andrew expected of her. But she knew this was impossible, for she'd tried. Obedient to his wishes in all things, she might be and would be, but there was something in her that demanded more of him than he was willing to give—or knew how to give.

<hr />

As Wesley dismounted from his horse at Marlborough, his watch fell out of his pocket.

Andrew, who had also dismounted, saw the watch hit the ground. The glass flew off and he picked it up. "It's not broken, Mr. Wesley," he said. "I think it can be reattached by a good watchmaker."

Wesley took the circle of glass and stared at it. He was extremely weary, even though this was only the second day of the journey. He had welcomed Andrew to join him on his trip to Bristol and the two had passed the two days amiably enough. Holding the glass in his hand, he studied it carefully before saying, "I think this is a sign, Andrew. I've been in poor health, wondering if I could endure what faces me in Bristol. But if this glass didn't break and the watch wasn't damaged, perhaps this is an assurance that the events ahead will not break me."

Andrew stared speechlessly at Wesley. *He really believes that,* he thought almost desperately. *That's more of the Moravian reliance on dreams and incidents.* It disturbed him greatly but he said nothing.

The two men spent the night at Marlborough. After supper,

Wesley preached to the people gathered in the inn. There was a slight disturbance when one well-dressed gentleman growled loudly, "Preaching is for church, sir—not for a tavern or an inn."

Wesley had merely said, "The gospel is for all times and all places."

Afterward, when the two men were preparing for bed, Andrew said, "I think you might consider the words of the gentleman, as rude as he was."

Wesley turned, his eyes narrowing. "You refer to preaching in the fields?"

"Yes, sir, I do. I'm not sure it's wise at all."

For a moment Wesley hesitated. "I'm praying on the matter. I must tell you that four times we consulted the oracle and each time the Scripture that came up spoke of death." He lay down on the bed before finishing his remarks. "It may be that God is saying this will be the death of me, but I must go on."

The next day they continued their journey along the Bath road and in the evening the weary horses made their way down from the hills into Bristol. It was the second largest city in England, humming with activity, and they made their way to the home of Mrs. Grevil, George Whitefield's sister.

Whitefield himself was there and greeted the two with joy. "I'm much refreshed by the sight of my friends. God's providence has sent you here."

The evening went well, for Andrew was happy to see George Whitefield. Whitefield spoke much of his imminent departure to the mission field, and early on the next morning he preached to a considerable crowd in the open air at Bowling Green.

Wesley stood off to one side, with Andrew beside him. The two watched as Whitefield's magnificent voice floated on the air and the crowd received his message with evident satisfaction.

Late in the afternoon, Whitefield preached again at Hanham Mount. The wind blew strongly but there seemed to be no limitation to the voice of the young minister. It rose up like a mighty organ and Andrew whispered to Wesley, "There must be twenty thousand people in this crowd and yet every one of them can hear George speak plainly."

Wesley seemed amused by the scene. "I can scarcely reconcile myself to this strange way of preaching in the fields." He hesitated, then met Wakefield's gaze as Andrew said, "I should have thought the saving of souls almost a sin if it had not been done in a church. But what do you think now, Mr. Wesley?"

Wesley's gaze took in the packed multitudes. He was silent for a long time. At last he said under his breath, "The fields are white unto harvest. The gospel must be preached to the poor and if they won't come to church, we must go where they are."

On the following day, Whitefield left to ride into Wales. That afternoon Andrew accompanied Wesley out to a brickfield at the farther end of St. Philip's Plain, which had been lent to Whitefield for preaching. Wesley's name meant little to the people in Bristol but the people were so hungry for the truth that several thousand people gathered to hear the sermon. Many of them had been so caught up in the revival that they had put down their tools, left their trades, and hastened to the brickyard.

At four o'clock the sun was sinking and the wind had died down. Andrew was nervous as John Wesley stood forth, wearing his cassock. There was determination on Wesley's face as he lifted his voice and said, "The Scripture I would have you hear today is taken from Luke chapter 4, verses 18 and 19." His voice wasn't the instrument possessed by George Whitefield; nevertheless, it was clear as he said, "'The Spirit of the Lord is upon me, because he hath anointed me to preach the gospel to the poor; he hath sent me to heal the brokenhearted, to preach deliverance to the captives, and recovering of sight to the blind, to set at liberty them that are bruised, to preach the acceptable year of the Lord.'"

As John Wesley preached, Andrew Wakefield watched the faces of the roughly dressed congregation who had gathered in the brickfield. It was so foreign to anything he'd understood a minister's sphere to be, but he was aware of the hunger in the listeners' faces. His eyes fastened on one poorly dressed man who held a little girl of no more than two years of age in his arms. The child was thin, her cheeks hollow. The man stroked her hair as he listened to John Wesley's words, his expression attentive and eager. Soon tears flowed down the listener's cheeks. As the little girl saw this, she reached up, touched the man's face, and whispered. The man shook his head, kissed her, and then turned his eyes back on the preacher.

Where does all this lead to? Andrew thought desperately. *What am I to tell the bishop—that we are to leave the churches? He will never understand a thing like this. . . . I don't understand it myself, but Dorcas would.* This thought disturbed him and he turned away from it as Wesley continued to speak of Jesus Christ to the crowds that listened so attentively.

***

Andrew remained in Bristol only two days. During this time, Wesley preached five times in the fields. He had quoted to Andrew the line he'd written in his journal concerning his field preaching: "At four in the afternoon I submitted to be more vile and proclaim in the high ways the glad tidings of salvation, speaking from a little eminence in a ground adjoining to the city to several thousand people." Before he took his leave, Andrew made one attempt to speak to Wesley. He'd packed his belongings and the two men were walking out of the house to where Andrew's horse was hitched to a post. "Mr. Wesley," Andrew said, stopping, "I have been much disturbed about all of this. I beg you to consider your ways."

"You mean," Wesley asked abruptly, "field preaching?"

"That and the other things that are causing unhappiness within the church."

"It cannot cause unhappiness to see men and women come to Christ, can it, Andrew?"

"I fear the methods cause unhappiness."

Wesley examined the young man. Andrew expected him to defend what he'd been doing but instead he said quietly, "Andrew, I've known you for a long time. I know, I think, your good qualities. But I want to ask you one question."

"Yes, sir?"

"Do you have the Lord Jesus Christ in your heart as your own Saviour?"

A cold shiver ran through Wakefield. He hadn't expected this, and anger followed surprise quickly. "I'm shocked you should have to ask such a question, Mr. Wesley."

"It's a question all of us should be willing to ask ourselves," Wesley said calmly. He had been over this ground in his own life so often that it was not a new thing for him. "Now," he said simply, "I won't preach at you, my boy, but I want you to let this question be part of your meditation." He put his hand out and when Andrew took it he said warmly, "God has great things in store for you but you must be the servant of the Almighty in your heart."

Andrew muttered his good-byes, mounted his horse, and rode out of Bristol at a fast trot. The question Wesley had put to him would not leave. On the three-day trip to London it came to him constantly. *Do you have the Lord Jesus Christ as your own Saviour?* He brushed it aside time and time again, only to have it come back. Finally he shrugged, saying, "I fear the bishop is right. Mr. Wesley is allowing Moravian doctrine to mislead him."

⚜

Two days after Andrew's return, Dorcas noticed he was more silent than usual. The two ate their meals together and communicated, after a fashion, but something was wrong with her husband, she well knew.

There was no one to talk to, to bring her problems to, at least not the larger problems. It was Beth Buchanan who said, "Is something wrong with Reverend Wakefield?"

The two women were in the kitchen, experimenting with a new way of roasting lamb, and Dorcas looked up with surprise. "Why do you say that, Cook?"

"He's so silent. 'Course he's a quiet man anyway but I have hardly heard a word out of him since he came back from Bristol. I hope there's nothing wrong."

For one instant Dorcas yearned to throw herself into the arms of the older woman. Beth Buchanan was not old enough, quite, to be her mother but there was a goodness, gentleness, as well as a wit in the woman, that drew Dorcas. Instead she merely said, "I suppose he has many things on his mind to trouble him."

Beth Buchanan had the wisdom often found in Welsh women. She was no gossip but she well knew that the relationship between the reverend and his wife was not good. "May I say something, Mrs. Wakefield?"

"Why certainly, Beth."

"I think your husband is a very lonely man. It's a woman he needs to comfort him—in every way."

Dorcas felt her face grow warm. She knew exactly what Beth Buchanan was saying. As little as she knew about men and women, she at least understood this, that God had made women to be a comfort to men—and she had been no comfort for Andrew Wakefield.

"I—I thank you for your concern, Cook," she said, "but I fear he is a hard man to comfort."

Wisdom was one thing but impertinence was another and Beth knew she'd said all that decorum would allow. But later on, when she went home to her husband, she poured out her thoughts before him. "They're no more husband and wife than they're birds in the air." Her husband had been a tall, muscular man but he'd been crippled in a cave-in and now his left leg was almost useless. Still, he knew this wife of his and for a time sat as she talked of her master and mistress at the rectory.

"What are you saying, Beth?" he demanded finally. Reaching over, he pulled her down into his lap. She squealed but he held her and kissed her firmly. "Are you saying Mrs. Wakefield is not a fit wife?"

"Stop that, Tom!" she said, slapping at his hands but pleased with his attentions. She put her arms around him and for a time sat there, her head on his shoulder. Finally she whispered, "He's left her bed, Tom, and that's no marriage."

"You think she kicked him out?"

"I don't believe so. She's a gentle, loving woman. Too sensitive about that bad hand of hers but enough woman for any man if she but knew it."

"Will she be having him back, do you think?"

"I don't know, Tom, but I know a man needs a woman and a woman needs a man—now, you take *my* man. . . ."

***

Thirty

As a counterpoint to this conversation, Dorcas had one brief word with her husband that same evening. He'd risen from the study and was leaving the room after a brief good-night when Dorcas suddenly rose and called his name.

"Andrew." She waited until he turned to her, a somewhat surprised expression on his face. Drawing a fortifying breath, she moved toward him, pressing on. "I have something to say. You may not want to hear it but I must say it."

"What is it?" He saw as she came to stand before him that her lips were trembling. "Is something wrong?"

"Andrew, I'm a woman and I need more than a house," she

said, waving her hand around the room indicating the fine furniture. "I could live in a shack, I could cook on a grate, but I can't—" She hesitated, then looking vulnerable, continued, "I can live anywhere and do without anything, but I can't live without love." She threw her arms around him and pulled his head down. Her lips were soft under his and shock ran along his nerves as she pressed against him. She held him tightly and he felt the inner hungers stir. For a moment he lost himself in the wonder of the sweet, feminine form that fit so well into his arms, and the tenderness she offered him.

Then she drew back and looked up. "Can you ever love me?" she asked simply. Tears glittered in her eyes and she waited with her lips slightly parted.

Andrew Wakefield put down every instinct that cried to take her in his arms. He was so confused that in that moment he made a terrible mistake. The thought intruded, *One woman has failed you. What makes you think this one will be different?*

Still he stood there, swept by desire, not only for the trim figure of his wife, but also by the almost agonizing desire for someone with whom to share his life. But he could not bring himself to say it. Licking his lips nervously, he said, "This is not fitting—it is not what I meant when I asked you to marry me. Please say no more of this, Dorcas, ever again."

She stood motionless, her face white, looking as if he'd slapped her. The door closed behind him and she hugged her arms about herself, shattered. She wanted to run, to flee this place and this man, but there was no place to go. The pain that raced through her was almost physical. Life stretched out in an endless procession of days and none of them meant anything. Her life had become a charade—a play in which she would take on a role but would never have what she longed for most.

She had asked him outright, and once again she had her answer. Once again Andrew had told her that love was the one thing he could not give her. A desperate hopelessness filled her, for if a man withholds his love, what is a woman to do? She moved almost mechanically through the house and went into her bedroom. Her mind was fragmented and a dull pain gnawed at her. A wild thought came: *I'll pack my things and leave—I'll never see him again. He doesn't need me!*

Then she fell across the bed and wept. The silence of the room was broken by her cries and sobs and finally she said softly, "I can't bear to live like this—but there's nothing for me to do."

END OF PART THREE

A New

1 7 3 9

Part
FOUR

1 7 4 1

Song

Nineteen

SARAH HEARS A SERMON

s Andrew Wakefield gazed around the dining-room table, his eyes came to rest on his sister-in-law, Lady Caroline Wakefield. He'd had grave reservations about attending the dinner for he knew, deep down in his heart, he had not forgotten how Caroline had treated him. Now, as he watched her laughing and talking to Major Ian Crenshaw, who sat across from her, he tried to push such thoughts away. *What's past is past,* he thought grimly. *A man must learn to set things aside and get on with life.* It was easy enough advice to give but not so easy to take. Andrew lowered his eyes to the table, a glum expression on his face.

But the rest of the guests seemed to be content. George and Caroline sat at the far end, well enough pleased with each other. Caroline had evidently made her adjustment into the Wakefield line with little trouble. George had already discovered to his chagrin that her tastes were rather expensive. He'd whispered to Andrew before the dinner, "It's a good thing you didn't marry Caroline. You'd never have been able to afford her style of living." George seemed to have no concept, at all, of Andrew's pain at losing Caroline, for never once had he alluded to his brother's attachment to the young woman who had become his bride.

The other guests included Sarah Lancaster and her parents, Sir Talbot and Lady Jane. The two were expensively attired, as always,

269

but there were rumors that Sir Talbot was in financial difficulty. These rumors spread quickly and had been attached to every nobleman, from the prince of Wales down to the latest knight who felt the touch of a blade on his shoulder. In many cases the rumors were true, for the nobility often had much land, but often it couldn't be sold or mortgaged to raise funds.

Andrew glanced at Major Crenshaw and back to Sarah, who sat on one side of him. *They're hoping to marry her off to Crenshaw,* Andrew thought. Crenshaw was the eldest son in a wealthy Welsh family. His father was aged and soon the major would resign from the army and take up his place—and a wealthy one it was.

The one figure who seemed out of place at the table was Bishop Alfred Crawley. Why he'd been invited Andrew couldn't understand. Perhaps so the two of them would have someone to talk to, being the only nontitled people at the dinner. The bishop, he saw, seemed to be enjoying himself. Despite his lean frame, he was a hearty eater and had worked his way with gusto through the seven courses that had been set before him.

Crawley raised his eyes when Major Crenshaw asked loudly, "What's all this going on in the church, my lord?" He took a long drink of the ale from the silver goblet, set it on the table, and demanded, "I mean all this business with John Wesley and those people of his."

"I suppose it's the sort of thing that happens in every structure," Crawley said mildly. He eyed the major, who was wearing a scarlet tunic that fit him like a glove. "There will always be those who are unhappy with authority. I suppose you find that's true enough in your profession."

"Well, sir," Crenshaw exclaimed, "we know how to deal with that sort in the army. Turn them over a barrel and beat them until they learn better sense—or have them shot if they keep on with their foolishness!"

Sarah Lancaster turned to stare at him. "I hardly think that would answer, Major. We can't have people shot because they disagree with our doctrine in church."

Crenshaw smiled. "Well enough you should think that, Sarah, but you can't run an army without discipline." His bright blue eyes settled on the bishop and he demanded, "I suppose you feel the same way, sir?"

Bishop Crawley picked up a cake that had been placed on a silver tray beside him and took a bite. Chewing on it thoughtfully, he nodded. "Naturally I am upset that some of our ministers have become enthusiasts, but the discipline, as you say, will be less severe than the death penalty."

Sir George Wakefield spoke up. "I understand this Wesley fellow has been blocked off in the churches. They won't have the fellow to preach for them. Is that by your orders, Bishop?"

"Each pastor must make that decision for himself. Mr. Wesley is still a member of the Church of England, as is his brother Charles. I'm hoping they will return to the flock."

"What about Mr. Whitefield? I suppose you've read what large crowds attend every time he preaches."

"He's an eloquent man and an able man. I have hope for Mr. Whitefield—more than I have for Mr. Wesley."

"Why is that, sir?" Dorcas asked. Sitting beside her husband, she'd said very little, but now at the mention of Whitefield she grew interested.

The bishop explained, "Mr. Whitefield, as he has told me, has firmly decided to remain within the Church of England. Mr. Wesley says the same but his societies are growing prodigiously." Bishop Crawley shook his head, a glum expression on his long, thin face. "They're spawning all over England— little groups of people. They are dangerously close to being illegal, for they are nonconformists, not licensed by the Church of England."

"You think they will unite and form their own church

under the leadership of Mr. Wesley?" Sir Talbot said, with a disapproving air. "The Church of England is good enough for our people!"

"I'm glad you should think so, Sir Talbot," Bishop Crawley answered instantly. His eyes rested on Andrew and it was to him he said, "You have had a great experience with Mr. Wesley. What is your feeling, Andrew?"

Andrew shifted uneasily. "I think Mr. Wesley is an honest man and a good man. But I think he needs to confine his activities to the Church of England."

"Well said!" Sir Talbot exclaimed. "I hear some of these fanatics are falling to the ground, barking like dogs. All sorts of things are going on at their meetings. Have you heard of this, Bishop?"

"It's common knowledge," Bishop Crawley said, shrugging, "and according to my reports it's much more common under Mr. Wesley than under Mr. Whitefield. Rampant emotionalism must be stopped."

The talk around the table went on for some time and finally the bishop brought up another matter. "I hear," the bishop said, "that Mr. Whitefield and Mr. Wesley are at odds with one another."

"I didn't know that, Bishop," Andrew said, with considerable surprise. "What is their problem?"

"It's a doctrinal matter. Whitefield, of course, is a Calvinist. He believes strongly in the doctrine of predestination."

"And what is that, if I may ask?" Lady Jane inquired curiously. "I'm not sure I understand it."

The bishop explained, "It lies back in the history of England, since the Reformation. The Calvinists put strong emphasis on Saint Paul's words about predestination: that God chooses what will happen to us. The doctrine of election is related: that God chooses certain ones to be saved."

"And what does Mr. Wesley believe?" Sarah asked with interest.

"He leans in the other direction: that whosoever, in what he calls free will, will come may be saved."

"And the two have fallen out about it?" Andrew inquired. "How did that come about?"

"As I understand it, Whitefield asked Wesley not to preach on free will to his people in Bristol. Wesley ignored his desires and not only preached on free will but also published a sermon on it. I understand it's caused quite a division in the ranks—some holding to Mr. Whitefield, some to Mr. Wesley. Perhaps this division will split them up and the whole movement will come to nothing," the bishop concluded. "At least I fervently hope so."

The conversation turned then to other matters and after dinner Sarah pulled Dorcas to one side. "Have you heard from your brother lately, Mrs. Wakefield?"

Dorcas was not surprised, for she knew Gareth had been writing Sarah frequently. Now she took in the tall, shapely woman, thinking, *How beautiful she is. She's rather spoiled but I think she has a good heart.*

"Why, yes. He's preaching constantly. He's been in Wales for some time but I'm expecting him home soon."

Sarah pursed her lips thoughtfully, then asked, "I suppose he'll do as your husband and get a church in London?"

"I'm not at all certain about that. You heard, of course, the talk of Mr. Whitefield and Mr. Wesley?"

"Yes, it's very interesting, but surely Gareth is not going in that direction?"

"I think he is, Miss Lancaster. He's spent considerable time with both Mr. Wesley and Mr. Whitefield and now he's preaching out-of-doors to large crowds. He writes that many are coming to know the Lord Jesus through his preaching."

Sarah seemed uncomfortable. "I'm sorry to hear it. The bishop is obviously opposed to such things. There won't be much future for Gareth, will there, unless he comes into the Church of England?"

"I don't think Gareth is interested in that."

Sarah's eyebrows lifted. "But a man must be interested in making a living."

"Ordinarily that's true," Dorcas admitted, "but Gareth has always been headstrong. When he throws himself into something it's never halfway."

"I've noticed that." Sarah smiled demurely and said, "He's bombarded me with letters. I had no idea he was so eloquent. I suppose that's his Welsh blood."

Dorcas said gently, "I know you may not care to hear this but it's the simple truth. He's very much in love with you, Miss Lancaster."

Sarah nervously moved her shoulders. "Well, he shouldn't be. You must tell him, as I've tried to do, that he would not find me suitable—not in the least. I'm too flighty a creature to be in the presence of a minister for long." She sighed and said, "What a shame!"

"Why is that?" Dorcas inquired.

"He's so handsome. He's the best-looking man I've ever seen. It seems a shame," Sarah added plaintively, "to waste such good looks on a man, especially on a preacher. I imagine the young women follow him around, constantly seeking his attention."

"He doesn't mention it," Dorcas said quietly. She felt a pang for Gareth, for this young woman was totally worldly. There was not an ounce of spirituality in her as far as Dorcas could tell and she determined to try to counsel him to turn his attentions another way.

The party broke up shortly after ten o'clock. Sarah was sequestered in a carriage with Major Crenshaw and as soon as they were under way, he suddenly put his arms around her and drew her close. He'd kissed her before and she'd allowed him to do so. He was a tremendously strong man and his embrace crushed her against him. His lips were demanding and there was a possessiveness in his embrace that frightened her.

When she drew back, Crenshaw said, "Sarah, you're playing games with me. When are you going to agree to marry me?"

"I'm not sure I love you, Ian."

"Well, I'm sure enough for both of us. I'll grow on you. You may not love me as much as you should now but after we're married I'll teach you to love me better." He kissed her again and as the carriage rolled along, Sarah suddenly thought of the kiss she'd received from Gareth Morgan. It had been gentle, tender . . . not like the major's kiss at all. And that realization troubled her greatly.

❦

The dinner had drained and disturbed Dorcas. After she and Andrew had arrived home, she'd gone to their room after their usual brief word of good-night. She dressed for bed, putting on a light cotton gown for the warm April weather, and for some time sat at her desk writing to Gareth. She spoke of Sarah Lancaster as tactfully as she could:

> Sarah Lancaster was at the dinner George gave tonight.
> Andrew and I were there. I had opportunity to speak to
> Miss Lancaster after the meal. I find her a most attractive
> young woman, as everyone does. However, Gareth, she
> seems very much attached to the things of this world.
> She has known great wealth all of her life and it was
> obvious her parents are pushing her into marriage with
> Major Crenshaw. As you know, he will come into a
> tremendously large estate on the death of his father—
> which will not be long, so I hear. Try to put her out of
> your thoughts, Gareth. She wouldn't be suitable for you.

I know you think you love her, and perhaps you do, but it would be a tragedy if you married her.

Dissatisfied with the letter, she put it aside and began to read. Over the next hour the house grew quiet and finally she went to bed. But sleep evaded her; her eyes simply wouldn't remain closed and she went over and over again the things she'd heard at dinner. Somehow she knew, in her heart, that John Wesley and George Whitefield were right and that Bishop Crawley and her husband were wrong.

The thought of Andrew reminded her of how strange her life had become. Her only problem at the rectory had been Mrs. Lesley and since she'd confronted the woman she'd ceased to be trouble. She knew Mrs. Lesley despised her but outwardly she was pleasant and that was all Dorcas could ask. She had formed a close relationship with Beth Buchanan, one that would have been closer except for the difference in their stations.

But Andrew—her heart smoldered as she thought of the fiasco her marriage was. *We are like two strangers. We live under the same roof, eat at the same table, but we're further apart now than we were on the day he walked into our cottage in Wales*. She remembered sadly the sweet times she and Andrew had had with Hope. "We were close then," she whispered. "Why can't we be close now?" She knew Andrew had been terribly scarred by Caroline Barksdale's rejection and her choice of George over him. Several times she'd tried to hint that such bitterness could only lead to spiritual problems but Andrew seemed blind to it. Again she remembered Sally Bradwell's advice to entice her husband and entertained the desperate thought, *Perhaps I should do that. . . .* But she knew that she would not. *He must love me for myself*.

At last she gave up trying to sleep. Getting out of bed, she tried to read and couldn't concentrate. Hoping a glass of warm milk would help, she moved to the chifforobe, removed one of the sheer dressing gowns Sally Bradwell had chosen for her wedding trip, and slipping it on over her gown, she put on her slippers and left the room.

The house was still as she went down the stairs. Not a sound broke the silence as she moved into the kitchen. Moonlight streamed in through the window and she didn't need to light a candle. Moving to the cabinet, she removed the heavy jug that contained fresh milk. She poured herself a glass, then replaced the jug.

After she drank the milk, she went to the door and stepped outside. The cool night breeze stirred the leaves of the trees that grew in the backyard of the rectory and there was a sweetness in the air that reminded her that spring was coming.

She stood absolutely still for a while, thinking, and then began to walk down the line of tile that wound around the section set off for a small garden. Once she stopped and plucked a flower, delicate and blue, and breathed its fragrance. Then she continued her walk.

She'd approached the house, intending to go in, when out of nowhere she heard a voice and felt a hand on her arm. "Who are you? What are you doing here?"

Fear raced through Dorcas and she cried out, "Don't—!"

Looking up then, in the moonlight, she sighed with relief when she saw the face of the man who held her. "I—I thought you were a burglar!"

Andrew held Dorcas's arm fast. The moonlight illuminated his face and he laughed shortly. "I thought the same about you. What are you doing down here this time of the night?"

"I couldn't sleep," she said. "I came down to get a glass of milk. It was warm in my room. What are you doing out here?"

Andrew shook his head. "The same for me. I guess I was disturbed by what I heard at the dinner tonight." He realized he was holding her arm and dropped his hands abruptly. "I'm sorry if I frightened you."

"You did, a little," she said, "but it's all right." She'd been frightened but now her sense of humor came to her aid. "We're a fine pair, aren't we, catching each other. If real highwaymen came, I suppose I'd run like a rabbit."

"So should I, I think," Andrew said and returned her smile, feeling a strange lightness in his heart at their shared sentiment. The garden was beginning to fill the summer air with the scent of roses. "I think I'll sit awhile. Better than lying awake staring at the ceiling." He hesitated, then said, "Will you join me, Dorcas?"

"Why—yes, I will."

The bench was so small that when Dorcas sat down beside him she could feel the touch of his arm on hers. She asked, "What did you think of what the bishop said?"

"I think Mr. Wesley and Mr. Whitefield are headed for trouble." He turned to her and said, "And Gareth, too. I know we've had our differences, Dorcas, but I've never forgotten what Aunt Hope asked. That I take care of you and Gareth as best I could." He looked down at his hands and shook his head sadly. "I've done a sorry job of it, I fear."

"No, that's not true." Dorcas put her good hand on Andrew's, squeezing it and saying earnestly, "You've done everything you could for Gareth . . . and for me, too."

Andrew turned to her. The quietness in the air somehow had moved into his spirit. As he looked down at Dorcas and saw the smooth contours of her face illuminated by the full moon's silver light, he realized that Dorcas was beautiful in her own way, although she sometimes had a stubborn spirit. She seemed to all but glow at this moment with a soft depth and a woman's fire that he'd never noticed before. Her features were relaxed and the curtain of reserve that normally fell over her was gone. He found her composure tremendously attractive for he had little of that himself. There was a fire in her that, Andrew realized, brought out the rich and headlong qualities of a spirit otherwise hidden behind a cool reserve. Suddenly he was swept with the unbearable desire to know she was not totally unhappy. "Are you miserable, Dorcas?" he whispered suddenly, thinking of how alone she must be.

"No, not at all. I only wish——" She broke off abruptly, lifting her face to his.

"You wish what?"

"I wish we could be closer, Andrew." Her voice was gentle and soft and, as though for the first time, Andrew realized the goodness and steadfastness of this young woman he'd wronged. He said quietly, "You're very lonely but so am I. A man needs someone to talk to." He wanted to say more—would have done so—but the cursed self-consciousness that plagued him filled him yet again. He'd never confessed this lack of self-sufficiency to anyone, thinking he was strong enough to stand alone. Now, as he looked down at his wife's face, vulnerable and bathed with the moonlight, he thought, *I wish I could tell her all the things that go on in my heart—how unhappy and miserable I am.*

Why not do so? a small voice from within him asked. And, his heart beating, he opened his mouth to try, when a voice broke into the silence. "Who's that? Who's out there?"

Both Andrew and Dorcas started and turned. A man stepped out from the corner of the house, holding a lantern high.

"Silas," Andrew said quickly, "it's just Mrs. Wakefield and myself."

Silas Wagner, the coachman and handyman, blinked owlishly at the pair. "Oh, beg your pardon, sir," he mumbled. "I heard voices and thought—well, beg your pardon, sir."

"It's all right, Silas, I understand. I appreciate your watchfulness."

"Well, good night, sir, and you, Mrs. Wakefield." The handyman disappeared but the moment was broken and Andrew drew himself up. "I suppose I'd better try and get some sleep. I have a busy day tomorrow."

Dorcas wanted to say something that would bring him back, that would restore the surprising closeness they had shared but a moment before. She'd seen a side of Andrew he'd not shown her since their marriage. There was a vulnerability in him and she longed to reach out to express her concern, but he left as if fleeing from her. As she stood in the garden awhile, then went up to her bed, she wondered if she'd missed a great opportunity to put her marriage together.

⁂

Rebecca Holden, an attractive young woman of nineteen, was Sarah Lancaster's closest friend and frequently spent weekends with Sarah. May had come and as the two walked down the streets of London, looking in shops, Rebecca said, "Let's stop and have a cup of tea. There's a nice restaurant around the corner."

"All right, Rebecca. Shopping is tiring, isn't it?" She followed Rebecca inside the restaurant and soon they were drinking steaming cups of fragrant tea.

Sarah cocked her head to one side as Rebecca said, "You told me so much about that young minister, the good-looking one."

"Oh, Gareth Morgan?"

"Yes. I'm curious. He still writes to you?"

"Yes, he does," Sarah said, smiling thoughtfully. "If he's as careful about the well-being of the flock as he is about writing letters, he's a wonder." She sipped her tea, then asked curiously, "Why are you asking about a minister?"

"I've heard so much about this revival and there's going to be preaching tomorrow afternoon out-of-doors. I've never heard preaching out-of-doors but I've heard a lot about Mr. Wesley. He may be speaking. Let's go, Sarah."

"Why, you've never gone to church in your life, Rebecca, when you weren't forced to go."

Rebecca laughed. "I know, but this is different. Let's make a holiday of it. I understand there's some interesting sights—people falling to the ground and screaming. It'll be fun."

Sarah was amused by her companion. She knew Rebecca Holden cared not one pin for religion in any form; the young woman was always looking for excitement. So at first she resisted, then finally agreed, saying, "I suppose I'm as bad as you are, Rebecca. I've heard a lot about these meetings. Bishop Crawley almost goes into fits when you mention them. All right, we'll go."

The next day the two of them left London in the Lancaster carriage. Sarah didn't actually lie to her father but left her destination for the day rather vague. Now, as they were helped into the carriage by Thomas, the driver, she paused and gave him a confidential smile. "You can keep a secret, can't you?"

"I trust I can, ma'am."

"Good, because you are going to have to keep our afternoon's activities a secret."

Thomas was somewhat apprehensive. "You're not going to a bullbaiting, I trust, Miss Lancaster?"

"Oh, no. Something much more cultured than that. We're going out to Moorfields to hear the Methodist preachers."

Surprised, Thomas commented, "I wouldn't think that would interest you, Miss Sarah. But I suppose it can't hurt. I hear there's quite some goings-on at those meetings. I'd like to hear 'em myself."

"Good—you know how to get there." Sarah got in the coach and leaned out saying, "Now, Thomas, if you see me showing any signs of throwing fits, just pick me up and carry me back to the coach." She laughed merrily as he winked at her, saying, "Yes, mum, I'll do that."

All the way to Moorfields the two girls talked excitedly about their outing. When the carriage stopped, Thomas jumped to the ground and opened the door. "I think you'll have to stand, ladies. There's no place to sit."

"That'll be fine, Thomas. You stay here and mind the horse. We'll be back when the service is over."

As the two moved away, they were the target of many eyes. Sarah wore an exquisite outfit, a rich burgundy dress, and Rebecca's was equally colorful—a light rose color. They stood out like bright butterflies amidst the soberly dressed crowd. Most of the congregation, they saw, were men, although some women were there— some even with children.

"Let's get closer," Rebecca urged. "Look, I think those are the preachers over there." She motioned to a rise of ground.

"Yes, I believe they are, but I'm not sure we want to attract attention."

Looking around, Rebecca laughed. "I think we already are. Not many of our class here today. Come on, Sarah, I want to get as close as we can."

Sarah allowed herself to be pulled along through the crowd, for Rebecca was determined. They squeezed through and finally stood on the verge of an open space. As soon as she stopped, Sarah gasped, "Oh my!"

Turning quickly, Rebecca said, "What's the matter, Sarah?"

"It's him. There. The black-haired one."

Rebecca wheeled and saw a tall, well-built young man with hair as black as a crow's wing. She whispered, "Is that him? Gareth Morgan?"

"Yes—I didn't think he'd be here. I thought he was in Wales," Sarah said. "What if he sees me?"

But Rebecca wasn't paying attention; she was examining the young minister, who was wearing a neat gray suit. "My, he *is* handsome! No wonder you thought about him so much!"

"Hush, Rebecca!" Sarah said nervously, for the other girl hadn't lowered her voice and several were smiling at her. "Let's get out of here."

"No!" Rebecca said, grasping Sarah's arm firmly. "I wouldn't miss this for anything—look, they're getting ready to start."

The service began very simply when someone started singing. Soon the air was filled with thousands of voices. Sarah didn't know the song but she was impressed with the fervency of the singing. There was nothing like this inside any church of her knowledge. The sounds seemed to swell and rise, filling earth and heaven, and she was moved by it.

After several hymns, Gareth Morgan stepped forward and began to speak. "We will pray before the gospel is preached," he said simply.

Sarah bowed her head but noticed that Rebecca was staring around, as if she were at a play of some kind. Sarah was embarrassed and angry at herself for coming. Earlier it had been a game to her but now she wished she'd resisted Rebecca's urging.

After the prayer was over, Gareth began to preach. His strong, clear voice carried well and there was an assurance in his manner that spoke of a much older, more experienced man. His dark eyes flashed and from time to time he'd lift his hands in a fervent gesture. The sermon itself was simple—so simple that Sarah understood it quite easily. He was preaching on the resurrection of Jesus Christ.

This was a subject she'd heard every Easter of her life. But there was a triumphant note in the preacher's voice and from all around she heard sighs and agreements, although silence reigned over the great congregation.

"I wonder when someone's going to fall down," Rebecca commented.

"Hush your mouth, Rebecca!" Sarah said fiercely and pinched the girl. "If you don't, I'll tear a plug out of you!"

Rebecca gave her a hurt look, then turned back to listen. "He's certainly dynamic, isn't he? Why, he could be a fine actor."

Sarah watched closely but saw no signs of people falling to the ground—which she had more or less feared. Then the sermon was over. After the prayer she saw Gareth coming straight toward her.

"Why, Miss Lancaster," Gareth said, a smile on his lips, "I'm so glad to see you—and is this your friend?"

"Yes, this is Miss Holden."

"I'm glad to see you, Miss Holden." Gareth smiled again at the young woman and asked, "Is this your first visit to one of our meetings?"

"Yes, it is," Rebecca said, "but it was so wonderful." She could no more help flirting than she could help breathing and stood there flattering the young minister for some time.

Finally Sarah said briefly, "We must go now." She turned to Gareth and said, "I've missed you. I thought you were in Wales."

"I just came back the day before yesterday. I'll be preaching now in the London area for some time. Perhaps I may call on you."

"Why—yes, that would be very nice." Sarah walked away, half pulling Rebecca after her. When they were back in the carriage and headed for London, Rebecca teased her unmercifully, "You've kept that good-looking man hidden but it's just as well."

Sarah looked at her. "What do you mean?"

"Why, that's the one man in London you couldn't have, Sarah."

For some reason this irritated Sarah Lancaster. "What do you mean I couldn't have him? He writes me all the time. He's done everything but propose."

"I don't believe it. He's too serious about religion. He wouldn't have a featherheaded thing like you or me."

Rebecca kept up with this line and finally Sarah was stung by her attitude. "I can see him all I want to! He'll come any time I ask him."

"Prove it!"

"I will!" Sarah said firmly. "I'll be one of his—what they call *seekers*. I'll ask him to come and instruct me in religion."

Rebecca giggled. "May I join in the class? I'm sure I need help as much as you do."

Both young women found the idea amusing. But Sarah liked Gareth and it was always interesting to have a good-looking man coming to call.

"I'll write him a note and tell him that two young ladies need instruction in the doctrines of the Bible."

"Be careful," Rebecca said, laughing, "he might make a preacher's wife out of you."

Leaning back against the carriage seat, Sarah Lancaster laughed too, finding the idea ridiculous. "No, he won't do that, but he'll make Ian jealous." Sarah actually looked forward to having Gareth come. It would annoy her parents, she knew, and her heart troubled her for a moment. *But I don't mean him any harm,* she said to herself. *Besides, it'll be good for him to spend time with me and Rebecca. . . .*

"ALL THE WORLD IS MY PARISH!"

At the root of the revival that swept England in the middle of the eighteenth century, two men stand out: George Whitefield, an enthusiastic twenty-three-year-old, and John Wesley, a calculating thirty-six-year-old. Whitefield's emotion and Wesley's logic formed the foundation of the movement. Since that first day in April 1739—which Wesley marked as one of the most important dates in his life—God worked mightily in England. Whitefield was the pioneer but Wesley donned the mantle and carried the gospel to those who had been, to a large extent, ignored.

Preaching in the fields stirred a tempest of opposition, for field preaching inevitably meant invading another man's parish because every acre in England was in a parish. Wesley had a general license to preach, as a fellow of Oxford College, but this implied the permission of the local minister and Wesley ignored this totally. He told a friend who objected to these proceedings:

> God in Scripture commands me, according to my power, to instruct the ignorant, reform the wicked, confirm the virtuous. Man forbids me to do this in another's parish; that is, in effect, not to do it at all;

saying that I have no parish of my own, nor probably ever shall, whom shall I hear, God or man? Suffer me now to tell you *my* principles in the matter. *I look upon all the world as a parish.*

From the moment John Wesley preached his first sermon in the open field, he never turned back. After his death, it was reckoned that he traveled more than a quarter of a million miles on horseback and preached more than forty thousand sermons—an average of about fifteen a week. He took no holidays, saying, "I'm not to consult my own ease, but the advancement of the kingdom of God." Little did even George Whitefield guess what God was setting afoot that April afternoon in Bristol in 1739. Considering John Wesley had always been a man of strict methodical habits, no one was surprised when he carried these principles into his life during the days after Whitefield left for America. His weekly plan emerged quickly, as was revealed by his journal:

> My ordinary employment in public, was now as follows: Every morning I read prayers and preach at Newgate. Every evening I expounded a portion of scripture at one or more of the societies. On Monday in the afternoon, I preached abroad near Bristol; on Tuesday at Bath, and Two Mile Hill alternately; on Wednesday at Baptist Mills; every other Thursday nears Pinnsford; every other Friday in another part of Kingswood; on Saturday in the afternoon, and Sunday morning, in the Bowling Green; on Sunday at eleven near Hanham Mount, at two at Clifton; and at five at Rose-Green. And hither to, as my days so hath my strength been.

The messages he preached were simple: basically, that the only way to heaven is to repent and to believe the gospel. He stressed the biblical truths he held so dear and was supported by the power of the Holy Spirit.

Soon the results of Wesley's labor began to appear; men and women were converted by the hundreds. Wesley saw them as sheep having no shepherd or a very feeble shepherd, for the Church of England, in his opinion, thought little of such poor lambs. As a result of this, he began to organize the people. Before Whitefield left Bristol, he suggested Wesley should write out orders for the "Bands," and soon the first little Band, consisting of three women, was founded. Their purpose was to meet together weekly in order to confess their faults to one another and to pray for each other. Others came, including four young men, although the two groups met separately. They were soon joined by others and subdivided into three Bands. Wesley felt that fellowship was all important to growth in the Christian life and crystallized his converts into a network of little cells. Other organizations or meetings soon came into existence. One of these was the "Society," which formed as a result of the people's desire to have Mr. Wesley address them on spiritual issues. This was inaugurated in London, and in Bristol the "Class Meeting" was formed. Those involved came together to pray and to help one another and soon Class Meetings were spawned all over England. One later historian said, "If it had not been for the Class Meeting, Methodism would have been a rope of sand."

Soon it became necessary to find accommodations and after seeking some advice, Wesley bought a piece of property in Bristol called "The New Room." He had no intention of setting up buildings in opposition to the Church of England. Apparently he couldn't see that, in some respects, he'd reached a parting of the way with that body and was advancing on a path that would lead to the formation of a totally new structure. He was busy with other things, including founding schools for unfortunate children—and these gave the first impulse to popular education in England.

John Wesley threw himself into the work of preaching the gospel in the open fields and then of gathering the fields that were ready for harvest, saving them. And all of England wondered at the growth of this new work called Methodism.

※

Dr. Joseph Butler was a celebrated philosopher and bishop of Bristol. He was eleven years older than Wesley, comparatively young for a bishop. Butler was concerned, as was every bishop in the Church of England, about the activities of John Wesley and sent for him to give account. They fell at once to disputing about justification by faith. The bishop contended that Wesley made God tyrannical. "If some people were justified without previous goodness, why were not all?" the bishop asked.

"Because, my lord, they resist his Spirit. They will not come to him. They cannot be saved because they have not faith."

"Sir, what do you mean by faith?" asked the bishop.

"By justifying faith, I mean a conviction wrought in man by the Holy Ghost that Christ hath loved him and given himself for him."

Wesley quoted Scripture after Scripture and finally the bishop said heatedly, "Mr. Wesley, I will deal plainly with you. I once thought Mr. Whitefield and you well-meaning men. But I can't think so now. For now I have heard more of you. Mr. Whitefield pretends to extraordinary revelations and gifts of the Holy Ghost. This is a horrid thing, sir. A very horrid thing!"

"My lord, for what Mr. Whitefield says, Mr. Whitefield, not I, is accountable. I, myself, pretend to no extraordinary revelations and gifts of the Holy Ghost."

"Ah, but I hear that people fall into fits in your Societies and that you pray over them."

"I do so, my lord, when any show by strong cries and tears that their souls are in deep anguish. I frequently pray to God to deliver them from it. And our prayers often answer to that hour."

"Very extraordinary! Well, I give you my advice. You have no business here. You are not commissioned to preach in this diocese."

"My lord, my business on earth is to do what good I can. At present I think I must do good here. Therefore, here I stay."

Wesley left the bishop's office and rushed at once back to London for he'd heard that the Fetter Lane Society was split by dissension. Some were following a French prophetess; some were leaning toward Moravian customs, which did not sit easily in the Church of England. Wesley tried to pour oil on troubled waters but the dissension was deep. They were mostly Whitefield's converts and Wesley sensed their loyalty to the man.

On the next Sunday, Wesley preached in the fields near London at Moorfields. In the crowd was Grace Murray, an unhappy woman who'd lost her child and husband at sea. When one of her neighbors had spoken of a comfort received from listening to John Wesley speak, she rose and set out for Moorfields. When Mr. Wesley stood up, she fixed her eyes on him and had a sudden inexpressible feeling that he was sent from God to heal her spirit. He preached on, "Except a man be born again, he cannot see the kingdom of God." She was soundly converted on the spot.

She didn't speak to Wesley and neither of them could foresee that the future would bind them together in the most solemn of all ties on earth.

The Evangelical revival was coalescing—spreading widely over the nation; Wesley made two preaching tours in Wales, where there was a great awakening under Howell Harris.

During this period numerous pamphlets were written to condemn or defend the Methodists, and violence began. Twice that year in London, Wesley was surrounded by howling ruffians as he got down from a coach to enter his house. He calmly faced them and preached the gospel to them until they listened quietly. In Bristol, on April 1, a mob came to disrupt the service at the New Room. The streets, court, and alleyways were filled with people's fierce shouts and curses. The mayor sent an order that they should disperse but they ignored him. At length the mayor sent officers that took the ringleaders into custody.

Shortly after this explosion of violence, internal disputes threatened to destroy what violence could not. A Moravian named Philip Molther had come to London. He'd visited the Fetter Lane Society and had spread the seeds of false doctrine among the people there. Molther had persuaded the people that if faith was not strong it was not faith at all. He also taught that those who lacked faith must not receive the sacrament or go to church but be "still." What this stillness controversy advocated was that people should do absolutely nothing at all but simply wait. Wesley did his best to bring order to this group. But on July 20, 1740, he went to Fetter Lane and after begging and warning the people, found them adamant. He said, "I believe these assertions flatly contradictory to the Word of God. You that are of the same judgment, follow me." He walked out without another word. Only eighteen people followed him and the next Wednesday the little company met in another place. Fetter Lane turned Moravian and later would be formally constituted as the United Brethren.

Added to this, during 1740 letters passed across the Atlantic between Wesley and Whitefield concerning their differences over predestination. The distance between the two men made matters worse, for both of them listened unadvisedly to gossip that ran rampant. Whitefield was fully engaged in the whirlwind preaching to New England, which more than any other factor, brought about the Great Awakening.

Wesley was in England, doing all that lay in his power to spread the gospel. The differences that separated the two men should never have caused a division, but sadly, they did.

England was shaken by the Spirit of God as John Wesley preached the gospel. America likewise was shaken as George Whitefield traveled incessantly day and night, proclaiming the riches of Christ. These two men and two nations were given the bounty from God of seeing how mighty and powerful the gospel of Jesus Christ is when simply proclaimed. Seeds were sown during these early years that would bring forth fruit for both nations in the centuries to come.

Twenty-One

"I NEED YOU, DORCAS—!"

O ld soldiers who have experienced the fiery trial of battle are agreed that one type of wound is common. During the battle, when bullets are flying and shot and shell fragments fill the air, some take effect immediately. Men take a bullet in the brain or in the heart and are killed instantly. They fall to the ground, motionless, assuming that strange eloquence of the dead, and speak their mystery to those who come to gather the grim harvest.

Another type of wound is that which is so slight it's not even to be noticed—a slight scratch on the cheek, scarcely showing blood; a bruise in the side; a fingertip sliced by a flying steel fragment. These, in the heat of battle, are ignored and not even cared for.

A third type of wound, however, is fairly uncommon. It consists of a soldier who is hit in the body by a bullet or steel fragment and is seriously wounded. In the frenzy of battle, however, he presses forward, shouting, firing his weapon, making a bayonet charge as though nothing had happened. But something has happened and sooner or later the terrible wound will bleed, perhaps internally. His fellow soldiers may not even know their friend has been shot. On he goes, fighting even more violently, urging others on into the fray—but all the time his precious lifeblood is seeping from the secret wound. Of course, there's only one end to this. No matter how fervent his desire to go on with the battle, he cannot overcome the wound that has touched his very life. Oftentimes such men stop in the midst of combat and look around, astonished, then down at their body where they discern for the first time what has happened to them. Then they suddenly lose all strength and fall to the ground, helplessly ruined by the bullet of which they weren't even aware.

Something like the wound of the third soldier had happened to Andrew Wakefield. For months he'd functioned as the rector of Redeemer Church. Those who sat and listened to his sermons were impressed by his zeal and his earnestness. Throughout the city he'd become a familiar figure who visited the sick and dealt out charity to the poor. There seemed to be no end to the energy he expended and Bishop Alfred Crawley had said proudly, "We need more young men who give themselves to the work like Andrew Wakefield."

But if Andrew had achieved a measure of success through sheer effort, there were times when he collapsed inwardly. At night he lay in the silence of his room, weary to the bone and at times sick of the paltry affairs people brought to him, clamoring for his attention. He felt drained, like a man on a treadmill. He'd seen one of these affairs at a prison: a huge treadmill where felons were, early in the morning, chained and made to walk on the large paddles. Hour after hour passed until their weary legs trembled, but they couldn't stop or they'd be dragged down by the paddle wheel.

There was no known cure for depression—indeed it was not recognized as a possibility for a rector of a large London church. But almost every moment seemed to consume Andrew with its incessant calls for duty. At night he'd lie awake trembling, dreading the morning, when he must get up and begin the round again. This was not what he'd pictured when he'd given his life to God!

There was a weariness in him that stretched him thin. The things he'd trusted to give him strength, the Bible and prayer, were now dry, tasteless duties. He listened to the stories of how godly men would pray all night with great joy—but this was not for him.

Andrew began to turn inward and became more and more disheartened, almost frightened at the life he now had. He was continually troubled by his relationship with his wife. His plan had failed utterly and miserably. He could not quell the longings, physical or emotional, that he felt for his wife—yet he would not give in to them. And so he stayed there, in a place of oblivion, neither giving nor receiving, watching all that he cared about decay. His marital life was a daily disaster. It was almost impossible for him to face Dorcas and she, too, seemed weary of the charade they presented to the world.

Is there another marriage under heaven as bitter and tasteless as the one I so foolishly put myself into? he thought one night as he lay awake. He had sought sleep and it had not come, so he went back over and over his life, wondering, *Where did I go wrong?* He thought of his Aunt Hope, of the joy and hope and faith that had been hers, and wished desperately she was alive so that he could lay his troubled spirit before her. He thought of Dorcas and her calmness, aware that he'd failed her miserably.

When dawn came, it was feeble and gray in the east. He arose and dressed, moving slowly, then knelt beside his bed and tried to pray. He said the prescribed words, the ritual having become almost hateful to him, and concluded bitterly, "God forgive me for my cold heart—but it's the only heart I have." He almost blamed God and the unspoken charge was, *God, I have given everything I have to you—even my life—but where* are *you? Why don't I know the joy and peace George Whitefield, John Wesley, and my Aunt Hope showed so clearly? Where is the joy in this life, God?*

He left the house early and spent the day among his parishioners. He'd learned to conceal his heart from people, keeping it locked carefully away. While his face was often touched with a smile, his heart was bitter and filled with a grim despair.

If Andrew hid his heart from his parishioners, he didn't succeed in doing so with Dorcas. She was very much aware that he was suffering inwardly but felt helpless to do anything about it. She herself had been given a peace from God and although she wasn't happy, still she had faith that somehow, someday, things would change.

She threw herself into her work with the poor and spent much time with Beth Buchanan, experimenting on new recipes in the kitchen.

She had had the coachman build a small shed for chickens and had taken great pleasure in raising them for the table. One bright sunshiny morning she came out to examine her small flock. She'd been raising three of them on crushed raisins, white bread crumbs, and milk, for she'd been assured this would produce a fowl delicious beyond compare. Examining the three, she made her decision and gave instruction for the hen to be dressed. All day she and Beth worked on a meal she hoped would please Andrew. The two of them had come upon a recipe in an old book, and with a great deal of laughter they stuffed the body of the hen with bread crumbs, mincemeat, herbs, and spices, including chestnut stuffing made from minced bacon and the bird's liver.

Beth laughed aloud at their concoction. "There never has been such a bird, so help me! I hope Mr. Wakefield likes it."

"We better have something else in case he doesn't. What about fish?" Dorcas asked.

The two of them experimented again, this time with a fish pie made from sturgeon. It was baked in an open dish after being covered with a protective layer of bread crumbs and dotted with butter. Dorcas spent most of the afternoon baking red gingerbread. Carefully she constructed it, flavoring it with cinnamon, aniseed, and ginger. She darkened it with licorice and a little red wine, then stirred the mixture together and rolled it thin. She baked it carefully and finally put it out to dry in a cool oven.

"Well, mistress," Beth said, looking over the food they'd worked on most of the day, "if Mr. Wakefield doesn't like this, there's no hope for him."

"Oh, I think he'll like it," Dorcas said, smiling. "You're a wonderful cook, Beth. I've learned so much from you."

Beth Buchanan flushed at the praise; then, as the young woman left the kitchen, she shook her head. "If that preacher doesn't like this supper, I'll dump it over his silly head!" she vowed sternly.

Andrew came down to supper but was so depressed that he didn't see the excited look on Dorcas's face. Dish after dish was put in front of him and he barely tasted them. His mind was wandering and he had no life in him so the two went through a silent meal.

Dorcas was terribly disappointed. *He doesn't care what he eats,* she said to herself. *I might as well put straw in front of him.*

The meal was almost finished and Andrew had eaten practically nothing. Lilly Jarvis, the mousy young maid, came in bearing a pot of fresh tea. She poured it into Andrew's porcelain cup and then, with an awkward gesture, knocked the cup over.

"Oh my—I'm so sorry, sir!"

The hot liquid splashed over Andrew's hand, burning him severely. He leaped to his feet, anger bursting forth like water over a dam. "You clumsy girl," he shouted, "can't you do anything right?"

He threw his napkin down on the table and rushed out of the room, his face pale with anger.

Dorcas at once got up and went to the maid. "There now," she said, "Mr. Wakefield is just upset. Don't let it trouble you, Lilly."

"I didn't mean it," she said, weeping. "He didn't have to be so mean."

Dorcas spent some time with the girl, then wearily sat back down in her chair.

When Lilly went back to the kitchen, Beth Buchanan asked her why she was crying.

"It's that Mr. Wakefield! I spilled his tea but he shouted at me awfully!"

"Never mind, Lilly," Beth said between clenched teeth. She continued cleaning up the kitchen and muttered, "I'd like to shove him in the oven and roast him!" The river never ran colder than the anger in her eyes and later, when she tried to talk to Dorcas, it was all she could do not to express this anger.

Dorcas wanted to accept the sympathy she knew would come from the cook but she knew she must not. She spoke a few words of commendation about the meal and said no more.

Andrew kept to his room that night and Dorcas went to bed filled with despair. She put on a simple, white cotton shift, fixed her hair, and then climbed into bed.

For a long time she lay awake thinking about how miserable her life was. *I was happier back in Wales when we were hungry, Gareth and I,* she thought suddenly. Then she shook her head, almost fiercely. *I'm sorry God, I don't mean to complain. Thank you for all the good things that have come into my life.*

***

At first it was only a small sound, so faint it barely disturbed her sleep, but then it grew louder and Dorcas awakened suddenly, a streak of fear running through her. The house was usually so silent and now she knew it was in the early hours of morning, not long past midnight.

"What is it?" she whispered. "It sounds like someone crying."

She couldn't imagine who it was but when the sound came again she got out of bed instantly. Picking up the sheer robe she almost never wore, she slipped into it and moved toward the door. Opening it, she hesitated for a moment. *Could it be someone in the house, a robber perhaps?*

For a moment the air was very still—and then it came again. This time there was no mistaking the sound; someone was crying out!

Slipping out into the hall, she moved toward the origin of the sound and found herself standing in front of Andrew's bedroom door. Then she heard the sound clearly; Andrew was crying out in a strange fashion. Cautiously Dorcas opened the door and whispered, "Andrew?" There was no sound for a moment, then she heard his voice mumbling incomprehensibly. Stepping inside, she held the candle high and saw that Andrew was in bed, thrashing around wildly. She heard the words, "Can't stand it—help! Where are you, Dorcas—?"

Dorcas put the candle she'd brought on the table beside the window where it cast its yellow gleams over the room. She hesitated for a moment but then he grew more violent. He was throwing himself around the bed, his voice rising in a crescendo of sound.

Dorcas at once made up her mind. Going to him, she reached out and grabbed his shoulders. "Andrew—Andrew, wake up! You're having a nightmare!"

He reached out and grabbed her, calling out wildly, and she continued to say, "Andrew, wake up!" Suddenly his eyes opened. He looked distraught, his face twisted with fear.

"What—what is it?"

"Andrew, you're having a nightmare. Are you all right?"

He sat up and looked around wildly. "I—I don't know."

There was something so vulnerable in his face that Dorcas was moved with great compassion. She sat down on the bed and brushed the hair back from his forehead. "You're all right, my dear. It was just a bad dream. Don't be upset."

The gentleness of her words and the stark fear of his dreadful nightmare did something to Andrew. To his horror, tears began to roll down his face. He tried to hold them back but he couldn't. All of the doubts, bitterness, and disappointment of the past months suddenly seemed unendurable. He stared at her face and managed to say, "Dorcas—!"

She reached out and put her arms around him. He came to her then and collapsed. Sobs began to wrack his body and she held him tenderly, murmuring endearments to him. She knew that something inside him had broken.

As for Andrew, he'd never endured such a time as this; he'd always been able to control himself. But the gates were down and he wept uncontrollably. He held Dorcas fiercely, crushing her in the midst of his fear and of his release.

Finally the sobs ceased, but still he held to her. Then something began to change. As he grew calmer and the emotional storm passed, he became aware of her softness and warmth. The sweetness of the scent she wore was intoxicating and her hair was down her back like a silken cloak. He leaned back, meeting her gaze, too well aware that he'd kept himself from her for weeks and months—but he found no condemnation in her gaze. Indeed, there was a tender willingness in her eyes as he stared at her.

Silence filled the room as she wondered at this man she'd married. She was filled with pity and compassion—and the love she'd felt for him for a long time.

"Dorcas—" he whispered her name, then broke off.

"Yes, what is it, Andrew?"

The words came haltingly and slowly. "I—I *need* you, Dorcas!"

At the words, a great joy rose in her and she whispered, "I'm here for you, my dear."

Andrew's arms tightened around her and she felt his lips seeking hers. As he pulled her even closer into his arms she gave herself to the joy of knowing she was, at long last, a woman desired by the man she loved . . . !

⁂

Sunshine came through the window and fell on the face of the sleeping woman. She lay there quietly, her hair spread out underneath her like a fan. There was a peace and a relaxation on her features. The sunlight grew stronger and she stretched in a catlike motion, her hands over her head until they touched the oak of the bed frame.

Then suddenly she gasped and her eyes flew open. She sat up and looked around the room. Her eyes took in the rumpled, empty bed. "Andrew—" she said softly, her hand touching her cheek. She thought of his embraces and kisses and her cheeks grew warm. For a time she sat there trying to put it all together and then she got up and opened the door. No one was in the hall so she hurried quickly to her own room and dressed. Her hands trembled as she thought of how she'd given herself to Andrew without reservation. She'd felt her need of him more than she thought a woman might and he'd responded.

"He does love me," she whispered. "He must. He couldn't have been so caring and tender unless he loved me."

She went downstairs after dressing and asked casually, "Is Mr. Wakefield having breakfast?"

"Why, no. He's already gone," Mrs. Lesley said in some surprise. "He ate an early breakfast and left."

"Thank you, Mrs. Lesley."

All day long Dorcas wondered about Andrew's leaving her without a word. *He shouldn't be embarrassed,* she thought. *At last we're really husband and wife.*

But when Andrew came home that afternoon, there was an odd, tense expression on his face. She went to him at once but her smile died as their gazes met.

"Hello, Dorcas," he said, the old, familiar strained tones in his voice.

They were alone in the foyer and Dorcas felt a sudden apprehension. "Andrew, about last night—"

He held up his hand at once. "I—took advantage of you, Dorcas. It won't happen again."

The world suddenly seemed to end for Dorcas. The joy that had been hers drained away, leaving her empty. She couldn't know what was in his heart but she saw he was somehow ashamed. "What are you ashamed of, Andrew?" she demanded. She reached out and took his arm angrily. "Is it ashamed of being a man, you are? I'm your *wife*, Andrew—it's right that you should love me—and that I should love you."

But Andrew was locked in some sort of emotional prison and he dropped his eyes, unable to meet those of Dorcas. He had found her love complete and whole, but still there was some sort of blockage in his spirit and he could only whisper, "I—I'm sorry—" Then he turned and stumbled away blindly.

Dorcas watched him go and her heart cried out. She'd been so certain that now they could love each other. Her touch had awakened him and she was aware she'd stirred him as a woman can stir a man!

But she also knew something in Andrew's heart and spirit was warped and twisted. Dorcas had seen the black agony in his eyes and knew he was a haunted man. She moved away slowly, despair crushing her. "God—help him! Help him become a man," she prayed, her voice thin and worn with pain.

Twenty - Two

A DIFFERENT NEW YEAR FOR ANDREW

"There—that ought to warm you well, Mrs. Wakefield."

Silas had dropped two heavy logs into the fireplace and stood watching with satisfaction as sparks swirled madly upward, disappearing into the cavernous heights of the chimney. He turned and nodded. "I kept some dry wood back for you, ma'am. That ought to do for a while."

"Thank you, Silas," Dorcas said, smiling. She watched as the tall coachman disappeared, then turned back toward the fire. The logs caught quickly and the crackling made a pleasant sound in the stillness of her room. She watched as the yellow flames licked greedily around the fresh fuel—almost like a hungry beast devouring a fresh meal. The amber coals threw off waves of heat and her face grew so warm that she pushed her chair back slightly and removed the woolen coverlet she'd drawn over her lap. The room was so large that the fireplace could heat only half of it so she had her choice of being too warm or too cold.

Dorcas rose from her chair and moved over to the window, which was composed of triangles of glass, leaded in. Now as she stood there, the reflection of the red and yellow flames was repeated in each triangle. Stepping closer she looked outside, studying the bare December sky listlessly. The heavens were slate gray, without a single cloud. The smoke from a thousand fireplaces

305

ascended, forming a canopy over London, and joined the fog to make an atmosphere like thin soup. It was depressing and Dorcas longed for the fresh greenness of spring—for trees and white blossoms and warm summer rains. She thought of the glorious springs in her native Wales and for a moment was swept with a great longing to see the scenes of her homeland again.

Soon, however, she grew cold, for the wintry wind sought every crevice of the house. She heard the whistling as it moved across the roof, almost like a wild beast, seeking entrance. She shivered, went back to the fireplace to get the coverlet, put it around her shoulders, then moved back to the window. She longed for the out-of-doors since she'd been indoors for more than two weeks with the damp, foul weather. First the ground had been soaked with a sullen rain and then a freeze had come with bitterly icy temperatures, dropping during the nights and scarcely leaving during the days.

Dorcas watched the streets, which were almost deserted; ordinarily they would have been busy. A single dray came down the streets, pulled by two miserable-looking shire horses. The poor animals seemed to be freezing with the cold and the driver sat bundled up from head to foot, apparently wearing every garment he had. A wool stocking cap was pulled down over his ears and a muffler wound around the lower part of his face so that only his eyes were visible. As Dorcas watched, he slapped the reins on the horses' backs and she assumed he was urging them on, but no sound came from the street below.

Finally she grew weary of watching, threw the coverlet down, and went downstairs. As she walked down the staircase, the front door closed and she saw that Andrew had entered. As he took off his hat and coat and hung them on the coatrack, he turned suddenly and his eyes met hers.

He acts almost ashamed to see me, Dorcas thought. It had been that way for months now. Their relationship had deteriorated further, something she'd once thought impossible. Andrew rose early and left the house, often staying away until past bedtime. She'd heard him tell the servants there was so much work to be done that he had to be busy—but she knew his real purpose was simply to flee the house.

Keeping her face emotionless, she said, "You're home early, Andrew."

"Yes, I am," he said, nodding slightly. "The weather's so bad I thought I'd come in before it got worse."

"Would you care for some hot tea—and I think Cook has made some tea cake you might like."

Hesitating for a moment, Andrew seemed about to refuse, then said quietly, "That would be very nice."

"Go into the parlor. I'll bring it there."

"Very well."

The fire was blazing in the grate of the parlor and Andrew put his hands over it, waiting for the warmth to thaw out his numb fingers. He flexed them and tried to put aside the cares of the church duties he'd pursued since early morning. He'd lost weight the past few months and there was a hollowness in his cheeks that made him look older. He leaned over and put his arm on the fireplace, then leaned his forehead against it. The heat waves wafted upward and he closed his eyes, soaking up the warmth. He was so tired that at moments like this, when he paused, he almost dozed off. So he was startled when he heard Dorcas say, "Here, come and enjoy your tea."

Andrew jerked his head away from his arm and walked over to where she sat. An elaborate table sat before her opposite another overstuffed chair and he took his seat and watched while she poured the tea. She put in the sugar and cream as he liked, then took a snowy white napkin off the silver tray. "These are very good. Beth always makes fine pastries."

"Yes, she does." Andrew picked up one of the cakes and bit into it. "Very good," he said quietly. He tasted the tea, then leaned back in the chair. "Have you been busy today?"

"No, just sewing a little." Dorcas examined his face and said, "You look tired. You're working too hard."

"There's a great deal to do." He began to tell her some of the minute details of his day. She always seemed interested to hear them although he himself was weary of the details of church administration. When he'd first come, over a year and a half ago, he'd been excited about every detail. Now it had become wearisome and he gestured impatiently with his hands and frowned. "It's nothing very important; it just takes so many hours to keep a church running, it seems."

"I wish I could help you more."

Surprised, Andrew looked up. "Why, that's not your job, Dorcas. Keeping the rectory is your responsibility and you do a fine job of it."

This praise caused her cheeks to warm slightly since he paid her few compliments. Now she dropped her head for a moment.

Looking at her closely, he asked, "Have you felt any better?"

"I'm very well."

Andrew's eyes narrowed. "You haven't been well for several weeks now. We better have Dr. Brown in."

"No need of that. I'm all right, just a cold and, perhaps, the grippe." It was true she'd been ill. But she was such a healthy young woman that she felt somehow that sickness was a weakness in which strong people need not indulge. "It's probably something that's going around. I'll get over it."

"As you say, but it wouldn't hurt to have Dr. Brown stop in." He examined her a little closer, noticing a strain in her face. He wanted to inquire further but he said instead, "You're not worried about Gareth, are you?"

"No, he seems to be doing very well." Gareth had been back in Wales for a short visit with several of the leaders there. She'd been pleased to receive cheerful letters from him twice, in which he described his work. "He'll be coming here for Christmas, if that's all right."

"Certainly—certainly!"

Dorcas looked down at the fine porcelain cup in her hand. It was decorated with tiny cobalt-blue birds that fluttered around the edges. She studied it carefully, thinking how delicate and pretty it was. "Back in Wales," she said, holding up the cup, "if we had a cup like this, we would have thought ourselves rich indeed. We had two cups that didn't match," she said, her voice low and quiet. Her eyes grew warm as she spoke of those days. "Mine was an off-white. It had a chip in the side, right where the lips meet, so I had to hold it with my left hand to avoid getting cut. Gareth's was dark blue and it wasn't chipped. But it was an awkward, ungainly thing, handmade, I think, by someone not very good at such things."

"You think of those days often, Dorcas?"

"Sometimes—but they were hard and we tend to forget the hard things and remember the good things."

"I think that's true," he said quietly. He leaned back in his chair, the weariness in his body draining him of strength. "I can remember so many, but on the other hand, I remember many of the difficulties." He looked at her and said, "I suppose that's one difference between you and me. You remember good things—and I the bad things."

Dorcas looked up at him quickly. They hadn't talked like this over a dozen times in the past months. A faint hope grew in her that somehow things would change. As he slumped in his chair, holding the cup in one hand and staring across the room into the flickering flames that cast their shadows on his face, she thought, *He's a handsome man but that isn't what draws me. There's something good in his face, something appealing.* She studied his neat features, admiring the broad forehead, the small ears, the firm mouth, and a short English nose. He had a pronounced chin, giving him a stubborn look. The hands that held the teacup were long and strong. At that moment he glanced up and caught her examining him. She grew flustered. "I—I will look forward to our second Christmas, Andrew."

"I remember last Christmas," he said. "We hadn't been here long, only about six months. It was a good time, wasn't it?"

"Yes, it was."

The two sat there for some time and silence fell between them. Dorcas desperately wished to continue the conversation but, as always, the wall between them seemed high and finally Andrew rose wearily. "I'll go get ready for supper. I think I'll work in the study afterward." He left the room and climbed the stairs, noting their steepness. When he was inside his room and had closed the door, he suddenly saw the room as plain and bare, with no mark of his personality on it. There were no pictures, no mementos, just stark furniture: a bed, a chest, a washstand, a chifforobe, nothing more. Somehow he was filled with disgust at himself, that he could live in a room like this alone and make no more impact on it. *A man ought to leave some mark,* he thought, *even on the room he lives in. This looks like a museum, not a place where a man lives.*

With a flash he thought of the last time he and Dorcas had been together and he stood stock-still at the memory. *I gave in to weakness,* he thought, still ashamed of his actions. But despite himself, the memory of her face and how he'd been stirred by her that night washed back over him and he longed for a different kind of life.

"I can't be anything but what I am!" he said aloud. His voice shook the silence from the room and almost violently he began changing clothes, dreading the ordeal of supper and the effort of making conversation. He knew his life was abnormal and wished desperately to change it but he had no power or knowledge to do so.

"Maybe Christmas will be better," he whispered. But he knew in his heart that it wouldn't be.

A week before Christmas Day the snow began to fall. Dorcas stood outside in the garden now occupied by faint brown ghosts of the summer flowers. She was caught off guard when something—a tiny, burning sensation—stung her lower lip, making her flinch. Looking up, she saw tiny dots of glittering particles drifting down. They touched her face like fiery fingers. Closing her eyes, she allowed them to fall on her for a time, then opened her eyes and searched the skies. "There's snow up there," she said, and sure enough, within a few minutes, the diamond points were formed into tiny flakes. They drifted down softly, like white feathers, and she drew her cloak about her and watched as the ground before her was magically transformed. What had been brown and dark and dreary was now striped with pale lines that widened as the snow continued to fall. Then, as the flakes grew larger, a white carpet was laid softly, silently, over the dead earth, making it look immaculate. The carpet followed every bump, every broken stalk at first, so it looked like a body under a white coverlet with bulges and lumps.

Still she stood there. There was something about the quietness of snow falling that seemed to mute all sound. And the flakes, as they grew larger, rounded off the cornices of the house, breaking their sharp projections. The trees assumed rounded shapes, their bare limbs softly modified by their ermine overcoats.

She was almost hypnotized by the snow as it fell and coated the yard, the landscape, the houses, the trees, the grass. Her face was numb, as were her fingers, but she watched until she heard a shout and the mad barking of a dog. Jerking out of her reverie, she headed toward the commotion, which seemed to be coming from the backyard.

As she turned the corner she saw Silas and Blackie, the dog, standing at the foot of an apple tree. Blackie was yelping frantically and leaping at the trunk, while Silas yelled, "Get down out of there!"

Looking up, Dorcas saw, in the crotch of the tree, a hissing, spitting, calico cat with enormous green eyes.

"Don't do that, Silas!" Dorcas said quickly. "Get away, Blackie!" she commanded and when the dog didn't obey, she walked forward and pushed him away with her shoe. "Get away, I said!"

Silas stared at her in consternation. "Ma'am, we don't need no cats around here and if I ain't mistook, that one's got kittens coming."

The coachman's words caught at Dorcas. She stared up at the cat for one moment, then said, "Get the ladder, Silas. And take that dog away!"

"But, mum—"

"Get the ladder, I said!"

"Yes, mum." Clearly irritated, Silas called the dog and stalked away indignantly, Blackie following obediently. Silas came back alone, carrying a short ladder, and at Dorcas's command laid it against the tree. "You'd better not fool with that varmint," he said. "She's liable to scratch you. She's a wild cat."

But Dorcas ignored him and carefully climbed up several rungs of the ladder. The cat's green eyes fastened on her strangely. "Come now, let's have none of this." Reaching up her hands, she paused and waited. She didn't hurry, for she knew the cat was frightened. She kept her position there, speaking softly, and finally climbed up two more rungs so that she was within arm's reach of the animal. Keeping her voice low and gentle, she crooned, "Come on now, there's the girl. Would you like some nice milk and to lie down in front of a nice fire? Of course you would."

Tentatively the animal crouched and blinked as Dorcas ran

her hand over the soft, feline head. The animal seemed to relax and Dorcas slowly reached out and put her hands under the cat's front legs. Carefully she lifted the cat and rested her on her shoulder. Holding to her with her bad hand, she descended the ladder.

"I'm telling you, ma'am, she's going to have kittens. We don't need a bunch of them! I'll just have to take them down to the creek and drown them," Silas protested.

"I want you to make a box and bring it up to my room, Silas. It will be the bed for my new friend." She held his eyes for a moment, expecting him to argue, but her gaze was so unyielding that he merely turned away muttering about worthless cats and disappeared around the corner of the house.

Dorcas walked to the back door, stroking the cat, who was trembling with cold, her back wet with snow. Dorcas could feel her full belly and she smiled. "Being a mother, are you, girl? Well, we'll see about that."

Entering the kitchen, she found Beth cutting up a chicken. "What's this?" Beth said abruptly, staring at the young woman and the cat.

"This is Lady Mary," Dorcas announced, her eyes glowing. "Isn't she a beauty?"

Beth came forward at once and stroked the cat's head gently. "Well, she is that. Lady Mary, indeed! What a name for a cat!"

"I'm going to keep her in my room until she has her kittens," Dorcas announced. "Silas is making her a box. Would you find an old blanket, Beth, so I could make some bedding for her?"

She spent the rest of the day getting Lady Mary in place. By the time she had fixed the bed out of a warm woolen blanket and had seen to it that Lady Mary was fed, she was pleased with herself. "You'll be company for me," she said, watching as the cat walked around examining every inch of her new domain. Finally, the cat came back to where Dorcas was sitting in a chair before the fire. With a *thripping* sound she leaped up suddenly, turned around three times, and then settled herself down in Dorcas's lap. Dorcas stroked the silky fur, a pleased smile on her face. "We'll have a good time, you and I," she whispered, then sat dreaming by the fire.

The house had been gaily decorated, with Dorcas instructing the servants, although she didn't feel well enough to do the work herself. Holly and ivy had been bought from a peddler who cried his wares from the street. Silas had stripped the apple trees of their leafy branches, and now greenery decorated almost every room. The windowsills were bowered with bay leaves, and rosettes made of dyed rags were strung down the hall. Some of the windows had been painted crimson, ochre, and vivid green so that during the day colored light fell in and in the night colored light shown out. Oranges and lemons were tied together in bunches and some crimson cloth was unearthed by Mrs. Lesley, who, strangely enough, gave herself almost cheerfully to the festivities.

Gareth arrived two days before Christmas and he and Dorcas had a fine time. He saw almost at once that she was ill and on his first opportunity asked, "What's the matter? You don't look well."

"I'm all right," she said smiling, "just a cold and perhaps bronchitis."

"Have you tried licorice? That's what we always used at home."

"No, but I will. Come, let's not talk about my ailments. Tell me about home."

As the two sat beside the fire in her room, Dorcas curled up with Lady Mary on her lap and listened as Gareth spoke of former neighbors. He gave her the little bits of gossip, some of it harmless and rather funny, some more tragic.

"What about Rhys Ellis. Did he ever get a wife?"

Gareth laughed abruptly. "That he did. Remember Marge Fenway?"

"The large widow who lived over by Kelloway?"

"That's the one. She had a little property and Ellis married her. I went by and visited them just out of curiosity."

"I don't suppose he was very glad to see you."

"Indeed he was, for he was greedy for someone to spill his woes to, and he's got woes enough." Gareth leaned back, his face warmed by the fire and his dark blue eyes merry. "That woman is a dragon! I never thought I'd feel sorry for Rhys Ellis but he put his foot in the trap this time."

"Very soft, you are, to feel sorry for him." With a shiver of fear, Dorcas still remembered how close she'd come to being forced into a marriage with the man.

"Don't say that —he's got his comeuppance this time. That woman makes his life miserable."

Dorcas sat there, stroking Lady Mary's smooth fur. Occasionally the cat would look up and make her peculiar *thripping* sound, upon which Dorcas would hold her finger and the rough red tongue of Lady Mary would caress it.

"Tell me about your preaching."

"Well, God has blessed," Gareth said. "People have a hunger for God and the churches aren't meeting their needs. I don't want to become an enemy of the church, for they're doing part of God's work, but they've lost their early fire."

"That's what I fear for Andrew," Dorcas said quietly.

Looking up quickly, Gareth saw her face was drawn. It was more than just the illness that had taken her; there was a sadness in her eyes. He reached over and put his hand on hers where it rested on Lady Mary. "I'm sorry for that. He has such potential. Such a good man, Andrew Wakefield is. Not many would have done for us what that man did." He hesitated, then said, "Is it better with you, Sister?"

She knew instantly that he was asking about her relationship with Andrew—her marital relationship. "No," she said quietly. "I'm still believing God will do something." Then, in order to shake off his attention from her own sorrows, she asked, "Will you be going to see Sarah Lancaster?"

"Oh, yes. I'll go."

Something in Gareth's voice caught at Dorcas. "I pray much about this." She was disturbed and it was reflected in her eyes. Hesitatingly she continued, "Perhaps you made a mistake. Perhaps she's not the woman for you."

After a moment of silence, Gareth answered, his voice terse, "I've thought of that also, Dorcas, but I love her and that's all there is for it."

Leaning forward, Dorcas touched his cheek. "I'll keep on praying. God can do anything."

<hr />

The Lancasters were not particularly happy with Gareth's visit. They said nothing, but their manner was distant. And when Gareth and Sarah were alone in the parlor he said, "Your parents aren't happy with me. I suppose, in their position, I wouldn't be, either."

Sarah had been very glad to see Gareth, although she'd been a little shocked when he'd appeared at her door. Sudden joy had run through her and she'd impulsively reached out her hands. He'd taken them and kissed them and she'd laughed excitedly, then drawn him inside. As soon as she'd closed the door, she turned to him and lifted her face. "I'd forgotten how tall you were," she said.

"Always makes me feel good to be taller than a woman. Makes me feel masterful," he replied with a grin.

Sarah had laughed at him, then reached out to touch his cheek. "It's good to see you again, Gareth."

Gareth had leaned over and surprised her with a kiss on her cheek. "Merry Christmas," he'd said, smiling.

Now, as they sat in the parlor after dinner, looking at some books Sarah had found in an uncle's library and saved for him, she was again confused by the warmth of her feeling for this young man. "I don't know if you can use these or not," she said aloud.

Gareth, who'd been examining the books with delight, looked up, a smile lighting his features. "Why, of course I can use them. These are all quite good and expensively bound, too." He shook his head ruefully. "I don't have much of a library, I'm afraid."

His words embarrassed her and she flushed slightly. "I'm happy they will be of some use," she murmured. Then a silence fell. Sarah was acutely aware of Gareth's masculinity. Strength emanated from him and her eyes rested for a moment on his strong neck and broad chest and shoulders, all outlined beneath his white shirt. Sarah wasn't easily intimidated and she couldn't imagine why she felt so speechless now, almost like a schoolgirl in the presence of an older, more sophisticated man. She lifted her eyes and met his deep blue eyes and was disturbed even more. The rugged planes of his face showed strength and confidence, and his eyes were the deepest blue she had ever seen. His hair was fresh and dark, a perfect match for the black, expressive eyebrows. She dropped her eyes to his hands and noticed that they were square and showed signs of rough use—the result of his years in the coal mines, she knew.

They look so strong, she thought, and an absurd impulse filled her to reach out and take them. But she didn't have time, for Gareth reached forward and pulled her close.

"Sarah," he said, his husky voice low and thrilling, "I can but tell you again how much I care for you." And then, almost against his will, he kissed her. The fragrance of fresh flowers mingled with the scent of the woman, stirring him as no woman ever had before. To him, she was rich in a way a woman should be—at times carefree and reckless, at other times possessed of the mysterious glow of a softer mood.

Sarah, if possible, was stirred even more deeply than Gareth. There was, in truth, a depth to this young woman that had never been plumbed because her life had been on a narrow plane. Brought up to wealth and position, Sarah considered manners and courtship part of an intricate ritual, much like the posturing of exotic birds. She expected men to play the game and she, herself, had responded in kind. But now as Gareth's lips pressed against hers and his hands caressed her back, she was shaken out of her complacence. Shock raced through her as she realized she'd reached up and drawn him closer, anxious and yearning for his touch, returning his passion.

Finally, with a gasp, she forcefully pulled her head away. Placing her hands on her chest, she whispered, "You—you mustn't do that, Gareth! My parents would be terribly upset if they found you had done so!" Turning from him, her hands trembling violently, she said, "You mustn't ever do that again. Not ever!"

"Why not?" Gareth forcibly turned her around. His hands, as she'd guessed, were strong and she was as helpless as a child. She would have dropped her head but he released one shoulder and tilted her chin up. "What are you afraid of, Sarah? Of being a woman? Of being alive? Is all of this," he motioned almost with disgust at the opulent room, "more important than what a man and a woman feel for one another?"

"I don't—I don't feel anything for you."

"Sarah, don't lie. You wouldn't kiss a man as you just kissed me unless you cared for him."

Sarah knew the situation was fast slipping from her control. She wrenched herself away and said, "I'll have to ask you to leave, Gareth." Her eyes were enormous and she was trembling as she said, "You know it's hopeless—we'd never be suitable for one another."

"Suitable? What does *that* mean? Is everything a matter of pounds and guineas?" His words angered her for she knew, deep down, that he was right. Infuriated, she lifted her chin. She tried to keep the robust energy that lay beneath the surface carefully contained, but Gareth saw a hint of her will and pride in her face.

"I would never make a minister's wife. . . . It's not a matter of money," she added quickly before he could protest. "I'm not a woman of God—not in the way you would have me be."

"You could be, Sarah."

"Would you have me make myself into a religious puppet to please you?"

"No, of course not, but—"

Her lips softened then and her eyes mirrored some deep wish, but her voice was even when she spoke. A tone of utter and absolute finality filled her words as she said, "Good-bye, Gareth. I wish you well—but I do not wish to see you again."

Gareth knew he'd lost. He stood silently for a moment, searching her carefully. He saw no break in her demeanor and finally said quietly, "I see your mind is made up." For one moment he hesitated, thinking to say more, but the adamant lines of her expression forbade it. "I will always love you," he said quickly, then left the room.

As soon as she heard the door slam, Sarah groped her way to a chair and fell into it. She was not a woman who wept easily but she did weep then, for somehow she felt that something had passed in her life and she'd be the poorer for it. "It's impossible," she said. Still, she felt empty as she arose and left the room with heavy steps.

⸺⸻⸺

The first day of 1741 passed slowly for Dorcas. She kept to her room during the morning, not coming down for breakfast. Late during the afternoon she did descend but said little to any of the servants. Dinner was a silent, glum meal. Andrew tried to make light conversation but Dorcas made only nominal responses.

After the meal Dorcas rose and excused herself. "I think I'll retire early. Good night."

"Just a minute, Dorcas."

Andrew rose to his feet, moved to her side, and searched her face carefully. "Come into the parlor," he said quietly. "I must speak with you."

Curiously Dorcas lifted her eyes and studied his face. "All right, if you wish." The two made their way down the hall. Once in the parlor, she asked, "What is it?"

"Sit down for a moment, will you?" Andrew seemed uneasy and Dorcas wondered if he had to break some bad news.

"Very well." She took her seat on the horsehair sofa and kept her eyes fixed on him.

He came over to sit awkwardly beside her. "Dorcas, something's wrong. I must insist we have Dr. Brown in. You've been ill for weeks now."

Dorcas hesitated. She'd been waiting for this moment for some time and yet, now that she had to speak, words failed her. Loneliness is not a disease, perhaps, but for her it had been almost as bad. She'd been almost isolated in the rectory during the winter season. She longed to see Gareth and, most of all, she missed Hope Wingate. She'd thought a thousand times, *If only Hope were here. I could talk to her.* Now, however, she knew that the time had come. "I don't need to see Dr. Brown," she said, "although I will."

Relief came to Andrew's lean face. He swallowed and nodded almost eagerly. "Good," he said, "I've been worried about you, Dorcas. There are so many diseases around these days that I've been concerned."

"I'm not ill—not in the way you mean, Andrew."

Her words puzzled him. "What do you mean?"

"I mean that—I'm going to have a baby."

Andrew thought at first he'd misunderstood her. He kept his eyes fixed on her lips, waiting for her to say more, but she remained silent. The impact of what she'd said struck him so forcibly that his expression resembled that of man who had taken a rough blow in the pit of the stomach. He opened his lips to speak and when nothing came, he licked them and stood there, staring at her.

"I—I assume you are certain." His voice was thin and strained and he found, suddenly, that he couldn't control his hands. Grasping them tightly together, he looked down at them as if they were not attached to his own body. In the silence of the room, the clock on the mantel over the fireplace ticked loudly, its rhythmic cadence echoing inside his head. The fire snapped and popped and he heard outside the rumble of a heavy dray over the frozen streets.

At long last he looked up and said, "I'm a fool about such things, Dorcas. Somehow I never thought . . . such a thing could happen."

Dorcas was absolutely still. From the moment she'd ascertained she was pregnant, she'd dreaded this moment. Having a child had been something she had always associated with joy. But she knew there would be no joy in Andrew and, looking at his face, she said simply, "I didn't tell you until I was sure. That's been some time ago. I knew it would be unwelcome news for you."

Andrew gathered himself together. Taking a deep breath he ran his hands over his hair helplessly. "I never considered such a thing," he said, his voice almost a whisper. "Are you all right? You've been ill for so long."

"I will see Dr. Brown tomorrow. I don't know much about having babies. I haven't felt very well, to tell the truth."

An agony struck Andrew. He'd always tried to be a kindly man, anxious not to give offense. He looked back now, with blinding clarity, on the months of their marriage and the loneliness he'd seen in Dorcas's face. As she sat there watching him, she looked so small and vulnerable that if Andrew had been a cursing man, he would have cursed himself at that moment.

He wished to speak, but no graceful words sprang to his lips. Finally he said lamely, "We'll have to see that you're taken care of. I'll call Brown tomorrow and have him come to the house."

"Thank you."

Dorcas's words were spare, devoid of any outward emotion, but as Andrew looked into her eyes, he saw a grief he couldn't deny. He was fully aware he'd brought hurt into this woman's life and quickly said, with as much fervor as he could manage, "This will change things for you a great deal."

Dorcas noticed he didn't say *for us,* and the oppressive doubt that was growing in her became even darker. "A child always changes things," she said, rising to her feet. "Good night, Andrew."

"Good night—" Andrew stood up, desiring to help her upstairs but knowing she would think this strange. As she disappeared he called up the stairs, "I'll call Brown tomorrow. It'll be all right— you'll see."

Andrew went back to the parlor and sat down, staring blindly into the yellow and red flames. But he wasn't aware of the fire or the room or anything else. All he could think of was, *O God, what a terrible wreck I've made out of my life! And Dorcas, how alone she must feel!* Andrew began to hate himself then and, lowering his face into his hands, struggled with the guilt that was as sharp and piercing as any sword ever forged by man.

Twenty-Three

A BLOW FOR GARETH MORGAN

N othing in Andrew Wakefield's life had come as more of a shock than Dorcas's announcement that she was bearing his child. He'd left the parlor in a daze and had gone at once to his study, where he stared blindly at the wall for some time. Once, Mrs. Lesley came to ask about a household matter and he'd automatically answered without coming out of the paralyzing, emotional shock.

Finally he muttered, "I don't know what to do."

He left the house the next morning and went to Dr. Brown's office, where he left word for the doctor to call. Afterward he moved back along the streets, reluctant to go to the church, and at last was drawn back to the house. He entered and attempted to work for two hours but his mind was driven back and forth as a leaf is driven by an erratic November wind. Finally Mrs. Lesley came to say, "Dr. Brown is here, Mr. Wakefield."

"Thank you." Andrew went at once to meet Dr. Brown. "I'm glad you came so quickly," he said.

Something in Andrew's face drew the physician's attention. Dr. Barnabas Brown was a young man for his profession, not yet thirty. He was small, with keen features and alert brown eyes. "What seems to be the trouble, Reverend?" he asked.

"It's my wife. She's—she's been having difficulty for some

time." Andrew stumbled, finding the words difficult. "She just told me she's certain she's expecting a child."

"I see. Well, that's natural enough. I assume she's not very far along?"

Andrew tried desperately to think of how many months had passed since the child had been conceived. He knew he looked like a fool in the eyes of the doctor and finally said lamely, "I expect she'll give you all the details."

"Very well, then, I'll see her now."

Andrew led the way up the stairs, knocked on the door, and when Dorcas answered he opened it and said, "Dorcas, the doctor is here." He stepped back and said, "I'll see you before you leave, Dr. Brown."

"Very well, Reverend."

Andrew took one look at Dorcas and saw she was examining him carefully. There was nothing of an accusing nature in her gaze but he couldn't meet her eyes. He turned and closed the door behind him. Going down the stairs, he didn't return to his study but paced the carpet in the receiving room until, after a relatively short time, he heard the doctor on the stairs. Quickly he moved into the hall and even as Dr. Brown reached the floor level, asked anxiously, "How is she?"

Dr. Brown didn't answer immediately. He seemed to be preoccupied with his thoughts and when he looked up, there was some doubt in his sharp brown eyes. "I wish I'd been called in earlier," he said. "It's unusual to wait this long. She's been carrying the child for about six months. I'm not entirely happy with her condition."

Andrew's face fell and he bit his lip. "What's wrong?"

"I'm not exactly sure." Brown's words were slow. He was a careful, methodical man and something about his face revealed his concern. "She hasn't been eating properly. She's far under-weight for what she should be at this time. She says she's been ill for some time, unable to eat. I'll talk with the cook about a better diet for her."

"Yes, Doctor, anything," Andrew said. "She'll be all right then, when she gains some weight?"

Again the hesitancy on the physician's part filled Andrew with apprehension. "I trust she will be, but she's a small woman and there's something unusual about her case. I'm not exactly sure what it is."

"But she will be all right?"

Dr. Barnabas Brown knew well the dangers of bearing a child. He wanted to prepare the rector for anything that might happen. "We will hope so and indeed pray so, Reverend, but I want to see her fairly often."

"Come back as often as you please. Money's no object, Dr. Brown."

"Very well. I'll talk with the cook now."

Andrew left the doctor with Beth Buchanan. When he'd announced the reason for the doctor's visit, something that he couldn't identify had leaped into Beth's eyes. He knew he wasn't her favorite and that she was very attached to Dorcas. "Do the best you can for Mrs. Wakefield," Andrew said. "If there's anything you need, be sure and let me know." He left the room then and waited until the doctor was through. When Dr. Brown left, he closed the door and looked tensely at the stairs. His lips tightened and he knew he must go at once to Dorcas.

When he entered the room, she was sitting in a chair, looking out the window. She greeted him, saying, "I suppose the doctor said the same to you as to me."

Andrew sat down across from her. "He said you were delicate, that you'd need special care."

"I don't want to be a bother."

"How could you be that?" Andrew sought desperately for some way to reassure this woman who sat so quietly examining him. There was no fear in her eyes but he'd been thoroughly frightened by the doctor's words. "You must be very careful," he said. "The doctor has given instructions to Cook about your diet and he'll be coming to see you very often."

Dorcas listened, her eyes never leaving Andrew's face. "This will make trouble for you," she said.

"Don't speak of that!" Andrew said quickly. He desperately wanted to break through the curtain that lay in her eyes and he awkwardly reached over and laid his hand on hers. She always kept the crippled hand covered by the one that was not maimed and surprise leaped into her eyes as his hand touched her. "We must—we must take very good care of you," he said, almost with an effort. "I would be very grieved if anything happened."

It was the closest thing to an expression of concern that Dorcas had heard from Andrew in months. His hand on hers was hesitant but at least he'd touched her of his own will. "That's good to hear," she said. When he didn't move his hand, she knew he was trying to find the words to say something. For a man who was so good with words, he was having great difficulty. Finally he pulled his hand back and said, "I'll have Cook fix us some of that India tea you like so much. And I think she has some fresh-baked cakes. I'll bring them up, if you don't mind."

Again his gentleness touched Dorcas's heart. Tears rose to her eyes and she blinked them away. "I would like that very much."

When he left the room, she stared at the door and thought of what the doctor had said. His words hadn't been encouraging and she knew she was not well. But Andrew's brief visit had encouraged her and she bowed her head to give thanks for his new air of concern.

***

"I'm glad to see you, my dear Andrew!" John Wesley had been in his study at the "Foundry," as his new center of operations in

London was called. "Come in and sit down. Let me hear what you've been doing."

Two weeks had passed since Dr. Brown made his first visit. During that time, Andrew had stayed at home more than in all the previous weeks. He'd gone quickly about his duties at church and then had rushed back. During that time he had surprised the entire staff with his obvious concern over his wife's condition.

Beth Buchanan had told her husband, "Well, it's good to see the man is finally awakened to what a gem he's married to. But the poor girl, she's just not well. She's not strong, I fear. We'll pray for the good Lord to bring her through this with a fine, healthy baby."

Now, at John Wesley's, Andrew sat down and said, "My wife is expecting, so I've been staying fairly close to home."

Wesley smiled. "Congratulations, my dear fellow! May mother and child be in the hands of the good Lord during this time."

"Thank you, sir. I appreciate your prayers. I've been meaning to stop by and visit you for some time. I hear things about your work but I'd like to hear it from you. How you see the revival."

Wesley at once began to relate his personal affairs, saying rather sadly, "Mr. Whitefield and I are not reconciled. He's apparently convinced of the doctrine of election and of the final perseverance, but I trust we'll be reconciled soon."

"I read he is doing great things in the Colonies."

"Yes, indeed. God is blessing him mightily. I rejoice in it, for despite our difference he's a good man."

"Unfortunate," Andrew said, shaking his head rather sadly, "that these differences have to be publicly aired. The papers, of course, printed the letter Mr. Whitefield wrote, rebuking you for your stand."

"Yes, it's unfortunate," Wesley agreed, "but we'll weather these things. I have sad news to report about the Fetter Lane Society. I had to sever my relationship with them. I expect they will go toward the Moravian persuasion."

"Mr. Wesley," Andrew said, "could I speak with you on a private matter? A personal problem has come into my life. I have no one else to talk to."

Wesley was surprised. "What is it, Andrew?"

"There are some who say that you believe in what you call 'Christian perfection.' I'm confused by this term and I don't seem to be anywhere close to such a state myself," Andrew said, grimacing. He looked at Wesley directly and asked, "Since you urge this on others, do you know it for yourself, sir?"

Wesley said quickly, "By the grace of God, I am what I am." He went on to explain that his whole life had been consumed by the desire and quest for holiness. "But," he explained, "I found that I was unholy, and could not become holy through my own works. Andrew, don't let words sidetrack you. My use of the term *perfection* does not mean I am reaching human perfection, or that of angels, or God himself. Christian perfection refers to the work of God in the heart. It is loving God with all your heart, mind, soul, and strength. It means your motivation is pure. Your thoughts, words, and actions are governed by pure love. Your heart is perfect before God and your life is full of joy." Although Wesley went on for some time, he never directly answered Andrew's question.

Finally Andrew said, "I'm not filled with the joy of the Lord as I'd like to be. Indeed, sometimes I wonder if I'm a believer at all."

Because Wesley had felt much the same way during the days before Aldersgate, he began to encourage Andrew warmly. "How does a man come to know Jesus Christ? By faith. And how are we to live our lives after we are converted? The same way, by faith. By the Scripture that comes often to my mind: Romans chapter 5, verse 10—"For if, when we were enemies, we were reconciled to God by the death of his Son, much more, being reconciled, we shall be saved by his life." Wesley's eyes lit up as he quoted the verse and said, "Do you see it, my boy? How are we reconciled?"

"By the death of Jesus."

"Exactly. And how are we saved? Do you see it? By his life?"

Andrew's brow furrowed and he asked, "Could you explain that a little more clearly, Mr. Wesley?"

"At the cross Jesus paid the price for our sins. When we come to him, by faith," Wesley explained, his voice warm, "we are reconciled to God. Our sins are forgiven. But," he said, spreading his hands wide, "that's not the end of our lives. No, we must go on some thirty, forty, sixty years. How are we to live then? The Scripture says it is by his life, the life of Jesus. We receive life from him and day by day we are saved from what we are, by the resurrection of Christ. Because he lives, I live also. That's what Paul meant, I think, when he said that Christ is our life."

"I find myself unable to enter into some of the Scriptures," Andrew confessed. "I've struggled with this for some time and I know you've struggled yourself. But you speak now in your preaching of the new birth and the new joy that has come to you."

"Yes indeed!" Wesley leaned forward and began speaking earnestly. For some time he pressed upon Andrew the necessity of trusting Christ only. "You see," he said, "it's a dangerous thing to trust Christ *and.* That means if we trust Christ *and* our baptism, we aren't really trusting Christ. If we trust Christ *and* our charitable works, we are depending upon our charitable works— at least in part—to save us. Only Jesus brings salvation; that's what the whole book of Galatians is about. But it's a hard thing, my boy, for us to put away our pride. We don't want to think we have nothing to offer God."

This was exactly what Andrew had felt and his face flushed warmly as Wesley touched on this sensitive spot of his theology. He sat there listening for over an hour while John Wesley spoke of the sufficiency of Jesus Christ. "He is all you need, all any man needs, and I urge you to throw away all else you have trusted in. Only the blood of Jesus pleases God."

When Andrew left Wesley's study, his mind was numbed by what he'd heard. He went back over his life, realizing he'd fallen into exactly what Wesley had described: trusting in his own works, at least in part, to please God. As he walked along under the gray skies of January he began to pray, "God, show me the way. I can't go on like this."

⌁⌁⌁⌁⌁⌁

Andrew Wakefield wasn't the only inhabitant of London who was struggling with a spiritual problem. Sarah Lancaster had been terribly shaken by her meeting with Gareth. She'd attempted to shake off the feelings that swept through her by throwing herself into a round of shopping and during the Christmas season had entered into the celebration as never before. She'd been loud and almost frantic in seeking to drown out the emotions that clamored for her attention.

But all had been to no avail. Finally, in desperation, she'd begun to read the Bible. It hadn't been a book she'd delighted in and now she found herself accused by so many verses. When Jesus said to forsake all and follow him, she realized she'd forsaken nothing. Wherever she turned, Scripture seemed to stress that every human being was called upon to make a choice for Jesus and against the world. The world had been a large part of her life, as natural a habitat as water is for a fish. Now, however, other voices were beginning to echo and she realized how shallow were most of her activities and dreams.

She'd begun attending some of the meetings that were becoming common around London. Mr. Wesley spoke often and he had several assistants who did the same. Sarah knew Gareth was one of these and had no desire to confront him again. She didn't tell her parents any of this. They were still clamoring for her to marry

Major Ian Crenshaw but she felt less inclined to do this than ever. Crenshaw was gone from the country to France for some military purpose and she was glad.

The worst, perhaps, for Sarah, was that she had no one to speak to. She well understood that her parents would be mortified if they knew she was attending the Methodist meetings. None of her friends were devout Christians; most of them, like Rebecca, were openly scornful of the religious revival. Sarah's face often burned with shame as she realized how she'd made a game of trapping Gareth's attention.

Finally, feeling a bit desperate, she called upon Dorcas Wakefield. She'd been impressed with the young woman's modesty and there had been a spiritual quality in her that Sarah didn't find in her own friends and family.

Since she hadn't seen Sarah for some time, Dorcas had been surprised when Sarah had come. She thought at once of Gareth but said nothing of this. Smiling warmly, she welcomed Sarah in and said, "Come into the receiving room. There's a nice fire and we can have tea." Dorcas stroked Lady Mary, saying, "Lady Mary gave birth to her brood not long ago. I hope I do as well as she did."

"You must think I'm dreadful, coming without notice," Sarah said when they were seated and tea was served. She was very nervous and didn't have the faintest idea of how to bring up such a subject since talking about religion was not done in her set. There was something in Dorcas's face—a gentleness and a kindness—that made her more bold and she asked, "How is your brother, Mrs. Wakefield?"

"Gareth is doing very well. Have you not seen him?"

"N-no." She stumbled over the denial. She couldn't meet Dorcas's gaze and turned the subject at once to Dorcas's pregnancy. The two women talked about children, babies, and families for a while, and then it was Dorcas who said, "You seem troubled, Miss Lancaster."

"Please call me Sarah."

"Of course, Sarah. You must call me Dorcas. What's the trouble, my dear?"

Sarah's fingers plucked at her skirt for a moment, then she looked up. "I'm so unhappy. Has Gareth told you anything about—about us?"

Instantly Dorcas understood something of the turmoil in this young woman's soul. "He's told me," she said gently, "that he's very fond of you. In fact, I think he loves you with all his heart."

The words, once spoken, seemed to strike Sarah. She dropped her head and clasped her hands tightly. A silence fell over the room, and Dorcas did not disturb it. She knew it was easy to talk too much and that this young woman had come to tell what was on her heart. So she waited until Sarah whispered, "I know he says he loves me, but it's so—so *impossible!* I'm quite spoiled. I've had my own way all my life. How could I ever live the life that would be called for by a minister?"

"If it's God's will, he will fit you to lead the life." She looked around the rectory and said, "I was living in a shack with Gareth when Andrew came, and now I have more than I ever had in the way of this world's goods. But all of this, this house, the servants, they're not what makes a family. They have nothing to do with love and concern for another."

"Are you happy, Dorcas?"

"A few weeks ago I would have said no, without a doubt. But," Dorcas continued, smiling, a peace and harmony in her eyes, "I feel God is doing something wonderful. For one thing, the child I'm carrying. The fruit of the womb is the reward of the Lord and I rejoice in that."

Dorcas regarded Sarah, then said almost bluntly, "And you, Sarah, how do you feel about my brother?"

It was a question Sarah couldn't even answer in her own heart. "I don't know, Dorcas—I just don't know. It all seems so impossible

. . . and besides, I didn't come to talk about Gareth so much as . . . well . . . well, I've been having great doubts about my own life."

Instantly Dorcas realized the girl was under conviction. "I'm so glad you came to me," she said warmly. "Let me get my Bible and I'll tell you how I found the Lord. Perhaps that will be of some help to you."

For over an hour Dorcas read Scripture after Scripture, giving her testimony in a quiet voice and Sarah drinking it all in. When Sarah got up to leave, she said, "It's been such a help, Dorcas. May I come back?"

"Certainly! God is reaching out for you. He's drawing you to himself and you will find the Lord Jesus, I know it."

Sarah had been so encouraged by her talk with Dorcas that she made regular visits. Her family was disturbed by this but they said nothing. They knew she was a stubborn girl at heart and the surest way to drive her into a marriage was to forbid it.

Rebecca Holden was puzzled as well but she was far more direct: "Sarah, why are you going to the rectory so much? You never were so religious before."

There was a worldly spirit in Rebecca that seemed almost hard. For a while Sarah tried to avoid the questions, then finally said, "I've been visiting with Mrs. Wakefield, the rector's wife. She's such a lovely young woman and she's having a hard time. It's her first child and she's not well."

"Oh, well then, I shall certainly go with you and give my condolences."

On the whole, Sarah wished Rebecca wouldn't, but Rebecca did go and when they were there Dorcas received her as graciously as she had Sarah. Rebecca sat and listened while Dorcas spoke of the things of God. Although Dorcas's face was pale and she seemed ill, still there was a quiet air of assurance about her.

The two women prolonged their visit. Sarah went into the kitchen to talk with the cook about a special dish for Dorcas while Rebecca remained in the study. She was there when she heard the door close, and when she looked up and saw a man pass by, she said, "Why, Mr. Morgan."

For a moment Gareth couldn't recall the young woman's name, since he'd seen her only once, that he could remember. Then it came to him. "Miss Holden, isn't it?"

"I'm pleased you remember, sir," Rebecca said, dimpling. "I'm sure you remember my friend, Sarah Lancaster."

"Why—yes, of course."

"She's out in the kitchen. She should be back in a moment." Rebecca saw a strange look appear in Gareth's eyes and said, "I want to apologize for the trick we played on you." Rebecca assumed Sarah had told Gareth about their foolish game of enticing a preacher.

"I'm not sure I know what you mean."

"Oh, it was the game Sarah decided to play." Rebecca had forgotten it was her idea and babbled on, "We thought it might be fun to see if we could entice a young minister, at least Sarah did." Rebecca's eyebrows arched and she continued, "I'm sure most men would be enticed by such a beautiful young woman."

As the woman continued to speak, Gareth realized what she was saying and grew angry. *So she was just toying with me—that's all it ever was!* He couldn't believe what he was hearing. He heard steps and turned to see Sarah enter.

"Come in, Sarah. I've just been telling Reverend Morgan how awful we were to play that game."

Sarah had never been happy with what Rebecca had called a game and now when her eyes met Gareth's, she saw pain in them. "Gareth—" she began and could speak no more.

Gareth was filled with hurt. His love for this girl had been greater than anything in his life except his love for God. Finding out it had been nothing to her but a farce was devastating.

"I just came to see my sister," he said quietly. "It's good of you ladies to visit her." He turned instantly and walked out of the room, his back straight, his head held high.

"Rebecca, what did you tell him?" Sarah asked tensely.

"Just that you were teasing him a little bit."

"You shouldn't have done that." Sarah suddenly felt she had to get out of the house. "Let's go. I can't stay here any longer." She ignored Rebecca's protest and as they left the house she remembered keenly the look in Gareth Morgan's eyes.

He's terribly hurt, she thought. *And I don't blame him. Oh, what a fool I was. Why did I ever listen to Rebecca? But I can't blame her because I agreed to it.* She got rid of Rebecca as soon as she conveniently could, but she couldn't rid herself of the humiliation that had come to her as she realized what a shoddy thing she'd done to a man she really loved.

Twenty - Four

An Interrupted Sermon

The established church had never been a particular problem for the criminals and lower orders that swarmed some sections of London. However, the Methodists had become a thorn in their sides, for so many of the prostitutes and fledgling young pickpockets were being converted, they felt their occupations threatened. Mobs were stirred by some of the gang leaders and pimps, who found their customers deserting them for prayer meetings, and by thieves, pickpockets, and louts who'd seen their fields less than white unto harvest. A mob had already tried to pull the roof off of Wesley's center. The rabble had brought in a bull, which ran wildly through the crowd when Wesley was teaching in Wiltshire upon a table. Wesley had stopped his preaching and handled the situation well. The poor animal had been used for baiting and wasn't difficult to lead away.

Later on, that same week, Gareth received his share of persecution. A mob attacked the congregation, throwing stones. One of them struck him in the middle of the back. It drove the wind out of him and made a large bruise but did no further damage.

Wesley applied to the authorities for protection. This was fairly easy to accomplish in London but the London mob would follow and create trouble whenever they could in the provinces. Sarah witnessed a mild form of this when one of the Methodist preachers inside the city was shouted down by a group of toughs. The minister was taken and shaken a bit by the mob but otherwise was unhurt.

The next day Sarah went to visit Dorcas and wasn't happy with her physical condition. Sarah found her in bed, being nursed by the maid, Bertha. When Dorcas asked at once about her spiritual condition, Sarah said, "Oh, Dorcas, you mustn't worry about me. It's I who am concerned about you." Looking over at the swollen body and pale face, she said, "Do you feel as bad as you look? Oh, dear—that was a terrible thing to say."

Dorcas managed a small laugh. "I think I look much worse than I feel. Never mind that."

"But I must mind it. What does the doctor say?"

Dorcas hesitated. "He is rather pessimistic."

Sarah stared at the features of the young woman, framed by the white pillow. Dorcas's hair was fanned out around her, and her face looked almost gaunt. Despite every effort, she hadn't gained enough weight and now there was a grayish pallor in her cheeks that frightened Sarah. *I'll have to talk to the rector before I leave here,* she thought. Aloud she said, "I've been going to hear the Methodists preach." She gave Dorcas, who was hungry for news, the results of her search, concluding with, "I'm afraid for the ministers."

"Gareth never mentioned such things," Dorcas murmured. "But then, he wouldn't."

"Where is he now, do you know?

"I got a letter from him two days ago. I think he will be preaching at Mileton tomorrow." A spasm crossed her face and she turned away until the pain passed. When she turned back, she smiled. "Now, have you found the Lord Jesus yet?"

Sarah shook her head miserably. "I don't know what to do, Dorcas. I've listened to you and everything you say is right. It works for you but perhaps I'm not meant to be saved."

"You haven't been listening to the Calvinists, have you?"

"What's that?"

"They believe God chooses only certain people to be saved."

"What about the rest?"

"They die and go to hell."

"But that's not fair!"

"So Mr. Wesley says. That's why he speaks so often of *free grace*. He says, 'whosoever will, may come,' and I agree with him." Dorcas reached out her hand and Sarah took it, squeezing it. "You may come to Jesus. The only thing that is standing in the way is your own will. . . ."

Sarah said nothing.

"I know it's hard," Dorcas continued, shaking her head. "I had nothing to give up—nothing of this world's goods, but you have wealth and position and everything the world holds dear. But let me ask you, Sarah, if you were to die tonight, how many of those things could you take with you when you went to stand before God?"

Sarah lowered her eyes and couldn't answer. There was a thickness in her throat, for she was struggling. "I will seek God more fervently," she said finally, "and I will pray more fervently."

Dorcas looked tired so Sarah rose and kissed her on the cheek. "I'll be back. I'm going to hear Gareth preach tomorrow."

"Give him my love."

"Well, I won't let him see me; I'd be too embarrassed. But I'll come and tell you all about it."

⌦⌦⌦

The next afternoon Sarah almost decided to stay at home. She felt miserable. Ever since her talk with Dorcas, she'd sunk into a deep depression. Just the mention of dying and going to meet God frightened her. But at last she put on her coat and hat and, as usual, had the coachman take her out to Mileton, a small village

339

outside London. Since it wasn't too far from the rectory, she decided to give Dorcas a report on the way back.

When the coachman drove up, he turned to her and advised, "Seems to be a rowdy bunch, Miss. You'd better stay in the carriage."

Sarah replied, "Can you pull around to that ridge over there? I think we can hear from there."

"Yes, mum, I think that's possible."

Sarah kept her seat in the carriage. There was a natural depression in the ridge and the preachers had put themselves in the center of it. Sarah saw Gareth, accompanied by two other ministers. One of them she recognized as none other than John Wesley. As she sat there listening, the crowd grew even larger. But she noticed there was a different atmosphere in this group. Many of the men looked as if they were from the worst parts of London. They were moving around, whispering to each other, apparently waiting for a sign.

Down in the center of the depression, Gareth had been watching the crowd closely. "I fear we may have trouble, Mr. Wesley," he said. "This is a rough crowd, I think."

"We will have to preach the gospel. God will take care of us, Gareth."

John Wesley soon began to preach and had no sooner started when cries broke out. "Shut your mouth! Keep quiet or you'll be the worse for it!"

John Wesley paid no attention to these cries but lifted his voice. His penetrating tenor tones rose above the threats and for ten minutes he preached without ceasing.

Then a ringleader, a hulking man with a prizefighter's battered face, stepped out. His face contorted with rage, he positioned himself in front of the preacher and yelled, "Shut your mouth, Preacher, or I'll shut it for you!"

Wesley simply looked at the man and said, "I must preach the gospel," and began once again where he'd left off. A great roar came from the toughs in the mob and suddenly there was a stampede. Many were flattened as the toughs struck out right and left.

Gareth stepped forward, putting himself between Wesley and the bully who towered over him, saying quietly, "It'd be best if you would allow the meeting to go on."

Instantly the huge man struck Gareth in the cheek. The blow drove him back against Wesley and blood trickled down from his cut lip. But he did not strike back because Wesley had instructed him not to. Once again the ringleader struck, this time numbing Gareth's arm. Then others came, so that not only Gareth but also Wesley was grabbed and overpowered.

Teeming mobs pulled Wesley, Gareth, and the third minister, an older man named Edward Fitch, roughly into the circle. Several of the men had bludgeons and they were striking out at the congregation. Gareth saw one man raise his arm and heard it snap quickly when he was struck.

Gareth cried out, "Mr. Wesley, are you all right?"

Wesley said "Yes!" then turned to the ringleader. "Will you hear me?"

"No! No!" the mob yelled. "Knock his brains out! Kill him!"

"What evil have I done? Which of you have I wronged?"

Wesley began to speak reasonably but the crowd screamed for blood.

Up on the ridge, Sarah watched with horror. She pressed her fist against her lips to keep from crying out. She saw the three men dragged roughly around. Wesley and the older man were punched repeatedly by blows they made no effort to block.

And then she saw one of the mob pick up a large rock. Even as she watched, he came up behind Gareth, who was standing helplessly, held by two members of the mob. Sarah cried out as the man raised the rock and brought it down on Gareth's head. He fell limply to the ground, obviously unconscious.

"Quick, drive the horses right down there, Thomas!"

"But we can't do that."

"Do as I tell you!"

Thomas stared at Sarah, then picked the whip out of the socket. "Yes, mum, but it'll be trouble."

Sarah repeated her commands. "We must help him. Go now!"

Thomas obediently struck the horses with the whip. Startled, the horses lunged forward. He drove them around a semicircle, following an old track. People were moving away from the mob in all directions.

Sarah held on with both hands, her face pale. Thomas drove directly toward the struggling ministers and one of the roughly dressed members of the mob screamed as he was knocked down by the flailing hooves of the horses. Others saw the team coming right at them and forgot their business. They lunged wildly to one side, trying to escape the horses.

Sarah waited until the coach pulled up beside the fallen man, then leaped out. Gareth was lying facedown on the ground. She went to her knees and turned him over. His lip was bleeding and a huge bump was beginning to form on the back of his head.

Suddenly a hand grasped her and she felt herself pulled up. The burly ringleader was glaring down at her. "What do you want here? This ain't no place for a woman."

Sarah stared at him fearlessly. "I assume you know I'm going to have you arrested. What's your name?"

"What's this?" he snarled, tightening his grip.

"Turn loose of my arm, you oaf!" she said clearly. She turned to Mr. Wesley and Mr. Fitch and said, "What's this man's name? I'll have my father see to it that he's put in jail at once." She turned back to the man and said, "Turn loose of my arm unless you want to stay in jail even longer. My father is Sir Talbot Lancaster and we'll see if you treat him as you do helpless men!"

A murmur went around the crowd and instantly some of the troublemakers began fading away.

The burly ringleader grew crimson with fury but when Sarah's eyes met his fearlessly, he knew he had met his match. "Come on!" he shouted. "We put the fear into them!" He glared at Wesley and said, "Keep up with your preaching and you'll wind up dead."

Even as the man walked away, Sarah was kneeling again by Gareth. He was breathing evenly and when Wesley and Fitch came over, she looked up and asked, "Are you gentlemen all right?"

"Yes, thanks to you," Wesley said. "How is our dear brother?"

"He's unconscious," Sarah said. "Help me get him in the carriage. His home isn't far. I'll take him there."

There were plenty of hands ready and soon Sarah was sitting in the coach, Gareth's head cushioned on her lap. "Drive home and drive easy, but be quick, Thomas!"

"Yes, mum, I'll do that."

<hr/>

Gareth awoke with a pounding head. Jagged streaks of pain made him shut his eyes and grit his teeth. He couldn't think for a moment because his head hurt so badly. Instinctively he reached up to touch it and encountered a bandage and a hand. His eyes flew open and a face formed in front of his vision. Slowly it cleared and he whispered, "Where am I?"

A voice said, "You're home, Gareth."

The face had been blurred and he blinked his eyes until finally his vision cleared again and he whispered, "Sarah!" Then it all came rushing back. "How did you get me here? I don't remember—"

"One of those villains hit you with a rock from behind," Sarah said. "How do you feel?"

Gareth looked down to see that he was lying in a bed and that no one else was in the room. Sarah was sitting beside him. She reached out and put a hand on his face. "Does your head hurt terribly?"

Gareth struggled and said, "Let me sit up."

"No, you shouldn't."

"I'm all right—just help me up." He struggled to a sitting position, the room reeling for a moment. Then he said, "That's better." He blinked as the pain came and reached up gingerly. "What a knot! It feels like a pumpkin."

"You've got a cut, too, but I dressed it for you. I'm not much of a nurse," she said.

"What happened? How did I get here?"

Sarah hesitated. "I went out to the fields to hear you preach and when you fell I had Thomas drive the carriage down. We put you in it and brought you here."

Gareth stared at her. "It wasn't that easy, not with that mob there. What about that monster who was egging everybody on?"

Sarah smiled, her eyes wickedly bright. "I threatened to have him put in jail. My father's name came in quite handy. He ran like a rabbit as soon as he heard that."

Gareth, feeling somewhat better, swung his legs over the bed and sat there for a moment, thinking about what had happened. Then he said quietly, "I know you risked your life."

"No, it wasn't that dangerous."

Silence took them both for a moment. Finally Gareth said, "Why did you come?"

"Oh, Gareth, I know the awful thing Rebecca told you about—how I led you on for a game. That was true enough at first . . . but I hated myself for it before long. And it's not a game anymore. Will you ever forgive me?"

"Of course, but that wasn't what I asked. Why did you go out to the preaching?"

"Gareth, I've been talking to Dorcas. I'm so miserable; I don't

344

know how to find God." Suddenly her face broke and she cried out, "I don't know what to do. Dorcas asked me what I would do if I died and had to go meet God. I know I'm not ready."

Gareth forgot the pain in his head, saying gently, "God has been calling you, Sarah. Will you let me introduce you to the Lord Jesus? He's been looking and longing for you and now it's time for you to find him."

Tears began to flow down Sarah's cheeks. "Will he have me?"

"He died for you, Sarah. Now let me tell you how much he loves you and how much he wants to give you peace in your heart. . . ."

Dorcas's eyes flew open when she saw Gareth walk into the room with Sarah by his side. She saw the tearstains on Sarah's cheek, and the triumphant look in Gareth's eyes and she cried out, "Gareth—Sarah—!"

"I want you to meet your new sister in the Lord," Gareth said. "Sarah has just taken the Lord Jesus as her Saviour."

Sarah ran over and threw herself into Dorcas's arms. She began to sob again but when she leaned back there was victory in her face. "Oh, Dorcas, it's true. I'm a Christian, now. I believe in Jesus, that he saved me from all my sins."

Gareth watched the two women as they rejoiced, a deep joy in his own heart because he knew somehow that this day's work was not over.

I had to get my head broken but it's worth it, he thought, smiling as Sarah turned to him. There was an expectant look on her face and when he went to her, she took his hand timidly and then met his eyes and smiled back. They didn't speak, but they both knew there was no longer a wall between them.

Twenty-Five

TWO ARE BETTER THAN ONE

George Whitefield landed in Cornwall in early March and reached London four days later. He'd been an astonishing success in America. The fires of the Great Awakening there had swept the eastern seaboard like nothing else ever had. Even Benjamin Franklin, who had practically no religion, became a warm personal friend of George Whitefield and supported him despite his own lack of convictions.

Whitefield longed to see the breach with John Wesley healed. He felt he'd been at fault for revealing, in a public letter, what he believed was Wesley's unwise use of the lot. He'd also been subjected to a constant stream of gossip concerning Wesley's actions from those who felt John Wesley had usurped Whitefield's ministry.

But the two men met at the Foundry and were frank with each other. Wesley approved Whitefield's plain speaking and later commented, "Integrity was inseparable from his whole character."

Whitefield respectfully spoke of their differences in doctrine. Both men were distressed. Whitefield showed it more openly for he had, as Wesley said, "a heart susceptible of the most generous and the most tender friendship. I have frequently thought that this, of all others, was the distinguishing part of his character. How few have we known of so kind a temper, of such large and flowing affections."

The two men made a beginning, at least, and as Whitefield said afterward, "Busybodies on both sides blew up the coals. We hearken too much to talebearers."

The estrangement, Wesley felt, put the Evangelical revival into danger. He was called to a tour in Wales, where he sought God constantly about the matter of George Whitefield. During that time, Howell Harris, the pioneer of the work there, came and spoke to Wesley, and God blessed his speech with healing words.

Harris wrote to Whitefield and in a little garret in the New Room the two men met. There they healed their long altercation and affection returned. The theological divisions that had weakened the Reformation two centuries earlier had divided their minds, though not their hearts, and each believed he was right. Wesley was tremendously relieved and wrote in his journal: "I spent an agreeable hour with Mr. Whitefield. I believe he is sincere in all he says concerning his desire of joining hands with all that love the Lord Jesus." Not long afterward, Whitefield wrote to Wesley and spoke of their reconciliation. He put it plainly,

> I say that old things pass away, and all things become new. Let the king live forever, and controversy die. It died with me long ago. God be praised for giving you such a mind. I subscribe myself Reverend and very dear sir, your most affectionate, though younger brother, in the gospel of our glorious Emmanuel.

Sarah had come to love Dorcas Wakefield as a dear sister. Since she'd become a Christian, she'd practically moved into the rectory, coming almost every day to care for Dorcas. There was no real need for physical care, since the servants all spent themselves freely on behalf of their mistress, but she was a consolation to

Dorcas. Dorcas had learned to lean upon Sarah and was always happy to see her.

Dr. Brown came one day in mid–April, staying longer at his examination than usual. Andrew paced the floor downstairs while Sarah sat tensely in a chair, her eyes going up, from time to time, toward Dorcas's room.

Andrew stopped his pacing and followed her glance. Meeting her eyes, he said abruptly, "I'm fearful for Dorcas."

"We must trust God, Reverend Wakefield, but, of course, you know that."

Andrew stared at her almost without comprehension. "I thought I knew that, but it seems I know little of God."

Sarah had been aware, as had everyone, of Andrew's almost frantic concern for Dorcas. He haunted the house, unable to work, and yet he couldn't visit Dorcas without being greatly disturbed. As a result, he became nervous and withdrawn. Sarah had seen him sit for hours in his study, staring out the window, his eyes blank and his hands locked fiercely together.

Dr. Brown appeared in the door and stepped inside. "May I speak with you alone, Mr. Wakefield?"

"You may speak in front of Miss Lancaster," Andrew said. "What is it?" He dreaded to ask the question for the doctor's brow was drawn up in a frown.

"As I told you from the beginning, your wife is having difficulty. I still am unable to fathom it, but she is undernourished and very weak. Also there is some difficulty I cannot pinpoint in the position of the child."

"What are you saying, Doctor?" Andrew demanded. "Can't you get more help? A second opinion?"

"Of course. I've thought of that. I will have my colleague, Dr. Callendar, come in. He's very good in affairs such as this. He'll be leaving soon, but not before the child comes, I trust."

"Do it right away!" Andrew said.

"Perhaps you'd like to go speak with her. I think she needs your comfort."

Andrew paused, stared at the doctor, then he licked his lips and tried to speak. At first he failed, and then he asked, "Doctor—will she live?"

Dr. Brown was an honest man. He stood considering the question for what seemed like an inordinately long time and finally looked Andrew Wakefield steadily in the eye. "I cannot offer false encouragement. Unless there's a miracle, I don't see how she can survive the birth of the child."

"Oh, no!" Sarah cried out without meaning to. She turned pale and sat back down in the chair. Her hands trembled and she shook her head, as if unwilling to receive the words of the doctor.

The doctor's words struck Andrew Wakefield harder than a bullet. He'd known, for some time, that Dorcas was not doing well, but he kept hoping and praying for improvement. Now Dr. Brown's words hung naked in the air, cold and full of menace. They could not be ignored or shrugged off. "Get Dr. Callendar—we must do something."

"He'll be here later this afternoon."

Dr. Brown left and Sarah rose from her chair. "We must not lose hope, Reverend Wakefield," she said. "I cannot believe God would let her die."

Andrew stared at her blankly, no recognition in his face. He turned and Sarah thought he was going upstairs, but instead he moved to the hall and passed through the front door without even pausing to get his coat or hat.

Sarah was astonished. *He's lost his mind,* she thought. She ran to the window and saw the rector walking down the street in his shirtsleeves. Although it was a mild April day, the pastors of large churches still didn't do such things.

Sarah knew she had to do something. Quickly she ran out the

door, holding her skirt, and caught up with him halfway down the block. "Reverend Wakefield!" she said, taking his arm. She forced him to turn around and froze when she saw his fixed face. "Reverend Wakefield, you must come inside!"

"What?"

"I say, you must come inside." She hesitated, then said quietly, "Please come inside. I know you're distressed but we'll talk about it."

Obediently Andrew allowed himself to be led back down the street to the house. Once they were inside, she said, "Come, let's sit down in the drawing room and talk."

For over an hour Sarah talked to Andrew. At times he seemed to hear her and responded with a slight nod, but his mind seemed unhinged. He'd stare over her shoulder at the wall without speaking and finally Sarah grew distraught. "I think you should lie down, Reverend Wakefield. I'll go sit with Dorcas."

"Yes—yes, I shall."

Sarah watched as he made his way, like an old man, up the stairs. She heard his door close, then hurried to Dorcas. Dorcas was asleep and Sarah sat beside her for some time. She thought she heard a door close, once, down the hall, but couldn't leave.

Finally Dorcas roused and asked for water.

Quickly Sarah filled the glass from the pitcher at the wash-stand. She helped Dorcas to a sitting position, seeing that her lips were dry and parched and that she was an unhealthy washed-out gray. The sick woman sipped the water until a spasm of pain gripped her, sending the glass flying and spilling the water.

"Are you all right?" Sarah asked anxiously.

"Yes—I think so. Just so very sick."

Sarah stayed with Dorcas until she fell asleep. She was tremendously worried. She'd never seen her look so pale—or be in such great discomfort.

When she passed down the stairway later, she said to Mrs.

Lesley, "We must get the doctor back. I think Mrs. Wakefield is worse."

"Why, Mr. Wakefield has already gone. Did he go for the doctor?"

"He left?"

"Why, yes, ma'am. He looked terribly distressed, so I thought he'd gone to seek the doctor."

"I don't think so. I'll have to go myself. Go and sit by Mrs. Wakefield, Mrs. Lesley."

"Yes, of course, ma'am." Mrs. Lesley stared after the younger woman, then turned and made her way to the kitchen, where she found Beth Buchanan peeling potatoes.

Beth looked up anxiously as the older woman entered the room. "And how is she, Mrs. Lesley?"

"Poorly." The single word was curt and inflexible. A light of satisfaction glinted in the housekeeper's cold eyes as she added, "I doubt she'll live."

Beth knew Mrs. Lesley had never forgiven their mistress for taking over the management of the household but she was shocked at the cruelty that she saw in the woman's face. Tightening her lips, she said, "I'd think you'd have a bit more kindness for the mistress. She could have sent you packing, you know."

Mrs. Lesley, her thin lips drawn into a straight line, stared at the cook. For a moment she appeared ready to lash out at Beth—then a slyness came into her gaunt face and she turned without a word and left the kitchen.

Once outside the room, however, she whispered fiercely, "Let her die!"

<hr />

Andrew walked down the street, oblivious to everything except what Dr. Brown had said. *She might not live!* Suddenly the thought of that was unendurable. He realized he wasn't thinking clearly and he tried to pull his thoughts together. *She'll be all right—she has to be!*

But the longer he walked, the more fragmented his thinking became. He finally went to the church, to a small office on the second floor that was never used. He didn't want to see anyone so he entered through the back door and was successful in finding his way without seeing anyone.

Once inside, he sat down on a chair by the wall and stared across the room. He began to pray. His prayers were not formal, but tortured utterances. Soon he found himself on his knees, crying out for God's mercy.

How long this went on, Andrew Wakefield never knew. He did know that, at some point, he stopped praying for his wife. There came a sudden knowledge in his spirit that he was in the presence of God and he began to tremble. "Oh, God," he cried, "show me what to do!"

From that moment on, God spoke to Andrew Wakefield's heart. It was like Jacob wrestling with the angel. Andrew was taken back in his mind to his early days and very clearly came to see how he'd been nothing more than a pharisee all his life. He'd kept the letter of the law but he hadn't sought the God who wrote the law.

Fragments of old sermons he'd heard came back to him as clearly as if they were spoken. All of them had to do with the blood of Jesus. He was shaken when he thought of other sermons that had to do with the doom of sinners—everlasting punishment for those who rejected Christ.

He was on his face for he knew not how long. He remembered his Aunt Hope reading the Scripture and her voice echoed in his heart over and over again: *Without the shedding of blood there is no remission.* She'd read that Scripture to him often. It had meant little to him, but now he knew it meant everything. *Behold the Lamb of God, which taketh away the sin of the world* was another favorite Scripture of his aunt's. And he remembered, as he wept, how she'd spoken of the time she'd beheld Jesus in her own spirit and had her own sins taken away.

In the semidarkness of that room, Andrew Wakefield was stripped of every hope. He saw himself not as an Oxford graduate or the pastor of a large church but as a man who'd never had faith in the Lord Jesus Christ. He felt alone—more alone than he'd known he could feel. This was the point at which no one could come with him because he knew every man and woman must come to God alone. Leaving behind friends, family, acquaintances, he knew he must stand before God and make his decision. And that's exactly what Andrew did that April day. At some point he cried out to God the simplest prayer he could think of: "God be merciful and save me by the blood of Jesus Christ."

Nothing seemed to change, but again and again Andrew prayed that simple prayer. Finally, exhausted, he collapsed facedown on the floor, sobbing. And as he did, he received the peace he'd longed for all his life and the joy of true salvation!

<hr />

The streets were dark when Andrew walked quickly toward his house. The lights were on and he entered at once. Sarah and Gareth met him.

"How is she?" Andrew said at once.

"Dr. Brown's been called to an emergency but Dr. Callendar came," Gareth said hesitantly. "He says it's in the hands of God."

Andrew looked at the two young people and they knew that something was changed about him. Sarah said, "You look much better, sir."

"Yes," Andrew said quietly. He stood there before them, a peace in his eyes that spoke of the end of the struggle. "I'm much better than I've ever been in my whole life." He smiled then and said, "I must go to Dorcas—"

He halted abruptly as a portly man in a dark brown suit

appeared at the top of the stairs. Andrew met him as he reached the top of the last step.

"Dr. Callendar?"

"Yes, I'm Callendar." The physician was short and round—he was one of those men who appear heavyset but actually are muscular and hard. He had a shock of rough brown hair and a pair of steady, deep brown eyes. "I'm glad you're back, Reverend."

At the tension in the doctor's face, Andrew drew back, filled with apprehension. "How is she?"

"She's having a difficult time, sir." For a moment the doctor studied Andrew's face, as though hesitant to impart the opinion he held. When he finally spoke, his voice was heavy. "Your prayers may do more for her than I can."

Andrew understood at once. Without another word, he took the stairs two at a time, opened the door, and saw Mrs. Lesley, who was standing beside the wall, her face cold and hard. She nodded to him as he entered, then left the room as though she couldn't wait to be away.

Andrew moved toward Dorcas, whose face was drawn with pain. When she saw him, she tried to smile.

"Dorcas!" he cried and went to her. He took her in his arms and held her gently. He could feel the life pulsing within her and held her as if she were very fragile and precious indeed. He buried his face against her luxuriant hair and stroked it with one hand.

"Andrew—what is it?" Dorcas whispered. When Andrew leaned back she saw something in his face that made her catch her breath. She couldn't speak but waited for him.

Andrew hadn't planned a speech. But his heart was more full than it had ever been and he could not keep himself from saying, "Dorcas, I found peace with God. . . ." He spoke quickly, with great fervor, all the time holding her, not letting her go. He saw her face light up, as if a candle had been lit inside her, and was glad.

"And I want to tell you that my love for God has brought me a love for you." He felt her tremble and saw tears come to her eyes. "Marriage is more than an agreement between two people. I have struggled for so long—" his voice caught but he pressed on. "I have fought off feelings for you, the longing to be near you, the need to let you come close to me both physically and emotionally. I-I was ashamed—" He looked away for a moment and she lifted one hand to rest it against his cheek. He pressed a gentle kiss on her palm, then took her hand in his own and met her tear-filled eyes. "I thought it was weakness to want you, to want to love you the way I did. But God has shown me that it's all a part of his design. He created us to become one, Dorcas. And that's what I want. I want us to become one, in every way." The glad light in her eyes stirred him deeply and he swallowed hard against the wonder and grati-tude that threatened to overwhelm him.

She still loves me, God! The prayer sang out from his heart. *Thank you! Oh, thank you!*

He leaned forward to touch her still-pale cheek gently. "You're so beautiful, Dorcas," he said softly. "In my eyes you're the fairest woman on the face of the earth—and to me the most precious. Having a child . . . it's . . . it's when two become one. I want us to become one, in every way."

The words sounded almost rough and awkward coming from Andrew, but they were enough for Dorcas. "Oh, Andrew," she said, putting her arms around him and drawing him down. She felt his lips on hers and tasted the salt not only of her tears but also his.

He held her for a moment, then pulled his head back. "You must get well. You are my life, Dorcas."

Dorcas Wakefield smiled sweetly, reached a hand out to touch Andrew's face gently, and said, "Now I really do have a husband!"

The silence in the rectory was almost palpable. The three who sat motionless in the parlor had spoken little for the past few hours.

Andrew had made a wild dash for the doctor when it was obvious Dorcas's time had come.

From time to time one of the three would look upstairs and they all listened for any sound that might give them a hint of the progress that was taking place.

The clock ticked slowly and ponderously. The sounds it made were heavy and slow, as was the time itself, as they sat there. All three seemed to be in their own universe. They were almost unconscious of one another, for they were praying desperately. Dr. Callendar had looked harried when he'd dashed upstairs. He chose to keep Mrs. Lesley in the room to carry out his orders, and the stern-faced housekeeper passed by the three once, staring at Andrew in a strange fashion.

Once, the doctor came down the stairs, his face even more strained. But he'd merely said, "You must pray. That's all I can tell you."

On and on the hands of the clock moved around and still nothing. Outwardly Andrew was like a figure carved in stone but inside, his heart and head were caught up with praying for Dorcas. Since he'd told her he loved her, she had brightened, as sick as she was. Now all he could think of to do was to pray, and so he did.

A sound finally came—that of a door slamming. All three—Gareth, Sarah, and Andrew—came to their feet at once. None of them were steady and all waited with both hope and dread for the doctor.

"You may come up now."

Dr. Callendar had stepped inside, his shirt wet with perspiration, the sleeves turned up. His hair was ruffled and there was fatigue etched in his eyes, but there was a tiny smile on his lips that made the hearts of the trio leap.

"How is she, Doctor?"

"She's doing miraculously well. It must be the hand of God."

The three at once exclaimed gratefully, "Thank you, Jesus! Praise God and hallelujah!"

Dr. Callendar smiled as they embraced each other. Then he said, "I think you ought to go upstairs. Mrs. Wakefield has a surprise for you, sir."

"Can we go, too?" Sarah whispered.

"Yes, just for a little while," Dr. Callendar said.

Andrew led the way upstairs but Gareth and Sarah were right on his heels. When he reached the door, he opened it and stepped inside, then paused.

"What is it?" Sarah asked. She pushed her way past and came to a halt beside Andrew while Gareth did likewise on Andrew's other side.

Dorcas looked up, her face thin, but victory was in her fine eyes as she said, "God has given us a double blessing, Husband."

Andrew stared at the two bundles she held, one on each side. "Twins!" he gasped, then dashed across the room and reached down to kiss Dorcas on the forehead. "Are you all right?" he asked quietly.

"Yes, I'm all right. How do you like your two sons?"

Andrew pulled the linen back from the babies' faces, one at a time. "Twins!" he said again in awe.

Sarah came over. "Oh, they're precious. Let me hold one." She took one of the babies and Dorcas said, "You should hold this one, Husband."

Andrew took the small bundle of humanity and held it almost fearfully. As he gazed at the tiny, wrinkled red face, the child opened his mouth and uttered an inordinately loud sound. Gareth came to look down. "He'll probably be an evangelist, Mr. Wakefield," he said, grinning.

Sarah was touching the soft cheek of the baby she held. "He's so beautiful!" she crooned.

Dr. Callendar turned to her, his coat in his hands. "My ship leaves in two hours. I must go at once." He took the hand Andrew offered, adding, "I'm sure Dr. Brown will call as soon as he can. A fine pair of boys you have there, Reverend." He moved to gaze down at the two tiny babies and smiled gently. "I wonder what these two will bring to the world." Then, as though embarrassed by this bit of philosophy, he finished brusquely, "You can always tell them apart if you take their shirts off."

Andrew looked up at the doctor, surprised. "What do you mean?"

"One of them has a birthmark." Callendar took one of the infants, pulled the blanket back, then nodded and held the babe out for inspection. "Looks like a four-leaf clover, eh? He ought to be a lucky fellow."

Andrew peered at the mark, which was just over the baby's left shoulder blade, then smiled down at Dorcas in wonder. She gazed up at him, clearly exhausted but pleased.

"I've already named them," she said, watching as Andrew took the baby from the doctor. "I hope you like what I've chosen."

"I would like anything."

"That's Paul you have there, with the birthmark." She pointed to the child in Sarah's arms and said, "And that's David."

When Dr. Callendar left the room, Andrew stood, holding his child and staring down into the tiny red face. "David and Paul," Andrew said gently, "what wonderful names." He sat down on the bed, taking both of Dorcas's hands in one of his. "I love you very much," he said simply. "I haven't said that enough, so I may have to say it many times to get caught up. Will that be all right?"

Dorcas smiled up at him. "Yes, that will be all right."

Gareth and Sarah had the same impulse. Sarah put the child down beside Dorcas and said, "I'll be back to take care of you. I won't be very far away."

After the two left the room, Andrew sat down beside Dorcas. Each of them held one of the babies and though Dorcas was exhausted, she was so happy that she almost burst with joy as she listened to Andrew speak of the future.

Mrs. Lesley stepped into the room but after one look at the two new parents, she turned to leave again.

"Dorcas, which is the oldest?" Andrew asked.

At his question, Mrs. Lesley paused, turning slowly, as though curious herself about the answer to the question. Dorcas looked at the two babes, then at her husband, a slight frown on her features.

"Why—I don't know."

Andrew glanced at the housekeeper, who watched him with the same impassive expression as always. "Mrs. Lesley, we forgot to ask Dr. Callendar which of the boys was born first. You were here. Surely you can tell us."

For a moment the woman remained perfectly still, her eyes fixed on her master's face. Then she spoke in even tones. "The one without the birthmark. He was born first."

Dorcas smiled and held David closer. "You're the elder brother, then, David." A tender smile tipped her lips as she looked at Andrew. "And you have the younger of the two." Her smile broadened. "The baby of the babies."

Andrew Wakefield studied the face of his son, tracing the smooth cheek with a gentle touch. After a moment he shook his head. "He's only a few minutes younger. I doubt that will matter greatly. Unless . . ."

"Unless?" Dorcas questioned.

His gaze met hers. "If these were George's sons, of course, those few minutes would matter greatly. The eldest would have claim to the title and the estate."

"Well," Dorcas said gratefully. "We do not need to contend with such things. Our boys will never be called 'Sir,' but they will have a goodly heritage, Husband. They have a father who loves God!"

"And a mother who loves the Creator even better."

❦

From their listening post just outside the doorway, Gareth and Sarah looked at each other with tender smiles.

"Isn't that sweet?" Sarah whispered, smiling.

"Yes, it is."

"Twins!" Sarah exclaimed. "Isn't that marvelous?"

Gareth suddenly took her in his arms. "I don't know about that," he said.

Sarah pulled back slightly, a reproachful smile on her face. "You shouldn't be holding me like this, you know."

"I'm trying to tell you something. Twins—" he tilted his head to one side—"aren't bad. But I think we can do better than that."

Sarah blinked in surprise. "What do you mean?"

"I'm expecting you to have triplets. We'll call them Abraham, Isaac, and Jacob."

Sarah laughed, trying to pull away gently. Gareth held her fast, and she protested lightly, "That's boastful talk for a poor Methodist preacher."

But Gareth knew the victory was his. He drew her close and kissed her thoroughly. Then he commented, "Whoso findeth a wife findeth a good thing, and obtaineth favour of the Lord."

Sarah Lancaster, not to be outdone, reached up and pulled his head down. She kissed him equally thoroughly, then, her eyes sparkling, said, "She that findeth a husband findeth a good thing, too. That's a free translation, I think, of the Bible."

They stood there, holding each other, and when two tiny voices began protesting, simultaneously, behind the door, they smiled and went inside, closing the door behind them.

THE END